# WHITE GHOST

# SHAUN HUTSON

WARNER BOOKS

A *Warner* Book

First published in Great Britain
by Little, Brown and Company in 1994
This edition published by Warner Books in 1995
Reprinted 1995 (twice)

Copyright © Shaun Hutson 1994

The moral right of the author has been asserted.

A CIP catalogue record for this book
is available from the British Library.

ISBN 0 7515 0768 7

Printed in England by Clays Ltd, St Ives plc

Warner Books
A Division of
Little, Brown and Company (UK)
Brettenham House
Lancaster Place
London WC2E 7EN

'We are satisfied too that there are no Triads operating in the UK, simply gangs using Triad nomenclature to inspire fear. Thus the shadow of the threat of retribution is disproportionately larger than its substance. The word Triad could be usefully dropped from the Police vocabulary.'

Excerpt from The House of Commons Home Affairs Committee investigation into the Chinese Community in Britain Report 1985.

'If you think you haven't got a problem, it's because you haven't found it yet . . .'

Anonymous Police Officer, London 1993

# Acknowledgements

I know these are shorter than normal but I was caught out by the printer's deadline (I hope those who I've forgotten to include believe me . . . ). Back to normal next time. For the time being, many thanks to my manager, Gary 'Moogler Boy' Farrow and everyone at 'the office'. To everyone at Little, Brown, especially my sales team.

Extra special thanks to Jill Freshwater and Carlsberg for making the dream come true. Thanks also to Sheila, Jenny, Edna and everyone in the Bob Paisley suite including Paul, and Steve 'I've got a bus' Lucas. Thanks also to Ray who showed us round on that memorable day, to Jimmy and to everyone at Liverpool FC. Come on you Reds.

Thanks, for various reasons, to Graham Rogers, Keith Elliott, Gareth James, Jo Bolsom, Caroline Bishop, Malcolm Dome, Jerry Ewing, Mick Wall, Neil Leaver, Alison Cole, Zena, Martin 'Gooner' Phillips, Bert and Anita at Broomhills Shooting Club, even to Maurice and his bloody scoreboard. Cheers.

To everyone at Sanctuary Music, especially Merck Mercuriadis. Many thanks to Steve, Dave, Nicko, Janick and Bruce and also to Rod Smallwood. As ever, to Wally 'lap top' Grove. Ring me during office hours when I've got my dictionary out . . .

Thanks also to Jack Taylor, John Mackenzie, Damian and Christina Pulle, Amin Saleh and Lewis Bloch. To Simon Drake, Everite Stationery in Bletchley, The Adelphi in Liverpool and the Holiday Inn, Mayfair. Yamaha Drums, Zildjian Cymbals, Pro-Mark sticks and Remo Heads. Rob, Steve, Andie and Nicola at Chas Foote's in Golden Square. To UCI The Point 10 in Milton Keynes. Duncan Stripp, *still* film critic *extraordinaire*. Julie and Mike, for the headaches and late nights. All those on the Birmingham 'death lists'. Your times will come.

My mum and dad I thank and always will and my wife, Belinda, for being there *every* time and *still* putting up with me.

And to my readers, old and new. Many thanks.

Time to pull the trigger.

Shaun Hutson.

# PART ONE

'Pleasure is oft a visitant, but pain clings cruelly to us.'

John Keats

'And when I'm walking the dark road, I am the man who walks alone . . .'

Iron Maiden

# One

The explosion blew him off his feet.

Sean Doyle hit the ground hard, rolling over, aware of the ringing in his ears from the incessant machine-gun fire. Deafened by the blasts, blinded by the clouds of smoke and choking on the stinging cordite fumes, he struggled upright.

The .44 calibre pistol which he held was hot in his hand from repeated use. Somewhere nearby he could hear shouting.

Screams of pain.

There was blood splattered across the floor, some even up the white walls of the hallway.

Doyle felt pain. Sudden excruciating pain.

He was flung backward by some savage impact to his shoulder. Blood burst from the bullet wound.

The staccato rattle of machine-gun fire filled his ears.

More smoke.

The only thing he could see was the bright muzzle flashes of the weapon that was trained on him. Everything else was a blur.

He ran through the smoke-enshrouded hallway and tripped headlong over a body. A uniformed man. Garda. Irish Police.

The man was dead, two bullets had ripped away most of his face. Doyle went sprawling, his hand sliding into the blood which had puddled around the man's pulverised head.

*Fuck it.*

To his right there was a staircase. He ducked that way,

taking the steps two at a time.

Bullets tore across the wall beside him, blasting great chunks of plaster away, showering him with a fine white powder.

He was hit again, his side punctured.

More pain.

The breath was torn from him as another of the high velocity shells snapped one of his ribs then punched through a lung.

He coughed bright red fluid down his chin.

*Fuck.*

Doyle fired twice into the heaving smoke.

The recoil of the .44 was massive, but he pumped the trigger.

More figures were dashing into the house now, spilling through the open doorway.

The roar of gunfire seemed to be building.

Doyle was shouting to make himself heard above the cacophony, but as he drew breath he felt it sear through the hole in his lung. Felt the pain enveloping his upper body.

Another explosion.

His head was spinning, he felt as if his legs would not obey him when he forced them to carry him further up the stairs towards the landing.

Deafened by the thunderous retorts, blinded by smoke and badly injured, he struggled on, aware that consciousness was beginning to slip away from him. He gripped the butt of the .44 as if to fight off the onset of unconsciousness. He felt as if he were standing on the edge of some huge dark pit, about to topple in.

Men were falling as they entered the house, brought down by the same weapon that had wounded Doyle. He took a couple more shots at the man who held that gun; one of Doyle's bullets struck him in the left arm.

Doyle grinned crookedly at his triumph, but then the gun was trained on him once more, bullets drilling into the wall and the stairs, a dotted line of death coming closer to him.

He squeezed the trigger of his pistol until the hammer slammed down on an empty chamber.

*Fuck.*

More pain.

*You're going to die.*

*So what?*

What was left to live for now?

She was dead.

He had touched her body only minutes earlier. Bullet riddled and broken. He had touched her face, felt the coldness of her skin.

*You're going to die.*

A fusillade of fire screamed across the wall above him ripping holes in brickwork.

Doyle reached into his jacket, struggled with shaking hands to push more shells into the empty chambers of his .44.

The pain was incredible.

*So much pain.*

He gritted his teeth against it, tried to will it away.

He wondered if *she* had felt pain before she died.

A bullet struck him in the leg, tore through his calf.

He bellowed in pain and rage and snapped the cylinder shut, squeezing the trigger almost immediately, feeling the pistol buck in his hand as the savage recoil slammed the butt back against the heel of his hand.

This was for *her*.

For himself. For all those who had died.

He saw two bullets strike their target. Saw a blinding white flash as the machine-gun was fired for the last time. Bullets drilled into wood and stone as they raked the area around him.

Coming closer.

He was deafened, blinded. The only sound he could hear now was his own roar of rage and pain.

Then the bullets began to hit him.

# Two

Sean Doyle sat bolt upright, dragged from the nightmare as if by unseen hands.

He was still shouting as he came out of it.

Both his hands were clapped to his bare chest as if to hold the blood in. Blood which, he slowly realised, had been flowing only within the darkened recess of that nightmare. He slumped back against the headboard, his breath coming in great racking gasps.

'Shit,' he hissed, bowing his head, trying to slow his breathing. He tried to swallow, but it felt as if someone had filled his throat with chalk. He raised both hands to his face feeling the perspiration as he drew fingers across his skin. His whole body was sheathed in sweat and Doyle flung back the sheets angrily, glancing down at his own nakedness. He sat motionless for what seemed like an eternity then swung himself onto the edge of the bed, his breath still rasping in his lungs.

'What's wrong?'

The voice came from behind him. Soft, heavy with sleep.

'Sean?'

Doyle merely shook his head almost imperceptibly and got to his feet, padding through from the bedroom to the bathroom.

He spun the cold tap and scooped a couple of handfuls of water into his mouth, then splashed more on his face already feeling his body cooling. The last vestiges of the nightmare were fading and he screwed up his eyes hard, as if to hasten that process. As he stood before the bathroom mirror he looked at his torso. At the scars which criss-crossed it. Reminders of his pain.

He looked directly into the eyes of the reflection which gazed back at him, wiping his mouth with one hand.

He was grateful he didn't feel as rough as he looked.

Doyle sucked in a deep breath and held it for a second.

Water was dripping from the ends of his long hair, some of it sweat, some of it from the tap when he'd splashed his face. He released the breath and ran a hand through his hair, sweeping it back from his forehead. The lines which creased his flesh there were not scars. They had been forged in the skin by years of frowning. He touched a particularly deep one between his eyebrows then glanced down at his body once more.

At the scars.

So many of them.

As he ran fingertips gently over one on his shoulder the hazy dream images seemed to resurface momentarily with renewed clarity.

How long ago had it been?

Four years? Five? Longer?

*A lifetime.*

He thought of the blonde girl in the nightmare. Dead. Bleeding.

Doyle gripped the edge of the washbasin as if to steady himself.

He exhaled wearily.

How long since he'd touched her bullet-shredded form?

How many years had passed since that night when his world had been shattered?

*A lifetime.*

Time didn't heal. It merely formed scabs over pain.

'Sean, are you all right?'

The voice was behind him now and he glanced into the mirror to see its source.

Karen Moss stood naked in the doorway.

'You scared me when you shouted out,' she told him.

He lowered his head.

'Go back to bed,' he told her. 'I had a bad dream, that's all.'

She hesitated.

'I'm okay,' he said, a little forcibly, and she retreated.

Doyle swallowed more water from the still-running tap then rubbed his face with both hands. Looking in the mirror he could see beyond and behind him into the bedroom where Karen was sitting up, the sheet around her breasts, her long blonde hair cascading over her shoulders.

The girl in his nightmare was blonde.

He closed his eyes tightly and spoke her name softly.

'Georgie.'

He turned off the tap and headed back into the bedroom.

Karen smiled as she saw him approach, trying to prevent herself from staring at the scars that covered him, but unable to control her curiosity.

Doyle slid into bed beside her and she rolled over, touching his chest.

'How did you say you got those scars?' she said, tracing the outline of one with her index finger.

'I didn't,' Doyle reminded her.

'Were you in an accident?'

'It's a long story.'

'I've got time,' she told him, smiling.

Doyle rolled over to face her, his body now pressed close to hers.

'Well *I* haven't,' he insisted and kissed her.

Karen responded fiercely, allowing one hand to slide down towards his groin. She felt him stiffening as she touched his penis and this seemed to increase her own excitement. He rolled her over onto her back so that he was above her, one of his hands now kneading her left breast, coaxing the nipple to hardness.

Doyle kept his eyes closed as he kissed her, their tongues meeting avidly.

He stroked her blonde hair but, in his mind, it was hair which belonged to the girl in his nightmare.

The girl he had known as Georgina Willis. The girl

whose death he had relived a thousand times in his nightmares.

Perhaps he should have died with her.

*Plenty of time for that.*

For now he abandoned himself to physical pleasure.

It would keep those particular demons at bay, at least until the next time.

And he knew only too well that there *would* be a next time. It was just a matter of time.

Time heals?

*Bullshit.*

# Three

*Aberdeen Street, Central District, Hong Kong*

The taxi slammed on its brakes, the driver blasting on his horn simultaneously. The man who had walked in front of the vehicle ignored the stream of abuse the driver shouted at him and ambled on. As the taxi pulled away the smell of exhaust fumes seemed to thicken, mingling with the already impenetrable curtain of odours that seemed to permeate the busy street like an invisible shroud.

The man stood on the pavement and reached into his jacket pocket for a Marlboro, which he lit with a disposable lighter. He sucked in a lungful of the smoke then walked on, past a tea vendor. The man stopped and dug in his pockets for some small change, scraping up enough for a drink. The vendor looked at him as he sipped at the tea, perhaps put off by the smell the man was giving off, and wrinkled his nose.

The man was in his early forties, shabbily dressed in a light blue nylon jacket which obviously hadn't been washed for months. Dark rings of sweat stained beneath both arms and down the back. It was this stale perspiration that gave off the most distasteful of the odours. The man wore a striped shirt that was similarly filthy, with food stains down the front. His trousers were too short, ending almost an inch above his grubby trainers. There was another dark stain on the front of the trousers and one knee was badly worn.

Blue Jacket took another drag on his Marlboro, his head bowed as if he were searching for something in the gutter. He finished his tea and handed the small cup back to the vendor who nodded cursorily and dropped it into a small tub of hot water that he kept warm by means of a Calor gas burner. He watched as Blue Jacket walked away up the hill, pushing through the people who crowded the pavement. There was a handful of tourists wandering about but, the vendor had found, they rarely frequented these streets. Some of the Japanese did but never the *gweilos*.

By the time he looked again, Blue Jacket had disappeared.

Still sucking on his Marlboro he wiped his face with the back of one hand. There had been a rain shower less than fifteen minutes earlier, and it had raised the level of humidity. He could feel the sweat soaking into his shirt and jacket but ignored it, aware of the rumbling in his stomach.

Further up the street was a restaurant; he could smell the food from where he stood now. The delicious aromas only served to remind him how hungry he was. He'd used the last of his money on the tea. He couldn't afford to eat too. He sucked on the cigarette instead.

He headed off up the street glancing at the sky which was cloudy, promising more rain. The signs that stood out proudly above every shop looked strangely muted during the daylight hours; only when night drew in and they flared with neon did they look spectacular. When darkness came the entire street would be awash with the multi-hued glows. Blue Jacket loved the city at night. He loved the multi-coloured signs but he loved the darkness too because it made him feel more comfortable. He could blend in more easily, move with more assurance. The daylight made him feel too exposed. And it hurt his eyes.

He passed the restaurant, his stomach rumbling protestingly. There was a clothes shop next door and he could see two women parading back and forth in dresses they had just put on. He stopped and watched until the shop assistant noticed his gaping and gestured angrily at him. Like so many others she didn't like his unkempt appearance. He moved on past a fresh-fish stall where an older woman, hunched over as if folded at the waist, was chattering in Cantonese about the quality of the carp. She was prodding the fish on the slabs, sniffing her fingers after each such action as if smelling her fingertips would tell her which of the fish to buy.

Across the street a lorry was being unloaded by men wearing only shorts, their bodies sheathed in sweat as they lifted boxes and crates from the truck and carried them into the shop. Music was blaring from the radio inside, competing with the racket pumping from the stereo within the cab of the truck.

Blue Jacket took one final drag on his cigarette and dropped the butt, grinding it out with his foot.

He moved on a few paces and leant in the doorway of a shop with a red and white sign that bore the legend, 'Super Fine Jewellery Store'. There was a door next to the shop. Just a glass door. It led through to a wooden staircase which disappeared upwards into a gloomy landing. Blue Jacket lit another cigarette and peered towards the door, trying to see past the frosted glass to what lay beyond.

He was still looking when he felt a hand on his shoulder.

Turning, he saw a young man dressed in a suit staring at him. The youth was in his early twenties, thin faced, almost anorexic in appearance, his bones pressing against his flesh as if threatening to burst through. He jerked his

11

head at Blue Jacket, gesturing for him to move away from the door. Blue Jacket obeyed, watching as the youth pushed open the door and disappeared up the stairs.

Seconds later two more youths joined him, both disappearing through that doorway.

Blue Jacket rubbed his rumbling stomach as he watched them. They too were smartly dressed, one had his hair in a long pony tail.

They looked as if they had money.

Blue Jacket needed money.

He sucked on his cigarette and watched as a Mercedes pulled up to the kerb and disgorged two more men, older this time. Mid-thirties. Well-dressed.

Blue Jacket stepped forward, one hand outstretched towards the leading man.

In an almost apologetic tone he asked if the man had a couple of dollars he could spare.

The first man merely brushed past him, the second dug a hand in his pocket and produced a five dollar bill, shoving it into Blue Jacket's hand before breezing past through the doorway. Blue Jacket smiled appreciatively and stuffed the note into his pocket.

He had seen these men enter this same building every day around this time. The same five men always came here, sometimes with others. He had known they had money, but he hadn't dared ask any of them for some before today.

The driver of the Mercedes switched off the engine and pulled a magazine from the glove compartment. He eyed Blue Jacket disinterestedly for a second then began reading.

There may already have been other men inside the building, but the five Blue Jacket always saw were now there. He reached into his pocket, pulled out the two-way radio and flicked it on.

'They're inside,' snapped George Lee. 'All units move in. Let's go.'

# Four

The cars appeared as if from thin air. Marked and unmarked vehicles belonging to the Royal Hong Kong Police sped into the street from both ends, some pulling across it, sealing the thoroughfare. At either end there were transit vans and, from inside each of these, uniformed officers spilled out and ran towards the doorway next to the Super Fine Jewellery Store.

Sergeant George Lee smiled as he saw them coming, pausing a moment before shoving open the frosted-glass door. He pounded up the stairs followed by a dozen officers.

At the top of the steps were two doors, both closed. Lee moved towards the nearest one, his right hand snaking inside his jacket, closing over the Smith & Wesson .38 that he had tucked there in a shoulder holster. Gun in hand, he drove a foot against the door. It slammed back on its hinges and he moved forward.

The room beyond was large and as well as the five men he'd already seen enter there were a dozen more, most of them seated on the floor around low tables. Cards were strewn across the tables and Lee saw piles of money there too. The room was thick with cigarette smoke.

Faces turned in surprise as the law officers crashed in and Lee swung the .38 up, drawing a bead on one of the suited men he'd seen earlier.

'Nobody move,' he shouted as the other officers filed in.

Shouts could be heard from the room next door as a similar scene was interrupted and Lee could hear footsteps on the stairs as the occupants of the room were hurried out. He heard shouting and swearing in two or three different dialects.

'On your feet,' he said to those men still sitting dumbfounded on the bare boards. They rose almost as one, standing bewildered until they were shepherded out by the uniformed officers.

The man who had given Lee the money moved slightly, his hand brushing his jacket.

'Don't move,' said Lee.

'Officer,' said the man, smiling. 'If there's a problem . . .'

'Shut up,' snapped Lee.

The youth with the pony tail eyed him malevolently, his gaze flicking around the room every so often.

'We'll be back on the streets in twenty-four hours,' said one of his companions. 'There's no way you can hold us.'

The thin man was smiling.

'Not this time,' Lee told him.

'Want to bet?' the thin man chuckled.

'Yes,' hissed Lee stepping towards him. He kicked over one of the boxes that had been used as a gambling table, the money spilling onto the floor. 'Cover *that* bet.'

'You've tried before, you and dozens like you. When are you going to learn your lesson?' the thin man chided, that sickly grin still hovering on his bloodless lips.

'You're finished,' Lee told him. 'And you know it. Not just you, but the rest of the gangs too. We're chasing you out. After all these years. For so long you've been like a fucking disease in this country. Well now we've finally found the cure.' He stepped closer to the thin man, pulling a pair of handcuffs from his jacket, snapping them on to the other's emaciated wrists with a grunt of satisfaction. The thin man's smile faded.

Pony Tail took his chance.

Lee turned in time to see him take a pace towards the door, his hand snaking inside his jacket. He pulled the Taurus PT-92 from its holster and fired off two rounds at the policeman standing nearest the doorway.

The first blasted a lump from the frame of the door, the second struck the officer in the arm.

Lee spun round and fired.

The retort of the pistols in such an enclosed space was massive, the sound throbbing in the ears of the men in the room.

The .38 calibre shell struck Pony Tail in the chest, staving in two ribs before bursting the lung. He dropped like a stone, blood blossoming on his shirt front and already spilling from his mouth.

His companions looked on silently as the roar of the shot gradually died away.

Lee walked across to the man and kicked at his hand, knocking the pistol from his grip, noting as he leaned closer that Pony Tail's chest was rising and falling slowly.

'He's still alive,' Lee said. 'Get an ambulance.' He looked across to the wounded policeman who was clutching his injured arm. 'But make sure this man is attended to first.' One of the uniformed officers helped his colleague out, another completed the job of handcuffing the men remaining in the room. Lee holstered the pistol. 'Get the rest of this shit out of here.'

## Five

Sergeant George Lee took a swig from the plastic coffee cup, wincing when he found the contents to be cold. He dropped the cup into a nearby bin and reached for his cigarettes, which were lying on the table in the interrogation room.

'Those things will kill you,' said John Ching without looking up. 'I know, I used to smoke forty a day.'

'And you've never stopped telling me,' Lee reminded him. 'If there's one thing in the world I hate it's a reformed smoker.' He blew a stream of smoke towards Ching who smiled. The two men glanced at each other for a moment then Lee nodded towards the pile of manilla files that lay before his partner. 'Do they all check out?'

'All five of them, including the one you shot,' Ching told him. 'Arrest sheets longer than your arm and all five admitted to membership of the Tai Hung Chai Triad.'

Lee nodded slowly.

Outside the sun was still shining, the bright light reflecting off the glass front of the police station in Gloucester Road. From the roof of the building there were clear views of Wanchai Stadium, the harbour and beyond to Kowloon. Lee himself had often stood up there looking out over the city, watching the boats that littered the dark waters of the harbour. By the Star ferry, Kowloon was less than ten minutes away. Lee had grown up there amongst the poverty and degradation. Now he saw that same poverty from a different side.

'The one you shot, you might be interested to know, will live,' Ching told him.

Lee merely shrugged.

'Next time I'll aim higher,' he muttered.

'He was big time,' Ching continued, flicking through the file. 'He'd been *Hung Kwan* for the last six months – an ambitious boy.'

Lee ground out his cigarette and reached for another.

'What's wrong, George? You don't look very happy,' Ching told him.

'Why should I be?'

'Jesus, we've busted more Triad operations in the last ten months than the Royal Hong Kong police have in the past ten years. They're moving out of Hong Kong and Kowloon in droves. We've got them on the run. At last, after all this time, they're losing power.'

'Do you honestly believe that, John?'

'It's a fact.'

'So we drive them out of Hong Kong or they move out of their own free will, what then? They turn up in Macau, Burma, Malaya and Singapore. You've been working

16

undercover with me for eight years now, we've run up against Triads from every part of Asia. Pushing them out of Hong Kong isn't going to stop them.'

'It gets them out of *our* hair,' Ching said, defiantly.

'It moves the problem elsewhere.'

'Fine. If it moves elsewhere, it's not our problem any more. Let somebody else deal with it for a change. But I tell you, George, we're pushing them out.'

'The Triads have run criminal activity here for thousands of years, do you think that smashing up a few of their drug rings, raiding some of their gambling houses or closing down a handful of their brothels is going to beat them?'

'The point is, up until the last ten months we haven't even been able to do that. The odd arrest here and there, and the bastards we pulled in were out on the streets again in a matter of hours or they got off with fines or small prison sentences. All the ones we've arrested during the past ten months, the charges have stuck, they've gone down for long stretches. I'm telling you George, we'll beat them.'

'When I first joined the force an older officer told me that the Triads would always be around. Along with the rising of the sun, he said, it was the only certain thing in life.'

'He was wrong,' Ching insisted.

Lee raised an eyebrow.

'I hope you're right,' he murmured. 'I hope to Christ you're right.'

# Six

*London*
They'd been following him for the last ten minutes, he was sure of it.

He'd first spotted them when he'd stopped for a coffee.

Standing in McDonald's in Shaftesbury Avenue he'd seen them outside, one tall and one slightly shorter, more stockily built. The taller of the two kept glancing in at him. Certainly there was no attempt to hide their pursuit.

The shorter one had come inside, ordered a couple of Cokes, then wandered back out to his companion and the vigil had continued.

Billy Kwan had sipped his coffee and glanced at them, trying to recognise them in the gloom outside but not able to put names to the faces.

He finished his coffee, dropped the cup into a waste bin and left.

They waited ten or fifteen seconds then followed him.

Kwan sprinted across the street, scuttling between cars as he did so.

The two men followed, moving more quickly now.

Kwan headed down Macclesfield Street and into Gerrard Street. He wondered if he should increase his pace, just to see if the other two did likewise.

He glanced back over his shoulder and saw that they were keeping up.

Now he did move more quickly, occasionally jogging a few yards at a time, anxious to put more distance between himself and the two men, not even sure why he was feeling so compelled to get away from them.

Maybe he should just stand still, wait for them and ask them why the hell they were following him.

*Then again.*

The taller of the two men suddenly broke into a run.

Kwan did likewise, bumping into a middle-aged couple as they emerged from a restaurant. The man gestured angrily at Kwan who ignored the motions and ran on, affording himself another look back to where his pursuers were now sprinting along the street.

Both of them were dressed in jeans and sweatshirts like him. Both were in their early twenties like him. Chinese too.

Kwan considered these niceties as he hurried round a

corner into Wardour Street. The bright lights all around were curiously forbidding now. The neon signs glowed like luminous spotlights intended to remove any enveloping darkness that may have hidden him.

He slowed down slightly and tried to blend into a large group of people crossing the street, moving towards Leicester Square.

Kwan jostled with them, pushing through them, irritating a blonde girl who muttered irritably as he stepped on her foot.

He stepped around two men seated at a metal table outside the Swiss Centre. Close by there was a man dressed in full Scottish attire playing the bagpipes. People were throwing coins into a small box at his feet and Kwan noticed that there was a dog lying motionless beside the man.

Odd that he should notice something so insignificant when the only thing that should have mattered was the progress of his pursuers.

He saw them hurrying along, eyes darting right and left as they sought him amongst the throng of people.

Kwan hurried through into Leicester Square, past a couple who were kissing passionately, leaning against one of the posts there. He passed a queue of people waiting to enter the Empire Cinema. Few glances followed his speedy progress towards Irving Street.

Perhaps he should duck into a building, melt into a crowd until he lost them.

*Hide or turn and face them?*

He decided just to outrun them.

The two men hurried across the crowded pavement towards him, intent on catching him. As determined as hounds after a fox.

Kwan hesitated for a moment, wondering which way to go.

The two men were less than fifty yards from him now.

*Which way should he go?*

Forty yards.

His breath was rasping in his throat.

Thirty yards.

He darted off to the left, towards St Martin's Street, his feet pounding the pavement as he moved more quickly.

The men following were running at full speed now, bumping into passers-by in their haste to reach Kwan.

He raced ahead of them, glancing back once again, perspiration beginning to form on his forehead.

Ahead of him was a darkened courtyard, no lights in it.

If he could duck in there . . .

He rounded the corner and looked back, smiling when he saw that he'd put a little distance between himself and his pursuers.

The courtyard was ten feet away.

He stepped round a high brick wall, pressing himself against it, trying to control his breathing.

The taller of the two men hurtled past and ducked into Orange Street.

Kwan smiled.

*Fuck you.*

He stepped out of the shadows, into the arms of the second man.

Kwan's smile faded, wiped from his face by the appearance of the second man.

'Who the fuck are you?' Kwan rasped, anger now overcoming his anxiety.

The other man didn't speak, merely stepped closer to him. Kwan saw his hand go to his jeans, to the waistband, to something hidden beneath his sweatshirt.

'I'll kick your fucking face,' Kwan hissed, none too convincingly.

The stocky man pulled a knife into view and the threat froze in Kwan's throat.

The weapon was nine inches long and broad bladed. In fact, as his pursuer approached him he could see that the gleaming steel wasn't a knife but a cleaver.

*One on one. At least he had a chance.*

The tall man rounded the corner and walked into the courtyard.

He was smiling.

Kwan's bravado drained from him. He felt his bowels loosen.

The tall man was carrying one of the cleavers too.

'Tell me what you want?' hissed Kwan, backing off as far as he could, hemmed in by the high walls of the courtyard.

Neither of the men spoke.

Kwan had one thought before they came at him.

Those fucking cleavers looked sharp.

Then they were upon him.


## Seven


Sean Doyle gritted his teeth as he lifted the barbell, the effort making the veins in his neck and temple throb menacingly. As he lowered it he felt a slight gnawing pain in his right shoulder, but he ignored the discomfort and raised the bar again.

And again.

The pain in his shoulder seemed to subside slightly or, at least, Doyle was less aware of it. He concentrated on the rhythmic lifting of the bar instead. Up and down it went in unwavering motions.

Sweat had already soaked through the grey T-shirt he wore, dark rings had formed beneath his armpits and there were streaks of it across the back of the top which bore the legend, DON'T TREAD ON ME.

Doyle could see his own reflection in the mirror before him, his biceps bulging as he lifted the weights.

He was the only one in the gym on Pentonville Road. The clock on the wall above showed 7.06 a.m. Doyle had already been in there for an hour. He'd jogged from his flat in Islington, less than half a mile from the gym and, when he was finished, he would jog back. Doyle had known the owner of the gym for many years now. A small, narrow-faced individual who he knew only as Gus. Doyle had never bothered to find out the man's second name. Gus unlocked the place for him every morning at six and let him work out in private for an hour or more. Doyle appreciated it.

The doctors had told him that exercise would be beneficial while he was recovering. He needed to build up his strength again.

*Recovering.*

The physical recovery was complete, apart from the odd twinges from joints or old wounds. But the psychological recovery. . .

Doyle gritted his teeth and decided to lift the bar for a little longer than usual. A bead of sweat trickled down his face and dripped from his chin.

Exercise could banish the stiffness from his bones, could endow him with strength once more, but how could it ever wipe out his memories? Doyle knew how to cope with physical pain, he'd always seen it as an occupational hazard, but his struggle with mental pain had been something else.

He dropped the bar, the clang reverberating around the deserted gym.

Doyle ran a hand through his long hair, smoothing it back, away from his forehead.

A punch bag was suspended from the ceiling close by and he stepped across towards it, shrugging his shoulders and flexing his arms before driving the first of a series of pile-driver blows into it.

He wondered why he hadn't died.

As he hammered the bag mercilessly, the thought occurred to him again and again.

Years before he should have died in a bomb blast in Londonderry. He'd recovered from that when, by rights, he should have been killed or, at the very least, crippled.

And then he'd fought his way back to fitness again, driven by his anger and his need to fight, once more, those men who had caused his injuries and nearly taken his life.

As part of the Counter Terrorist Unit he'd risked his life a dozen times in the last ten years.

He pounded the bag with relish, each blow rocking it.

After the bomb he'd been advised to retire. However, Doyle was never one for advice, either giving it or taking it. He'd gone back to work, back to Ireland, and it had happened again.

He'd suffered wounds which, rightfully, should have seen him consigned to a wooden box and six feet of earth, but something had pulled him through. Some spark, some desperate need to survive and, at times, he cursed that ferocious streak of self-preservation. There was no one left for him to care about. All those he'd worked with, those he'd been foolish enough to care about, had all died. But not Doyle, he remained. Alone. Driven only by his anger and his need for revenge against those who had hurt him, and if that need led to his death then so be it. Not that he invited death, but he wasn't afraid of it. When a man cared so little for his life, a life that held nothing but pain and memories, then that final blackness was a relief.

Doyle drove a succession of blows into the punch bag, moving around it as he would an opponent, striking into it with bone-jarring force.

The image of that blonde girl flashed into his mind again.

*Georgie.*

He spoke her name silently.

*Forget her. Forget the hurt.*

But it was easier said than done.

*You always said you wouldn't get involved and you did. It's your own fault.*

He struck the bag with even more ferocity.

They'd told him to retire. *They.* The suits. The men who gave him his orders.

*Who the fucking hell were they?*

23

Without his work he was nothing, he might as well be dead. If he'd retired he'd have been chewing the barrel of a gun within a month. He'd seen it happen to others like him. Doyle wasn't made for that way of life. He couldn't just sit back and wait for life to ebb out of him, even if it was with a good pension from his former employers. And that was what it amounted to, pure and simple. Retire, sit around, vegetate, live on your memories, wait for death in your fucking armchair. Perhaps the memories would drive you insane first, transform you into a gibbering idiot to be pitied. Doyle didn't want pity, not from anyone, and he wasn't about to put himself in a position where it was offered.

He slammed his fist one last time into the bag, then stood there, watching as it swayed back and forth. He wiped his forehead with the back of his hand and headed for the door, picking up his sweatshirt on the way. Pulling it on, he used one sleeve to remove perspiration from around his eyes then he walked slowly down the stairs.

'Cheers, Gus,' he called as he reached the bottom. 'Same time tomorrow, right?'

Without waiting for an affirmative answer, Doyle pulled open the door and wandered out onto the street.

There was a chill, early morning breeze whipping along the street, disturbing discarded newspapers and disposable drink cartons, rolling them across the tarmac like bizarre tumble weeds in a Western. Doyle set off for home, jogging at a brisk but even pace.

He passed a few people on the way, some heading towards King's Cross. He noticed another jogger and smiled as the man passed by. He was badly overweight and the effort of the run was clearly causing him some distress. Doyle smiled and ran on.

He felt a twinge in his left leg. Another legacy of that night when he'd come so close to death yet again.

He wiped the image from his mind, ignored the slight pain.

If only he could wipe Georgie's image so easily from his consciousness.

If only. . .

*Fuck it.*

He glanced down at his watch, quickening his pace.

He had to get home, shower, change.

There were things he had to do.

# *Eight*

*County Down, Northern Ireland*

'Does it ever stop raining in this fucking country?'

Private Stewart Crichton peered myopically through the windscreen of the Scania lorry as it rumbled along, its windscreen wipers struggling to clear the rain from the glass such was its intensity.

'Christ, it's been raining ever since we got here,' Crichton continued, irritably.

'You talk as if it never fucking rains in Glasgow,' said the man seated to his right. Private Ray Fairbridge grinned at his colleague and glanced down at the map spread out on his lap. He traced their route with the index finger of one hand then looked into the wing mirror of the truck.

Behind them, two similar trucks, both ten tonners, rumbled through the Ulster countryside. To one side of them, the river Bann, swollen after so much recent rain, coursed past. The heavens had opened two nights before but despite torrents of rain that suggested the clouds had emptied for ever the weather was still appalling, the rain driving in so hard that it was difficult to see more than twenty or thirty yards up the narrow road.

As they turned a corner the river disappeared behind thick clumps of trees and the ground rose up on either side to form gently sloping banks. Rivulets of rain water coursed down them in places, having cut furrows in the soft earth.

The Scania lurched to one side as the offside wheel hit a pothole and Crichton muttered irritably as he struggled to jerk the lorry back on a level course.

There were several loud bangs on the partition of the cab, the men inside the lorry itself letting him know of their displeasure at the sudden bump.

There were four men in each lorry. Two in the cab and two in the back with the cargo.

The small convoy had left Newry more than thirty minutes earlier. It would take another couple of hours before they reached Portadown, possibly longer if the bad weather continued.

'What are you so happy about anyway?' Crichton said, wiping condensation from inside the windscreen. 'You've been like a dog with two dicks since we left Newry.'

'I've got leave coming up in two days, Jock, that's why,' Fairbridge told him, still looking down at the map. 'While you're mincing about out here in this pissing rain, moaning about how much you'd like to be back in Glasgow, I'll be down the pub with my mates and looking forward to giving my old woman one. Eat your heart out.'

Crichton muttered something and gripped the wheel more tightly, anxious not to lose control of the lorry on the slippery road. Mud was spattered across the tarmac in places, carried down the banks on either side by the rain. Behind him, the drivers of the other two trucks were encountering the same problems and the convoy was forced to slow even more.

'Isn't there another route we could take?' the Scot demanded. 'These fucking roads are murder.'

'We go through a town called Scarva in about half an hour, after that it should be plain sailing,' Fairbridge told him. 'We can't change routes halfway, you know that. Some engineers checked this route last night and gave it the all-clear.'

The high banks to their right and left began to slope less

severely and, gradually, they gave way to a stretch of flat land. Trees grew thickly on the right-hand side, but Crichton felt a little happier at not being so hemmed in. He, like his companions in the third battalion Grenadier Guards, had served long enough in Northern Ireland to know that there was more safety in open areas. That applied to cities and the countryside, and Crichton and his comrades had been on numerous patrols in both. The battalion had lost four men on this tour: one killed in a shooting incident, the other three badly injured in a bomb blast in Armagh. Crichton himself had received minor injuries in that explosion but a small scar on his left cheek was the only physical reminder he carried. He had worse scars from his youth, growing up in Glasgow.

'Car,' said the Scot, noticing a vehicle approaching from the other direction.

Fairbridge nodded and sat up slightly in his seat, watching as the blue Nova drew nearer, forced to drive onto the grass verge at the side of the road in order to pass the huge vehicles.

Crichton watched it in the wing mirror as it eased past the other two Scanias.

There was a junction ahead.

'Take the road to the right,' Fairbridge said and the sound of crashing gears reverberated through the cab as the Scot changed down to negotiate the turn.

'Are gear boxes cheap to replace?' Fairbridge chuckled.

'Fuck you.'

'Thanks for the invitation, Jock, but you're not my type.' He drummed agitatedly on the door. 'I tell you something, I'm dying for a fag.'

'Well you'll just have to wait won't you?' Crichton said smugly, noticing with irritation that the road was once more beginning to wind between thickly wooded high banks. The rain continued to pound mercilessly against the windows and, once more, Crichton wiped condensation from the glass with the side of his hand. 'Christ, I feel as if I've been driving for fucking hours. It must be your company making the time go so slow.'

'It could be worse, you could have Malcy boy in here with you,' Fairbridge reminded him.

'How did that prick ever get to be a sergeant, eh?' Crichton asked.

'Your guess is as good as mine, Jock. Shall we ask him?' Fairbridge hooked a thumb over his shoulder to the rear of the truck where Sergeant Malcolm Turner and another of their companions sat with the cargo. 'If you went round a corner quick enough, perhaps you could tip him out.'

'Don't tempt me,' Crichton laughed.

Both men began laughing.

They were still chuckling when the windscreen was blown in.

## Nine

Glass exploded inwards, showering the two men. The strident sound of shattering crystal was suddenly drowned by the rattle of automatic fire.

'Jesus,' yelled Crichton, struggling to keep control of the Scania as it swerved across the road, heading for the bank on the right.

Fairbridge put up a hand to protect his face, aware of the wind and rain lashing into him as well as fragments of glass. He felt something warm and wet running down his face, saw blood on his hand.

'What the fuck's happening?' he shouted, gripping his rifle.

Crichton was too busy wrestling with the steering wheel to answer and as the vehicle skidded he thought for one terrible instant that the entire thing was going to tip over.

The side window was blasted in.

More glass hurtled into the cab.

Crichton put up a hand to shield his eyes and let go of the wheel. Fairbridge shot out a hand and grabbed it, trying to keep the vehicle steady. Behind him, the other drivers were doing the same. The last truck of the three came to a halt, the second skidded as the driver slammed on the brakes.

Crichton was bleeding badly from a gash on his temple.

'Fucking bastard,' he shouted in rage.

The bullet which struck him entered his open mouth, exploding from the base of his skull.

A sticky slop of brain and pulverised bone splattered Fairbridge, coating his face and the upper part of his tunic with a pinkish grey porridge.

Crichton slumped forward across the wheel, his foot pressed hard on the accelerator.

The Scania hit the bank, shot about fifteen feet up it, wheels churning the earth to mud, then seemed to rise vertically before crashing back down on its side.

Fairbridge felt a massive jarring impact as the truck hit the ground then suddenly he was gasping for air as the dead bulk of Crichton fell onto him, what was left of the head still spouting blood. Fairbridge heaved himself free, pulling at the driver's door, which was now his only way out. He pushed it open and hauled himself up towards the rain.

His head had scarcely left the confines of the wrecked cab when a bullet struck him in the right eye, drilled the socket empty and took away most of the back of his head.

He slid back into the cab, his body twitching madly.

From the back of the truck two other figures stumbled, one of them bleeding from a cut on the face.

There was a sudden deafening explosion at the side of the road.

'Mortar,' screamed Sergeant Malcolm Turner, ducking as a shower of wet earth came raining down.

There was more small-arms fire, the crack of a rifle mingling with the rattle of automatic weapons.

From the second truck Privates MacMahon and Andrews scrambled down, running towards the banks looking for what little cover was offered there. They pinpointed their attackers by the bright muzzle flashes.

'They're in those fucking trees,' shouted Andrews as another explosion shook the ground. Where the mortar bomb landed a great geyser of earth rose into the air, accompanied by a cloud of greyish smoke which hung in the air like noxious fog.

'Get the trucks off the road,' Sergeant Andy Coles roared to the drivers as he leapt from the back of the third Scania. As he hit the tarmac a bullet tore through his left leg, smashing the femur. He went down heavily, seeing the gouts of crimson shooting from the wound. It felt as if his leg was ablaze. As he dragged himself towards the second truck he prayed that his femoral artery hadn't been hit. Like some kind of human slug he left a slime trail of bright blood behind him as he crawled.

Bob Mackenzie dashed towards him, trying to pull him away from the open space now left on the road.

Bullets spun off the ground around them, singing away as they ricochetted. Mackenzie grabbed Coles' outstretched hand and pulled him to the roadside.

They both threw themselves to the ground, hugging the wet earth as they heard the arc of a mortar shell.

This fucker was *really* close.

The same blast killed them both.

'Get help,' shouted Turner to Andrews who was struggling with a radio, trying to find the frequency. 'Give them our position.'

Andrews continued to struggle.

'Move it, for fuck's sake,' Turner bellowed.

There was another explosion. More gunfire.

The smoke that rose from each successive blast was quickly dispersed by the driving rain, making it even more difficult for the soldiers to see their attackers. Crouching on the sodden mud they had to tilt their faces up into the downpour to catch sight of the telltale muzzle flashes.

Private Ross Williams was trying to apply a tourniquet to the arm of his colleague, Tim Daniel. His right hand had been pierced by a piece of shrapnel, the palm holed by the lump of hot steel. Daniel was struggling to keep a hold on consciousness, his arm numb with pain.

Bullets suddenly struck the bank beside them and both men flung themselves down.

'They're on both sides of us,' Turner roared.

Two or three of the men turned to catch sight of more blinding flashes coming from the line of trees topping the left-hand rise.

Andrews was still struggling to contact someone, his frantic attempts cut short by a bullet which smashed his left clavicle. Another splintered his right shin.

He fell backwards screaming, rain pouring into his open mouth.

Turner himself moved towards the radio but another explosion sent him hurtling into the road, his ears ringing, his eyes seared by the blast. He lay helplessly on his back clutching at his face, blood pumping through his fingers from the wound which had taken away most of his bottom jaw.

'Get the trucks away,' shouted Corporal John Turnbull, hauling himself up into the cab of the second vehicle.

Bullets sang off the bonnet, one of them hitting Turnbull in the side. It tore through the fleshy part and exited carrying blood and flesh with it. He hauled himself into the cab and twisted the key in the ignition, flooring the accelerator.

The juggernaut roared into life, leaping forwards, narrowly missing Turner who was still lying in the road clutching at his shattered jaw.

There was a huge explosion only feet from the truck and Turnbull put up a hand to shield his face as the windscreen was cracked, the glass spider-webbing. He punched a hole in it just in time to see the ten-ton Scania heading into a crater. The truck pitched forwards and Turnbull grunted in pain as the steering column shot back to slam into his solar plexus. As his breath was torn from him, he toppled to one side, falling heavily from the cab.

Andrews was still screaming.

MacMahon and Williams were firing back as best they could, the Sterling ARs slamming into their shoulders as they spat out their lethal load.

'Come on you fuckers,' roared Williams, his finger tightening around the trigger.

'I can see them,' snarled MacMahon, pointing towards a shadowy figure amongst the trees.

The next explosion seemed more powerful than the rest combined. A searing eruption rocked the earth and sent a mushroom cloud of red and black fire screaming into the air. Smoke billowed out, spreading over the scene of devastation like a filthy shroud.

Apart from the rain beating its incessant tattoo on the tarmac, there was silence.

# Ten

The first of the Ford vans came careering down the slope at speed, its tyres struggling to gain purchase on the slippery earth. Mud sprayed up along both sides of the vehicle as it skidded to a halt close to one of the five craters that now pockmarked the road.

The second van followed, the rear doors hurtling open even before it had stopped moving.

Figures clambered out, scurrying amongst the wreckage, stepping over the prone forms of soldiers.

Four of them, dressed in dark clothes and wearing masks, moved swiftly through the rolling banks of smoke that wreathed the road, moving like spectres in some dim nightmare, heading for the Scanias.

One of the figures stood close to the largest shell crater, looking around at the fallen soldiers.

The uniformed men lay still, dead or wounded or just too terrified to move.

The figure close to the crater gripped an AK-47 assault rifle firmly, gently sweeping it back and forth, watching for any signs of movement from the uniformed men.

The other three were clambering into the closest Scania, moving over the juggernaut like scavengers on some piece of carrion.

What they sought was in the back.

The wooden crates, sealed and unmarked, were lifted quickly but carefully from the rear of the truck and loaded with equal speed and efficiency into the vans.

Three crates came from the first truck and they moved to the next.

The contents of each crate were such that it took two of the dark-clothed figures to move each one, but they moved with a single-mindedness which belied the effort of the task.

Three more crates were taken from the second truck.

The leading figure, the tallest of the four, glanced at his watch and tapped the face agitatedly.

They must hurry.

The ambush had gone well, as well as they'd hoped, but speed was now essential. They had to be clear of this place as quickly as possible if the plan were to succeed.

The figure clutching the Kalashnikov took a step forward, surveyed the soldiers once more, and saw movement.

Through the slits in the mask the figure saw one of the men move a foot. Both his legs were broken, probably by shrapnel, and a length of bone protruded through the shin, the sharp end having sliced through the trousers. It gleamed whitely. The soldier moaned quietly.

The figures moving the crates from the lorries to the vans were sweating from their exertions, trying to move with even greater haste now and as they loaded one of the wooden containers into the second van, they dropped it.

One of them cursed as it hit the road, but it was hurriedly retrieved and pushed back into the van. The figure held up an index finger and pointed to the last crate in the back of the overturned Scania.

Even through the driving rain they heard a low rumbling sound.

It was coming closer.

'Move,' shouted the first, taller, figure.

The one with the assault rifle stepped back and forth, looking up at the sodden clouds then at the fallen soldiers, aware that the rumbling was growing louder.

The last crate was moved with difficulty and, again, almost dropped.

As the two figures hurried back towards the waiting van they were forced to tread close to two of the wounded soldiers.

It was Ross Williams, bleeding badly from two wounds to the neck and shoulders, who shot out a hand and grabbed the taller figure's ankle.

The man went down heavily, the crate falling from his grip. He sprawled on the wet tarmac, trying to roll away from Williams, but the wounded soldier seemed to find fresh strength and lunged desperately towards his attacker's face.

His bloodied fingers gripped the woollen mask and pulled it free, exposing the man's face.

'You fucking bastard,' snarled Williams, blood gurgling in his throat.

The man kicked out, rolling away from Williams, feeling the rain splash against his exposed face.

The roar of automatic fire deafened him and he looked up to see the figure with the AK-47 standing over him, finger on the trigger, drilling shots into Williams. Each impact made the soldier's body jerk and blood burst from the holes torn in his chest and stomach.

The dark-clad figure kicked at the dead soldier then stepped back, almost slipping in the blood which was puddling around the body.

Without a word, the unmasked man grabbed the end of the crate and lifted, running with his companions towards the waiting vans.

The last wooden box was pushed in, then the figures leapt inside the vehicles as the rumbling sound drew ever closer. The engines started almost simultaneously and the vans hurtled down the road, away from the scene of devastation, peeling off in separate directions as they reached a fork in the road.

The rumbling was reaching deafening proportions now – not the approach of thunder, but the sound of helicopter rotor blades cutting through the air.

The Lynx came into view like some huge mechanical puppet suspended on invisible wires. It hovered over the site for long moments before slowly descending.

Private Nigel Andrews heard it coming closer, just as he'd heard the vans scream away, heard the roar of automatic fire as Williams had been shot.

In terrible pain he lay still, unable to move, aware only of the searing agony that seemed to envelop his entire body. Apart from his legs. He couldn't feel them at all.

The word cripple suddenly flashed into his mind like a neon warning.

He was bleeding too, he could see the crimson fluid on the road around him. Some of it his, some of it Williams'.

Andrews lay still, just as he had done when the dark-clad figures had come so close to him. He had watched, his eyes open very slightly.

He'd seen Williams pull the man down, seen him rip off the mask, seen him riddled with bullets.

Seen the face of the tall man.

He knew he had to try and remember that face. It might be important. He tried to file away the memory, but his brain seemed to be rejecting everything except the word cripple.

*Remember the fucking face.*

He couldn't feel his legs.

The rain was beating against his skin so hard it felt like needles jabbing him.

*Cripple.*

At least he could feel the rain on his face.

*Pity about the legs.*

That cunt in the mask had such vivid blue eyes.

He remembered that.

*Not bad for a cripple.*

The Lynx had landed now. He could hear shouts.

Such blue eyes.

*Cripple.*

He passed out.


# *Eleven*


The driver pressed down harder on the accelerator, anxious to put as much distance as possible between the approaching helicopter and the fleeing van.

The Ford sped along doing seventy, weighed down to a degree by its new cargo.

Paul Riordan looked behind him, trying to catch sight of the Lynx, but there was no sign of it. He wiped rain from his face.

It had gone well.

The entire operation had been planned methodically and carried out with maximum efficiency. He was glad. Despite the incident with the soldier. Why didn't the bastard just lay where he was? There always had to be a fucking hero somewhere.

Riordan felt his heart beating hard, thudding against his ribs as if it were going to burst. He felt light-headed, the adrenalin still coursing through him.

He glanced across at the needle on the van's speedo and

saw it nudge eighty. They'd be miles away before the fucking chopper even touched down. He hadn't anticipated the convoy getting off a distress signal, but he'd known even when he began planning the job that the closest British army base was in Portadown. He'd known that no help would have been able to arrive for a good ten minutes. That was exactly how it had worked.

Riordan smiled again and glanced into the back of the van at the three wooden crates there. They could be unpacked later. For now he banged the top of one triumphantly and chuckled.

The van's driver merely concentrated on the road, guiding the vehicle expertly towards its appointed destination.

Another three or four minutes and they would be there. They'd rendezvous with the others later.

'Thanks for stepping in back there,' Riordan said. 'That bastard took me by surprise.'

The driver didn't reply, merely reaching for the mask and pulling it free, tossing it into the back and shaking the head to release a cascade of flowing blonde hair.

'You did well. Thanks,' Riordan said.

Marie Leary smiled.

# Twelve

*Norwood Cemetery, London*

Doyle had parked the Datsun close to the main entrance and headed off up the main gravel path, the stones crunching beneath his feet.

There was a strong breeze and spots of rain intermittently splashed his leather jacket as he walked. The wind blew his long hair back from his forehead, the thick strands trailing behind him like dancing snakes. He pulled up the collar of his jacket with one hand, clutching a small bouquet of red carnations with the other.

The fresh graves to his left and right were covered with flowers, some still wrapped in their cellophane, a sign of newly felt grief. The card on one bouquet fluttered away in the wind, the writing on it already smeared by the rain, the dark ink trickling down the card like black tears.

As he moved through the area of new graves he noticed how the others round about were less well-tended. The headstones of many were grubby, the inscriptions on some already faded. Some of the pots set into the plinths were rusted slightly, either empty or filled with dying flowers.

He took a path off to the right where the grass grew more thickly. It wasn't a designated pathway, rather a track where the grass had been trodden down by the passage of so many feet. Further ahead of him were graves as old as fifty or sixty years. There was no one to tend these and Doyle wondered if the people who used to visit were now themselves resident in the same necropolis they'd visited as mourners.

One of the stones had a picture set into it. A locket-type photo that bore the image of a man in his mid-thirties. A little older than Doyle himself.

He walked on, aware that he was approaching the grave he sought.

The black marble headstone seemed to stand out like a beacon amidst the profusion of white stones and crosses that surrounded it. Doyle slowed his pace as he approached, glancing down at the inscription:

GEORGINA WILLIS
AT PEACE

He looked at the dates on the grave, which testified that she'd been just twenty-eight when she died.

He looked down at the grave for long moments, the

38

wind rustling the cellophane around the carnations, then knelt and began his chores.

He took a damp rag from his pocket and wiped the headstone, removing any traces of dirt from it. He did the same with the plinth, then took out the pot and emptied out the rancid water within.

There was a tap a few yards away and Doyle walked to it, washed the inside of the pot then returned with it now full of clean water.

It had been a long time since he'd been back here. Two months, perhaps longer. Time didn't seem to matter much to him any more. He knew no one else came to the grave. Georgie had been without family. He was the only one who visited now.

Doyle placed the carnations carefully in the pot, balling up the plastic covering and stuffing it into his pocket.

As he straightened up he saw a woman at a grave twenty yards from him. She was crouching close to it, talking softly to the stone as if expecting it to reply.

She was an attractive woman in her thirties. He wondered who was buried there. Her husband? Father or mother? Perhaps a child? Doyle watched her for a moment longer then returned his attention to Georgie's grave.

Perhaps he should stop coming here. Bury the memories as surely as Georgie had been buried.

Why did he return here?

Maybe to remind himself that it could just as easily have been him lying beneath six feet of dark earth.

*Perhaps it should be.*

How long had it been since her death?

Five years? Six?

*Longer?*

It didn't seem to matter. She was dead, that was that. Whether it was ten minutes or ten fucking years, she was gone forever.

The wind seemed to intensify, blasting across the cemetery so strongly it almost rocked Doyle where he stood. The branches of some nearby trees shook frenziedly and leaves were pulled from their branches, tossed through the air.

The whine of the breeze through the trees sounded like mournful cries, perhaps a testimony of how much grief this place had witnessed over the years.

Doyle closed his eyes momentarily, his mind struggling to seize control of the thoughts tumbling there, flying about as wantonly as the leaves in that wind.

*Georgie.*

He saw a vision of her face in his mind, smiling.

Then another of it covered in blood.

'Shit,' he murmured.

The woman at the other grave was making her way back to the main pathway. She nodded politely at Doyle as she passed him and he returned the gesture, watching her walk away.

The wind gusted even more strongly and he winced at the onslaught, feeling the moisture forming in his grey eyes.

*Tears?*

He shook his head almost imperceptibly then turned to go, allowing himself one last look at the stone. At her name.

Then he walked away.

The wind swept remorselessly across the cemetery, stirring the carnations that Doyle had just left. One of them toppled out of the pot and lay on the marble plinth where it remained for a second before the wind blew it away. It disappeared into the long grass nearby. Gone, like a forgotten memory.

# Thirteen

*Portadown, Northern Ireland*

The office was on the third floor of the administration block, overlooking the remainder of the barracks. As Major John Wetherby stood peering through the rain-flecked glass he watched as two Scania lorries drove past below. Similar to those . . .

Wetherby stroked his chin gently.

*Similar to those in the convoy.*

'How many did we lose?'

The voice startled him from his silent musings but he didn't turn around, merely continued peering through the window.

'Five killed, seven wounded,' Wetherby said, distractedly. 'Two of them seriously; it's unlikely they'll pull through.' Only now did he turn, glancing at a map of Ireland in the process. It was tacked to a notice board on his right. He looked at it briefly then turned his attention to the other three men in the room.

'And what equipment was taken?' asked the same man. He was tall, his thinning hair brushed back severely from his forehead.

Wetherby consulted some notes lying on the table in front of him.

'Seventy-five Enfield L70E3 rifles, seventy-five Sterling AR-180s, four L7A17 GPMGs and six thousand rounds of ammunition,' he announced curtly.

'Jesus Christ,' murmured the man who'd asked the question. Colonel Laurence Faulkner smoothed his hair back with both hands.

'I think the problem isn't just *what* was taken but *how*?'

said the man on his left. Captain Edward Wilton shuffled uncomfortably in his seat and looked at his companions for affirmation.

'I would have thought the how was pretty obvious,' said Faulkner, irritably. 'They hit the convoy with mines and automatic fire.'

'There were no reports of mines, sir,' Wetherby interjected. 'Just mortar fire and small arms. Obviously they didn't want to damage the trucks or their cargo too much.'

'How did they know we were using that route?' Faulkner wanted to know. 'Perhaps that's the real question we should be asking ourselves.'

'Are you suggesting there was some kind of breach in security, sir?' Wetherby said, a note of irritation in his voice. As head of Army Intelligence he didn't like the inference that the attack could have been due to the failings of *his* men.

'I'm suggesting that perhaps we underestimated the IRA this time,' Faulkner said.

'It was an unusually bold move on their part, attacking a fully-armed convoy,' Captain Simon Young added.

'They were well organised,' Wetherby said. 'They knew they had the advantage of surprise.'

'Even so, even if they were so bloody sure of their success, why hit an armed convoy?' Faulkner said. 'It's not their style.'

'There are a number of possible reasons why they attacked the convoy,' Wetherby offered. 'Firstly, they knew if they were successful they stood to acquire more weapons at a stroke than they normally would. Over a hundred and fifty weapons in one haul is pretty good going.'

'And the other reasons?' Faulkner wanted to know.

'I think the main one was a kind of reprisal attack,' Wetherby began. 'As you know, we seized a shipment of weapons only a few days ago, intended for them.'

'What was their origin, sir?' asked Wilton.

42

'We think Libya. It's difficult to tell sometimes. They get their equipment from such a wide range of sources. I would hazard a guess that they attacked the convoy to replace the weapons we prevented them from receiving in that shipment.'

'That still doesn't explain how they knew the route of the convoy or what it would be carrying,' Faulkner said, irritably.

Wetherby could only shrug.

'I agree, sir, but I can safely say that they didn't obtain their information through any fault of *my* department.' He looked at his superior challengingly.

'What kind of back-up did they have?' Young wanted to know.

'There was a Lynx there within ten minutes,' Wilton said, sheepishly.

'Ten minutes *after* it happened wasn't much bloody use was it?' snapped Faulkner.

Wilton lowered his gaze slightly and began fiddling with his pen.

'Any idea how many were involved in the attack?' asked Faulkner.

'Three or four. Less than that and they couldn't have loaded and unloaded the weapons in time, the Lynx was there very quickly after the signal was received from the convoy. They must have known how long it would take a chopper leaving here to reach that position.'

Faulkner nodded slowly.

'It's a bloody shambles,' he said, angrily. 'The whole thing. A shambles, not to mention an embarrassment. They've made us look like idiots.'

'Where do you think the weapons are by now?' Wilton mused.

'Probably in the Republic,' Wetherby said.

'Where we can't find them,' Faulkner added, his face darkening. 'Christ,' he banged the table top. 'This is the worst incident I can remember here since Crossmaglen. We lost seventeen then.'

'But we didn't lose any weapons,' Young offered, quietly.

'I think there's something that none of us are considering,' Wetherby began, looking round at his companions.

'Such as?' Faulkner interjected.

'Irrespective of where those weapons are at the moment,' Wetherby began, 'I think it's safe to assume that it's only a matter of time before they're used against us.'

# Fourteen

*London*

Sean Doyle pinned a target to the black foam backing board and stood back, inspecting the shape.

He jabbed the red button beside him and the target whirred away, carried on its trolley. Doyle stopped it at fifteen metres. He adjusted his ear protectors and looked down at the guns that lay on the counter before him. The polished steel of the barrels and frames glinted in the fluorescent light. Doyle reached for the first weapon and began thumbing cartridges into the cylinder.

The .357 Charter Arms Bulldog fitted snugly into his hand and he hefted it, feeling the weight of the revolver.

Through the thick, reinforced safety-glass partition that separated the lanes from the reception area of the shooting range on Druid Street, he could see the receptionist sitting chatting on the phone. Pretty girl. Dark haired. Doyle watched her for a moment, seeing her turn towards him, aware of his gaze upon her. She smiled and waved to him. Doyle smiled back then turned to face the target.

He was the only one in the range; more often than not

he had the place to himself and that was how he liked it. If there were other people there, invariably they would want to start a conversation, enquire about his guns, want to show him theirs. Doyle didn't come to the range to make friends, he came to shoot. It was one of the few places where he could come even close to relaxing and yet there was purpose in his frequent visits too. He was honing a skill.

He thumbed back the hammer of the Bulldog, took aim and fired off three shots in quick succession.

Each was accompanied by a loud bang and Doyle gripped the pistol tightly as it recoiled, the bullets striking the target low. Doyle murmured something to himself and readjusted his sights. He fired off two more rounds, smiling as he saw the second clip the outer rim of the bull's-eye. He flipped open the cylinder, ejected the spent cases and reloaded.

After his last brush with death

(*five years ago, longer?*)

he had set himself rigorous exercise routines to recapture the fitness level he'd had before the incident. The daily workouts at the gym in Islington, his runs and his weight-training had been hard at first, often causing him great physical pain, but he'd refused to give up, pushing himself mercilessly in his quest to recapture the fitness he'd lost during the months of recovery.

All the doctors had said to him that he should retire, get out of the job, leave the Counter Terrorist Unit.

*The same old shit.*

The unit had offered him a desk job.

*Big fucking deal.*

Doyle squeezed the trigger of the Bulldog and put five shots into the chest of the target, which shuddered with each impact.

The smell of cordite stung his nostrils as he emptied the gun, tossing the shell cases into the nearby dustbin. He pressed the 'Return' button on the console beside him and the target whirred back towards him. Doyle pulled white sticky paper circles from a roll and stuck them over the bullet holes in the target then sent it away once more.

He turned and glanced back through the glass partition to look at the receptionist. She was still talking on the phone but every now and then she would look at him and smile, flicking her hair with a carefully manicured hand.

Doyle ran appraising eyes over her.

She was wearing jeans, short suede boots and a baggy jumper.

He approved and made a note to try and remember her name in future. She'd been at the range the last three or four times he'd been in. He would ask her name.

*Why?*

She was good looking; she seemed very confident.

*Don't bother getting involved. Not with her not with anyone.*

He decided to ask her out for a drink sometime.

*What's the point?*

Doyle wanted her and the more he looked at her the more he realised it.

*Forget it. You'll lose her. Just like all the others.*

*Just like Georgie.*

He turned back to face the target, picking up the second gun on the counter, pulling back the slide of the Beretta 92F Burst Fire automatic, chambering a round.

The memories of the wounds were fading, the recollections of the pain were diminishing. Why the fuck was it so difficult to forget one single woman?

He squeezed the trigger and the first three shots ripped a hole in the target, drilling across it, the rounds expelled in a three-shot burst. Doyle worked the trigger, sending more shots from the fourteen-round clip into the target.

He reloaded, pushing the slugs into the magazine, slamming it into the butt when he was ready.

Doyle knew that one of the reasons he could never have a lasting relationship was that he would never be able to wipe out his memories of Georgie. She was there with him constantly, imprinted not just on his mind but on his fucking soul.

He blasted off another full magazine at the target, his teeth gritted, the pistol bucking in his grasp. Spent cartridge cases pumped from the breech, raining down around him, one of them landing on his hand where the hot metal burned him slightly, but he ignored it and continued firing.

Even if she'd lived would there have been a future for them? Doyle was committed to his job, driven by hatred and anger which he found impossible to express or explain, and it was that inability to share the rage that fuelled his ferocious attitude to life. He'd been convinced for many years now that he was living on borrowed time. The only way he knew how to live life was to extremes, whether passion, pain or anger. How could he expect anyone to live like that but, then again, if they wouldn't, fuck them.

*Even Georgie?*

She'd tried to understand him, perhaps she'd got closer than anyone he could remember, but now she, too, was gone. He was alone again.

Alone with his anger.

His work gave him an outlet for that rage. Without it Christ alone knew where he would be. Prison? A madhouse?

He reached for the last of the guns and held it in his hand.

The pistol was awesome both in appearance and power.

Its barrel was a black maw within the triangular frame, the muzzle large enough for Doyle to fit the end of his thumb in.

The .50 calibre Desert Eagle automatic was one of less than a dozen in the country. Doyle ran one index finger over the gleaming barrel then began sliding shells into the magazine. The weapon fired .375 cut-down rifle cases, filled with 400 grains of power. The nitro-express bullets moved at a speed in excess of 2,500 feet a second.

He steadied himself and squeezed off two rounds.

The noise of the retort was massive, the shock waves

bouncing off the wooden walls of the cubicle in which he stood.

A hole the size of a fist was punched in the head of the target and a blinding white muzzle flash illuminated the range as Doyle felt the savage recoil slam the pistol back against the heel of his hand.

He nodded approvingly.

Time had wiped away the memories of his suffering. Perhaps it would remove the thoughts of Georgie too. Something had to.

*Either time or death.*

He emptied the remainder of the magazine into the target.


# Fifteen


*Kai Tak International Airport, Hong Kong*

The flight had been late and the two middle-aged men who climbed into the back of the Mercedes moved with the stiffness that accompanies long flights.

The driver knew better than to speak to them. He felt it prudent to remain silent rather than ask them about a journey it appeared neither had enjoyed. He glanced at them occasionally in the rear-view mirror as he drove away from the airport, seeing how pale they both appeared. One of them, the man he knew as Chan Lu, lit a cigarette and drew on it, as if the inhalation of nicotine would somehow fortify him. The men spoke only briefly as the car passed along the busy streets of Kowloon, sometimes nodding towards something beyond the tinted glass of the Mercedes.

On both sides of the road there were market stalls, crammed close together, sometimes threatening to spill over from the pavement. Tourists mingled with the locals and the clicking of many camera shutters was lost beneath the constant cacophony of shouts, blaring hooters and roaring engines.

The driver guided the car expertly through the traffic, pulling at his tie occasionally, more from nervousness than from the heat. Although the humidity was high and the day was hot, the car was fully air conditioned and comfortable enough inside. The two men in the back seat made him nervous though. Despite the fact that he'd been driving for them for over six weeks now he still felt uneasy in their presence and he wasn't sorry when he saw the road signs announcing that the Harbour Tunnel was less than half a mile away. Five minutes through the tunnel to Hong Kong island and he'd be able to drop his passengers off.

They were chatting more animatedly now but their conversation was still conducted in an almost conspiratorial whisper, as though they didn't wish him to hear what they were discussing. Chan Lu lit up another cigarette, the smoke filling the inside of the Mercedes. His companion, an older man who the driver knew as Huang, also lit a cigarette and they seemed to disappear beneath a bluish-grey cloud of their own making.

The driver turned up the air conditioning in an effort to clear the air somewhat. He wanted to clear his throat, but wondered if the gesture might be construed as an unspoken complaint about the fumes. He glanced in the rear-view mirror again and saw that the two men were looking out of a side window, one of them pointing at a group of youths standing on a street corner playing dice. The two men chuckled and the driver took his opportunity to cough lightly as the smoke continued to fill his nostrils and throat.

He almost smiled when he saw the Harbour Tunnel entrance approaching.

The traffic had slowed to a crawl as vehicles got into lane in preparation for entering the tunnel.

There was a taxi to one side of the Mercedes and the driver could see three Japanese in it, gesturing excitedly around them at the tenements and shops of Kowloon, which crowded in on all sides.

A dark blue Nissan moved across in front of the Mercedes without signalling, causing the driver to hit his hooter angrily.

In the back Chan and Huang muttered irritably and the driver apologised, gesturing towards the offending blue Nissan.

As they entered the tunnel a red Subaru pulled in behind them, close to the rear bumper of the Mercedes, but the driver paid it little attention. He was more concerned with the taxi on his right which was pulling uncomfortably close to him once more. He banged his hooter and gestured at the driver to move over.

The cab dropped back slightly.

Inside the tunnel the roar of car engines seemed to reverberate off the walls and roof, echoing around within the submerged tube that amplified every sound. The tunnel was bathed in a sickly yellow light from the banks of fluorescent lights fixed to the roof and walls, and traffic travelling in the other direction roared past adding to the din.

Ahead, the Nissan was speeding along, as if trying to outpace the Mercedes and, more than once, it pulled out to overtake only to drop back, causing the driver of the Mercedes to brake harder than he would have liked. Each time he did so he glanced at the faces of his two passengers, watching for any signs of displeasure.

The two men merely sat back in their seats, as anxious to reach the end of their journey as their driver.

Traffic seemed to speed up as the road rose upwards and daylight flooded in, replacing the fluorescent glow.

The Mercedes was coughed forth from the tunnel mouth and the driver glanced to one side towards the Royal Hong Kong Yacht Club. The taxi sped up and passed him, but he ignored it this time.

In the back Huang and Chan began talking again, Chan laughing at something his companion said.

The blue Nissan stopped so quickly the driver of the Mercedes barely had time to step on his brakes.

There was a squeal of rubber and the crunch of buckling metal as the two vehicles collided.

The driver gritted his teeth angrily, wondering what the hell had made the man ahead stop so suddenly.

He was so preoccupied with the possible damage to the Mercedes that it took a couple of seconds for him to realise that the two men who'd leapt from the rear seats of the Nissan were carrying guns. Small, compact weapons, he recognised them as Ingram M-10s.

Instinct took over immediately and he jammed the Mercedes into reverse, anxious to escape these men who were now only yards away.

The red Subaru slammed into the back of the Mercedes, shunting it forward two or three feet.

Men were clambering out of there too.

The driver of the Mercedes threw himself down across the front seats, scrabbling to open the glove compartment, trying to pull out the gun he kept there.

The first concentrated fusillade of fire hit the Mercedes at once.

The 9mm bullets ripped through the chassis as if it had been cardboard. Windows were blasted inwards as the hail of bullets raked the vehicle.

The driver was vaguely aware of car hooters being sounded, then he heard nothing but the deafening roar of automatic fire.

The windscreen was blasted to fragments, some of those crystal shards raining down on him, cutting his face and hands as he tried to protect himself.

In the back Huang ducked down, crouching on the floor of the car as bullets ripped into it.

Chan saw one of the back doors being pulled open and shot out a hand to lock it, but he was too late.

The door was wrenched open.

Two bursts of fire raked the inside of the car, blasting lumps from the leather seats, drilling into upholstery and bodies alike.

Chan was hit in the face, chest and neck, his body jerking madly as the heavy grain shells powered into it.

Beside him, Huang, still crouching on the floor, was killed instantly by two bullets which took off most of the right side of his head. He fell backwards as more and more shots were poured into him.

The driver pushed open his door and slid out onto the road which was covered by spent cartridge cases.

He barely had time to straighten up before a burst of fire spattered the road and the side of the car, putting more holes in the vehicle, which was already smoking in several places.

He was hit in the chest and face and, as he crashed backwards against the car sliding off the bonnet, he was vaguely aware of the men in the Nissan running away, leaping back into the vehicle and driving off.

The Subaru also sped past, missing him by inches.

He smelled exhaust fumes and something else, something which seemed to be stronger than the stench of cordite in the air. It was a coppery odour which he finally recognised as blood. There was a huge puddle of it spreading out around him as he lay there.

He rolled over onto his back, his sightless eyes gazing at the sky.


# Sixteen


*London*

The police car drove into Leicester Square, up onto the pavement, parking outside the Empire Cinema.

Detective Sergeant Nick Henderson sat still in the passenger seat for a moment, looking out into the grey morning. Rain flecked the car windows and many of the people moving through the square were carrying umbrellas. Some glanced cursorily at the police car, but most were content to hurry about the day's business, some heading towards the tube station, others away from it. Life went on. It was just another day in the capital.

Maybe not so for Henderson.

He finally swung himself out of the car, pulling up the collar of his coat as he straightened, gazing around.

With its hoardings and neon signs unlit in the daylight hours this normally vibrant area of London looked strangely muted. It was as if all the life had been sucked from it, all the energy drained. Only when night fell and the multi-coloured signs were lit did it truly find animation. Henderson glanced at his watch as if to reinforce his observation that, at 8.20 a.m., Leicester Square was no more vibrant than a dud light bulb.

He dug a hand into his coat pocket and pulled out a mint, which he unwrapped and pushed into his mouth.

Give up smoking, save money someone had told him. Christ, he was spending ten quid a day on bloody sweets now. Thirty Rothmans a day might fuck up your lungs, but at least they didn't rot your teeth. He was sure he was putting on weight too. He had checked the height-to-weight table last time he'd had a medical and come to the conclusion that he wasn't overweight. It was just that, at fifteen stone, the correct height for a man like him was ten foot four. Henderson smiled thinly to himself and set off across the square.

He could see two or three uniformed constables on the far side and it was towards them that he walked, seeing the temporary cordon that had been erected as he approached.

The sheet of drizzle, driven by a breeze, swept across the square and Henderson ran a hand through his hair, smoothing it back from his forehead.

He saw that the uniformed men had noticed his approach and they straightened up as he drew nearer.

As well as the cordon there was a tent-like contraption which covered two or three feet of the railings around the centre of the square. Plastic curtains were drawn across, hiding whatever lay beyond from view and from the curious looks of passers-by, more of whom were slowing down now as they passed the clutch of policemen.

Probably hoping to get a glimpse of what lay beyond the curtains, thought Henderson. Human curiosity never ceased to amaze him, especially in this job. He'd been present at the aftermath of road accidents where traffic jams had formed, so anxious were other drivers to get a glimpse of the wreckage. He remembered a shooting in Camden Town only months earlier when it had taken nearly thirty minutes to remove the body from the block of flats in which it had been discovered because so many onlookers had blocked the stairways and surrounding paths. All desperate to get a look at the corpse.

He'd heard rumours that newspaper sales the day after the King's Cross fire were higher than any for forty years. But how could that be when everyone said they didn't like reading about that kind of thing? The general public weren't morbid. No, they were just curious.

Henderson swung his leg over the cordon and headed towards the plastic curtains. As he drew nearer, one of the constables pulled the curtains back and Henderson walked through into another area which was completely surrounded by the hastily erected screens.

There was another man waiting for him inside, a man dressed in a dark suit, the trousers of which needed turning up. He turned to face Henderson, seeing the look of distaste on the face of the D.S.

'Have the lab boys seen this?' Henderson asked, his gaze fixed on the object ahead of him.

'Been and gone, Nick,' Detective Constable John Layton told him. 'There's an ambulance on the way to collect. . .' He allowed the sentence to trail off.

Henderson reached into his pocket for another mint and pushed it into his mouth, his eyes fixed on the sight before him.

On the railings, jammed there like some monstrous jack-o'lantern at Hallowe'en, was the severed head of Billy Kwan.

## Seventeen

'Who is he, do we know?'

D.S. Henderson stood beside the slab looking down at the shape that lay there, covered by a white sheet.

On the opposite side of the body the chief pathologist, Phillip Barclay, was glancing at his notes. D.C. Layton nodded and looked across at his partner.

'His name is Billy Kwan,' Layton said. 'We found some I.D. on him – a driver's licence – but it could be fake. That's the only other thing we know.'

'The only *other* thing,' Henderson mused.

'He was a member of a Triad gang.' Layton flipped open his notebook. 'The Tai Hung Chai, or however the fuck you pronounce it. We'd pulled him in before, about six months ago, for causing a breach of the peace at some chinkie in Gerrard Street.'

'Let's have a look, Phil,' Henderson said and the pathologist pulled back the sheet.

'Jesus Christ,' murmured Henderson. 'What got him? A fucking combine harvester?'

'It's a Triad killing,' said Barclay, pointing towards the body. 'No question.'

'How can you be so sure?' Henderson wanted to know.

'Look at the cuts.'

'I'm looking.'

The headless body lay stiffly on the slab, arms outstretched, already rigored. There were deep gashes, the flesh split to the bone, across both arms, legs and the stomach. The wounds were still clogged with congealed blood.

'The Triads always cut across the main muscle groups,' said Barclay, pointing towards the savage gashes that bisected the dead man's arms and legs. 'They call it a "chop" or to "wash body". A hit in our parlance.'

'Thanks for the translation, Phil,' Henderson muttered, running his eyes over the ravaged corpse. 'What about his head? Why cut it off?'

'It's a final insult to the dead man,' Barclay told him.

'There wasn't much blood at the actual scene.'

'He was killed elsewhere, then the body was carried or dragged to Leicester Square and dumped, the head was probably severed immediately after he was killed. Although, to be honest, I doubt if he was actually dead when it happened.'

'Shit,' murmured Henderson.

'These cuts would have bled profusely, he would have been unconscious, in shock from blood loss. He wouldn't have known much about it. Besides, the wounds on the neck indicate that it only took two blows to sever the head. It was hacked off, not sawed off.'

'Well, I'm sure he feels much better about that,' Henderson remarked, nodding towards the body. 'What about the murder weapon?'

'Large knives and from the different angles and depths of the cuts I'd say there was more than one attacker.'

'John, get onto Bow Street nick, they deal with Chinatown. I want as much information as possible about any inter-Triad aggro they've come across in the past few months.'

'Already checked it,' Layton told him. 'According to them, there hasn't been a peep out of any of them for more than ten months. Just the odd bit of rough stuff between members of one particular Triad, but no hint of anything like a war.'

'This one might have been killed by members of his own Triad,' Barclay offered.

Henderson nodded almost imperceptibly.

'Maybe,' he said, quietly. 'But it seems a bit extreme if this was done by his own blokes. What the fuck could he have done that'd make them do this to him?'

'So what do you reckon, Nick?' Layton asked. 'Have we got a war on our hands?'

'It's too early to say,' Henderson told him. 'But if we have, then there's going to be more than fucking chow mein lying around in the gutters of Chinatown.'

## Eighteen

The bar of The Three Bells was crowded. Nearly every table was occupied, the occupants of the pub forced to raise their voices over the constant throb of the jukebox which seemed to be turned up to maximum. A chorus of shouts and cheers accompanied a darts match on the far side of the bar, the raucous sounds merely adding to the overall discord.

The barman pushed another vodka across the bar towards Doyle who handed him a five pound note and waited for his change, his eyes darting furtively around the crowded bar, checking each face until he found the one he sought.

The man was sitting with his back to Doyle, facing the door of the Gents' lavatory.

He'd been there for the past hour. Doyle had followed him into the pub and parked himself at the bar. Watching and waiting. It was all part of the job.

*'She's told so many guys to sling their hook. . .'*
roared the jukebox,

*'but I been watching her eyes and I've seen that look. . .'*
Doyle tapped his foot in time to the music.

'Aren't you going to buy me one then?' a voice asked from one side of him.

Doyle turned to look towards the source of the enquiry.

She was smiling broadly at him.

He ran appraising eyes over her.

Tight black leggings, suede boots, a black jacket over a white blouse. About twenty-four. Blonde.

*She had to be blonde.*

'I said. . .'

'I heard what you said,' Doyle told her, nodding towards her glass. 'You've still got a drink.'

She picked up the glass and downed what remained in one swallow.

'Now I haven't,' she grinned.

He ordered her another gin and tonic.

'Where did you say you're from?' she wanted to know.

'I didn't,' Doyle told her.

'You're not from around here are you?'

'Do you know everyone around here then?'

'I've lived here for the last three years; I've got a flat round the corner in Kilburn Lane, near to the church.'

'It must be handy for the confessional,' he said, smiling thinly.

She laughed loudly.

'If I confessed to the priest in there he'd have a heart attack, some of the things I could tell him,' she said, wiping her eyes with one long nailed finger.

'Why don't you tell me?'

'Maybe later,' she said, sipping at her drink.

They locked stares for a moment.

'Do you come in here a lot?' Doyle wanted to know. 'You said you knew most of the people around here.'

'That's almost as original as "Do you come here often",' she chuckled.

'All right then. How about "What's a nice girl like you doing in a place like this?"' Doyle smiled too. 'You obviously like a drink, I just wondered if you knew any of the other regulars in here.'

'Like who?'

'Like that guy there.' He nodded towards the man close to the lavatory door.

'I know him,' she said, smiling.

'How well?' Doyle enquired, raising an eyebrow, quizzically.

She shot out a hand and playfully slapped his knee.

'Away with you,' she chuckled, 'I'm not that kind of girl.'

Doyle looked disappointed.

'You're not that kind of girl. Shit. Does that mean I'm wasting my money buying you drinks?'

She laughed and slapped him on the knee once more. This time he gripped her hand and held it there, feeling her long fingers stroking at his thigh.

'Why do you want to know if I know him? You ask a lot of questions,' she told him.

'I'm a nosey bastard,' Doyle told her. 'Besides, I want to make sure I'm not trying to pick up his girlfriend. You're not his girlfriend are you?'

'I'm not anyone's girlfriend,' she told him, still stroking his leg.

'Good. I wouldn't want to step on anyone's toes. Especially not his.'

'How do you know him?' she wanted to know.

'He tried to steal my girlfriend,' Doyle said, smiling.

She laughed again.

Doyle took another sip of his drink, his eyes flicking briefly back to the man sitting close to the Gents'.

'His name's Neeson, isn't it?' he said. 'Michael Neeson.'

She nodded.

'Why is it so important to you?'

'Now who's asking questions?'

'It must be catching.'

'Yeah, and so is flu.'

'I don't even know your name,' she told him.

'Frank,' Doyle lied.

'I'm Angela. Nice to meet you, Frank.'

Doyle kissed her outstretched hand.

'You smoothie,' she giggled.

Doyle ordered them more drinks, glancing over as Michael Neeson got to his feet and wandered into the Gents' toilet. He returned moments later and sat down in the same place.

'Cheers,' said Angela, raising her glass.

Doyle returned the toast and shifted slightly on his stool so that Neeson was always in view.

Behind them, the jukebox thundered out another tune.

Doyle slipped one hand inside his jacket, his hand brushing lightly against the butt of the Beretta which nestled there in its shoulder holster.

# Nineteen

*County Armagh, Northern Ireland*

From outside the building looked deserted. Standing alone in one of the more thickly wooded parts of the forest it was accessible by the narrowest of dirt tracks, these known only to those who knew the existence of the building itself.

It was little more than a wooden hut, its windows so caked with dirt they looked opaque. One or two were boarded up, slats of wood hammered across the openings.

Rain hammered the roof, puddling around the hut, forming pools in the ruts made by the van wheels.

The vans, too, looked unused, their sides splashed with mud and rusted in places.

There were footprints in the mud leading to the front door of the hut. Four sets of prints.

Inside, illuminated only by the dull glow of hurricane lamps, Paul Riordan slammed an empty magazine into the AR-180 and raised it to his shoulder, squinting down the sight. He drew a bead on one of the other occupants of the hut and squeezed the trigger.

Declan O'Connor turned as he heard the metallic click and he saw Riordan grinning at him.

O'Connor ran a hand through his curly black hair, feeling the sweat that sheathed his forehead. Moving the guns had been hard work. He and his three companions had been at the hut for more than two hours now, working solidly to stow their precious haul in the cellar. Perhaps cellar was a rather grand term for what was a boarded over hole in the dark earth, but it served its purpose.

From below O'Connor heard a voice shouting to him to hand down more of the rifles and he did so, passing them to James Christie who carefully stacked them with the others already laid there, covered by a sheet of tarpaulin to protect them from the damp. Christie shone a torch over the piles of weapons and smiled to himself, then he clambered up the wooden ladder from the cellar, closing the hatch behind him.

'Done,' he said, wiping his hands on his jeans.

Riordan nodded.

'What now?' asked Marie Leary who was seated across the table from Riordan.

'We wait,' he told her. 'Let the fuss die down a bit, let the Brits comb the area. They're going to be pretty anxious to get these guns back so we'd best lay low for a few days.'

'Head back home?' Marie asked.

Riordan nodded slowly.

'Are you sure the guns will be safe here?' O'Connor wanted to know.

'No one knows about this place except us,' Riordan told him. 'They'll be fine here. Until we need them.' He laid the weapon on the table and Marie picked it up, raising it to her shoulder and testing the weight of the weapon. Satisfied, she handed it back to Riordan.

'And when will that be?' Christie wanted to know.

Riordan could only shrug.

Marie smiled.

'The Brits must have been really surprised. They can't have expected us to hit anything as big as an arms' convoy.'

They all chuckled.

'That'll cheer my brother up when he hears about it,' Christie said, smiling. 'He doesn't have much to fucking laugh about in the Maze.'

Riordan looked at his watch.

'We'd better move,' he said. 'The Brits will have tightened up their border patrols.'

'What about the meeting?' Marie enquired. 'You said you were going to call. . .'

Riordan cut her short.

'It can wait,' he said, holding her gaze. 'Let's get across the border first.'

They left the hut quickly, locking it up behind them, Riordan fastening the door with a rusty padlock before pocketing the key.

The two vans drove off in opposite directions, one to the west, one to the south. They were swallowed up by the trees and darkness.

The hut was deserted once again. As if no one had ever been there.

# Twenty

*London*

Doyle lay on his back gazing at the ceiling.

The flat was silent, but for the low breathing coming from beside him. He sat up slightly and looked across to where Angela Piper lay motionless, one hand gently gripping the corner of a pillow.

Doyle watched the slow rise and fall of her chest, allowing his gaze to stray to her breasts for fleeting seconds. She stirred slightly in her sleep then rolled over onto her side.

Doyle waited a moment longer then slipped out of bed, pausing to ensure he hadn't woken her.

He gathered up his clothes and laid them on a chair, smiling thinly as he looked at Angela's clothes still scattered over the carpet. They'd undressed quickly, pulling at each other's garments with reckless abandon, eager to feel the touch of the other's skin. Doyle had been careful to remove the Beretta in the toilet as soon as he'd entered the flat, hiding it beneath his jacket. The last thing he wanted her to do was stumble upon the pistol during the throes of their passion.

When she'd pulled off his shirt she'd paused momentarily, shocked by the sight of so many scars, but her reticence had soon disappeared as her lust overcame her.

They'd stumbled into the bedroom, Doyle ripping the thin material of her knickers in his haste to see her naked. His own eagerness had served to inflame her more.

They'd made love furiously.

*What the hell. They'd fucked. As simple as that.*

There had been no tenderness, just the desperate desire to satisfy a mutual craving.

They'd fucked twice before she'd drifted off to sleep.

Now Doyle pulled on his jeans and padded into the sitting room.

Her handbag was on a table beside the television and he crossed to it, glancing over his shoulder as if to ensure she wasn't standing there watching him. He pushed open the bag and began rummaging around inside.

Some make-up. Half a packet of Polos. A wallet containing some cards. Doyle flipped it open. There was an Access card, a Travel Card bearing her photo (not a very flattering one), a video club membership card and a business card. For a hairdresser, he noticed. He pushed them back into the bag, noticing as he did that there was another pocket inside. Doyle slipped his hand in and pulled out a small black diary. He flipped it open, scanning the entries: 'Meet Carol at 5.30', 'Pete ringing'.

He flipped to the back. There were addresses there. But only three or four.

Perhaps she didn't have many friends, he mused but then spotted a slim red booklet in the same handbag compartment from which he'd taken the diary.

An address book.

*That's better*.

Doyle flicked through.

He saw names.

Adrian Foxman. Barry Gray.

*This was a popular girl*.

Michael Neeson.

Doyle smiled and looked around the room for a piece of paper. There was a copy of the Thomson Local lying close by the phone. Doyle tore off a corner of the back cover and, taking the small pencil from Angela's diary, he scribbled down Neeson's address, quickly sliding the diary and the address book back into the bag. Then he pulled on his cowboy boots and shirt and crept through into the bathroom.

There he slipped on his shoulder holster and hurriedly pulled his jacket over the top, heading back towards the bedroom.

She was still asleep in there, the sheet pushed back to reveal her nakedness. Doyle nodded approvingly then turned away, smiling.

He wondered how well she knew Neeson.

Well enough it appeared.

Doyle wondered if the address Neeson had given to Angela may have been false.

It was unusual for members of the IRA to be so forthcoming with details such as that.

Doyle headed for the front door and eased it open. He waited a moment, listening for Angela's low breathing then, as silently as he could, he slipped away.


# Twenty-One


*Wanchai District, Hong Kong*

Sergeant George Lee pushed another tangle of noodles into his mouth then wiped his lips with the back of one hand. As he stood watching the Hennessy Road exit of the MTR he glanced at the sea of faces emerging from the underground railway as if seeking one particular visage in the crowd.

Beside him Officer John Ching was smoking a cigarette, watching his colleague.

'Whoever hit them knew what they were doing,' said Lee. 'It was a professional job.'

'And you say they were both members of the Tai Hung Chai?' Ching muttered.

Lee nodded.

'High up too,' he told his colleague. 'Chan Lu was the

*Heung Chu*. He'd been in since the early 1960s. Huang was rumoured to be *Fu Shan Chu*, second in command for the entire Triad.'

'It had to be another Triad. Who else would know who to hit?'

'But why, John? It doesn't make a lot of sense,' Lee offered, pushing more noodles into his mouth. 'The Tai Hung Chai, all of the other Triads too, are pulling out of Hong Kong. The last thing any of them need is a war.'

'Okay, maybe it wasn't another Triad that hit them,' Ching offered, dropping his cigarette and stubbing it out beneath his foot. 'But if not, then *who*?' He looked at his colleague. 'Who could possibly gain by killing two of the top men in Hong Kong's leading Triad. Other than another Triad?'

Lee nodded thoughtfully, his eyes still on the streams of people emerging from the subway, swarming up from the subterranean depths as if spewed from the earth itself.

'You're right. It just doesn't make any sense,' Lee said.

'Since when does anything the Triads do make sense?'

'The killers certainly didn't take any risks. The coroner said they dug twenty-six bullets out of Lu and nineteen out of Huang.'

'What kind of weapon?'

'Mach 10s he thinks. Ingrams.'

Ching frowned.

'I suppose if they're wiping each other out it saves us a job,' Lee observed. 'Let's just hope no innocent bystanders get caught in the crossfire.'

'Or policemen,' Ching said, smiling.

Lee nodded.

'Amen to that,' he said, quietly.

'Any idea which of the other Triads might have been responsible?'

'The others weren't as powerful,' Lee told him.

'But with so many of the Tai Hung Chai leaving Hong Kong, perhaps one of the smaller Triads thought they'd try to take over.'

'Take over what? There's nothing left for them.'

Ching shrugged.

'You might be right though,' Lee continued. 'If the Triads are relocating, and Christ knows why they are, then this attack on the Tai Hung Chai might be an attempt to win respect elsewhere, to show that wherever they settle, they're not going to have it all their own way.'

'So, which Triad is your money on? Who do you reckon blew away Lu and Huang?'

Lee took one last mouthful of noodles then tossed both bowl and chopsticks into a nearby bin.

'I wish I knew because you can bet your arse that the Tai Hung Chai are going to try and find out and when they do, the only money I'd bet is that we're going to be picking bodies off the streets by the truckload.'

## Twenty-Two

*London*

He heard the phone as he stepped from the shower. Doyle turned off the stinging spray and sprinted through to the sitting room of the flat, water dripping from him. He snatched up the receiver, glancing across at the clock on the video as he did. The luminous green letters were flashing 7.46 a.m.

'Hello.'

'Doyle, it's Parker,' the voice at the other end said, and the counter terrorist recognised it immediately as belonging to his superior. Jonathan Parker.

*Hardly worth rushing to pick the fucking thing up.*

'Hold on,' Doyle said and dropped the receiver, padding back into the bathroom over carpet already soggy from his initial dash. He picked up a bath towel and began wiping the moisture from his skin finally wrapping it around his waist as he returned to the phone.

'What do you want?' Doyle enquired. 'It's a bit early for a social call isn't it?'

'I want you here at the office at nine this morning,' Parker told him.

'What for?'

'I'll explain when you get here.'

'Listen, I was in a pub in Kilburn last night, tailing Michael Neeson. I picked up some girl . . .'

'What a surprise,' Parker said, sardonically.

'Do you want to hear what I've got to say or not?' Doyle snapped. 'I went through an address book she had, it'd got Neeson's address in it. I'm going to check it out today.'

'It's probably a fake address.'

'Yeah, that's what I thought, but I'm going to check it anyway.'

'No you're not, I told you, I want you here at nine.'

'What the fuck is so important?' Doyle rasped. 'I've been tailing Neeson for the past three weeks and last night was the first break I've had. I'm going after him.'

'You're off the case, Doyle, I've already assigned another agent. You'll hand over all information you have on Neeson when you get here.'

'Fuck you.'

'I'm giving you an order, Doyle.'

'Just in case you've forgotten, Neeson is wanted in connection with two bomb blasts in London, one of which killed two people. It's taken me three weeks to get anything like close to this bastard and now you're pulling me off the case. Why?'

'I told you, I'll explain everything when you get here.'

'Explain it *now*.'

'Be here at nine.'

'You . . .'

Parker hung up.

'Cunt,' snarled Doyle at the receiver then slammed it back down onto the cradle.

*Taken off the case.*

He turned and stalked back towards the bathroom.

*There'd better be a fucking good reason.*

Doyle pulled off the towel and hurled it angrily into the bath.

He began to dress.

# Twenty-Three

*County Donegal, Republic of Ireland*

Crossing the border had been easier than she'd expected. The patrols that Riordan had warned of had not been in evidence and Marie Leary had been unhampered on her drive.

Above her the early morning sun cast its watery rays over countryside glistening with a combination of dew and rain. The roads were slick with the covering of moisture and once or twice she'd felt the brakes struggling to get a grip as she'd rounded corners, but the roads were virtually deserted and she'd only seen two or three people in the last twenty minutes. A farmer walking across one of his fields had waved to her as she'd driven by and she'd acknowledged his greeting happily. With his ruddy complexion and thick growth of beard he'd reminded her of her own father.

The memory of her father brought the usual mixed emotions. A sense of happiness at times remembered, tempered by the knowledge of his passing, the realisation that there had been so many things unsaid between them.

He'd died three years earlier, taken by a massive heart attack on Christmas Eve. She still had that vision of him now, slumped in his chair surrounded by the gaily coloured lights and the festive decorations which had suddenly seemed so incongruous.

It had taken an age for the ambulance to arrive that night and Marie still wondered if he might have been saved had the emergency vehicle got to their house sooner.

Perhaps they knew who he was. Perhaps they wanted him to die, she had thought as the ambulancemen lifted him onto a stretcher and carried him out to the waiting vehicle.

Could they have known that he had been a member of the IRA? Many times over the years she'd heard him talk about the injustices which went on all around them. The domination of the Province by the Protestants. The indifference of the British Government to the situation in the North. She had heard his words, but they'd had little impact on her. Both she and her younger sister, Colette, had endured his passionate tirades but neither had felt that same passion. Colette in particular, at twenty-two, had other things on her mind. She had been studying for a degree at Belfast University. It was there she'd met Colin Maguire, the man she was to marry.

Marie had watched her sister's progress, both academic and romantic, with an almost maternal pride. Since the death of their mother five years earlier, Marie had become the matriarch in the family. Despite being only twenty-seven at the time she had shouldered many responsibilities ordinarily the domain of her mother.

She'd worked in a factory in Belfast until the owner (a Protestant as her father had been quick to point out) had made her and twenty other women redundant. So Marie had looked after the home instead, working nights in a pub around the corner.

She never asked her father what he did or where he went. When he disappeared for days at a time she never questioned why, never asked for explanations. He never spoke of his whereabouts when he returned either. His passion for a United Ireland never wavered and although Marie could understand his views she could never find it in her heart to become a part of the organisation her father loved.

Not until her sister was shot.

The men who put five shots into her sister and three into Colin Maguire one night were arrested within a day of the shooting.

They claimed, or rather those around them claimed, that the shootings had been retaliatory, revenge for the killing of a Protestant man the week before.

Colin had been killed instantly.

Colette survived, despite a bullet which lodged in her brain and turned her into a paraplegic, damaging her so badly that it robbed her of the power to speak all but a few mumbled syllables.

Marie still remembered visiting her soon after the shooting, staring into the blank eyes, watching spittle run slowly from one corner of her mouth as she flapped her hands uselessly. Marie had been glad her father hadn't lived to see it.

Three years had passed since the shooting and she'd visited Colette only twice in those intervening years. The sight of her younger sister transformed into a helpless caricature of her former self was too much to take.

The attackers had been members of the Ulster Volunteer Force, so the police had informed her.

They'd been tried.

Marie smiled bitterly at the recollection.

It had hardly been worth it. The case against both of them had been dismissed because of insufficient evidence. She could almost hear her dead father's words echoing around the courthouse as the men walked free.

*Protestant judge, Protestant jury. What did you expect?*

She had cried. Not just for Colette but for herself. She had wished that she could have told her father just once that she knew him to be right. That all the things he'd said over the years had been true.

What else was there for her to do but join the organisation he had so proudly championed?

71

She had sought out a friend of his, an older man. He had helped her enlist, kept in contact with her during her training.

Eight months ago she'd joined an IRA active service unit. The transition was complete. She found it a little sad that it had taken the shooting of her sister to cause such a transformation, sad that she hadn't been able to share her father's passion until it was too late.

But that was in the past now. The regrets would always be there, but at least she felt she could go some way to removing them.

She knew he would be proud of her. He was watching her from somewhere, she was sure of that, and he was proud.

She glanced down at the dashboard clock.

Another thirty minutes and she would be at her destination.


# Twenty-Four


*London*

As he guided the Datsun up Hill Street, Doyle scanned the roadside for a parking space, muttering irritably to himself when he saw there was none. On his left-hand side a man was feeding coins into a parking meter, glancing at the Datsun as it rolled past, windows slightly open, cassette blasting away:

*'You take a mortal man and put him in control . . .'*

Doyle looked at the man feeding the parking meter, watching as he pushed the last coin in then retreated into the building behind.

There was one space right outside the building he sought, but it was on double yellow lines.

*Fuck it.*

Doyle swung the Datsun into the space, switched off the cassette and fished in his glove compartment, scrabbling about amidst the empty cigarette packets and sweet papers. He smiled as he found what he sought.

He stuck the orange 'Disabled' sign on the windscreen, clambered out and locked the car.

The building that rose above him was an imposing edifice. Three storeys of dark stone with a high walled garden at the rear. It had been the townhouse of millionaire John Paul Getty back in the 1930s. Now it was the headquarters of the Counter Terrorist Unit.

Doyle pressed the buzzer beside the ornate front door and leant close to the intercom, which crackled loudly a second later.

'Identify,' a metallic voice said.

'Doyle, 23958,' he said sharply and waited.

Another few seconds passed and the door was opened, the lock sliding back with a loud burring sound. Doyle walked in.

There was a wooden desk to his right, an officious-looking woman seated behind it. She looked Doyle up and down as he passed.

To his left there were dark wooden doors, straight ahead some stairs led down into the basement of the building and ahead, rising from the main reception, was a large staircase. The entire hallway was dominated by a massive chandelier, attached to the ceiling by a thick chain. The huge crystal shape hung there, light dancing off the glass droplets.

Doyle made his way up the stairs, his footsteps muffled by the thick carpet. He turned left at the top, peering briefly over the ornate bannister and back down into the foyer.

The officious-looking woman was still watching him.

Ahead of him was another door which he opened, walking through into a small anteroom, barely large enough to accommodate the desk and secretary within.

The secretary looked up, a little bewildered by Doyle's appearance, taken aback by the long hair, worn leather jacket and jeans.

'Can I help you?' she said, rising from her seat.

'Is Parker in his office?' Doyle said, without breaking stride. He was heading for the door beyond the secretary and she tried to step in front of him, realising his intention.

'Mr Parker is busy,' she said.

'Good,' Doyle told her.

She stepped in front of him, trying to prevent him turning the door handle.

'He's expecting me,' Doyle told her as if it excused his abrupt entrance. He pushed the door open and stepped into the office beyond, the secretary close behind.

'You said nine o'clock,' Doyle announced. 'It's nine o'clock.'

'I'm sorry, Mr Parker,' the secretary stammered. 'I tried to stop him but . . .'

'That's all right, Judith,' Jonathan Parker said, smiling thinly.

The secretary retreated a couple of paces.

'Yeah, thanks, Judith,' Doyle echoed, watching as she closed the door.

Jonathan Parker was standing behind his desk, framed by the light from two large French doors which looked out onto Hill Street. He was a tall man, almost six five and his physique was impressive. His body was heavily muscled – something that was evident despite the folds of his impeccably cut suit. Yet even Parker was dwarfed by the vastness of the room. The office seemed gigantic, part of the illusion created by the high vaulted ceiling that rose above them like the inside of a small church. Thick carpet covered the floor, dampening every movement made upon it. Doyle could see motes of dust twisting in the rays of light coming through the windows.

Parker was not alone.

As Doyle sat down opposite the desk he cast an appraising eye over the other occupant of the room.

Tall, powerfully built, thin faced and a little pale. Doyle immediately thought there was something official, no, something martial about the man.

Major John Wetherby was doing his own inspection of the newly arrived counter terrorist and he wasn't impressed by what he saw. He stroked his chin thoughtfully as he scrutinised Doyle, his eyes flicking from the scarred face framed by long hair to the leather jacket, the jeans and the cowboy boots, which looked as if they hadn't tasted polish for months.

Wetherby sipped at his coffee and then looked at Parker.

'Okay,' Doyle began. 'What's the deal? What's so important that you took me off the Neeson case?'

'I see time hasn't blunted your insolence, Doyle,' Wetherby said.

'And who the fuck are you?' Doyle snapped. 'Do I know you?'

'I've not had that dubious pleasure so far,' Wetherby told him.

Parker completed the introductions.

'Major Wetherby is head of Military Intelligence in Northern Ireland,' he added.

Doyle raised an eyebrow.

'As the song says, "*Military Intelligence, two words combined that can't make sense*". It is a bit of a misnomer isn't it?' He smiled.

Wetherby held his gaze icily.

'I still don't know why I'm sitting here when I should be tailing Michael Neeson,' Doyle continued.

'It's being taken care of,' Parker assured him. 'This job is far more important.'

Doyle didn't answer, merely settled himself in his seat and reached for his cigarettes.

'I'll let the Major explain,' Parker said, sitting down behind his desk.

'As you may or may not know,' Wetherby began, 'three days ago an army convoy was ambushed by the PIRA resulting in heavy casualties and the theft of a number of weapons.'

'How many?' Doyle wanted to know.

'One hundred and fifty rifles and six thousand rounds of 5.56mm ammunition.'

'Jesus,' grunted Doyle. 'Are you sure they were provos?'

'Who else would it have been?' Wetherby snorted.

'INLA, IRM. How many more do you want me to name?'

Wetherby eyed him warily for long seconds then continued.

'We're as sure as we can be it was PIRA.'

'Even if it was, what's that got to do with me?'

Parker and Wetherby exchanged glances and it was Parker who finally broke the silence.

'That's your new mission,' he said, quietly. 'Find those guns.'

## Twenty-Five

Doyle laughed.

He reclined in his seat, tilting it backwards so that it was balanced on two of its polished wooden legs.

'What's so funny?' Wetherby snapped.

Doyle's gaze was directed at Parker; he chose not to look at the army officer.

'You pulled me off the Neeson case for this shit?' he said, scornfully.

'This "shit", as you put it, cost the lives of five British soldiers,' snarled Wetherby.

'Then call a fucking undertaker. What's it got to do with me?' Doyle countered.

'We want you to work with the army getting the guns back,' Parker told him.

'I don't work with *anyone*,' Doyle reminded him. 'Besides, why come to the Counter Terrorist Unit for help?' he said, his words and his gaze now directed towards Wetherby. 'Why can't you use your own men? Or get the fucking SAS in on it.'

'We need your . . . expertise, Doyle,' the Major told him. 'No one knows the IRA as well as you, no one's had as much experience with them as you have.'

'Even though my "experience" extends to having been blown up and nearly killed by them, right?'

'You seem to understand how they think, you're aware of their pyschology,' Wetherby said.

Doyle shrugged.

'They're no different to groups like the Red Army, Black September or the French Resistance,' he said flatly.

'The French Resistance weren't terrorists,' Wetherby said.

'They were if you were a German,' Doyle told him.

'Doyle, I didn't call you in here to discuss the merits of the political struggle in Ireland. I'm telling you, you will help the army retrieve those guns. I'm not offering you the mission, I'm giving you an order,' Parker said, defiantly.

'Considering you're supposed to hate them, you seem to have a remarkable ability to understand the IRA's motives,' Wetherby said.

'It's best to know your enemy,' Doyle told him.

Wetherby flipped open the manilla file he'd taken from Parker's desk. He scanned the contents, nodding to himself occasionally.

'You've worked undercover both here and in Ireland on numerous occasions,' the Major said. 'The last time was in the Republic five years ago.'

*Five years. A hundred years.*

Doyle lit another cigarette.

'You were almost killed, you suffered bad injuries,' the officer continued. 'Another operative you were working with, Georgina Willis, was shot to death.'

'I didn't lose my memory over there,' Doyle snapped. 'Why the fucking refresher course?'

'Just reacquainting myself with the facts,' Wetherby said quietly, his eyes still flicking over the contents of the file. 'Four years previous to that you were almost fatally wounded in a bomb blast in Londonderry. After both incidents it was recommended to you that you retire but you refused. Why?'

'What difference does it make?' Doyle wanted to know.

'You said it was important to understand the psychology of your enemy, I'm just trying to understand yours,' the Major told him. 'Twice you were hospitalized. On each occasion you were lucky to escape with your life. Both times you were offered the option of retirement and turned it down. You've been involved in numerous incidents in between, any one of which could have caused your death. What drives you, Doyle? Revenge?'

'I like my work,' the counter terrorist said, flatly. 'I get to meet such interesting people.' He blew a stream of smoke in Wetherby's direction.

'Your parents were both Irish,' the Major said, as if it were an indictment.

Doyle nodded.

'Any other family?'

'It's in the file, read it.'

'You never married, you live alone. You're unpredictable, don't respond well to authority,' Wetherby tapped the file. 'So it says here.' He smiled thinly.

'Have you finished?' Doyle asked.

Wetherby nodded. 'All you need to know now are the details of the mission,' he said.

'You said find the guns, right?'

'Yes, but . . .'

'That's all I need to know,' Doyle told him. 'Just give me some information about where they were taken from and I

78

might need to talk to some of the men who were on the convoy, other than that I'll manage.'

'You're to report in every second day . . .' Wetherby began.

'Bollocks,' snapped Doyle. 'I'll report in when and if there's something worth reporting and I don't want anyone tailing me for back-up. If I need it I'll be in touch. I work alone.'

'Is there anything I can do to help you?' Wetherby wanted to know.

'Yeah,' Doyle told him, 'you can stay off my fucking back.'

He got to his feet.

'When do I leave?' he asked.

'As soon as possible,' Parker told him.

Doyle nodded at each of the men in turn.

'I'd like to say it's been a pleasure,' he said, smiling, 'but it hasn't, so I can't.' He headed for the door. 'I'll be in touch.' And he was gone.

'Jesus Christ,' snapped Wetherby. 'Why the hell do you put up with his insolence?'

Parker raised an eyebrow.

'Because he's the best we've got,' he said, quietly. 'If anyone can find those guns, Doyle can.'

Wetherby exhaled.

'I hope to Christ you're right.'

## Twenty-Six

*County Donegal, Republic of Ireland*
Marie Leary could see no signs of movement as she approached the house.

She slowed the car down, peering through the

windscreen towards the building, watching for any indication of life inside or out. There was a short driveway leading up to the front of the red brick building and she guided the Peugeot to a halt about ten yards from the front door.

Marie sat behind the wheel for a long time, eyes scanning the windows.

She saw nothing.

The house stood alone, the closest neighbour over half a mile away towards the town of Cloghan. Here, high banks and gently sloping hills seemed to push their way out of the earth, as if to protect the anonymity of the piece. Further to the west she could see the dark shape of the Blue Stack mountains pushing their way upwards into the banks of low cloud which scudded across the sky. There was a scent of rain in the air and she felt the first fine droplets as she moved around to the rear of the car and unlocked the boot.

There were half a dozen carrier bags inside, most stuffed with clothes. Shirts, jeans, trousers, T-shirts. The others held food and she could smell the scent of fresh fruit as she lifted the bags out onto the tarmac drive.

She heard a sound behind her.

*Footsteps?*

Marie spun round, her hand sliding inside her jacket.

Her hand closed over the butt of the CZ automatic and she pulled it free.

The man who had approached her saw the weapon and took a step back, his gaze flicking from the barrel to Marie's face.

They stood facing each other for a second then the man smiled. She returned the gesture, dropped the hammer on the pistol and slid it back inside her jacket.

'Help me get these inside,' she said, pointing towards the carrier bags.

The man nodded and picked four of them up, turning and heading for the front door. Marie followed with the other two.

As she drew nearer she saw a face at one of the upper windows of the house, looking out curiously, watching her. The face remained there for a moment then was gone.

Marie stepped inside and followed the man into a kitchen area. A Formica-topped table still bore dirty plates, as did the draining board. They were stacked up beside the sink which was already full of saucepans and rancid water. Marie could only guess at how long the unwashed pots had been there.

'Nice to see you're keeping up the usual standards of hygiene,' she said, dumping the food bags on top of the worktop nearby.

The man didn't speak, merely watched her as she pulled the clothes from the bags and laid them out on the floor.

'There are enough clothes here for all of them,' she said. 'Wash the others in the machine. I'll bring more in a week. If you need more food you'll have to get it yourself. I don't have the time to keep running backwards and forwards after you.' She looked at the individual piles of clothes. 'Riordan says you're to make sure they don't leave the house.'

The man nodded.

'Any problems, get in touch with either me or Riordan,' she told him, then turned and headed back towards the front door.

The man watched her as she climbed into the Peugeot. He stood at the door leaning against the frame.

Marie looked up at the first floor window and, this time, she saw three faces gazing down at her.

'Remember,' she called to the man at the door. 'Don't let them leave the house. No matter what.'

She started the engine, swung the car round and headed back onto the road, looking at the house in the rear-view mirror. The image of those pale faces in the window was still on her mind.

She smiled and wondered how long it had been since they'd seen a woman.

Or indeed, how much longer it would be.

It would be a long time before they would be allowed to leave the house.

# Twenty-Seven

*Gerrard Street, London*

The ages of the seven men in the room ranged from twenty-eight to sixty-two. But to look at all but one of them, they didn't seem to be separated by more than five or six years here and there. Some of the faces bore extra etchings of lines across the forehead or beneath the eyes, but there was a uniformity to their appearance, even down to the suits they wore, which made them look like the offspring of some huge amoebic mass that had merely cloned itself numerous times. Each one was impeccably dressed in dark colours, the profusion of grey and black in the material adding to the sobriety within the room itself.

Three tables had been set up in the room, each covered by a white tablecloth, and the seven men sat at these tables ranked according to their importance.

Their eyes were turned towards one of their number just as their thoughts were focused on a particular event. They were as one in their appearance and in their intent.

Joey Chang wandered slowly back and forth as he spoke, hands occasionally clasped together as if in prayer, the gesture designed, albeit unconsciously, to add weight to the pauses in his speech, so as to let his colleagues know that the importance of the matter he discussed was not lost on him.

Chang was in his mid-thirties, stocky and compact, his eyes constantly flicking from one man to the next as if to gauge each of their responses.

'We know of the murder of Billy Kwan, here in London, just days ago,' he said. 'We also know of the murders of Chan Lu and Kan Huang in Hong Kong. From simple foot soldier to *Shan Chu*, it seems our enemies do not discriminate. What we don't know is why they have chosen to attack us.'

'The reason isn't important. The fact is, they have insulted us with these attacks.'

The voice belonged to the youngest man in the room, Frankie Wong.

'We are being made to look like fools,' he continued. 'We must strike back.'

'Strike back against who?' Chang wanted to know. 'We don't even know who is responsible for these attacks.'

'The longer we wait the more foolish we look. They are laughing at us now,' Wong insisted, his gaze drawn to the older men in the room.

Three of them sat at one of the tables, a greying man flanked by two thin figures, one of whom was tapping his fingers constantly on the linen cloth.

'As *Shan Chu* it is up to you to give the word, Master Wo,' Wong said, looking at the older man. 'We respect your knowledge, your wisdom. The Tai Hung Chai will be laughed at by both friends and enemies if this goes on any longer.'

'Chang is right,' the older man said, his voice slow and deliberate. 'We cannot fight against an enemy whose face we do not know.'

Wong sat back in his chair and exhaled wearily. 'I'm surrounded by old women,' he muttered, irritably.

'What would you have us do?' Chang snapped at him. 'Go out and slaughter every other Triad in London to gain vengeance? We don't need a war, Frankie.'

'Well it looks as if we might have got one,' Wong rasped. 'And I for one will not sit around and wait to be the next one killed.'

'You will do nothing until a decision is made,' Wo Fen told him flatly.

'There are a number of issues to be considered here,' Chang continued, still pacing slowly back and forth. 'Who would want to cause trouble against us? What do they hope to gain by it? We have been the most powerful Triad here and in Hong Kong for many years now, we must think who would try to gain from attacking us.'

'The Hip Sing,' Wong offered.

'It's possible,' added the man seated next to him. He was only four years older than Wong but his face was more heavily lined. 'We've had reports from our operations in Amsterdam that the Hip Sing have been causing trouble there, trying to move in on some of our concerns.'

Wong nodded in agreement.

'The Hip Sing have more to gain from attacking us,' he said. 'They are a newer Triad, they do not have the history that we do. They are ruled by money, not by honour.'

'I agree,' Jackie Ti said, shaking his head. 'They are all young boys, they know nothing of honour, they care nothing for their homeland.'

'Most of them have never even seen Hong Kong,' Chang reminded him. 'Many were born here, they know nothing of the old ways because they do not *wish* to know.'

'Our organisation is based on religion, as you all know.' Wo spoke quietly. 'From the very beginning, our fore-fathers were freedom fighters, they had the best interests of their families and their homeland at heart but as each new generation comes along, it becomes more difficult to instil in them that sense of history and of worth. They see no further than the next dollar bill. Some would make the Triads as corrupt as every other organisation if they were allowed. In America the Tongs trade with the Italians, but they at least understand the concept of honour within the family. Here we are alone.'

'To accept these attacks would be to lose face,' Wong said, unimpressed by Wo's ramblings.

'We would lose even more face if we were to strike at

the wrong opponent,' Chang told him defiantly.

'Chang is right,' Wo said. 'We will wait until our enemy reveals himself.'

'How many more of us will have to die before you give the order to act?' Wong snapped.

All eyes turned on him and he lowered his head in supplication.

'My apologies, master,' he said, softly.

'When we know who our enemy is,' Wo continued. 'We will strike. This is my judgement.'

Beneath the table, Wong clenched his fists angrily.

## Twenty-Eight

Joey Chang reached for the sliver of beef, dropping it into the bowl of rice. He inhaled deeply, enjoying the aromas which came from the food laid out before him.

The restaurant was quiet and he sat alone, gazing out into the street beyond where the neon signs outside shops and other restaurants buzzed and hummed like captive fireflies, casting their multi-coloured glows in the blackness. He watched people walking past, Chinese and white. Chinatown was as much a tourist attraction as a home to the thousands of Chinese who lived and worked within its relatively narrow boundaries. It was nothing like the overcrowded slum in Kowloon which he had called home until ten years ago. There was poverty in London, homelessness and all the attendant problems associated with big cities, but Chang had never seen anything in the place to compare with the soul destroying squalor in which he'd grown up.

The Triad had offered him a way out and he'd taken it.

Both his parents were dead; he'd come to England

shortly after the death of his mother. He had no family back in Hong Kong. London was his home now and it had been good to him.

He pushed the strip of beef into his mouth and chewed a couple of times before reaching for his tea. He was about to take a sip when the table was knocked hard by someone sitting down opposite him unbidden.

Chang looked up to see Frankie Wong lowering across at him.

'I thought I'd find you in here,' Wong said.

'What do you want, Frankie?' Chang said, wearily.

'You know I'm right don't you? About the Hip Sing.'

'I wish I did.'

'I thought you had more sense than Wo Fen. He's too old, he's out of touch, but you . . . I expected more from you, Joey.'

'And what *did* you expect? That I was going to talk the old man into a war? My job is to mediate, Frankie. To advise. To look at every side of the situation, not jump in with both feet. I wasn't elected for that.'

'You know I'm right though.'

'Bring me the proof and I'll believe you.'

'What if the proof is your wife and children. If they're that intent on a war then they won't care who they kill – members of the Tai Hung Chai or our families. Is that what it's going to take to convince you that we're all in danger?'

'One man has been killed in London, two in Hong Kong, it's hardly the beginning of a bloodbath is it?'

'How can you be so sure?' Wong demanded.

'Frankie, when we have proof of who is attacking us then I'll gladly advise Wo Fen to go to war, but until then it doesn't make business sense to start fighting another Triad. If we get involved in a war our businesses become targets as well as ourselves; if we lose financially the entire Triad is at risk. It's simple economics.'

'You sound like one of the men Wo was talking about, those who love the dollar more than honour,' Wong hissed, scathingly.

'Don't talk to me about honour, Frankie,' Chang snapped. 'My position as *Pak Tsz Sin* is founded on honour and knowledge. I handle the thinking, you take care of the violence. That's your job.'

'I can't move until I get the order from Wo. He won't give that order until you persuade him.'

'Wo will give the order when he feels it is time. Nothing I do or say will change his mind.' Chang took another sip of his tea, watching as Wong picked up a piece of corn with his fingers and pushed it into his mouth.

'You can persuade him,' the younger man said.

'Why should I persuade him? I agree with him this time. We need more proof that it is the Hip Sing attacking us.'

Wong shook his head.

He sat looking at his companion for a moment longer then got to his feet.

'Just remember what I said, Joey,' he said. 'Think about your wife and children.'

And he was gone.

Chang watched him stalk off past the window of the restaurant, then he returned to his meal, picking at the meat with his chopsticks agitatedly. After a few moments, he put the pieces of wood down, reached into his pocket and pulled out his mobile phone.

Perhaps he would ring home, just to see if everything was all right.

*Stop overreacting.*

He administered a mental rebuke, annoyed with himself for allowing Wong's paranoia to affect him.

*Your own wife and child.*

There was nothing to fear from the Hip Sing.

*Unless. . .*

He picked up the phone and dialled his home number, waiting while it rang, was finally picked up and answered. He recognised Su's voice.

'It's only me,' he said, quietly. 'Just checking if you're okay.'

She giggled. She was. She wanted to know why he'd rung.

'Because I love you,' Chang said. 'See you later.'

He pressed the 'End' button and dropped the phone back into his pocket.

# Twenty-Nine

*Portadown, Northern Ireland*

That smell.

Always that fucking smell.

Doyle hesitated at the entrance to the ward, the antiseptic odour making him recoil. The smell acted like a Pavlovian trigger, causing the memories of his own hospitalisation to come flooding back.

*Which memories? After the bomb? After the shooting?*

Or the dozens of other times he'd been inside hospitals for injuries ranging from a bullet wound to a broken finger.

The nurse with him noticed his hesitation and glanced at his face, seeing the knot of muscles at the side of his jaw pulsing.

'Are you okay?' she asked.

Doyle nodded, irritated that she'd spotted his reaction. He pushed the door and strode through into the ward.

There were twenty beds stretched the length of the ward, ten on each side. Seven were occupied.

'I was told to stay with you while you questioned the men,' said the nurse.

'Why?' Doyle wanted to know.

'They mustn't be overtaxed, Mr Doyle, they're still very ill.'

He nodded and moved towards the first bed.

The man was in traction, both legs raised above the bed and bandaged heavily. There was a saline drip running into one of his arms. Doyle glanced at the bag of clear fluid suspended above him, watching as regulated amounts of it trickled down the tube and into the waiting vein.

*Looks familiar.*

The counter terrorist walked closer, peering at the man's face, and saw that the eyes were half closed. He seemed to be watching Doyle beneath the hooded lids, struggling to open them fully to look at his mysterious visitor. Doyle saw the patient's eyes flicker and perched on the edge of the bed, looking down at the wounded man.

*He looks better than you did,* Doyle thought.

'He's heavily sedated,' the nurse told him, never moving more than a foot or so from Doyle.

'Can you hear me?' Doyle asked, watching for some sign of recognition or reaction from the man.

The wounded soldier opened his mouth to speak and forced out a dry croaking sound.

'Yes,' he murmured.

'When the IRA hit your convoy, how much can you remember about it?' Doyle asked.

'Who are you?' the soldier wanted to know.

'Counter Terrorist Unit, my name's Doyle. Tell me what you can?'

Corporal Turnbull tried to swallow but his throat was as dry as chalk.

The nurse filled a plastic beaker with water from the jug on the bedside cabinet and offered it to him. He took a few sips, wincing as he swallowed.

'Did you see any of them?' Doyle said. 'Any of their faces?'

'They were wearing masks,' Turnbull said. 'They caught us fair and square, they'd obviously planned it carefully. We didn't have a chance. We're just lucky we got out alive.'

Doyle nodded slowly.

*Lucky?*

Two broken legs and Christ alone knew what other

injuries. If that was lucky then Doyle decided he didn't want to know. The doctors had told him the same thing after his own brush with death. Never mind the numerous fractures, the punctured lung, the pulverised kidney and the other catalogue of injuries.

*He'd been lucky.*

He regarded the man impassively for a moment then got to his feet and moved to the next bed.

The occupant was asleep, his chest rising and falling slowly. His face and hands were bandaged giving him the appearance of an Egyptian mummy. There was just one slit through which his left eye could be glimpsed.

'Most of his lower jaw was blown off,' the nurse told Doyle, 'He wouldn't be able to tell you anything even if he was conscious.'

The counter terrorist looked at the sleeping man briefly then passed to the next bed.

The occupant was sitting up, propped upright by the pillows wedged behind his back. Doyle noticed a tube running from his side. It was draining some dark fluid into a catheter which was choked with blood. There were thick patches of gauze over both his eyes.

'He may have lost his sight in both eyes,' the nurse said, softly.

'It's all right nurse,' said Private Daniel. 'I might be blind, but I can still hear you.'

Nurse Midgley blushed slightly and lowered her gaze momentarily.

'What can I do for you, whoever you are?' said Daniel.

'How much can you tell me about the attack on the convoy?' Doyle asked him.

'I heard what John said, there's not much I can add to that. They took us by surprise, they were using mortars. They hit us hard. What more can I say?'

Doyle looked at the gauze patches which covered the man's eyes. His roving gaze moved from there to the other beds. To the soldiers with broken arms, damaged legs, shattered jaws. The words of a song pushed their way unwanted into his mind:

*'Landmine has taken my sight, taken my speech, taken my hearing. . .'*

He got to his feet.

*'Taken my arms, taken my legs. . .'*

More dark fluid oozed along the catheter tube. Doyle could smell the pungent odour of blood and urine.

*'Taken my soul, left me with life in hell. . .'*

'I don't know what you expect them to tell you,' Nurse Midgley asked as they moved past the next bed.

'I need to know what they saw,' Doyle said, sharply.

'Then talk to me.'

They both turned to find the source of the voice.

Private Andrews was on his side, the dressings on the backs of his legs and the base of his spine preventing him from lying on his back.

Doyle looked at the stricken soldier.

'What did you see?' the counter terrorist asked.

'One of their fucking faces,' Andrews told him flatly.

# *Thirty*

Doyle crouched down, looking into the eyes of the wounded man. He could see the pain in his expression, made worse by every movement, no matter how small. He held Doyle's gaze.

'What did you see?' the counter terrorist asked.

'I saw one of them,' Andrews said, breathlessly, trying to suck in the air as if to inflate his lungs. 'They were wearing masks but Ross, Private Williams, he managed to pull one of their masks off.'

'Did you get a look at the man's face?' Doyle demanded.

'They fucking shot him,' Andrews wheezed, his eyes

misting. 'One of the other cunts shot him.'

'Did you get a look at the bloke's face?' Doyle snapped.

'Yes. He was about your age. Brown hair and the brightest blue eyes I've ever seen in my life. Bastard.'

Doyle nodded almost imperceptibly.

'How tall was he? About five ten, slim?'

'I think so.'

'About my age and about my build?'

'A bit taller than you, I think.'

'Did you hear any names mentioned?'

Andrews shook his head as best he could and closed his eyes momentarily.

'I just remember his eyes,' he said, softly. 'I can remember laying there and thinking about them. I don't know why that stuck in my mind.'

Doyle straightened up, ran a hand through his long hair.

'Have you finished now, Mr Doyle?' Nurse Midgley wanted to know.

'There's nothing else you can tell me?' Doyle said, looking down at Andrews.

'Isn't that enough?' said the nurse, angrily.

Doyle turned and headed for the exit.

'You'll never find them,' Andrews called after him.

Doyle didn't answer, he pushed through the doors and was gone.

He made the phone call thirty minutes later from one of the intern's rooms, perched on the corner of the desk watching the smoke of his cigarette rise into the air as he waited to be connected.

When he was he recognised the voice on the other end immediately.

'Wetherby, listen to me,' he snapped before the other man had finished speaking. 'I think I know who one of the IRA men was who hit your convoy.'

'How?' the officer wanted to know.

Doyle relayed the conversation with Private Andrews.

'The man he saw had vivid blue eyes, he said that was the most striking thing about him,' Doyle continued.

'What makes you so sure who it is just from that?' Wetherby said, sceptically.

'Check the fucking files,' Doyle snapped. 'I think it's Paul Riordan.'

'It's very thin, Doyle,' Wetherby told him. 'One eyewitness, and a badly injured one at that, God knows what was going through his mind at that time. He was hurt—'

Doyle cut him short.

'Look, you've got fuck all else to go on have you?' he rasped. 'The description I was given matches Paul Riordan, I don't care how fucking sketchy it is. This is a hunch, Wetherby, and, at the moment, that's all I've got.'

'Assuming it *is* Riordan, what then?'

'He's been part of an active service unit for the past two or three years, operating here and in Britain. He usually works with two other guys, Declan O'Connor and James Christie.'

'Reports say there were four men who attacked the convoy,' Wetherby interrupted.

'Four or a hundred and four, what's the fucking difference? If I'm right about Riordan then it's a fair bet I'm right about O'Connor and Christie too.'

'All right, assuming you are, what next?'

Doyle sucked on his cigarette, blew out a final stream of smoke then stubbed it out.

'Christie's got a brother, Dermot,' the counter terrorist said. 'He's doing a ten stretch in the Maze. I might be able to find out from him where his brother is. If I can find James Christie then I can find Riordan.'

'And you think Christie will talk to you?'

'I can be very persuasive when I want to be. Now I need you to clear it for me to go into the Maze and talk to him.'

'That's no problem,' Wetherby said. 'I just hope this idea works, Doyle.'

'Unless you can come up with another one then we'd *all*

93

better hope so, but since you needed my help in the beginning I think it's fair to assume you haven't got any ideas of your own. You're stuck with this, Wetherby.'

'Anything else I can do?' the officer said, irritably.

'Yeah,' Doyle told him. 'Try crossing your fingers.'

He hung up.

## Thirty-One

*London*

'Nine hundred, nine fifty, one thousand.'

Lee Chau picked up the bundle of fifty pound notes and tapped them on the table top, straightening the edges before he slipped an elastic band around the wad.

Chau grinned across the table and dropped the money into his pocket. Seated behind the table a large man in his early fifties watched impassively as Chau and his companion glanced around the office.

'How's business?' Chau asked, peering at the rows of videos decorating the walls.

'Good,' said the fat man. 'Just as well it is, the money you take from me every month is enough to bankrupt me.'

'Don't exaggerate,' Chau said, smiling. 'This tea money is money well spent and you know it.' He patted his pocket. 'It's cheap and it gives you peace of mind. There are a lot of criminals out there who would try to take your business away from you, Chi.' He grinned even more broadly.

The office was located towards the rear of the shop in Shaftesbury Avenue and as the three men sat there they could hear sounds of chattering coming from beyond. The video shop owned by Chi was one of many in and around Chinatown stocking exclusively Chinese language films, and the turnover was huge.

Chau and his companion, George Hung, had been collecting protection money from it for the last eighteen months, just as they did from numerous other video shops, restaurants and businesses in the area. Protection money was a large part of the Tai Hung Chai's income.

'You could at least offer us a drink while we're doing business,' said Hung, glancing along the line of videos, picking out titles, scanning the cases.

'I wouldn't call this business,' Chi observed, quietly.

'Why are you so hostile to us? We're here to help you,' Chau told him. 'If it wasn't us it would be someone else and others would take more money from you than we do.'

'I think Fat Chi is upset with us,' Hung said, grinning. 'Perhaps we'd better go.'

The two younger men got to their feet.

'When we come back next month we'll have that drink with you,' Chau said.

'Perhaps your daughter would like to serve it to us,' Hung added, laughing.

'You keep away from my daughter,' Chi said, his jowls wobbling as he rose to his feet.

'Where is she today, Chi?' Hung wanted to know.

'She's at home.'

'We'll see her next time then,' Hung said, heading for the door.

Chi followed the two men, anxious to see them off his premises. The customers inside the shop paid them only cursory attention as they emerged from behind the counter.

One of Chi's sons was serving, taking change from the till; Chau looked into the money drawer and saw it bulging. He grinned.

'Your business is doing very well,' he said. 'May it continue to do so.'

Chi didn't answer. His attention had been drawn towards two young Chinese who were entering the shop. Both were in their early twenties, one bore a scar on his left cheek. They both wore zipped-up leather jackets.

Chau and Hung seemed unconcerned by these newcomers, Hung in particular, more interested in the young woman with her boyfriend who was scanning the shelves of videos.

Chi saw the other two men slip hands inside their jackets.

He saw the guns first.

Chi opened his mouth to say something, but the words froze in his throat.

The two men in leather jackets opened fire.

The first couple of retorts from the 9mm Mambas were deafening within the confines of the shop. Great ear-splitting discharges drowned out even the terrified screams of the customers and of Chi himself who threw his considerable bulk to the floor, covering his head with both hands.

A bullet struck Chau in the stomach, the impact doubling him over. Another ploughed into the counter top, blasting a portion of it free. A third shot blew part of the glass frontage out, pieces of shattered crystal spraying everywhere.

Hung shot a hand inside his jacket, trying to drag his own pistol free.

Two bullets powered into him, one catching him in the back of the leg hamstringing him, the other thudding into his right shoulder. It smashed the scapula as it exploded from his back, splattering one wall with pieces of pulverised bone and blood.

Chau tried to straighten up, lifting his face towards his attackers.

A bullet hit him in the eye, drilled the socket empty and erupted from the base of his skull.

He slumped forward, blood spreading out in a wide pool around him.

Hung raised a hand as if in surrender but a bullet blasted through his palm, tearing off his index finger in the process.

Stray shots struck the walls and floor but, mostly, the men in the leather jackets made their shots count.

The first of them put another six shots into Hung; his companion only stopped pumping bullets into Chau when the slide flew back to signal the Mamba was empty.

The two men turned and walked out of the shop.

Chi remained where he lay, his head still covered, his ears ringing from the thunderous retorts, his nose and mouth choked with the stench of cordite and blood. Tiny fragments of glass were sprinkled over him like crystal confetti.

The young girl and her boyfriend were also lying on the floor, the girl crying loudly.

Chi's son was the first to move. From where he lay he could see that the attackers had left the shop and now he rose slowly up onto his haunches, his ears ringing, his eyes blurred. There was a dark stain across the front of his trousers and he could smell the acrid odour of urine where he'd wet himself when the shooting had begun. He was breathing heavily, perspiration beaded on his top lip and forehead.

Thin grey smoke hung like manmade fog in the shop and he coughed as he smelled cordite.

There were people gathering outside too, and he could hear shouts and screams.

Chi rolled over and saw the bodies of Chau and Hung, shredded by so many bullets.

Blood had already covered most of the floor as it pumped from their bodies. Some had even splashed up the walls.

Chi saw that there were crimson slicks on his own arms, pinkish grey globules which felt like thick mucus.

It took him only a second to realise they were pieces of brain.

He vomited.

# Thirty-Two

Joey Chang glanced down at his watch, tracing the sweep of the second hand as it moved around. It felt as if they'd been in this room an eternity, voices raised in anger and dismay.

'How much was taken?' David Lun asked.

'Nothing was taken,' Chang told him. 'This wasn't a robbery.'

'No, it was another attempt by the Hip Sing to dishonour us,' shouted Frankie Wong angrily. 'And they have succeeded. The longer we sit around here like washerwomen, the greater the damage we suffer.'

'I agree wih Frankie,' Cho Lok added. 'They have made us lose face. We must strike back.'

'It seems to me we've had this conversation before,' Chang said, wearily.

'And how many more times will we have it?' Wong demanded. 'How many more of our men will die before something is done?'

Eyes turned towards Wo Fen. The eldest of the six men gathered in the room had his head slightly bowed as if in meditation.

'Only you can give the order, master,' said Wong.

Wo Fen nodded, as if stirred from his silent contemplation. He looked at the faces of the men around him.

'Two more killed?' he said, vaguely.

Chang nodded.

'Do we know it was the Hip Sing?' Wo continued.

'Not for sure,' Chang told him.

'They were always our greatest enemies in Hong Kong,

98

we always had more trouble with them than anyone else,' Wong said.

'The attack took place inside a video shop, the Hip Sing own many such shops, it could have been an attempt to intimidate us,' Jackie Ti added.

'Then why not kill a member of the owner's family, or the owner himself?' Chang mused.

'What is it going to take to make you act?' snarled Wong.

Wo drummed gently on the table top with his fingers and looked at Chang.

'What is your opinion on this, Joey? We all look to you for guidance,' the older man told him.

Chang shrugged.

'I fear we have no choice but to strike back at the Hip Sing,' he said, quietly.

'You said before that we should not,' Wong said, accusingly.

'I advised against it for financial reasons,' Chang countered. 'I still fear the economic consequences of an all-out war with the Hip Sing, but if we do not make some retaliatory gesture then we run the risk of losing face and they will attack us again.'

'If it does come to war how will we be affected?' Wo Fen asked, his fingers now pressed together before him.

'It depends how long the war goes on,' Chang told him.

'It will go on until the Hip Sing are crushed,' Wong shouted.

Wo Fen raised a hand to silence the younger man.

'If we strike back and damage the Hip Sing badly enough then they may not want war, they may back off. If they do decide to go to war then they will suffer losses as well. They cannot afford to lose money either,' Chang said. 'The only problem I see is that the other organisations may see the dispute between the Hip Sing and ourselves as a chance to push their way into our concerns.'

'More excuses,' snapped Wong.

'It is not an excuse,' snarled Chang, angrily. 'I do not want to lose face any more than you do, but there are many matters to consider. Too many for your small mind to comprehend.'

The two men eyed each other malevolently then Chang continued.

'Frankie Wong's solution is too simplistic, he does not understand anything except force.'

'And force is what the Hip Sing have been using against us,' Wong reminded him.

There was another prolonged silence, this time broken by Wo.

'So, what do you advise?' he asked Chang.

'We have no alternative,' Chang said. 'We must strike back at the Hip Sing. You, master, must agree to that. It is our only course of action.'

'Does anyone else want to say anything,' Wo enquired, gazing around at the other faces in the room.

No one did.

Frankie Wong sat back in his chair smiling broadly.

'So be it,' Wo said, with an air of finality. 'The Hip Sing will pay for their aggression. How soon can you organise this?' His question was aimed at Wong.

'Days,' he replied. 'I will report back to you when everything is ready.'

'Then the matter is closed,' Wo added.

Joey Chang exhaled deeply and sat down. He glanced across at Wong and the other man held his gaze, the smile still on his lips.

Chang knew that there had been no other answer. The threat from the Hip Sing must be met with similar force. That much he understood, but what he felt came somewhere between anticipation and anxiety and he wasn't sure which of the two emotions he experienced more strongly.

Time would tell. And that time was close.

# *Thirty-Three*

*Long Kesh Prison, County Down, Northern Ireland*

It was like walking through some huge overcast concrete cloud, Doyle thought, as yet another metal door was unlocked ahead of him.

The entire building was grey. The walls, the floors, the ceilings, the doors. Doyle expected even the warders to have grey skin.

He walked briskly behind the warder, hands dug into the pockets of his leather jacket. As they reached each door the warder would select a key from the chain hanging from his belt, insert it in the appropriate lock and then lead the counter terrorist through into another corridor. Doyle was beginning to wonder if the whole fucking thing was a wind-up. There were no prisoners in here, no cells. Just miles and miles of grey corridors. No wonder they called the place the Maze.

The warder glanced round once or twice, as if to make certain Doyle was still following. His face was expressionless as he continued on through the labyrinthine structure finally opening a door that led to yet another corridor, but this one had more doors set in each opposing wall. Cells.

*At last.*

Doyle saw that the iron doors were sealed but for a tiny viewing slot which was also closed. He could hear little sound from inside any of the cells, the only noise in the corridor coming from the warder's heavy boots as he tramped along ahead of the counter terrorist.

There were no names on the cell doors, no hint as to who might be inside but Doyle knew that this particular part of the Maze housed convicted IRA prisoners and, more particularly, the man he sought.

'Bobby Sands died in that one,' said the warder, hooking a thumb towards the door behind him, looking at Doyle then at the door of the cell, nodding as if he was pointing out some monument of great historical interest.

Doyle ignored his remark. He was interested in living IRA men, not dead ones.

'Here you go,' said the warder, motioning towards another cell.

Doyle stood back as the man inserted the key, unlocking the door.

'I can stay if you want,' the warder informed him.

Doyle shook his head.

'I'll call you when I've finished,' he said.

The warder pushed the door open and Doyle stepped in. Immediately the door was closed and locked behind him. The counter terrorist looked around.

The appraisal didn't take long; there wasn't much in the cell to see.

It was less than fifteen feet square. Grey, like the rest of the prison. The room contained a bed, a slop bucket, a plastic basin and jug, a mug and toothbrush. There was a small table and one wooden chair in a corner. A couple of books were lying on the table. A wooden locker was attached to the wall above the bed, home to what few personal items the prisoner was allowed.

The single barred window in the wall was high up and covered on both sides by mesh which seemed to allow little light through.

Dermot Christie was lying on the bed reading a newspaper. He lowered it slightly as he heard the door slam, aware of another presence in the room.

Doyle merely stood still, looking at the IRA man, his face impassive.

Christie turned another page, finished reading it then looked up.

'Who the fuck are you?' he said, disinterestedly.

Doyle didn't speak. He merely ambled over to the small table and looked down at the books lying there. One was a detective novel, the other a book about car maintenance, which Doyle picked up and waved in front of him.

'You'll have forgotten what a car looks like by the time you get out of here,' he said, smiling thinly. He dropped the book back onto the table. 'Right, I'm not going to fuck around, I'm not here because I want to be, and the quicker I'm out again the better. According to the rules I'm supposed to identify myself officially. I'm with the Counter Terrorist Unit and that's all you need to know. I need your help.'

'Fuck off,' snorted Christie, picking up his paper once again.

Doyle took a step forward and struck the paper from the other man's hand.

'I'm in a hurry,' he snapped. 'The quicker you cooperate the better. I want to know where your brother is.'

'I've been in this shithole for two years, how am I supposed to know where he is?' Christie said, scornfully. 'And even if I did know there's nothing you could do. . .'

Doyle overturned the table, kicking out at it, snapping one of the legs.

'Where is he?' he rasped.

'Fuck you.'

Doyle swept the plastic jug and bowl from its shelf. It flew across the cell and bounced against the far wall.

Christie smiled.

'Stop,' he said, chuckling. 'You're scaring me.'

The counter terrorist glanced down at the slop bucket, saw that there was dark fluid in it and something solid floating there. He grabbed the handle and hurled the contents over Christie.

A shower of excrement splattered the Irishman, some of it showering the bed, pieces of soft faeces dropping to the concrete floor with a soft splat.

'You fuck. . .' Christie snarled and hurled himself at Doyle, but the counter terrorist sidestepped, bringing one foot up, kicking hard across the Irishman's shins. Christie went down heavily, rolling in the spilled faeces. Doyle spun round and drove a pile-driver kick into the prisoner's groin.

Christie doubled up in pain and clutched at his throbbing testicles but Doyle dropped to one knee beside him and grabbed his hand, pulling it away from his injured genitals.

'Where's your brother?' he rasped.

'Fuck you,' Christie croaked, his eyes screwed up in pain.

The stench from his excreta-soaked clothes was appalling, but Doyle barely seemed to notice as he leaned closer to the Irishman.

'Last chance,' he said.

'What are you going to do if I don't tell you?' Christie said, his voice high and reedy. 'Kill me?'

'No, *I'm* not going to kill you; when word gets out that you've turned tout your own boys will be queueing up to do it for me.' He slammed Christie's head back against the concrete floor hard enough to split his scalp. Blood dripped into the urine covering the floor. 'Word travels fast in here doesn't it? And when I walk out of this cell that word is going to be that you grassed your own organisation. You told me everything I wanted to know. Names, places and times.'

'You wouldn't do that,' Christie said, the first notes of apprehension in his voice.

'Just fucking watch me.'

'No one would believe it.'

'And you're going to take that chance are you? When the word gets round that you've dropped your mates in it you'll be lucky to last a fucking week.'

Doyle grabbed the Irishman by the collar and hauled him upright, slamming him against the wall.

'Where's your brother?' he snarled.

'I don't know,' hissed Christie.

Doyle drove one knee hard into the Irishman's groin.

'Where's your brother?'

There were tears in Christie's eyes as the pain seemed to envelop his whole body, swelling outwards from the raging agony between his legs.

'Where's your brother?' Doyle repeated the question robotically, still glaring at his quarry.

'It's two fucking years since I saw him,' Christie blurted. 'He'll have moved by now.'

'Where did you last see him?'

'I don't remember.'

'Where?' snarled Doyle, pressing one forearm across the Irishman's throat. 'Tell me, *tout*.'

The word seemed to galvanise Christie.

'He had a place in Andersonstown,' he said, his face still screwed up in pain.

'Address?'

'How do I know you won't tell anyone what I've said in here?'

'You don't. Now give me that fucking address or else you can *count* on me telling. Come on, tout. The address.'

Doyle was pressing so tightly across the Irishman's throat that Christie could hardly force the words out, his head felt as if it was swelling, and he was close to fainting.

'Twenty-six Crown Street,' he croaked.

'Again.'

He repeated the address.

Doyle stepped back, releasing the pressure on Christie's throat. The Irishman fell forward, landing heavily on the floor. Doyle noticed that his face had squashed a lump of soft excrement beneath it.

The counter terrorist stepped over the body and banged on the cell door.

A moment later the warder opened it, glancing in at the prone body of Christie.

'Fuck me,' murmured the warder.

'You'd better clean him up,' said Doyle, pushing past the warder.

'What have you done to him?'

'I was sent here to get information and that's what I've done,' Doyle said, glaring at the warder. 'Now get me the fuck out of here.'

# Thirty-Four

Marie Leary twisted the tuner knob on the radio, the band selector moving from station to station. She picked up a talk show, some static, some classical music, more static. Marie finally settled for a pop station, easing down the volume as the latest one-hit wonders blurted out their instantly forgettable offering.

There wasn't much traffic on the M1 leading into Belfast from the North and what little there was moved with the desired speed to cope with what were rapidly becoming treacherous conditions. Rain was falling fast, spattering the windscreen of the Peugeot so rapidly that even the brisk sweep of the windscreen wipers seemed not to help.

Marie slowed down slightly, glancing at her speedometer, watching the needle nudge sixty. She still had plenty of time. She wasn't due to meet Paul Riordan for another hour. He'd called her that morning and told her that she, Christie, O'Connor and himself had to meet; there was something he needed to discuss with them.

Marie had a good idea what it was.

Five days had passed since their successful attack on the British arms convoy. The guns had lain hidden for almost a week.

It was time to move them.

The rain eased slightly and Marie pressed her foot down on the accelerator, coaxing more speed from the car, happy to see that the motorway was clear for a few hundred yards ahead. The outside lane was closed, but the volume of traffic was not large enough to impede her progress. She leant forward to adjust the volume on the radio.

As she did so she glanced into her rear-view mirror.

The RUC car was fifty or sixty yards behind her.

Marie felt her stomach tighten and she swallowed hard, but the reaction was not one of fear. It was anticipation.

She looked again at the police car behind her, tucked in to the rear of a white Montego.

It was making no move to pull alongside her or even draw closer.

She snapped off the radio, the pop music suddenly an intrusion. Silence descended inside the car as she drove, her eyes flicking every few seconds to the mirror.

*Were they following her?*

Up ahead was a lorry, the huge wheels throwing up vast sprays of water. Marie accelerated past it.

The police car also moved out into the middle lane.

Should she slow down a little, see if it passed her?

She moved back into the inside lane and watched the speedo needle settle on fifty-five.

The RUC car also moved back to the inside.

Marie felt a stab of angry paranoia.

*Why should they be following her?*

She hadn't done anything.

(Apart from helping to kill or maim a dozen British soldiers.)

There was no reason why they should be tailing her. If indeed they were.

*Come on, calm down.*

A slip road off the motorway was coming up, and she decided to take it. The motorway was too open should they decide to pull her over.

She signalled as the turning approached, her eyes fixed on the reflection of the police car in the mirror.

It was less than thirty yards back now, but seemed to be moving closer.

Marie turned off onto the slip road.

The RUC car followed.

She murmured something under her breath and reached forward to the glove compartment, flipping it open.

The blue steel frame of the CZ automatic pistol gleamed amongst the discarded tissues and sweet papers inside.

She closed it again, feeling happier that the pistol was there.

She sped up the slip road, stepping on the brake to slow the car as she approached a roundabout.

The police car stayed five or six car lengths back but, even from that distance, Marie could see the officer in the passenger seat turning to speak to the driver. Perhaps he was discussing the number plate, saying that he was sure the Peugeot was stolen. Perhaps he'd already radioed through to base to check the registration and found that the car had indeed been taken from a street in Derry two weeks earlier.

*But how could they know? Riordan had changed the plates.*

She administered a swift mental rebuke at her own growing paranoia.

The road she drove down was flanked on both sides by trees and, beyond them she glimpsed the odd house here and there. She hadn't reached the estates that made up the outskirts of Belfast yet and there weren't too many other vehicles on the road.

No witnesses if it came to *that*.

She glanced at the glove compartment and its lethal load.

There were traffic lights ahead and she slowed down.

Behind her the police car also slowed.

Should she speed up now, shoot through while they were on amber and see if the car followed her. At least that way she would be sure.

And if they followed? What then? Why alert them when they may not even be following?

*Get a grip*.

The RUC car moved closer; she could see the faces of the officers inside.

The police car accelerated, overtook her then pulled back so that it was level. The officer on the passenger side held up a hand then pointed towards the side of the road, inviting her to pull over.

She nodded and pressed on the brake, bringing the car to a gentle halt, the windscreen wipers still moving backwards and forwards, one of them squeaking loudly.

The police car pulled up a few yards ahead.

Marie flipped open the glove compartment and reached for the CZ.

*Wait.*

One of the officers stepped out of the car.

*Wait until he's closer.*

She glanced around.

The policeman was less than twenty feet from her car now, walking purposefully through the rain, running appraising eyes over the Peugeot.

A car sped past. Other than that there was nothing on the road.

*No witnesses.*

He was drawing closer.

Fifteen feet.

She felt her heart thudding more heavily in her chest.

Ten feet.

She could kill this one then sprint to the police car, put two shots into the head of the other before he had the chance to radio through.

Five feet.

She ran a hand through her hair, looked at her reflection in the rear-view mirror as if checking she was presentable enough. Not that it was going to matter much to this man she was about to kill.

She smiled up at him as she wound down her window.

*Keep calm.*

Rain was bouncing off his cap as he leaned close to her.

She could take the automatic and press it against his face from here.

'Good morning,' said the officer, looking at her then allowing his eyes to flick around the interior of the Peugeot.

'Morning,' she replied.

'We spotted your car a few miles back there,' he said.

*Now. Shoot him now.*

'Is something wrong?' she asked, trying to sound nonchalant, hoping he didn't notice the slight breathlessness in her voice.

'Yes there is.'

The glove compartment was open. She could see the butt of the CZ.

*Grab it now. Shoot him.*

'One of your brake lights isn't working,' he said. 'You should get it fixed as soon as you can. It *is* an offence you know.'

'I didn't realise it was broken,' she said. 'Sorry.'

'You're lucky it was us that stopped you. Someone else might have given you a ticket.' He smiled broadly. 'Get it fixed before they do.' He tapped on the top of the car then turned and headed back towards the waiting police car. Marie watched as he climbed in and the car moved off.

It was a few moments before her breathing returned to normal. She closed the glove compartment, sitting behind the wheel motionless, collecting her thoughts.

'Jesus,' she whispered under her breath.

The windscreen wiper continued to squeak as it brushed away the rain.

Marie waited a moment longer then started the engine and drove off.

## Thirty-Five

There was a uniformity about the houses in Crown Street which was echoed across Belfast as well as here in Andersonstown: two-up-two-down terraced dwellings of red brick, most in need of some kind of repair either to paintwork or structure. They reminded Doyle of lines of building bricks, each dwelling indistinguishable from the next, different coloured front doors here and there the only attempts at individuality. Otherwise, uniformity blurred into anonymity. These streets bore little joy for their inhabitants whose hopelessness seemed to be mirrored in the stark sameness of the places where they lived.

Less than half a mile to the south was Milltown cemetery. Doyle wondered how many of the previous residents of Andersonstown were buried there; how many still living here had laid someone close to rest there?

Doyle took one last drag on his cigarette, his musings snuffed out as surely as the dog-end he stepped on. He crossed the street to 26 Crown Street, glancing at the house as he advanced.

The paintwork was chipped and flaking, particularly around the window frames where it was blistered in several places. The curtains were drawn both up and downstairs, the windows dirty. Doyle wondered how long it must have been since they'd tasted water.

If James Christie *did* still live here then he wasn't too fucking houseproud, thought the counter terrorist.

He gripped the knocker and rapped four times, loudly.

As he moved his arm, Doyle could feel the bulk of the .50 calibre Desert Eagle close to his body. If Christie was inside and wouldn't come out, he could use the Eagle to blow the hinges off.

There was no answer.

He banged again.

Nothing.

Perhaps Christie was still in bed.

Doyle glanced at his watch.

Unlikely at 2.30 in the afternoon.

He banged again.

Maybe his brother had lied. He said he hadn't seen Christie for two years. Or perhaps the man had simply moved.

*IRA members didn't usually leave forwarding addresses did they?*

Doyle exhaled irritably and kept on banging.

The door of number 24 opened and a tall, willowy woman in her late thirties emerged, still wiping her hands on a tea towel.

'What the bloody hell is all this noise?' she said, glaring at Doyle.

He met her stare but didn't speak.

'Are you trying to wake the dead?' she challenged. 'Because you're going the right way about it the bloody noise you're making.'

'I'm looking for the guy who lives here,' said Doyle, slipping into an Irish accent. 'Do you know him?'

'What if I do? Who are you?'

'I want to know if you've seen him, he owes me fucking money,' the counter terrorist lied.

'Will you watch your language, there's kids around here.'

'Where's Christie?'

'I'm not his mother. I hardly ever see him.'

'But he does live here?'

'Aye, he lives there, but he's hardly ever home.'

'Shit.'

'I told you to watch your bloody language,' the woman rasped. 'He's after spending a lot of his time round at the snooker hall in Donegal Street.'

'How do you know?'

'Because my bloody husband spends most of *his* time round there too. As if there isn't enough here for him to be getting on with,' the woman said, irritably. 'So if you're looking for James Christie I reckon you're better off looking there instead of kicking up a fuss here.'

'Thanks,' said Doyle, turning to walk away.

'If he comes back, shall I tell him you called?' the woman wanted to know.

'No, that's okay,' said Doyle. 'I'll surprise him.'

The tricolour had been spray painted on the wall of the shop, with cans, Doyle guessed, looking at the uneven lines of the shape. Beside it, in large green letters, someone had painted NO SURRENDER.

The shop itself had grilles across both front windows and the door. There were two or three women standing outside the shop chatting animatedly. Doyle could hear their laughter even from across the street.

Two young girls dressed in maroon school blazers wandered past his car, part of a steady trickle of similarly attired children who had been making their way down the road for the last fifteen minutes. All of them looked immaculate in their uniforms and Doyle noted the pride which was obviously engendered in them, their parents probably making financial sacrifices to ensure their kids were adequately clothed. It was a curious contrast to the poverty around him.

He massaged the back of his neck, feeling the beginnings of a headache gnawing at the base of his skull. He had pins and needles in one leg from sitting too long. Every so often he would get out of the Volvo and make a show of checking under the bonnet, wondering if the ruse would work. No one had bothered him yet, not even to ask if he needed a hand with his supposedly stricken car. Perhaps no one had even noticed him.

At least no one he'd spotted.

In the past ninety minutes he hadn't seen hide or hair of James Christie either entering or leaving the snooker hall. Plenty of other men had come and gone but so far not the man he sought. Doyle had thought briefly about going over there, wandering up to the first floor and taking a look for himself but he realised that a strange face in these surroundings was as noticeable as a Rabbi at a Nazi rally. He knew that he and his car had probably already been noted as intruders but, so far, his guise of stricken motorist seemed to be appropriate. But for how much longer?

*Where the fuck was Christie?*

Doyle thought he could afford to give it another fifteen minutes then he'd be forced to drive at least round the block a couple of times, possibly even head back to Crown Street and wait for Christie there.

He glanced across at the snooker hall entrance and spotted a figure.

It was a youth in his late teens, his hair slicked back to reveal a forehead dotted with spots.

Doyle sighed wearily.

Two more of the uniformed school girls passed his car, peering in at him, one of them giggling when Doyle winked back at her. She and her companion glanced over their shoulders as they walked on, wondering what the man with the long hair and the leather jacket was doing sitting in his car. He watched them disappear around a corner out of sight.

The women over the road had finished their conversation and went off in different directions, one of them into the shop. Doyle flipped open his cigarette packet and noticed he was out. He swung himself out of the car, locked the door and headed towards the shop, glancing briefly towards the snooker-hall entrance.

Still no sign of Christie.

If he was even *in* there.

It was warm inside the shop and Doyle could smell an almost overpowering aroma of coffee. The shop was a cross between a convenience store and a paper shop. He wandered over to the magazine racks, easing his way past the youth he'd seen leave the snooker hall. He was thumbing furtively through a copy of *Penthouse* but when Doyle brushed past him he coloured and jammed the magazine back onto the top shelf, leaving hurriedly. Doyle smiled to himself, took a paper from the rack then crossed to the counter to pay, picking up a Mars bar and a tube of mints.

'Twenty Rothmans, please,' he said to the rotund man behind the counter, his eyes straying to the front of the shop, out into the street. The shop owner took the five pound note Doyle offered and gave him his change. The counter terrorist nodded and headed back towards his car deciding now that he would drive back to Crown Street. If he sat around here for much longer then he was going to become conspicuous. If he hadn't already.

Might as well wait for Christie there.

He paused to light a cigarette, cursing as he dropped his lighter.

He bent down to pick it up then turned and headed back towards the car.

Had he turned at that moment he would have seen James Christie leaving the snooker hall.

The Irishman left alone, turned left and headed towards the end of the street, hands dug deep into his pockets.

Doyle slid behind the wheel and settled into the unwelcome embrace of the Volvo's driving seat. He glanced in his wing mirror when he heard a car hooter. Saw an Escort driving by, the man behind the wheel waving to someone on the other side of the road. Saw that man wave back.

Saw James Christie.

*About fucking time.*

Doyle reached for the ignition key, relieved that he could finally drop the stranded motorist guise.

In the rear-view mirror he could see Christie turning the corner, heading out of sight.

The counter terrorist turned the key.

The engine gave a strangled sound and died.

Christie had almost reached the end of the street.

Sod's law? Tempting fate? Or just fucking bad luck? Whatever the case, Doyle gritted his teeth and turned the key again.

Christie disappeared around the corner.

The car wouldn't start.

# Thirty-Six

Doyle saw the red battery light flicker on the dashboard and it seemed to galvanise him. He pulled out the choke so far he almost tore it off then hit the accelerator.

The engine burst into life.

Doyle pressed down harder, holding his foot there, ignoring the puzzled looks of passers-by who watched as clouds of exhaust fumes billowed from the tail pipe. He jammed the Volvo in gear and swung it round in the street, heading after Christie.

As he reached the end of the road he slowed down, peering right and left in search of his quarry.

The Irishman was nowhere to be seen.

'Fuck,' rasped Doyle, banging the wheel angrily.

*Take it easy. He can't have disappeared.*

Ahead of him a dark blue Ford Escort pulled out into the road and moved off slowly.

Doyle followed at a safe distance, peering towards the car in an effort to get a look at the driver. He saw the broad shoulders, the bald patch at the crown of the head.

It was Christie. He was sure of it.

*Now you've found him, don't lose him.*

At first Doyle thought that the Irishman was heading back to Crown Street, but then he dismissed the idea. Why bring a car four blocks when he could have walked. Christie drove on, heading for the city centre.

Doyle followed, dropping back one car length as they drew nearer to busier roads. He allowed an Astra to pull between him and his quarry, anxious not to alert the other man to his presence.

As they passed the City Hall the Astra moved off into

another lane. Doyle kept his distance from the blue Escort. He could see Christie tapping his fingers on the wheel rhythmically, possibly following the beat of the music coming from his radio.

They swung right at the next roundabout and Doyle glanced to his left at the Divis flats. Great grey monoliths, they seemed to have pushed their way up from beneath the ground, jabbing at the sky like probing fingers. At the top of each one, ringed by barbed wire, was a security position. Doyle saw two soldiers moving about in front of the flats.

He allowed another car to pull between him and Christie, careful never to let the Escort get too far in front.

They were heading out of Belfast now, he noticed, leaving the bustling city centre behind.

There were traffic lights ahead. They were still on green when Christie went through.

Doyle noticed, with exasperation, that they were changing to amber.

If he wasn't careful he'd get stuck at these lights and Christie would be long gone; he had already rounded a bend on the other side of the junction.

Doyle glanced in his rear-view mirror, saw the lane on his right was clear and pulled out, flooring the accelerator.

He sped past the car in front and hurtled across the junction as the lights slipped to red.

Someone coming from the opposite direction gestured angrily at him but Doyle ignored it, thankful that his enforced manoeuvre had been unseen by Christie. If the Irishman had seen the Volvo speed across the lights he may well have been alerted that something was wrong. As it was, Doyle eased up on his speed as soon as he caught sight of the Escort again.

They were still heading away from the city centre.

*Where the fuck was he going?*

For one absurd moment Doyle wondered if Christie was going to lead him to Riordan, the rest of the active service unit and the entire stock of stolen army weapons. He smiled to himself. No. That kind of thing only happened in films. This bastard was for real.

Subconsciously he slipped one hand inside his jacket and touched the butt of the Desert Eagle, as if making contact with the weapon would prepare him should it be needed. He had little doubt that Christie would be armed.

Doyle saw the Irishman was turning to the left, the indicator on the Escort flashing.

He slowed down, dropping back a few more yards as he tried to see where Christie was going. The Irishman pulled the Escort into a petrol station.

Doyle drove past, not wanting to pull into the forecourt too. He drove on two or three hundred yards and swung the Volvo into a side street, sitting there with the engine idling. The street entrance was narrow and he reversed in as far as he could, waiting for Christie to resume his journey. Even if he saw the Volvo pull out of this turning there was no reason to suspect it would be following him.

Doyle sat and waited.

Two minutes passed.

Five.

The Escort sped past.

Doyle waited a moment then followed. If Christie knew he was being followed he certainly showed no signs of it.

The road became a dual carriageway then a motorway. They increased speed, moving further away from Belfast.

It was as they passed one particular road sign that Doyle finally realised where Christie was heading.

He allowed a car to move between him and his quarry, confident now of their destination.

It was less than a mile to Belfast airport.

# Thirty-Seven

The child wouldn't be quiet.

No matter what its mother did to placate it, the baby kept on crying.

Doyle sipped his coffee and glanced across at the woman who was rocking the baby back and forth in her arms in a desperate attempt to still its yells. Other eyes also looked in her direction, nerves already frayed by the thought of boarding a plane agitated further by the constant sound.

From his position at a table in the small café at the airport, Doyle had a clear view across the departure area. There were a number of shops frequented by those who preferred to spend the time leading up to embarkation with more on their minds than the flight. Some were buying gifts, others books or magazines for their own journeys.

Doyle looked across at the crying baby and wished its mother had bought it a gag.

He finished his coffee, pushed the cup away then went and got another.

James Christie was sitting in the other part of the café, in the non-smoking area. He had spent most of the last thirty minutes wandering alternately between the Arrivals board and the newsstand. He sat with a glass of milk and a newspaper in front of him, every now and then looking at his watch and then at the board.

Checking the times of incoming flights? Doyle wondered.

The counter terrorist returned to the table where he'd been sitting, the sound of the crying baby still echoing around the terminal. He lit up a cigarette and sat back in the plastic seat.

A loud clicking sound came from the Arrivals board, like several huge playing cards toppling over. He looked round to see that another flight had just been posted on it.

BA 127 was due to arrive in ten minutes from London.

Doyle drank more coffee and looked across at Christie who was on his feet again, walking slowly towards the board, squinting up at it myopically. As Doyle watched he turned and headed towards the exit.

The counter terrorist waited a moment, not wanting to spring up in pursuit of his quarry in case his movement was spotted by the Irishman.

Perhaps he was just going for a piss, the toilets were in that direction.

Doyle waited a moment longer then got to his feet, his cup still full.

It didn't look like Christie was coming back.

The Arrivals area was a short walk away and Doyle didn't want to lose the Irishman. He glanced disdainfully at the mother and her howling baby as he passed, the sound echoing in his ears as he walked out.

He saw Christie as he emerged and quickened his step until he was twenty or thirty yards behind the other man, eyes fixed on him like some of kind of homing device. The Irishman entered the Arrivals area and Doyle followed.

There were a couple of RUC men inside, arms folded across their chests. Apart from the uniformed men Doyle saw a number of other people, doubtless all there to meet those leaving the plane that had just touched down. He saw Christie leaning against the wall close to a couple of payphones, his hands buried in his pockets, eyes scanning the doors through which the disembarking passengers must come. Doyle reached for a cigarette but decided against it when he saw the disapproving look given him by one of the RUC men. The last thing he wanted now was to draw attention to himself. He slipped the pack back into his pocket and leaned against one of the concrete pillars instead, eyes flicking back and forth from Christie to the doors ahead.

The first of the arrivals came through. A man alone carrying just an attaché case. He was followed by a woman and two small children. An elderly couple. Then the trickle became a flow of people.

*Jesus, which one is Christie waiting for?*

Doyle glanced back towards the pay phones.

Christie had gone.

Doyle scanned the crowd hastily.

There was no sign of the Irishman.


# *Thirty-Eight*


Doyle pushed his way through the throng of people, searching desperately for Christie, but still he couldn't see him.

He could feel the anger building inside him.

*To get this close and now lose the bastard . . .*

Someone bumped into him and Doyle spun round angrily. It was a woman with a large suitcase, she murmured an apology but the counter terrorist merely stepped around her, his eyes roving back and forth over the sea of faces.

*Where are you?*

He headed back towards the pay phones where he'd last seen Christie.

Still no sign.

He could see the uniformed RUC men through the crowd, but not the man he sought.

People were still coming through the doors that opened into the Arrivals area, a steady stream of faces.

He decided to head for the door, there was only one exit

from the building, if he covered that he couldn't avoid seeing Christie as he emerged. Doyle scuttled through the crowd, bumping into an elderly man in the process, ignoring the harsh words that accompanied the collision.

The RUC men glanced at Doyle then returned their attention to the flood of arrivals still filing out into the night.

Doyle reached the door and turned.

Christie was less than ten feet behind him, walking briskly, another man with him.

Doyle smiled to himself and bent his head as he lit a cigarette. When Christie and the other man passed him, Doyle noticed that the Irishman was gripping his companion's forearm, digging his fingers into the man's coat and almost dragging him along. The man looked pale, his eyes red-rimmed.

This didn't look like an emotional reunion, Doyle thought. As he followed them outside he saw Christie pull the man sharply in the direction of the car park and the man almost stumbled.

*What the fuck was this all about?*

The other man was tall but thinly built, his pale complexion made to look waxen by his ginger hair.

Doyle didn't recognise him from any mug shots he'd seen. He wondered if he was IRA. He wondered *who* the hell he was.

The man followed Christie's lead almost reluctantly, standing obediently at the passenger side of the car while the Irishman unlocked it, practically pushing the ginger-haired man inside before walking round and sliding behind the wheel. He started the engine of the Escort and pulled out of the parking space.

Doyle sprinted over to where his Volvo was parked, hoping that the bloody thing would start without any trouble. He twisted the ignition key and the engine burst into life. He stuck it in gear and pulled out, glancing ahead, seeing the brake lights of the Escort flare as Christie stopped to allow a woman by.

Then they were moving again.

He could see Christie turning to look at the passenger every so often, obviously speaking to him. The ginger-haired man merely sat gazing out of the front window, not moving.

Who the fuck was he?

Major Wetherby had said that the arms convoy had been hit by four armed attackers. He knew one was Paul Riordan, chances were that Christie and Declan O'Connor were two of the others. Could this man be the fourth?

If he was, why the apparent hostility from Christie?

*So many questions.*

The roads leading from the airport back towards the motorway were dimly lit and flanked on both sides, for the most part, by tall hedges which added to the overall gloom. Doyle switched his headlights to full beam, making sure he kept a good distance between himself and the Escort.

But not *too* great a distance.

There was a junction up ahead and Doyle slowed down, watching the Escort carefully.

Some cars turned right, others left.

The Escort went left.

Doyle followed.

# Thirty-Nine

'Did you have any trouble?'

James Christie guided the Escort skilfully along the narrow roads leading out of Belfast airport, glancing at his passenger every so often.

'I said, did you have any trouble?' he repeated, irritably.

In the passenger seat Stephen Murphy shook his head almost imperceptibly, his eyes blank and staring through

123

the windscreen. As he looked to one side he could see his own gaunt face reflected in the window of the car.

'You were late,' Christie told him.

'The plane was delayed,' Murphy said, apologetically. He spoke softly, the words barely audible above the drone of the engine. As he sat he had his hands clasped together in his lap. He could feel the perspiration on them and also on his face. 'There was something going on at Heathrow, some kind of strike. . .' He allowed the sentence to trail off.

Christie seemed uninterested and turned his attention more fully to driving. He glanced in the rear-view mirror and noticed that there was one solitary car following the same route. A Volvo he thought. Whoever was driving it, the bloody fool had his lights on full beam. They were shining brightly into the Irishman's eyes every time he looked in the mirror. He decided to turn off, try and find another route, perhaps this fucking idiot behind would be going some other way.

There was a crossroads coming up. Christie turned right.

A moment later the Volvo swung round too, the lights shining in his eyes.

Christie muttered something under his breath and drove on.

'I thought we were heading back into the city,' said Murphy, quietly, noticing that they were still on a country road, hedges rising on either side of them.

Christie didn't answer at first then he glanced across at his companion almost disdainfully.

'What's your rush?' he said.

'I just thought. . .'

'Well fucking don't,' snapped Christie, cutting him short. 'You don't have to think. All you have to do is what you're told. Right?'

Murphy nodded.

'There might be another job for you,' Christie continued.

'When?' Murphy said, his voice frantic.

'Whenever we fucking decide.'

They rode for a way in silence, Christie still irritated by

the glare of the Volvo's lights in his rear-view mirror. He slowed down a couple of times, pulling into the side of the narrow road in an effort to encourage the driver behind to overtake but it didn't work. The Volvo stayed close behind.

Christie frowned, wondering why the driver behind was so reluctant to pass him.

Up ahead he saw a lay-by, or what passed for one. It was little more than an area of mud, rutted and water-logged, pressed into the bank beneath the hedge but it was sufficient. He swung the Escort into the gap and brought the car to a halt.

The Volvo swept past, spattering mud and rainwater into the air, some of it showering the side of the Escort.

'Prick,' muttered Christie as the car disappeared around a bend in the road, tail lights swallowed by the gloom. He waited a moment then swung the car round and drove back the way he'd come.

It was only a matter of seconds before the Volvo reappeared, headlights still glaring.

Christie pressed his foot down on the accelerator, the needle on the speedometer touching fifty.

The Volvo kept close.

Jolted in his seat by the sudden increase in speed, Murphy looked at the driver with concern.

'What's wrong?' he said, his voice catching.

'You tell me,' snapped Christie. 'I'm sure this fucking Volvo is following us.'

'How do you know?'

'Take my word for it.'

Christie swung the car to the left.

The Volvo followed, now moving closer to the rear of the Escort.

'Fucker,' Christie snarled, his hand sliding to the inside of his jacket. He touched the butt of the Taurus automatic jammed in his belt.

Murphy turned in his seat, trying to see the pursuing vehicle. The headlights dazzled him.

'Sit still,' snarled Christie, pulling the gun free. He jammed it into Murphy's groin hard enough to make him grunt in pain. 'Do *you* know who he is?'

'No. I swear it.'

'You fucking liar. If you've set me up I'll kill you here and now.'

'I don't know,' Murphy said, despairingly.

'Shit,' hissed Christie.

The Volvo was right on his tail now. He knew his only choice was to run.

He pressed down harder on the accelerator.

The Volvo sped after him.


# Forty


Doyle had known when Christie pulled into the side of the road that he'd been on to him.

When he'd turned the car and driven back the same way, the counter terrorist had realised that the time he'd been waiting for had come. In a way he had provoked the response in Christie. Doyle knew that he could only tail the IRA man for so long. Eventually he'd have to move in on him.

Now he was about to make that move.

The Escort sped away, mud spraying up behind it, spattering the front of the Volvo.

Doyle pressed down on the gas and gave chase, never more than ten or fifteen yards from the fleeing car. In the darkness on these back roads he couldn't afford to let Christie get too far in front. But he couldn't pull alongside the Escort on such narrow thoroughfares. He would have to find a different way of bringing the Escort to a halt.

Doyle floored the accelerator and the Volvo shot

forward, slamming into the rear of the Escort.

One of the car's tail lights was shattered by the impact and Doyle smiled to himself.

The Escort turned sharply to the left, skidding on the mud in the process.

Doyle struggled to control the Volvo which also skidded, the rear of the vehicle swinging wildly as he took the corner in third.

On the straight once more the two cars speeded up again, hurtling down the muddy roads like rally cars.

Doyle thought about shooting one or more of the tyres out but if he did that the Escort might flip, crash and even kill the passengers and, as much as it galled Doyle to consider it, he knew he needed them alive if possible.

There was another junction up ahead and the Escort sped across, in front of a car coming from the left whose driver hit the horn.

Doyle shot past the junction on the tail of the Escort, causing the driver of the third car to brake hard. He heard the squeal of brakes as he drove on, speed increasing.

Mud sprayed up from the rear wheels of the fleeing Escort momentarily blurring Doyle's view. Cursing he flicked on the windscreen wipers, watching as they brushed away the mud.

He accelerated and slammed into the rear of the Escort once again, this time cracking one of his own headlights as well as putting a dent in the rear bumper of the Escort.

The road ahead was widening slightly and Doyle decided to try to pull up alongside the Escort.

If he could draw level he could perhaps push the vehicle off the road. He stepped on the pedal and the Volvo raced forward.

Christie saw what was happening and spun the wheel, smashing the Escort into the Volvo.

The two cars skidded then sped on.

Doyle could see the face of the passenger in the other car, ashen and terrified.

*Who the fuck was he?*

Christie was shouting something, gripping the steering wheel tightly. Doyle saw him gesturing angrily at his passenger.

He turned his own wheel and hit the Escort broadside, the two vehicles scraping together, paint ripped from them by the friction.

Doyle, no more than six feet from Christie, kept his eyes fixed on his quarry, who kept looking across at him angrily.

*You're not getting away you fucker.*

He saw Christie's hand go to his inside pocket.

Saw the Taurus pulled free.

Doyle swung the Volvo into the other car again, the impact making Christie drop the pistol on the floor of the Escort. Doyle smiled to himself and looked ahead, noticing that the road was narrowing once more.

He saw headlights coming straight for him.

The car heading towards him was flashing its lights madly, the driver sounding his horn in an effort to warn the oncoming vehicles of the imminent collision.

Doyle twisted the wheel to the right, Christie sent the Escort hurtling off to the left.

The Volvo crashed through a hedge and into a field, skidding in the mud, huge geysers of the filthy matter spraying up as the wheels churned.

Through the broken hedge, Doyle could still see the Escort, speeding along on a parallel path to him. He floored the accelerator and raced along through the field, keeping the hedge between himself and Christie for the next few hundred yards, then he swung the car back towards the road, smashed through the hedge and powered into the side of the Escort. This time the collision was strong enough to knock the other vehicle through the hedge on the far side of the road.

Both vehicles hurtled through, flattening the branches.

Christie steered away from the Volvo, guiding the Escort into the field away from the road.

Doyle followed.

128

The field was uneven and Doyle felt the Volvo leave the ground more than once, slamming back down with jarring impact as he fought to pull alongside his quarry again.

There were lights up ahead in the distance. A house.

Christie might be trying to reach it.

Doyle slammed into the back of the Escort again. And again.

Each impact sent a shock wave through the car and the counter terrorist had to grip the wheel tightly to retain control of the Volvo, but he persisted with the buffeting, aware of the ever approaching lights.

There was a low stone wall ahead with a gate set into it.

The Escort burst through it, pieces of shattered wood flying into the air.

Doyle shot through the gap behind noticing that the lights were now much closer. They burned inside a house.

He saw a barn to the right. A pig-sty. Some farm machinery.

Doyle sped up alongside the Escort and wrenched the wheel across, bumping the other car, pushing it towards the large wooden doors of the barn.

Both vehicles crashed through.

Doyle shouted aloud and stepped on the brake, the Volvo skidding to a halt.

Christie wasn't so lucky.

The Escort skidded across the floor of the barn and thudded to a halt in a pile of straw bales which promptly collapsed upon it.

Doyle was out of the Volvo in seconds, pulling the Desert Eagle from its holster.

He saw Christie push open the driver's door and stumble out, blood running from a gash on his forehead.

He looked up at Doyle and gritted his teeth.

'Don't move,' shouted the counter terrorist.

'Fuck you,' Christie roared back, his hand going to the inside of his jacket.

Doyle saw the Taurus swinging into view.

He fired twice.

The roar of the Eagle was thunderous within the confines of the barn.

The first bullet hit Christie in the chest, splintered the sternum with ease and ripped through a lung before exploding from his back, spraying the Escort with blood and lung tissue. The bullet punched through the side window as it exited and the sound of shattering glass mingled with a sickening thud as the Irishman was thrown back against the car.

The second shot powered into the driver's side door, missing Christie's left leg by inches.

He fell forward, the pistol falling from his hand.

Doyle scurried forward, the Eagle held ready, trying to get a look at the passenger who was slumped against the dashboard.

The engine of the Escort was still running, exhaust fumes filling the barn.

Doyle ducked low and drew a bead on the passenger.

He could hear a dog barking somewhere close by.

'Get out of the fucking car,' Doyle rasped, glancing down quickly at Christie who was motionless close by, blood soaking into the ground around him.

'Move it,' Doyle hissed, but the passenger remained motionless.

'You've got three seconds,' Doyle told him. 'Get out of the fucking car.'

Then he heard the loud double click and recognised it immediately.

The twin triggers of a shotgun being pulled back.

Doyle turned slightly and saw a figure silhouetted in the barn doorway, the double barrelled shotgun held firmly in his grip, the yawning barrels aimed at Doyle. He heard a voice.

'Drop the gun or I'll blow your fucking head off.'

# Forty-One

Doyle thought that the man holding the shotgun was in his early fifties, but it was difficult to tell. He was tall and powerfully built, his hair greying at the temples, his thick fingers gripping the Rossi tightly, the barrels wavering slightly.

There was a waver, too, in the man's voice, which Doyle put down to fear, and the way he kept shifting from one foot to the other seemed to reinforce the counter terrorist's theory.

*Be careful. Don't alarm him.*

The farmer kept looking at Christie's body and Doyle could see him shaking almost imperceptibly.

*Just hope his fucking trigger finger doesn't start shaking.*

A frightened man with a gun was as likely to blow a hole in you as miss. Doyle couldn't afford to take any chances.

He stood his ground, the Eagle aimed at the farmer, the other's shotgun pointed at Doyle.

Like two gunfighters in some Wild West scenario they looked at each other.

'Put the fucking gun down,' said the farmer again, that quaver in his voice.

Doyle didn't move.

'Just take it easy,' he said, slowly.

Doyle was suddenly struck by the awful irony of the situation. He'd survived bomb blasts and numerous bullet wounds during the course of his career. Was he now to be shot by some nervous farmer?

Outside the barn he heard the dog barking again.

'I'll shoot, I'm telling you,' the farmer assured him.

Doyle held his own gun in position, ready to kill this pain in the arse if he had to. But he didn't want to unless he was left with no other choice.

Behind him he heard a low groan as Murphy stirred in the passenger seat of the Escort. Doyle glanced round, saw the man slump back in his chair. Blood was running from his mouth and nose.

'Did you shoot him too?' the farmer asked.

Doyle returned his gaze to his opponent, his own pistol still gripped firmly in his fist.

'Look, just turn around and walk away, I'll handle this,' he said, quietly.

The farmer shook his head.

'My name's Doyle, I'm with the Counter Terrorist Unit.'

'My arse,' snapped the farmer.

'It's the truth. These men are IRA. I chased them here.'

The farmer was breathing more heavily now, his eyes wide with panic and confusion. He lowered the shotgun slightly as if the weight were suddenly too much for him.

Doyle took a step forward and the farmer hastily raised the gun up high once more.

The counter terrorist gritted his teeth.

'Go inside and call an ambulance for this one,' he said, nodding in the direction of Christie.

'Its a bit late for that isn't it? He's fucking dead.'

Murphy glanced myopically around him and coughed, tasting blood in his mouth. He could smell the fumes from the engine of the Escort.

'Please,' Doyle said. 'Go in and call an ambulance.' He was having trouble controlling his temper now, but knew he must for fear of panicking the farmer even more. The barrels of the shotgun seemed to yawn at him like defiant mouths.

'How do I know you're what you say you are, where's your identification?' the farmer asked.

'I don't carry any. You'll have to believe me.'

'Like hell.'

'If I'd wanted to kill you I'd have done it as soon as you

walked through that fucking door.'

The farmer looked across at Murphy who was struggling to get out of the car. He was moaning loudly in pain.

'What's wrong with him?' the farmer demanded.

'That's what I'm going to find out,' Doyle told him and stepped towards Murphy.

'Get back,' the farmer said.

Doyle ignored him, taking another step towards the Irishman.

Murphy pushed open the door and fell out onto the floor of the barn.

'Call that fucking ambulance,' Doyle hissed.

The farmer hesitated a second then lowered the shotgun.

'Do it.'

He turned and sprinted out of the barn.

Doyle pushed the Desert Eagle back into his holster and ran over to Murphy, pulling him upright, gazing into his eyes.

He groaned loudly.

Doyle saw the blood on his face, the pain etched across his features.

'Who are you?' he asked.

Murphy screwed his eyes up as another wave of pain hit him.

'Your fucking name,' Doyle snarled. He grabbed the Irishman by the lapels and slammed him against the side of the car.

Murphy coughed, more blood spilling over his lips. It hung like a crimson ribbon from his chin, mixed with saliva, dangling there like a liquid pendulum.

'Help me,' Murphy croaked then turned his head to one side and vomited close to Doyle's foot. Murphy sagged in his grip, but Doyle held him up.

*Internal injury?*

The Irishman's skin was the colour of rancid butter.

Doyle dragged Murphy across to the Volvo, wrenched

open the passenger door and pushed him in, pulling the seatbelt across him, then he hurried round and slid behind the wheel, starting the engine.

He reached across and fumbled in Murphy's pocket, pulling out his boarding pass from the flight into Belfast.

It bore his name.

Doyle looked at his captive and stuck the car in reverse. He had to get Murphy to a hospital and fast.

'Please help me,' the Irishman groaned and Doyle thought that he was going to vomit again, but Murphy clenched his teeth and merely allowed his head to loll back against the seat.

The Volvo sped out of the barn and Doyle headed back towards the road, each jolt of the car causing fresh pain to Murphy.

Doyle glanced across at him, at his waxen features and the blood and bile which had spattered his face and shirt.

'Hold on, you bastard,' hissed Doyle. 'I'm not losing you too.'

# Forty-Two

*London*

Traffic was heavy in Park Lane, even at such a late hour. Frankie Wong tapped agitatedly on the steering wheel of the Scorpio, waiting for the two taxis in front to move off.

The driver in the car behind him sounded his hooter but Wong ignored it, pulling out into traffic only when he was ready. He drove steadily, glancing to his left at the array of fine hotels which vied for position on this most exclusive of thoroughfares.

Beside him he heard the metallic click of an automatic slide being worked and he glanced down to see Cho Lok checking the hammer on the Smith & Wesson 459.

In the back seat a similar ritual was being performed as two other men of the Tai Hung Chai ensured that their weapons were in perfect working order.

The car smelled of cigarette smoke and perspiration.

Wong cruised along, glancing across at the Hilton hotel as they passed. He slowed down slightly, peering at the imposing frontage of the building, the flags that adorned it blowing gently in the breeze. A number of cars were parked in front of the hotel and a steady stream of taxis dropped off and picked up passengers, shepherded by uniformed doormen.

'What if he uses a different hotel?' asked Cho, running a hand through his hair.

'He won't,' Wong told him with assurance. 'He always uses the Hilton. He thinks it's good for his image.'

They drove on, Wong guiding the Scorpio along the one-way system and back up Park Lane, growing impatient with the slow-moving traffic. To the left was the great expanse of Hyde Park, swathed in darkness now, a startling contrast to the dazzling array of lights that shone on the edifices of the hotels opposite.

'Chi will arrive at the Hilton at about 12.45,' Wong said. 'He usually has two or three men with him. He'll go inside for maybe two or three hours.'

'What the fuck does he do?' Cho wanted to know.

'He gets his brains fucked out by two whores. High-price call-girls. He always has two.'

'He's lucky,' Cho mused, sliding the automatic back into his belt.

The men in the back chuckled, too, but Wong could hear the tension in that sound.

'You hit him when he comes out, got it,' Wong said.

'You've told us enough times,' Cho reminded him.

'We can't afford this to go wrong. If one of their top men is killed by us, the Hip Sing will stop this fucking war. They'll know they can't fuck with us. Chi is their *Fu Shan Chu*. By hitting someone so senior we'll show them we haven't lost face.' He tapped slowly on the wheel. 'This should have been done days ago. If the others had listened to me.'

'What about Chi's men?' Cho asked.

'I want them taken out too. But leave one alive, I want them to know who did it.' He glanced into the rear-view mirror at one of the two men seated there. 'When you chop him, don't kill him, right? Cripple him, but don't kill him.'

One of the men, a tall wiry individual in his mid-twenties reached into his jacket and pulled out a large, viciously sharp cleaver. The broad, flat blade gleamed in the dull light inside the car. He pressed his thumb gently against the razor edge, leaving a small red indentation on the pad.

'How much longer?' Cho enquired.

Wong looked down at the dashboard clock.

'Chi should be arriving any minute,' he said.

He muttered to himself as the car was held up once more. A taxi trying to edge its way into the traffic was causing the hold up.

Wong blasted on the hooter and gestured angrily at the car in front which had paused to let the taxi out.

The traffic finally moved on.

Wong slowed down as the Hilton came into view once again.

'There,' he said, jabbing a finger towards a brand-new Jag pulling in at the main doors of the hotel. 'That's Chi.'

A short, grey-haired man stepped out of the Jag, flanked on either side by bigger men who seemed more intent on watching those around them. They walked with Chi to the main doors but one of them paused, leaning up against the wall. He pulled out a pack of cigarettes and lit one.

Wong reached for the car phone and stabbed the digits he wanted, waiting for it to be answered at the other end. He flicked on the speaker and heard a familiar voice filling the car.

'Go ahead, Frankie,' said Joey Chang.

'Chi's just arrived,' Wong told him. 'He's inside the hotel with one of his men.'

'Are you ready?'

'We're ready.'

'Stand by.'

The line went dead.

Wong pressed the 'End' button on the phone and replaced it, then he glanced down at the clock once more.

It was 12.52 a.m.

'What now?' Cho demanded.

Wong looked up at the front of the Hilton, wondering which room their enemy was in.

'We wait,' he said, softly.


# Forty-Three


*Northern Ireland*

Doyle fed coins into the vending machine and punched the button claiming COFFEE WITH SUGAR. He watched the small plastic cup drop into place then heard the whirring sound as it was filled.

As he took it from the machine he cursed as the heat from the cup burned his fingertips. He put it down on the nearby table, shaking his hand angrily in the air.

*Bloody plastic cups.*

From where he stood in the waiting room of the hospital he could hear the sound of sirens, approaching ambulances bringing people into casualty he assumed. How blasé one became to that strident sound after a while. Doyle remembered when he'd been the one *inside* the emergency vehicle. So close to death, so many times..

*He suddenly thought of Georgie.*

The vision of that young woman with long blonde hair,

her body riddled with bullets.

*Fuck it.*

He picked up the plastic cup, holding it in his hand long enough to feel the burning sensation against his palm and fingers. The pain became more intense, but he held onto it.

*Georgie.*

Doyle squeezed his eyes tight shut.

*Forget it.*

He put the cup down and looked at his hand, the skin now mottled red from the heat of the liquid. He sighed then walked across to the door of the waiting room and looked out.

The hospital was about two miles outside Belfast. It was large and modern in design, constructed of great grey concrete blocks, its expanse of stonework broken up by areas of glass which now reflected the watery moon like dull mirrors.

Doyle had delivered Stephen Murphy to the casualty department over two hours ago and the Irishman had been hurried off to surgery immediately. Doyle hadn't been told what was wrong, despite his lie that he was Murphy's brother. He'd told the doctors he knew nothing of Murphy's condition, merely that he'd complained of stomach pains. Whether they believed him or not, the doctors had whisked Murphy away and a nurse had shown Doyle to the waiting room, telling him she'd let him know when there was any news. Doyle was suitably convincing as the concerned brother and he complimented himself on his own powers of deception.

It all went with the job.

He wondered if James Christie had been brought to this same hospital.

*Fucking idiot.*

Doyle had been annoyed that he'd had to shoot Christie purely and simply because it made his task of tracking down Riordan more difficult.

Unless Murphy could tell him something.

*Was Murphy the fourth man?*

Doyle sipped his coffee and reached for a cigarette, ignoring the NO SMOKING sign nearby. He looked at his watch then checked the time against the wall clock opposite.

3.06 a.m.

*What the fuck were they doing with Murphy?*

Doyle had wondered at first if the Irishman had been shamming, but he'd gradually realised that his pain was genuine. Perhaps sustained when the Escort crashed? And yet, the impact hadn't been *that* bad.

He heard footsteps coming towards the waiting room and tensed, but they passed by. Doyle opened the door and peered out to see an intern pushing a gurney disappearing up the corridor. The counter terrorist stepped back inside the waiting room, pacing agitatedly back and forth, his eyes straying to the posters that adorned the white walls, posters he'd already scanned a dozen times since he arrived.

Multiple Sclerosis. Aids. Cancer.

Just the thing to cheer you up while you were waiting for news of a loved one, he thought.

He took another sip of his coffee, heard more footsteps. This time the door opened and a doctor stepped in, a man no older than Doyle with neatly combed hair and deep-set eyes.

'Mr Murphy?' he said.

Doyle nodded.

'It's about your brother,' the doctor said, swallowing hard. 'He died on the operating table. I'm very sorry.'

Doyle turned away from the doctor in an attempt to hide his irritation.

*Fuck it. Two leads. Both of them dead.*

'There was nothing we could do,' the doctor added.

Doyle held up a hand in mock acceptance and despair.

'Listen, Mr Murphy, perhaps this isn't the time, but do you know what was wrong with your brother?'

'You're the doctor not me,' Doyle said in his faultless Irish accent. He hoped his façade of bereaved family

139

member was still convincing.

'We need you to identify the body anyway, just to make things official, but. . .' the doctor allowed the sentence to trail off.

Doyle looked puzzled.

The doctor frowned and licked his lips.

'Well, there's something I think you ought to see. Perhaps *you'll* be able to explain it.'


# Forty-Four

*London*

'He's coming out.'

Two of Chi's men emerged, checking to the right and left as they exited. One of them signalled to the Jag driver who guided the majestic vehicle over to the entrance, another stood close to the door looking back and forth.

In the passenger seat of the Scorpio Cho Lok eased the .459 from his belt and gripped it tightly, glancing round at the two men in the back seat. Both were armed with Smith & Wesson .38s. But it was the cleaver that one of them held firmly in his fist.

Wong watched the movement outside the hotel for a moment, waiting for sight of their real quarry.

There was no sign of Billy Chi.

'Where the hell is he?' said Cho, sharply.

'What if he's gone out another way?' asked one of the men in the back.

Wong swallowed hard.

*Surely not.*

One of the bodyguards climbed into the car, another stood close to the door.

Still no Chi.

'He could have gone out the back way,' the man in the rear suggested again.

'He's in there,' Wong rasped. 'He must be.' His own breathing was laboured now, his heart beating hard in his chest. 'Come on. Come on.'

The bodyguard by the door reached into his jacket and pulled out a two-way radio. Wong saw him speaking into it.

The Jag pulled away from the entrance.

'What the fuck *is* this?' Cho Lok said, quietly. 'He's not in there, I tell you.'

'We have to see if he's there,' Wong snapped.

He looked round to reverse and the headlights behind blinded him.

He couldn't even make out what kind of car it was that had pulled in behind him. All he knew was the other vehicle was little more than a foot from his back bumper and the lights were glaring madly into the Scorpio.

'It's a fucking police car,' snapped Cho.

And now Wong saw the uniformed men clambering out, walking towards the car.

Wong stuck the Scorpio into reverse and stepped on the accelerator.

The car shot back, slamming into the police car, shattering one of the headlights, splintering the radiator grille and pushing the vehicle back ten or fifteen feet.

The uniformed men threw themselves sideways to avoid the Scorpio. Wong twisted the wheel and jammed the car into first. It hurtled forward a few dozen yards and he slammed on the brakes, the scream of tyres cutting through the night.

Outside the Hilton the Jag reversed to the door, Chi's bodyguards looking round to see what the commotion was.

Chi himself ran from the hotel and leapt into the back of the Jag.

Wong saw him and forced the Scorpio forward once more.

It slammed into a parked car, skidded then sped towards the Jag.

'Take him,' Wong shrieked. 'Kill Chi.'

He hit the brakes again and Cho Lok leapt from the Scorpio, the .459 gripped in his fist.

He got off two rounds, both of which missed, the second punching a hole in the rear of the Jag.

The two men in the back of the Scorpio also jumped out, the first of them pulling the cleaver clear of his jacket as he ran at the nearest bodyguard.

He raised it high in the air, ready to bring it down but the bodyguard slipped a hand inside his coat and pulled out what looked like a small metal box.

Wong recognised it.

It was an Ingram M-10 submachine-gun.

The bodyguard fired two short bursts, the spent cartridge cases flying into the air, arcing there before bouncing on the tarmac.

Bullets struck the Tai Hung Chai man in the face and chest and he went down in an untidy heap.

Cho swung the automatic up and fired at the bodyguard, the retort of the pistol deafening in the stillness.

The burst of fire that answered the shot was even more devastating.

Most of the left side of Cho's head was blown away as the 9mm slugs hit him.

He pitched backwards onto the bonnet of the Scorpio, blood spilling across the paintwork, his body sliding off onto the ground.

More bullets struck the car itself, shattering a headlight and punching holes in the windscreen.

Wong ducked down and jammed his foot on the accelerator.

The car rocketed forward and hit the bodyguard, catapulting him several feet into the air. His body twisted then crashed down on top of the Scorpio before sliding off.

Across the street, the police were clambering into their car.

Wong could hear shouts from all around, then they were drowned out as another burst of automatic fire hit the car, drilling lines along the side panels and door.

He sat up in time to see the other Tai Hung Chai man take two shots in the back, one of which pulverised his kidneys. He dropped to his knees, blood spilling from the wounds.

Wong knew he could not help the man.

Perhaps he could still get to Billy Chi.

He sent the Scorpio crashing into the back of the Jag but the larger vehicle merely accelerated away, tyres squealing. It shot out into Park Lane, narrowly missing a car.

The police were close now, their car screaming into the car park of the Hilton, blue lights spinning madly.

One of the bodyguards raked it with fire, bullets shattering the windscreen.

The glass spiderwebbed. It looked as if the screen had been suddenly covered by a thick frost.

Blinded, the driver couldn't avoid the prone body of Cho.

The police car rolled over what was left of his head then skidded into a Bentley that was parked close by.

The bodyguards began running towards Park Lane, both of them still gripping their machine-guns.

There was a car coming down the road and the first of the guards ran into the street, waving his arms. The driver hit his horn at the sudden appearance of the man in the road, but he slowed down long enough for the other guard to wrench open the Sierra's door and pull him out.

The terrified driver was sent sprawling across the road as the two bodyguards clambered into the car.

Wong looked round to see one of the policemen running towards him. He pressed down hard on the accelerator and guided the Scorpio out of the car park and into Park Lane, racing towards the lights at the bottom, roaring through them and right up Piccadilly.

'Call for help, quick,' shouted one of the policemen to his colleague.

He looked down at the four bodies lying around him. Blood and shattered glass were everywhere. The air smelt heavily of blood and cordite and something stronger, which he realised was excrement.

People were peering out of windows above, trying to see what had happened.

The policeman looked around at the carnage once more and shook his head in disbelief.

Already he could hear sirens, but it seemed that they were a little too late.

# Forty-Five

*Northern Ireland*

As the lift descended, Doyle kept his eyes fixed firmly at the floor, trying to conceal his agitation. As the supposed brother of the deceased his expression was meant to be one of devastation rather than annoyed frustration.

Murphy had been his only link with the IRA men he sought and now that link was gone too.

*Inconsiderate bastard, dying like that.*

The doctor stood opposite him, glancing down at a clipboard which he carried, it seemed, to avoid looking at Doyle.

Every now and then the counter terrorist would glance at the other man, noting how pale and drawn he looked, his eyes framed by dark rings, the veins in the whites of his eyes standing out vividly. He looked as though he hadn't slept for days.

The lift bumped to a halt and the doors slid open. Doyle followed the doctor out into a corridor which was deserted but for a couple of empty gurneys. One had a sheet laid on it and, as he passed, Doyle noticed that there was a large bloodstain on the material.

The door leading into the morgue was a few yards ahead.

The doctor led the way, pushing open the door, and immediately Doyle was enveloped by the pungent odour of chemicals and death. That sickly sweet, cloying scent he'd come to know only too well over the years.

The morgue was tiled white, the harsh brightness made all the more striking by the banks of fluorescent lights which cast a cold glow over everything. To the right there were cabinets where bodies were stored, to the left six stainless-steel slabs.

On the closest of these was a body covered by a white plastic sheet.

The doctor moved hesitantly towards it, glancing at Doyle to ensure that he was still in attendance.

'I'm sorry, but this has to be done,' he said, softly, and reached for one corner of the sheet, pulling it back slightly.

Doyle looked down at the face of Stephen Murphy and nodded.

'What I said to you upstairs, Mr Murphy,' the doctor continued, his eyes averted. 'About there being something you should see . . .' He allowed the sentence to trail off.

Doyle moved closer, looking first at Murphy's waxen features then at the doctor.

'The police will have to be informed, you understand,' the doctor continued. 'I thought it only right that you should see this first.'

He pulled the sheet further back, exposing Murphy's torso then his stomach.

Even Doyle couldn't conceal his surprise.

'Jesus Christ,' he murmured.

Murphy's abdominal cavity was open from sternum to pelvis, the internal organs on view. Thick, bloated snake-like intestines bulged from the rent, the stench of blood and something more rancid was almost overpowering, but it was what was within the cavity that had caused Doyle's exclamation of surprise.

Dozens of cylindrical shapes filled the stomach.

They looked like purulent worms, thicker than his index finger and a little longer.

Doyle leaned closer to inspect the objects that clogged Murphy's stomach.

'I removed one,' said the doctor, reaching for a glass dish nearby. He pushed it towards Doyle.

The counter terrorist inspected the object more closely: the sleek contours, the glistening surface, the small teat-like appendage at the end.

'It's a condom,' Doyle said, quietly.

The doctor nodded.

'I found twelve inside the stomach, including the one that had burst,' he said. 'It was that which caused your brother's death. Or more to the point, the substance inside it. He died of a massive internal haemorrhage.'

Doyle looked at the condom that had been taken from Murphy and at the powder, most of which had solidified and congealed with the blood it had mixed with.

The doctor took a pen from the top pocket of his white coat and prodded the condom. Some of the powder spilled out and he stirred it around with the tip of the pen.

Doyle looked at him quizzically.

'What is it?' he wanted to know.

'Heroin,' the doctor told him. 'The condoms are full of it. As far as I can see your brother swallowed them after he'd filled them with the substance. It's not an uncommon way of transporting drugs.'

Doyle ran a hand through his hair, his eyes still fixed on the bulging contraceptive and its deadly load.

*What the fuck was Murphy doing with drugs like this?*

'You can see why I have to inform the police, Mr Murphy,' the doctor said, almost apologetically.

Doyle nodded.

'Did you have any idea your brother was involved in this kind of thing?'

'None at all,' said Doyle with genuine vagueness.

The IRA and drugs. This didn't add up.

Questions were already beginning to tumble through

his mind. Questions he knew had to be answered. And quickly.

'I think the police may want to speak to you too,' the doctor intoned.

Doyle nodded, struggling to keep up the façade of grieving brother.

'Just before you call them,' he said, motioning towards Murphy, 'I'd like to inform our mother. I don't want her to hear about his death from the police.'

The doctor nodded.

'There's a phone in the office along the corridor,' he said.

'Just give me ten minutes,' Doyle said. 'I appreciate it.'

He walked out and headed towards the office, his face set in hard lines.

Stephen Murphy. Who the hell was he? IRA? If so why was he carrying drugs?

*So many questions.*

And he needed answers.

He found the phone and jabbed out the digits, waiting impatiently for it to be answered.

*So many questions.*

He drummed on the desk top until he heard a familiar voice on the other end.

'Wetherby,' he snapped. 'It's Doyle. Listen to me. I need some information and I need it fast.'


# Forty-Six


Major John Wetherby listened patiently as Doyle recounted the chain of events that had led him first to Belfast airport and now to the hospital. When the counter terrorist finally paused in his staccato tirade, the intelligence officer muttered something which was lost in a hiss of static on the phone line.

'Did you hear me?' Doyle snapped.

'Yes, I heard you,' Wetherby told him. 'It doesn't make any sense.'

'I didn't call you to find out if you thought it made fucking sense or not. I need to know something about Stephen Murphy. You said four men hit that arms convoy, perhaps *he* was the fourth man and if he was, what the fuck was he doing with a stomach full of bloody heroin?'

'You know, that name rings a bell.'

'Probably because it's one of the most common Irish names around,' Doyle said, sardonically.

'I don't think he's PIRA.'

'How can you be sure?'

'It's my job.'

'Then do your fucking job and tell me something about him,' Doyle said, exasperatedly. He fumbled for his cigarettes and lit one, ignoring the NO SMOKING sign in the office. Perched on one corner of the desk, the phone wedged between his ear and his shoulder, he watched the door for the arrival of the doctor. At the other end of the line he could hear the tapping of computer keys, the rattle of a printer.

'Got him,' Wetherby said, finally. 'Stephen James Murphy. Born Carrickmore, County Tyrone in 1951. Divorced. No children.'

'I don't need his fucking life story,' Doyle snapped. 'Has he got any form?'

'Known member of the Provisional IRA, arrested two years ago for possession of explosives. Escaped from police custody. Arrested again six months ago . . .' The words tailed off.

'And?' Doyle snapped.

'I thought that name rang a bell,' Wetherby said, quietly.

'Is he the fourth man or not?'

'I doubt it, Doyle. He's been working for *us* for the last

148

five months. Murphy was an informer.'

It was Doyle's turn to be silent.

He sucked hard on his cigarette then blew out a stream of smoke, watching as it dissipated in the air.

'That's impossible,' he said, finally. 'If Murphy had turned tout he'd have been found and bagged inside a week.'

'Apparently not.'

'You're telling me the IRA let an informer walk about unharmed. Fuck off.' He ground out his cigarette on the desk top.

'Perhaps the most important thing is *why* the IRA let him live.'

'They must have been using him to transport drugs, that's the only explanation. They let him live because he was more use to them alive than dead. More use as a fucking mule. That's why he had a gutful of heroin.' The counter terrorist frowned even more deeply. 'But why drugs? That's not the IRA's game.'

'Doyle, drugs are not your concern. You were sent to track down those missing guns.'

'Don't tell me my fucking business, Wetherby. I know why I'm here. There might be a link.'

'How, for Christ's sake? Look, you forget about Murphy.'

'Forget him? He was the only link I had with Riordan and O'Connor after I killed Christie.'

'Perhaps you should have thought more carefully before you killed Christie.'

'He was pointing a fucking gun at me. What the hell was I supposed to do?'

'Just find the others.'

'As easy as that?'

'I was told you were the best Doyle. You'd better prove it.'

'Fuck you, Wetherby.'

Doyle slammed down the phone and moved to the office door. He peered out into the corridor and saw that it was still deserted. He guessed the doctor must be in the morgue, no doubt giving him the allotted ten minutes he'd requested. Doyle smiled to himself and headed for the lift, jabbing the 'Call' button. When it arrived he stepped in, rode it to the ground floor then made his way out of the hospital.

As he drove back towards Belfast the few facts he had kept swirling around in his head like dirty water gurgling down a plughole.

Why would the IRA be using Murphy, a known informer, to carry drugs for them?

And why drugs?

Was there a link with the attack on the arms convoy?

*So many questions.*

He'd lost two possible leads. The game was turning full circle. He was back to square one.

He had to find Paul Riordan and Declan O'Connor.

*Were they involved with the drugs too?*

And he had to find those fucking guns.

Time was running out.

## Forty-Seven

'That's him,' said Paul Riordan, nodding in the direction of the individual who'd just left the pub. 'That's Jimmy Robinson.'

Marie Leary squinted through the darkness and ran appraising eyes over the man. He was young, early twenties she guessed. Thick set, dressed in a white sweater and jeans. He wore chunky, multi-coloured trainers.

She watched him as he stopped and lit a cigarette then set off towards the end of the street.

Riordan started the car and swung it around in the road, the wheels squealing slightly.

Ahead of them, the younger man heard the sound and looked over his shoulder. He saw the car cruising slowly towards him and slowed his pace for a moment. He tried to see who was driving, wondering what they wanted.

*Nice car.*

It pulled up alongside him and Jimmy could see who was driving.

'Fuck it,' he hissed and bolted.

Riordan stepped on the accelerator, swung the car in front of Robinson and leapt out of the vehicle, catching the younger man by the scruff of the neck.

'We want a word,' Riordan snapped, pushing Robinson into the alleyway at the end of the street.

'Look, I haven't done anything,' he blurted, the fear evident in his voice.

'You lying fucker,' Riordan rasped.

Robinson saw Marie slide out of the car and advance towards him. She slid a hand inside her jacket and the younger man felt his bowels loosen as he saw her pull the CZ automatic free. She pushed the barrel against his temple.

'I swear on my mother's life, I haven't done anything,' Robinson uttered, closing his eyes as he felt the CZ pressing harder against his flesh.

'You stole a car in Ballymurphy two days ago,' Riordan told him. 'Showing off to your fucking friends, weren't you? You nearly hit a little girl, didn't you?'

Robinson was whimpering softly now.

'I'm sorry,' he said, breathlessly.

'It doesn't look good on us, Jimmy, when you do things like that. You know how we feel about fucking joyriding. You should know by now,' Riordan said, flatly.

'Jesus, I'm sorry.'

'You could have killed that little girl, Jimmy,' Riordan persisted, stepping away from the terrified younger man.

'Don't move,' Marie said, as Robinson watched Riordan

cross to the boot of the car.

'Look, I didn't mean to do it . . .' Robinson began.

'Shut it,' Marie hissed.

Riordan returned carrying a claw hammer.

'Please,' Robinson blubbered. 'Don't hurt me, I'll do anything you want, I swear.'

'Don't hurt you?' Riordan said. 'Like you could have hurt that little girl? Roll your fucking jeans up.'

Robinson hesitated.

'Do it!' Riordan snarled.

Marie pulled back the hammer on the automatic, the metallic click echoing in the alleyway.

Robinson pulled his jeans up as far as his knees, exposing his shins.

Riordan nodded.

'These fucking streets are dangerous enough,' he said, 'without fucking idiots like you, Jimmy.'

He struck with tremendous power, smashing the hammer across Robinson's shin just below the knee.

The first blow cracked the tibia, the second one broke it.

Robinson screamed but Marie clamped her hand across his mouth, feeling the spittle and warm air against her palm as Riordan hit him again, pounding at the shin bone until the skin split and a portion of tibia tore through the flesh.

Robinson went down in a heap and Riordan set to work on his left leg.

Four heavy blows and a length of bone several inches long, splintered from such furious impacts, had torn through the skin and was dribbling marrow from its shattered tip.

Riordan stood up and he and Marie walked back to the car and climbed in, oblivious to Robinson's screams of agony.

Riordan tossed the bloodied hammer onto the back seat.

Marie Leary pushed the CZ back into her jacket.

They drove off.

# Forty-Eight

*London*

Spots of rain were beginning to fleck the windscreen of the Daimler as Joey Chang eased the car towards the car-park entrance.

He glanced down at the dashboard clock and saw that it was 11.07 p.m. He felt the stiffness in his back. It had been a long day. The headache that had begun gnawing at the base of his skull a couple of hours earlier had taken a firmer hold now and Chang rolled his head gently back and forth in an effort to ease the tension there.

Knightsbridge was relatively quiet now. He'd driven past Harrods on his way home, seen late-night diners leaving the many bistros and wine bars that nestled around the building in side streets. But Chang had paid them little heed. He had more important things on his mind.

The block of flats in Cadogan Place was six storeys high with its own underground car park, and it was towards this subterranean cavern that he now guided the car.

Chang saw little of the other inhabitants of the block. They were all wealthy, that much he knew. They would have to be to afford the rates on such a property. He had bought the flat two years ago and it had cost him over a quarter of a million then. He wondered what his parents would have said had they lived to see it.

He'd come a long way. From a one-roomed shithole that he, his parents and six brothers and sisters had shared in Kowloon to the height of opulence here in London.

He had a lot to thank his organisation for, not least an income approaching half a million every year. It paid for everything he had and, when the time came, it would pay for the private education of his children. Chang cared about their futures, he worried about their futures, but then part of his job was coping with worry. It showed in the odd grey hair at his temples, the extra few lines around his eyes. He wondered how many more lines would find their way onto his features before this business with the Hip Sing was settled.

The failure of the attack the other night had only served to make everyone else in the Tai Hung Chai more certain that the only recourse for them was all-out war. Chang knew it too, but still resisted recommending it to Wo Fen. He knew when war came it would be swift and bloody and no one would be safe.

*No one.*

He swung the car into the garage, pressing down on the brake as the Daimler negotiated the ramp leading into the underground car park.

Apart from the beams of his own headlights, there was very little illumination down there. A faulty fluorescent tube sputtered erratically, casting a kind of mock strobe light over the darkened cavern.

Chang glanced into his rear-view mirror.

*Afraid someone's following?*

Then he parked in his usual place and sat motionless behind the wheel for a moment, massaging his neck with one hand. He took his briefcase from the passenger seat and swung himself out of the car, locking it.

The sound of the key turning in the lock echoed throughout the car park, the click amplified in the subterranean den. There were slicks of oil on the concrete around him and the place smelt of petrol.

There were half a dozen other vehicles parked nearby. A Rolls-Royce, a couple of Jags, a Ferrari.

Chang turned slightly, hearing something.

He stood motionless, ears attuned to the silence.

Was it breathing?

He realised it was the slight breeze blowing through the

154

car park, tossing a couple of sweet wrappers into the air, and Chang watched them skipping across the stained concrete.

The fluorescent tube buzzed somnolently, flickered then went out.

The whole garage was plunged into impenetrable blackness. Darkness broken only by the subdued street lighting which trickled through the car-park entrance like dull yellow water through a drain.

Chang walked hastily away from his car, his footsteps echoing loudly in the stillness.

He was irritated with himself for his nervousness but did not slow his pace, his eyes fixed on the door of the lift which would take him out of this gloom.

The light came back on again, flashed brightly then went out.

Chang made a mental note to complain about the fault.

He reached the lift door and jabbed the call button, turning to look out into the gloom.

The darkness seemed to be a living thing, filling the garage, crushing any light, slithering over the cars, masking everything.

He heard footsteps and looked anxiously back and forth.

The fluorescent light flashed on, brightly for a second.

Chang peered into the void.

He could see nothing. No tell-tale shadows. Nothing.

And yet he could still hear footsteps.

The light went out again.

As it did he realised that the footsteps were coming from the street above, echoing in the stillness, carried on the night. Amplified by the solitude.

The lift bumped to a halt behind him and the doors slid open. Chang stepped in gratefully and pressed button five, muttering to himself when the lift doors took so long to close. He stood with his back pressed against the rear wall of the lift car, gazing out into the blackness.

Waiting.

The doors finally closed and Chang couldn't resist a slight murmur of relief.

The lift began to rise.

## Forty-Nine

As the lift reached its appointed floor, Chang fumbled in his jacket pocket for his key.

He stepped out into a plushly carpeted corridor and made his way along to the far door. It was quiet inside the block and the only sound he heard was the muffled noises of a television set as he passed one of the other doors.

Chang let himself into his own flat and closed and locked the door behind him.

'You're late.'

He heard her voice from his left and smiled, turning to face her.

Su Chang stepped from the kitchen, her thin face wreathed in smiles.

She put out her arms and embraced Chang and he responded warmly, holding her to him tightly.

'I was getting worried,' she said, still clinging to him. 'The children wanted to wait up for you, but I said it was too late.'

Chang kissed her tenderly on the lips and nodded, stroking her long black hair with one hand.

When he'd first met her, twelve years ago in a bar in the Mandarin Oriental hotel in Hong Kong, he'd been hypnotised by her beauty – her slender features, her exquisite figure. Now, ten years of marriage and two children later, she was still as radiant and fragile, still exquisite in his eyes. Su was a couple of years younger than Chang and from the beginning she'd known what he was. In the early days he had been a humble foot soldier in the Tai Hung Chai, a 14K desperate to improve himself and his position. Over the years he had done just that and she'd been with him through it all. On more than one occasion only her willingness to provide him with an alibi had prevented him serving time in jail. It was one of the many things he had to thank her for.

He wandered through into the sitting room and poured himself a drink.

'That bad, is it?' she asked, sitting down in front of the sofa, her long legs curled beneath her.

'It's every bit as bad as that,' Chang said, quietly, refilling his glass. He motioned to the bottle of Martell and Su nodded. He poured her one and handed it to her, watching as she warmed the balloon in one delicate hand.

'What's going on, Joey?' she wanted to know.

'I wish I knew,' he said, vaguely, sitting down on the sofa, stroking her hair with one hand.

She swung round so that she was resting on his knee, looking up at him.

'The Hip Sing are leaving Hong Kong, just like the other organisations. The new regime there is no good for business, not ours, not anyone's,' he told her. 'They seem to be stronger than us, better prepared, better equipped and they're ready for a fight.'

'And you're not?'

He shrugged.

'If war is the only answer then so be it,' he murmured.

'Be careful, Joey,' she said, squeezing his leg.

He leaned forward and kissed her on the lips.

'It's *you* who I want to be careful,' he said. 'You and the kids. I don't worry about myself, but the Hip Sing have no honour. They will strike at us and our families. I don't want anything to happen to you or the children. You're everything to me.'

She gripped his hand and squeezed tightly, with a strength that belied the fragility of her pale hand.

'What do the others say about a war?' she asked.

'The elders will be guided by me. Frankie Wong, I'm sure, is looking forward to a war when it comes.'

'Is there no way of preventing it?'

He shrugged, then, as if tiring of the subject, 'I want to look at the children, I won't disturb them.' Chang got to his feet and headed towards the hallway. Su watched him go and smiled.

The flat had four bedrooms and Chang paused at the door of the first of them, listening for any sounds from inside before edging in a fraction.

His daughter, Anna, lay sleeping, clutching a large teddy-bear.

Chang crossed to the six-year-old and knelt beside her, watching her for a moment, listening to her low breathing, then he leant forward and kissed her very lightly on the top of the head. She murmured something in her sleep and rolled over onto her back, the teddy-bear falling from her arms. Chang retrieved it and placed it carefully back in bed with her then he tiptoed out of the room, closing the door behind him.

His son's room was opposite and he moved with similar stealth as he entered that one too, careful to avoid stepping on the toys scattered over the floor like some kind of playful minefield.

Michael was lying with his face in the pillow, his sheets pushed back.

Chang pulled the sheets up and gently covered the five-year-old, tucking them around him to keep out draughts, then he gently touched the boy's head before retreating from the room.

He found Su outside the door and smiled at her.

'They're both asleep,' he said, softly.

'Good,' she murmured and took his hand, leading him towards the bathroom. As he entered he saw the bath taps running, smelled bath oil and heard the water filling the peach-coloured receptacle.

'I thought a bath might help you relax,' Su said.

Chang smiled and began unbuttoning his shirt, his grin

broadening as he saw Su undoing her blouse, pulling it free of her leggings which, a second later, she slipped off.

She wore nothing beneath and he looked admiringly at her slim hips and thighs, and the small triangle of dark hair between them.

She shrugged off her blouse and moved closer to him, her breasts pressing against his chest, the nipples already erect.

'That bath is so big,' she said, smiling. 'I just thought you might want some company.'

Chang laughed.

Something he hadn't done for a while and something he feared he may not do too often in the coming days.

Outside, the rain began to fall more swiftly.

Inside, the water continued to fill the bath. The smell of bath oil seemed almost intoxicating to Chang and he laughed again.

Su was chuckling, too, as they stepped into the welcoming warmth of the water.


# Fifty


*Northern Ireland*

The guns were hidden beneath the floorboards.

One of the first tasks Doyle had undertaken upon entering the room, after securely locking the door, was to loosen one of the floorboards and check that there was a cavity which would house the weapons. He'd placed the Desert Eagle and the Charter Arms .357 in the hole along with ammunition for both pistols. The Beretta he'd kept out, secreting that inside the small wardrobe behind the few clothes he had hanging there: three shirts, a couple of pairs of jeans and a leather jacket. There was a chest of drawers, too, and into this he'd laid socks and underwear and a couple of T-shirts.

He hadn't had to search hard for the boarding house in Malone Road. Like most counter terrorist or undercover agents working in Ireland, Doyle was aware of such places and, stuck in the heart of the Republican part of the city, it was perfect.

His reasons for being there, for needing lodging, were carefully rehearsed too.

He'd told the landlady, a small woman with an abundance of facial hair, that he'd come to Belfast from the South to work for his brother in a plumbing business, only to discover on his arrival that his brother had been murdered by the UVF. Doyle had told her he needed somewhere to stay while he sorted himself out and decided what he should do next.

The ruse had worked like a charm, not only had she agreed to let him have one of the four rooms she let, she'd also offered him her sincere sympathies and told him he could have the room as long as he wanted it. She had taken to him and Doyle was grateful for the bustling little woman's concern.

He hadn't seen the other lodgers. The landlady was a widow, a fact she mentioned every day without fail, usually pointing to the photo of her deceased husband, which occupied pride of place on the mantelpiece, every time she saw it. The monochrome visage of Mr William Shannon gazed back blankly each time it was indicated.

Mrs Shannon talked a lot, usually to herself, Doyle had noticed, but she was a likeable enough woman. She didn't bother him and that was what mattered most.

He sat on the uncarpeted floor, listening to the steady drip of one of the sink taps, looking down into the hole where his guns were kept, each one wrapped in a plastic bag to protect it from dust and dirt.

The room was small, less than fifteen feet square and, apart from the wardrobe and chest of drawers, it contained a wall-mounted sink and a single bed. The paper on the walls was yellowing in places and the mat beside the bed was threadbare, but the place was adequate for Doyle's needs. He'd slept in worse.

*He and Georgie had . . .*

He closed his eyes tightly and tried to force the thoughts of her from his mind, wondering why they had suddenly resurfaced again unbidden.

*Forget her.*

He continued pushing shells into the magazine of the Beretta, breathing heavily as if in some kind of meditative state.

*She's fucking dead. Forget her.*

Doyle allowed his head to loll backwards, the sound of the dripping tap ever present in the room. There was a dark stain around the plughole and a crack in the porcelain of the discoloured sink. It looked like a scar on the white surface.

From downstairs he could hear the television set blaring away and wondered if it was Mrs Shannon watching one of her beloved soap operas.

Doyle finished cleaning the Beretta and slammed in a full magazine, satisfied. As he held the pistol before him he caught sight of his reflection in the polished chrome. Unshaven, dark beneath the eyes. He looked like shit.

*Fuck it.*

He crossed to the wardrobe and pulled out a shirt, slipping it on.

He tucked it into his jeans then pulled on a pair of baseball boots and began tying them.

*Drugs.*

What did the IRA want with drugs? And how was this linked with the attack on the arms convoy? Or maybe it wasn't. Indeed, the more Doyle thought about it, the less sense it made to try and connect the two events. The IRA had dozens of scams going; within their organisation there were subdivisions, offshoots all doing their own thing. Why the hell should the drugs and the guns be linked?

Perhaps if he found Riordan and O'Connor the knowledge he sought could be found. Or, more to the point, the missing guns could be found.

Doyle stood before the mirror over the sink and ran a hand through his long hair, not bothering to comb it. He pulled on his leather jacket, slipped the Beretta into its shoulder holster and headed for the door, flicking off the light, careful to lock up securely.

As he descended the narrow staircase towards the hallway, the noise of the television grew louder and he passed the sitting-room door which was half-open.

Mrs Shannon was seated on a fading green sofa gazing fixedly at the images on the screen before her. She didn't see Doyle leave, only heard the click of the front door as he slipped out.

The counter terrorist paused for a second outside the front door, looking around him at the terraced houses that lined both sides of Malone Road. Lights burned in most of the windows, the street lamps – those that were working – cast a dull sodium glare over the road.

Doyle knew that the first of the pubs he intended calling into was less than twenty minutes' walk away.

He pulled up the collar of his jacket, dug his hands into his pockets and set off.

As he walked, he could feel the Beretta pressed against his side.

Doyle wondered how soon he'd need it.

## Fifty-One

*London*
The ringing of the phone woke him. The strident sound cutting through the darkness, through the veil of sleep.

Joey Chang murmured something and flailed a hand towards the receiver, anxious to stop it before it disturbed Su or the children.

He rolled over, snatching at the phone, his sleep-laden eyes trying to focus on the glowing red digits of the electronic alarm.

For a second he wondered if he'd in fact heard the alarm, but the phone continued ringing.

He saw the time.

4.03 a.m.

*What the hell was this?*

He finally snatched up the phone, hauling himself up in bed, propping himself against the headboard.

Beside him, Su stirred, reached out for him with one arm.

'Hello,' Chang said, clearing his throat.

'Joey.'

The voice at the other end was agitated, excitable.

'Joey, listen to me.'

He recognised it as Frankie Wong's.

'What's wrong?' Su purred from beside him, her eyes still closed.

Chang merely reached out and squeezed her hand.

'Frankie, it's after four in the morning—'

'Those fuckers have done it again,' Wong shouted into the phone. 'Now will you believe me, now will you tell the elders what must be done?'

Chang sat up further in the bed.

'Calm down, for Christ's sake. And *slow* down. Tell me what's going on.'

'The Hip Sing,' Wong rasped. 'They hit one of our gaming clubs in Newport Court this morning, about an hour ago. They killed three of our men and stole some money.'

Chang exhaled deeply.

'Where are you now?'

'I'm at the club,' Wong told him. 'This is it, Joey. You've got no choice now, you have to tell the elders to go to war against the Hip Sing.'

Chang listened, glancing down at Su occasionally. She was looking up at him blearily, her face set in hard lines as she tried to catch the gist of the conversation.

'Are you listening?' Wong snapped.

'Just calm down, Frankie, I'll take care of it,' Chang told him. 'I'll get in touch with Wo Fen and the others.'

'And what will you tell them?'

'I'll tell them that we have to meet. That we have no other alternative now but to go to war against the Hip Sing. I will persuade them.'

'Let them come here and look at our dead if they need any fucking persuading.'

'Frankie, listen to me. I want bodyguards sent to the houses of each of the elders right now, understand?'

'Why?'

'Just do it. If the Hip Sing are that bold they may try to strike at them.'

'What about you, do you want men at your place too?'

'Yes.'

He swung himself out of bed and flipped open the top drawer of the bedside cabinet.

Inside, nestling amongst the handkerchiefs, lay a Star PD .45 automatic. He looked down at the pistol, as if seeing it reassured him.

'What else do you want me to do?' Wong asked.

'Nothing until you hear from me again, got that? I'll call you there in about two hours. And Frankie . . .'

'What?'

'You watch yourself too.'

He hung up.

For a long time Chang didn't speak, he merely sat, head bowed, on the edge of the bed until he felt Su touch his back.

'It's bad, isn't it?' she said.

He nodded.

'It's war,' he said, flatly.

# PART TWO

'You should seek your enemy, you should wage your war.'
Nietzsche

'Gone insane from the pain they must surely know. . .'
Metallica

# Fifty-Two

*Northern Ireland*

The door creaked loudly as he closed it and Doyle muttered irritably to himself as he paused on the landing to lock it, dropping the key into the back pocket of his jeans.

Inside, the guns were safely hidden beneath the floorboards once more. As far as he knew, Mrs Shannon didn't have a pass key to the rooms she let. She provided food for her tenants, but that was it. Cleanliness was their own responsibility. This insistence on her lodgers' independence suited Doyle, after all, he didn't want her snooping around his room when he was out and stumbling across the weapons and ammunition.

He made his way down the stairs, the smell of frying food reaching his nostrils.

There was a small kitchen to the rear of the house and what passed for a dining room to the left at the bottom of the stairs. He wandered in and sat down, glad to see that he was the only one present.

Since moving into the boarding house three days earlier, Doyle hadn't even seen his fellow tenants other than to nod in passing to an elderly man as he left on the first day. They were obviously as solitary as Doyle himself – something else which suited the counter terrorist. He wasn't here to make friends.

The tour of the local pubs the previous night had been largely fruitless. A few whisperings about the IRA here and there, but nothing more than he would have expected in such a strong Republican area.

He had not heard the names Riordan or O'Connor mentioned and, as yet, he'd not found the right circumstances to mention them himself. But he was sure that someone somewhere around here had heard of them or, more to the point, knew where they might be found. For a man of such little patience, Doyle realised that he could do nothing other than bide his time and that frustrated him but he knew there was no other way.

There were a couple of dirty plates on the table set in the middle of the dining room and, beside one, a newspaper. Doyle reached across and picked it up, scanning the headlines, flicking through then pausing to read the back page, a match report about the Liverpool versus Manchester United game from the previous night. The game had been shown live on the television and Doyle had caught bits of it in some of the pubs he'd visited, his attention drawn to those watching the screen rather than the action on it, but he'd seen nothing familiar, no faces he recognised. The only thing familiar had been the fact that Liverpool had won.

'Good morning, Mr Fagan. How are you?'

Doyle looked round to see Mrs Shannon bustle into the room clutching a large plate which she set down in front of him.

'I heard you coming down the stairs,' she told him then retreated back out of the dining room allowing Doyle time only to smile a greeting.

He began eating, joined a second later by Mrs Shannon who entered carrying an enormous tea pot. She filled his cup and her own and sat down opposite him.

'You don't mind if I join you? I wanted to talk to you about something,' she informed him.

'You're putting the rent up, is that it?' he said, smiling.

'Away with you,' she said, waving a hand dismissively at him. 'I wanted to talk to you about a job. I was thinking what you said about your brother being killed and all. If it hadn't been for that you'd be working now. It's not right that a man should go without work. My husband, God rest his soul, was out of work for two years before he died. It takes a man's self-confidence if he's got no job. He feels useless.' She sipped her tea.

Doyle listened intently, a slight smile on his lips.

'My brother runs a pub in the city centre, close to the Europa hotel. I rang him last night and asked if he needed any help. He said he could use a cellarman. If you're interested.'

Doyle smiled.

'That's very kind of you,' he said.

'I hope you don't think I'm sticking my nose into your business, but I just thought I could help. It must have been bad enough for you losing your brother.'

Doyle nodded.

The disguise of grieving brother seemed to be one he slipped into easily enough.

'It's touched everybody, Mr Fagan,' she continued. 'This bloody business here. I don't think there's a person in this street who hasn't lost someone or knows somebody that has. I used to live next door to a Protestant girl when I was a child, I still write to her every now and then, but if we were to walk down the street together now. . .' She allowed the sentence to trail off. She shrugged philosophically. 'It's a sad business.' Mrs Shannon took another sip of her tea then raised her hand again as if to wipe out the words she'd just spoken. 'I'll give you the address of my brother's pub, you can go along and see him if you want to.'

'Thanks very much,' Doyle said. 'It's very kind of you.'

The landlady bustled off to fetch the address while Doyle finished his breakfast.

A pub in the city centre.

It could be useful.

# Fifty-Three

The explosion had happened two days before, most of the destruction having been cleared away, but Doyle could still see fragments of broken glass and concrete in the gutter.

The cavities that had once been windows were boarded up, as was the main entrance to the wine bar. Across the wood someone had painted FUCK THE IRA in large red letters.

Doyle stood in the remains of the doorway looking across the street towards the Europa hotel, or rather, to the pub a few yards down from it.

The sign outside The Bowman was swaying in the strong wind. There were no signs of movement inside, nothing visible through the frosted glass of the windows. The counter terrorist took a drag on his cigarette and remained where he was, scanning the building, taking in as many details as he could.

Outside the Europa taxis came and went, people clambered in and out, luggage was ferried back and forth. He could see some guests sitting in the foyer, others in the coffee shop eating breakfast.

He finished his cigarette and strode across the road, heading for the main door of the pub which he knocked on three times. When there was no answer he knocked again, this time hearing movement from inside. He could see the shadowy outline of a figure on the other side of the opaque glass.

Doyle knocked again.

'Who is it?' the voice on the other side said. 'We're not open yet.'

'My name's Fagan,' Doyle lied. 'Your sister sent me, Mr Binchy.'

There was a moment's silence then Doyle heard the sound of bolts being drawn back, a chain being slipped. The door opened slightly and he found himself looking into the face of a large, heavy-set man with pink cheeks.

'Have you come for the job?' Jim Binchy asked.

Doyle nodded.

'You'd better come in.'

The counter terrorist stepped inside and Binchy locked the doors again.

The bar had that distinct pub smell of stale smoke and drink, an odour which seems to seep, over the years, into the walls and furniture of the place. There was a jukebox, a couple of fruit machines, the obligatory video game and, for those who sought entertainment of a less mechanised variety, a dartboard on the far wall at one end of the bar. The bar itself curved around in a U shape, curling from the public bar through to the lounge beyond.

'Jack Fagan,' Doyle lied easily, extending a hand which Binchy shook.

'My sister told me about you,' the landlord said.

'She's a kind woman. So, how many others are there for the job?'

'Just you. It'll break your fucking back but it's yours if you want it. I might need you to do some bar work too. Serving and that. It's only temporary, I know, but it's better than nothing.'

'Do you want any references?'

'If you can walk straight, carry a barrel of beer and add up they're all the qualifications you need,' Binchy told him, smiling. 'When can you start?'

'Right now if you want me to.'

'Good. Come on, I'll show you round.'

Binchy led Doyle through the pub, chatting about the business, his other staff, customers. The usual chit-chat. When he asked details of Doyle's life the counter terrorist was ready with the appropriate lie.

'I wouldn't normally do this, Fagan,' the landlord said, 'but if my sister says she trusts you, that's good enough for me. Don't let me down.'

Doyle smiled.

By one o'clock the pub was buzzing. Laughter, shouting, talking, accompanied by the ever-present jukebox and electronic noises of the fruit machines and video game.

Doyle went about his new-found business efficiently enough, spending most of his time moving back and forth between the bar and the cellar. He chatted briefly with those customers who spoke to him but, for the most part, he was content to do his work unobtrusively, ever alert for any snippets of information he could pick up.

The bulk of the clientele were from nearby offices. Clerks and secretaries.

Doyle caught the eye of a young woman in a rust-coloured dress who kept smiling at him over mouthfuls of sandwich.

He winked at her a couple of times as he continued with his duties.

'Clear some tables, will you, Jack?' Binchy asked, pulling another pint.

Doyle nodded and headed straight for the one where the woman in the rust-coloured dress sat. She was with a friend. A taller, thinner woman with straight black hair. They both smiled at him as he took away their empty plates.

'A woman's work is never done, is it?' he said, smiling.

They both laughed.

Doyle moved through both bars collecting empty glasses and plates, piling them on the counter.

As two o'clock arrived the office-based customers began to drift off.

Doyle waved to the young woman in the rust-coloured dress, watching as she wiggled out of the door.

He made a mental note to keep an eye open for her the following day.

Behind the bar, Binchy's normally pink face had turned the colour of beetroot and there were spots of perspiration on his forehead.

'Get me another barrel of Guinness up, will you?' he said to Doyle who wandered off to the cellar obediently.

It was cold down there. Not pleasantly cool after the heat of the bar. It was downright fucking cold. His breath clouded in the air as he exhaled, moving around the underground room with the assurance of a man who has been engaged in such a task his entire life. He could feel the chill even through the soles of his trainers, so cold were the flagstones he walked upon. The cloying heat of the bar was welcoming when he returned, looking around to see that even more customers had left.

Less than a dozen now remained, dotted around the two bars.

Two old men, in their seventies, were playing darts. Three youths stood around the fruit machines, feeding in coins almost non-stop.

Other drinkers sat quietly at their own tables, some reading the day's papers, others content merely to sit and enjoy the atmosphere. The air was thick with cigarette smoke.

Outside Doyle heard a siren and crossed to the door, glancing out to see an ambulance speed past.

As Doyle returned to the bar Binchy patted him on the shoulder as he passed.

'A good lunchtime's work, eh?' he said, smiling. 'I'll be through there if you need me.'

He disappeared through a door at the rear of the bar, closing it behind him.

Doyle picked up a cloth and began wiping down the bar.

He heard the main door open, saw two more of the customers leave. The sounds were still coming from the fruit machines, sometimes accompanied by yells of triumph when the youths playing them won.

Doyle continued with his cleaning.

'Excuse me.'

He looked up when he heard the voice.

The young woman who faced him smiled.

'I'm looking for Jim Binchy,' she said.

'He's out the back,' Doyle told her. 'Can I help you?'

'I need to see Mr Binchy,' she said, shaking her head.

'Can I tell him who's here?'

'If you just get him it'd be easier, thanks.'

'Okay, I'll just tell him there's a beautiful woman to see him, how's that?'

'Are you the new barman?' she wanted to know.

Doyle nodded. 'Well, you could say that,' he told her. 'Barman and general dogsbody really.'

'You've got something the last guy didn't have,' she told him.

'What's that?'

'Bullshit.'

Doyle smiled broadly.

Marie Leary smiled back.

## Fifty-Four

Doyle lifted the bar flap and ushered her through.

'This way, Miss. . .'

She smiled, ignoring his prompting.

'I know the way, thanks,' Marie told him and headed through the door at the rear of the bar.

Doyle saw her turn to the right, to the sitting room Binchy had retreated to. The counter terrorist took a couple of steps closer, moving nearer to the door, glad to see that it was open an inch or two.

'I didn't expect to see *you*,' Binchy told her, his voice catching slightly.

'You expected to see one of us though,' she said, flatly.

There was a moment's silence, broken by Binchy.

'I haven't got it all yet,' he said.

'You've had enough time.'

Doyle leaned closer to the door, anxious not to miss any of this conversation.

'I want it today,' Marie told him.

Another long pause.

'Don't fuck me about,' she snapped.

'I'll get it,' Binchy told her, nervously. 'If you come back later. . .'

She cut him short.

'Get it now, I'll wait,' she demanded.

Doyle heard footsteps coming towards the door and he ducked away, bending to pick up a crate of bitter lemon from a stack nearby.

When the sitting-room door opened he was heading back to the bar with it. Binchy and Marie emerged and also walked back into the bar. Binchy was wearing his coat, his face flushed pink once again.

'Jack, I have to go out for a while, look after the place, will you?' he said, pulling the belt tight on his coat.

Doyle nodded.

Binchy shot a wary glance at Marie then walked out.

She seated herself on a bar stool and ran a hand through her long blonde hair.

*The way Georgie used to?*

Doyle administered a swift mental rebuke, angry that thoughts of the dead girl had passed through his mind, but it was a forgivable mistake.

'Can I get you a drink?' he asked, running appraising eyes over Marie.

When she looked at him he was struck by the colour of her eyes. They were light brown and they seemed to burn into him as if lit from within.

'I'll have an orange juice,' she said, fumbling in her purse.

'Have it on me,' he said, pushing the juice towards her.

He watched as she sipped it.

'Do you know Jim?' he wanted to know.

'You could say that.'

'How long?'

'You ask a lot of questions.'

'I'm nosey.'

'I'd noticed.'

'Did I tell you my name?'

'I don't think I asked you.'

'Jack Fagan,' said Doyle, extending a hand for her to shake.

'Hello, Jack Fagan,' she said, smiling.

He felt the smoothness of her skin against his own flesh.

*Who are you?*

'How long have you been working here?' she asked him.

'I started this morning. Mr Binchy's sister recommended me for the job. I'm lodging with her. It's just a little place in Malone Road. I should have been working with my brother but. . .' He allowed the sentence to trail off, his face crossed with mock sorrow.

'What happened?'

'The fucking UVF murdered him,' Doyle rasped, his display of angry pain suitably convincing. 'Because he wasn't scared to say what he thought of them. So they killed him. Bastards.'

Marie looked impassively at him.

'UVF, fucking Brits, what's the difference?' he continued. 'They're all the enemy. My brother believed that and now he's dead.'

'And what about you?' she asked, quietly. 'What do *you* believe?'

'I think the IRA have got the right idea,' he said, lowering his voice.

'There's a lot of people who'd disagree with you.'

'Fuck them. Anybody who'd disagree with me doesn't care about Ireland. The fucking politicians do nothing. The IRA are the only ones with the guts to fight for what they believe in.' He leant across the bar, his face only inches from hers. 'I'll tell you something, if they put a gun in my hand and showed me the bastards who killed my brother, I'd shoot them myself.'

Marie sipped at her orange juice and eyed Doyle appraisingly.

'Which part of Ireland are you from?' she asked, finally.

'Ennis, County Clare, do you know it?'

'I've been through it, I think.'

'Everyone's been through it, it's just that no one stops,' he said, smiling.

Marie laughed.

'What about yourself?' he asked.

'I was born here in Belfast.'

'Any family?'

*Only a sister who's a vegetable.*

'No,' she said, lowering her voice. 'No family.'

Doyle reached out and took her left hand, running one index finger over the smooth skin and slender fingers.

'What are you doing?' she asked him, smiling.

'Checking for a wedding ring,' he told her.

She laughed.

'There's no husband either,' she told him.

'Good, I didn't want him to get angry when I took you out for a drink.'

She shook her head, fixing him in an unblinking gaze.

'You're full of it, aren't you?' she said.

'That depends on what the "it" is.' He winked. 'You said you were born in Belfast. Did they give you a name when you were born?'

'Marie Leary.'

'Hello, Marie Leary.'

She drained what was left in her glass.

'Can I get you another or would you rather wait until tonight?'

She looked quizzically at him.

'Tonight, tomorrow night, whichever night you're free. Which night do you want me to take you out?'

She got down from the bar stool.

'Thanks, but no thanks,' she said, smiling.

'Is it something I said?'

She pulled up the collar of her jacket.

'Marie, you wouldn't go out with a man out of pity, would you?' he asked.

'Why do you ask?'

'Because I was just going to beg.'

She laughed.

'Jack, I'm sorry about your brother,' she said, softly.

'Yeah, so am I. Like I said, if only there was something I could do about it.'

She nodded and headed for the door.

'Tell Binchy I'll be back,' she said.

Doyle nodded and watched her walk out.

'I'll be waiting,' he murmured under his breath.

Marie Leary.

*Who the fuck are you?*

# Fifty-Five

'Jesus Christ,' muttered Jim Binchy sliding the top bolt on the door. 'You practically have to hold a gun to their bloody heads to get them out come closing time.'

He exhaled deeply and walked back towards the bar where Doyle was drying glasses. Doyle watched as the landlord dropped the door keys in front of him then went round switching off the jukebox, the video game and the fruit machines. A pleasing quietness settled on the pub.

Doyle finished drying the glasses and replaced them in their appointed places behind the bar.

'Will you join me?' said Binchy, appearing at his side.

He took down two whiskey glasses and motioned to the Bushmills' optic.

Doyle nodded and gratefully accepted the glass of fiery liquid.

'Here's to your first day,' said Binchy.

Doyle echoed the toast and drank.

'Jim, can I ask you something?' he said, finally.

Binchy was taking money from the till, sorting the notes out into denominations, constantly tapping the wads on the counter to keep them neat.

'If you're after a pay rise this quick you can forget it,' Binchy told him, smiling.

'That girl who was here this afternoon, the blonde one. Who is she?' Doyle asked.

He saw the muscles at the side of Binchy's jaw tighten.

'Tell me to mind my own business if you like, but. . .'

Binchy didn't look at him.

'Mind your own business, Jack,' the landlord said, still taking money from the till.

Doyle eyed him warily.

'And if you've got any ideas in *that* direction,' Binchy told him, 'I'd recommend you keeping it in your pants.'

'She said she wasn't married.'

'Have you been talking to her then?'

'After you went out. Do you blame me? She's fucking deadly looking.'

Binchy was counting a pile of pound coins, his hands shaking slightly.

'If you want to chat her up then do it somewhere else, not in my fucking pub,' the landlord snapped.

'If I'm treading on somebody's toes you only have to tell me, Jim.'

The pound coins slipped out of Binchy's hands and went spilling over the counter.

'Fuck it,' he snarled and set about picking them up.

Doyle helped, standing them in small piles on the bar top.

He held Binchy in a questioning stare.

'Oh Christ, what the hell,' the landlord said, wearily. 'If

you're going to work here you're going to find out the truth eventually.' He looked directly at Doyle. 'She's IRA.'

Doyle raised an eyebrow slightly.

'Don't look so surprised, Jack. They come in all shapes and sizes,' Binchy told him. 'They don't all walk around in fatigues and fucking balaclavas.'

'The money she wanted, is it protection?'

'Protection my arse,' said Binchy indignantly. 'I borrowed some money off them. Gambling debts, I got behind. You know how it is.'

'I didn't think the IRA were into loan-sharking,' Doyle said with suitably convincing naivety.

'The IRA are into everything, Jack. They run this fucking city. Not the RUC, not the army, the IRA. Everything that goes on in this city they've got a finger in it. And do you know what I say? Good luck to them.'

Doyle drained what was left in his glass and set down the empty receptacle.

'You can get off if you want, Jack.'

Doyle fetched his leather jacket and slipped it on.

'If you want to hang on I can drop you at my sister's,' Binchy told him.

'No thanks, Jim, I think I'll walk. I need to clear my head.'

'You need to clear Marie Leary out of it for a start.'

Doyle nodded and opened the door. 'See you in the morning,' he said and he was gone.

As he stepped out onto the pavement he felt the cold wind which had been building up steadily during the evening. Doyle pulled up the collar of his jacket, dug his hands into his pockets and headed off towards the bus stop, intent on catching some transport at least part of the way back to Malone Road.

So, Marie Leary was IRA was she?

Doyle smiled.

*Bingo.*

She could be his way in. Maybe even a path to Riordan or O'Connor.

Or the guns eventually.

*Don't get ahead of yourself. One step at a time.*

What if he didn't see her again?

*She had to come back to collect Binchy's money.*

Just a matter of time.

He crossed the street, trying not to attach too much importance to his meeting with her, but nonetheless happy. Christie was dead. *She* might well be his next lead.

And she did look like Georgie, didn't she?

He kicked out angrily at a crumpled Pepsi can nearby, sending it flying into the road.

The blonde hair. The figure.

Even her eyes were the same colour weren't they?

*Weren't they?*

What colour had Georgie's eyes been?

Green. Blue. Brown.

She's only been dead four years. Come on, think.

*Four years, five years. A fucking lifetime.*

Doyle pulled his cigarettes from his jacket and paused to light one, glancing around.

A dark blue Austin Maestro passed him and turned into the street on the left.

Doyle kept walking.

He reached the bus stop. The shelter was broken, the glass gone, as if someone had sneaked up and skilfully cut away the entire pane which held the Adshel poster. He leant against the remains of the shelter, glancing occasionally at his watch.

IRA or not, Marie Leary was a good-looking young woman, thought Doyle. And if she was going to be useful to him, even better. But he would have to be careful.

The dark blue Maestro passed him again.

Doyle watched it more closely this time, stepping back towards the low wall behind him.

He felt the hairs at the nape of his neck rise. His heart was thudding harder against his ribs.

He heard tyres squeal and looked round to see the Maestro heading towards him once more.

It was slowing down.

*Come on then, you fuckers.*

It stopped.

The passenger door was pushed open.

Doyle could see inside.

Marie Leary smiled thinly.

'Get in,' she said.

# Fifty-Six

*London*

'If we are to win this war we must pick our targets carefully before we strike,' said Joey Chang, pacing backwards and forwards before the watchful eyes of the room's other occupants. 'The Hip Sing have struck only at our foot soldiers so far, and at some of our businesses.'

'They are afraid of us,' Frankie Wong interjected.

'Then why begin a war in the first place?' Chang demanded.

'Perhaps they knew we would take our time hitting back.'

'You would have had us hit back without even being sure it *was* the Hip Sing who were our enemies,' Chang rasped, glaring at Wong.

The younger man held his gaze.

'Remember, Frankie, the one attack we have tried against them so far has failed,' Chang said.

'Do you blame *me*?' Wong snarled, angrily.

'I blame no one,' Chang told him.

'Let us not fight amongst ourselves,' Jackie Ti interrupted. 'We know who our enemy is, all that matters now is defeating him.'

There was a rumble of agreement from the other men in the room.

'So how do we defeat the Hip Sing?' Cho Lok added.

Chang stroked his chin thoughtfully. 'If we strike at their business interests we cripple them financially,' he began. 'We destroy them not just now but in the long term. We force them out of London completely. But, and you all know this was my fear from the beginning, the other organisations will not look kindly upon all-out war. When war begins the police will crack down on everyone's operations, not just ours and the Hip Sing's, but those of the Wo Shing Wo, the Shui Fong and the Sun Yee On. All of us. The other organisations *might* join forces with the Hip Sing to prevent a long war destructive to everyone.'

Wo Fen nodded sagely and glanced at his old companions. 'You have thought carefully of this matter, Joey,' he said. 'We were right to choose you as *Pak Tsz Sin*. We will be guided by your wisdom. How should we fight this war?'

'It sounds as if you're trying to tell us *not* to fight it,' Wong snapped.

Chang ignored the interruption and addressed Wo. 'The Hip Sing are better equipped than we are, more heavily armed. If our soldiers strike at theirs then we will lose. We must arm ourselves more adequately.'

'And then?' Wo wanted to know.

'We strike at their businesses, quickly, and inflicting the maximum casualties. Then we strike at their officers.'

There were more murmurs of approval.

Frankie Wong smiled.

'At last,' he said, quietly.

'The weapons are the most important thing,' Chang repeated.

He looked at Wo for long seconds then the old man nodded.

Chang crossed to a phone in one corner of the room, picked it up and jabbed out the digits he wanted, waiting for it to be picked up at the other end.

When it finally was, his expression didn't change.

'We need to speak with you,' he said to the person at the other end. 'To meet.'

The others watched him, his face unmoving.

'As soon as possible. We have business to do,' he continued. 'You know where to contact us. We will make the other arrangements.'

The others saw Chang nodding as he listened to the voice of the person at the other end.

'We'll discuss that when you get here. We'll take care of that from this end.'

He put the phone down, ending the conversation abruptly.

'It's done,' he said, looking at Wo Fen.

'When?' the elder man wanted to know.

'Two days from now,' Chang told him.

Frankie Wong smiled.


# Fifty-Seven


*Northern Ireland*

The house was neat, clean and tidy and relatively uncluttered by too many ornaments or mementoes.

Doyle crossed to the window and pulled back one curtain a fraction, peering out into the darkness. Terraced houses exactly the same as this one faced him on the other side of the street. Most of the poorer parts of Belfast were identical as far as the architecture went. Belfast, London, Liverpool, Glasgow: any city in the country, any city in the world, Doyle thought, grouped its poor together then tried to lose them in the anonymity of uniformity.

Some things never changed.

'What are you looking for?'

He turned as he heard Marie's voice. She entered the

room carrying two mugs of tea, one of which she set down on the table in the centre of the room.

Doyle watched as she sat down in one of the chairs, drawing her slender legs up beneath her, the mug held in both hands.

'I was just being nosey,' Doyle said, picking up his own mug.

'Do you want something in it?' she said, smiling, nodding towards the steaming brew.

Doyle looked puzzled.

'A drop of the hard stuff,' she continued, chuckling. 'That's what my father always used to say.' The smile faded.

'Is that your father?' Doyle said, noticing the photo which stood on the mantelpiece between a carriage clock and a chipped vase.

Marie nodded.

Doyle got to his feet and crossed to the picture.

'Yeah, that's my daddy,' she said, smiling again.

'Who's that with him?' he asked, pointing to the other young woman in the picture. The first he recognised as Marie.

She lowered her gaze, staring into the depths of her mug.

'My sister, Colette,' she said, quietly.

'She looks like you.'

'She's dead,' Marie snapped. 'What about you?' she added, as if anxious to avoid the subject. 'Any family? Anyone close? I was thinking as we drove back here, I don't know anything about you.'

'You should be careful about picking up strange men then, shouldn't you?' he said, smiling. 'You don't know who I might be.'

*A counter terrorist?*

'I know your brother was killed by the UVF, that's *all* I know.'

He glanced at the photo again.

At Marie.

'What do you want to know?' he asked.

'Is there anyone close? A woman?'

He shook his head.

'There must have been,' she offered, smiling. 'Or are you saving yourself?'

'There *was* somebody,' he said, quietly.

*Georgie.*

'She died.'

'I'm sorry,' Marie told him.

'So am I.'

For long seconds they locked stares, held the gaze.

'She looked a little like you,' he told Marie, finally.

*Until they shot her.*

He took a sip of his tea.

*Forget it.*

'You said there must have been someone,' he said, quietly. 'What makes you so sure?'

'Come on, Jack. A fella like you. With your line of chat. The girls must have been falling over themselves.'

'Like you?' he said, softly.

Marie got to her feet and walked across to the sofa where he sat. She perched on the edge, gazing into his eyes.

'Yeah, like me,' she said and leaned towards him, her mouth searching for his.

They kissed deeply, her tongue probing into his mouth, stirring the warm wetness there. Doyle responded fiercely, pulling her down with him, one hand stroking her long, silky hair.

She broke the kiss and reached out with one hand, running her fingertips over his cheeks and chin, feeling the stubble there. She traced the outline of his lips with her index finger and Doyle flicked at the end of the probing digit with his tongue for a second before trying to sit up.

Marie did not budge. She sat on his lap, one leg each side of him, her crotch pressed hard against his groin, rocking gently. She could feel the stiffness of his erection through his jeans and she moved back only long enough to unbutton his flies, pulling at the fastenings, then she snaked her long fingers into his underpants and gripped his erection firmly.

Doyle groaned as she ran the pad of one thumb over his swollen glans.

She stood up and, as he watched, pulled off her sweater, tossing it to one side, then she undid her jeans, sliding them down, stepping out of them until she stood before him, naked but for her panties.

Doyle slid off the sofa and knelt before her, his hot breath warming her pubic mound which pressed so invitingly against the thin material of her briefs. He smelled her musky scent and it excited him even more. He kissed her through the material, pressed his mouth to her cloth-clad vagina, his own saliva now dampening the already moist cotton. Then he gripped both sides of her panties and pulled them down, allowing her to step out of them before he pushed his tongue through the tightly curled down which was her pubic hair.

He tasted moisture on his tongue, probed her clitoris with deft strokes that made her gasp and pull his head harder into her.

Despite the pleasure she was feeling she pulled back from him and sat on the edge of the sofa, her slim thighs parted, her labia swollen and slippery.

Doyle removed his clothes quickly and knelt between her legs, the head of his penis nudging the slippery opening to her cleft. He eased his erection forward a fraction, sliding into her an inch then he withdrew, his own bulbous head now coated with her liquescence. Again and again he repeated that action until she looked at him imploringly, needing the deeper penetration he promised but denied.

Gripping his penis in one hand he rubbed the swollen head over her clitoris, his own excitement growing stronger, his own desire building.

'Fuck me,' she whispered, hoarsely.

Doyle slid into her with one deep thrust and she gasped, pulling him down on top of her, gripping his arms as he began to move more rhythmically inside her.

He felt her inner muscles closing around his shaft and the sensations made him groan approvingly.

She raised her legs and locked them around the small of his back, allowing him deeper penetration.

He kissed her again, one hand stroking her face, then her hair, then her breasts. Doyle felt the hardness of her nipples between his fingers and she placed her own hand over his, encouraging him to squeeze the swollen bud more tightly as she felt her orgasm drawing closer.

Marie arched her back as the first wave of pleasure swept over her, her whole body stiffening as her climax enveloped her and she gasped aloud as Doyle kept up his powerful thrusts inside her, feeling her muscles tighten, seeing the pleasure on her face and in the reddish-pink flush which covered her face, neck and breasts. He slowed his rhythm, looking down at her, taking in every detail of her body: her face, beaded with perspiration; the silky strands of hair which had flailed across her neck; the firmness of her breasts and her stiff nipples; the smooth flatness of her belly, leading down to the matted triangle of light hair between her legs where he still pushed his erection firmly in and out, seeing it coated with her liquid pleasure.

Marie reached down with one hand and gently gripped his penis, preventing him from penetrating her.

She sat up, smiling, still holding his throbbing stiffness, moving her hand up and down the shaft more quickly now until she felt him tense then she removed her hand, leaving him gasping, on the verge of his release.

Marie slid onto the floor then turned away, raising her buttocks towards him as she crouched on all fours.

'Now,' she whispered.

Doyle entered her from the rear, feeling her push back to meet his thrusts.

'Go on,' she gasped as he speeded up, his desperation

for release reflected in the urgency of his movements. 'I want it.'

Doyle gripped her hips and tensed up, the pleasure building to a peak.

He saw the perspiration glistening on her back, her blonde hair trailing through it.

*He thought of Georgie.*

Marie reached back with one hand to touch her own clitoris and, as she did, she brushed the base of Doyle's shaft with her fingers.

It was enough to push him over the edge and he climaxed gushingly, gripping her so hard he almost bruised her skin.

'Jesus,' he hissed through gritted teeth, his thrusts slowing down as the last glorious sensations died away.

Marie was breathing heavily too, her hands balled into fists on the carpet. She felt him withdraw and she turned to face him, kissing him.

From the mantelpiece the photograph of her father looked on impassively.

She wondered what *he* would have thought of Doyle. Would he have wanted to know more about this man about whom she knew so little?

This stranger.

Doyle smiled down at her, brushing some strands of hair from her face.

When the time came, he wondered, would he find it difficult to kill her.


# Fifty-Eight


'You didn't get these working in a pub.'

Doyle felt her finger tracing the outline of a particularly deep scar on his right calf.

Marie was lying with her head close to his feet, looking up at him.

Her own left foot was against his armpit, her right on his chest.

Doyle gently stroked the sole of her foot, occasionally tilting his head forward to kiss her toes, licking gently at the nails or the flesh between the digits.

Marie sighed approvingly each time he did so.

Her bedroom was small but, like the rest of the house, neat. The walls bore only one or two pictures. Another of her sister and herself in school uniform was propped on the dressing table to his right.

'Where did you get these scars?' she wanted to know.

Doyle had the lie ready.

'I was working in Dublin a few years ago, a shop just off Grafton Street,' he told her. 'We were putting in part of the skylight and the fucking roof gave way. I fell through. It was the glass that did that.'

She eyed him blankly for a second then touched another scar in his thigh. A rounded hole.

She thought about mentioning that it looked like a bullet hole.

Doyle continued massaging her foot.

'Your sister . . .' he said, nodding towards the photo on the bedside table, 'what did you say happened to her?'

Marie was silent.

'I said. . .'

She cut him short.

'I heard what you said,' she snapped, rolling away from him.

'Okay, don't have a fucking fit about it,' he said as she swung herself onto the side of the bed.

'She *isn't* dead,' Marie said, flatly. 'At least she wasn't the last time I saw her. Not that the way she exists could be called living.'

Doyle sat up, reached for her, his show of false affection having the desired effect. She lay back on the bed and he pulled the sheet up over her stomach.

'What happened?' he wanted to know, listening as she told him about the shooting of her sister and her sister's boyfriend. About Colette's continuing existence in a hospital.

'They killed your brother too, Jack,' she said, angrily. 'You know what it feels like, you said how much you wanted revenge against the UVF, the Brits, the whole fucking lot of them.' Her eyes were blazing. 'But it isn't just sadness that I feel, sadness and anger, I feel ashamed too. She's my own sister and yet I can't even look at her. I can't bear to touch her. She can't even go to the toilet on her own and it's all because of them. What they did to her.'

Doyle nodded slowly.

'Is that why you joined the IRA?' he said, flatly.

She sat bolt upright, pushing him off, her eyes burning into him.

'How did you know?' she rasped.

'Binchy told me. After you came to collect the money off him, he told me you were with them.'

She looked questioningly at him.

'I admire you for it,' he lied. 'At least you've done something.'

'Binchy's got a big mouth,' she said, finally, lying down beside him again.

Doyle rolled over and reached for his cigarettes, sitting on the edge of the bed, his back to her.

'He didn't mean anything by it,' said the counter terrorist, drawing in a lungful of smoke.

He heard the drawer open behind him, heard the metallic click.

Doyle realised at once that it was the sound of a hammer being pulled back.

When he turned his head, Marie was holding a CZ automatic on him. He stood up slowly.

'I really wish he hadn't told you, Jack,' she said, softly.

Doyle looked briefly at the barrel of the pistol then at Marie.

If he was concerned it didn't show on his face.

'Are you going to kill me because I know about you?' he said.

*You fucking bitch.*

She held his gaze.

Doyle didn't move an inch.

*Come on. Do something.*

He had two choices. Rush her, take the gun from her and kill her, thereby losing another lead or. . .

*Or what?*

Or wait for her to pull the trigger.

*And get your fucking head blown off.*

'How do I know I can trust you?' she said.

'You don't and if that's the way you feel, you'd better kill me.'

*One chance.*

She raised the pistol so that it was pointing directly at his head.

*Take her out now. She isn't going to miss from three fucking feet.*

'I don't want to do this,' she said.

'Then don't,' Doyle said, quietly. 'No one's forcing you.'

'I *daren't* trust you, Jack.'

'What if you could?'

She looked puzzled.

'There *is* a way,' he assured her.

'Then you'd better tell me.'

The sudden banging on the front door surprised them both.

# Fifty-Nine

Neither of them moved.

Doyle and Marie faced each other, the pounding on the door growing louder, more insistent.

'What are you going to do?' said Doyle. 'Shoot me or answer the door?'

Marie kept the barrel of the CZ aimed at his head.

Like two naked statues in some bizarre tableau they stood with only the bed between them.

The banging continued.

Doyle glanced at the bedside clock.

1.56 a.m.

It must be important.

'If it's the police . . .' she said, quietly, her eyes narrowing.

He shook his head almost imperceptibly.

She took a step back as Doyle sat down on the edge of the bed.

'Answer it, Marie,' he said, quietly. 'I'm not going anywhere.'

She hesitated a second longer then snatched up her jeans, pulling them on hurriedly. She pulled a T-shirt over them and stuck the CZ in the waistband, covering it with the material.

Doyle turned his back as she headed for the stairs, scurrying down them as the banging continued.

As he heard her reach the bottom he quickly pulled on his own jeans and crept towards the bedroom door.

From downstairs he could hear the sound of bolts being pulled back, the lock being turned.

Then voices.

'You took your time,' said a man's voice.

'What the hell are you doing here at this time?' Marie asked, irritably, closing the door behind her visitor.

Doyle crept closer to the landing ballustrade, cursing when one of the floorboards creaked loudly beneath his feet.

The voices beneath him had moved into the sitting room, he guessed. It was hard to pick out all but the odd word or sentence here and there.

Fragments of the conversation drifted up to him, like dialogue heard via an ineffective radio transmitter.

'. . . at this fucking time of the morning . . . phoned first . . .' He heard Marie's voice, she was angry.

'. . . earlier . . . meeting . . . interrupting something?' The other voice was male, that much was obvious.

'. . . of your business. . .'

Doyle moved towards the top step, intent on descending a small distance in an effort to pick up more of the conversation.

One step.

The words were still difficult to pick out.

Two steps.

He could actually see the sitting-room door from his perch now. The door was slightly ajar.

He saw Marie walk past it, gesturing towards her visitor.

*Who the fuck was it?*

The sitting-room door suddenly opened.

Doyle retreated hastily back up the stairs as he heard movement in the narrow hallway below, then he heard the door being opened.

'I'll let you get back to whatever you were doing,' said the man's voice. 'Is it anyone we know?' the visitor chuckled.

'None of your fucking business,' Marie snapped and closed the door.

Doyle looked round. There was another door to his left, leading into the front bedroom. He bolted for it, slipped inside and crossed to the window, peering out into the darkness, trying to spot the man who'd just left.

He saw a shape moving on the pavement in front of the house, saw the man moving towards a car parked nearby.

'I know you,' murmured Doyle, a slight smile on his lips.

He recognised the powerful build, the curly black hair.

Declan O'Connor slid behind the steering wheel, started the engine and drove off.

Riordan, O'Connor and Christie. The three men he knew had worked as an active service unit.

*Bingo.*

Doyle was heading back towards Marie's bedroom when he heard her padding back up the stairs.

'Are you going to kill me now?' he said, flatly.

She pulled the CZ from her waistband and pointed it at him, her face impassive.

'Tell me how you can make me trust you,' she said.

'It's simple,' he told her, smiling. 'Let me join you.'

# Sixty

*London*

The school was at the corner of Cadogan Street and Draycott Terrace and as Chang brought the Daimler to a halt he could see dozens of uniformed children running about in the playground at the front of the building.

It was a short distance from their apartment and Su usually walked the children to the school, but he preferred to bring them by car. Especially as it was raining this morning. But it gave him an excuse too. A reason for keeping them close to him.

He saw other cars, some belonging to parents who had

come much greater distances. There were the usual groups of them standing about outside the gates, chatting amiably. He recognised a couple of young nannies who had safely escorted their wards to the school and who were now walking away, both puffing on cigarettes, something, he presumed, they would be forbidden to do in the company of their charges.

In the back of the Daimler, Michael Chang was pulling at his seatbelt and glancing out of the side window.

'Can *I* sit in the front next time, Dad?' he asked.

'You have to sit in the back because you're the baby,' Anna told him haughtily from the passenger seat.

'I'm not a baby,' he snapped.

'But you're younger than *me*,' she reminded him. 'I'll be seven in a few weeks.' She looked up at her father. 'Can I have a party, Dad?'

'We'll see,' Chang told her, scanning the pavement outside the school for any unfamiliar or curious faces.

'Michael had a party for *his* birthday,' she said, indignantly.

'And you'll have one for yours,' Chang said, turning and poking his daughter playfully in the ribs.

She giggled.

He prodded her again and she squirmed in her seat.

'Go on now, or you'll be late,' he said.

They both undid their seatbelts and slid out.

Chang kissed Anna on the forehead and then patted Michael, watching as they sauntered across to join the other children in the playground.

The rain spattered the windscreen and Chang pressed a button, allowing the wipers to brush away the moisture.

He saw a white BMW drop off another child, saw the mother step out with the boy to straighten his tie. She kissed him and Chang grinned as he saw the boy wipe the kiss away with the back of his hand before running into the playground.

The BMW drove off.

Two more cars dropped off their little passengers. He

saw a small minibus arrive with at least eight children inside.

A black Cortina passed by and Chang gave it only a cursory glance.

Had he seen it slow down at the far end of the street he may well have paid it more attention.

He sat for a moment longer then started his engine.

At the end of the street, the black Cortina turned and headed back towards him, moving slowly.

Chang swung the Daimler round in the road and drove off, glancing one last time towards the playground.

He saw Anna chatting to some of her friends. Of Michael there was no sign.

He heard the bell sound for the beginning of school and checked the dashboard clock.

9.00 a.m.

The black Cortina drew closer to him and, as he glanced in his rear-view mirror to check the traffic behind, he saw it.

Chang turned left.

The Cortina turned right.

Five minutes later it drove past the school again.

The passenger wrote something down.


Su Chang pushed the last of the plates into position in the dishwasher then closed the door and pressed the required button. The machine sprang into life.

She barely heard the phone above its loud droning.

Crossing the kitchen she picked up the receiver.

'Hello,' she said.

Silence.

'Hello,' she repeated.

Still nothing.

Perhaps it was a wrong number or. . .

'Su Chang,' the voice said.

'Yes, who is this?'

'After we kill your husband we will cut off his head,' the voice said, flatly.

Su felt the colour draining from her face. When she tried to speak again it was as if someone had filled her throat with chalk.

'And you will watch,' the voice continued.

She leant against the wall, as if needing the support for fear of falling.

'And when that is done we will kill your children,' the voice told her. 'Split them wide open and then you, we will fuck you and—'

Su slammed the phone down, nearly tearing the bracket off the wall.

She stepped away, her eyes fixed on it as if it were some dangerous animal.

Her breath was coming in gasps, her whole body trembling.

The phone rang again.

Su remained pressed against the far wall, her heart thudding against her ribs.

The ringing continued.

She gritted her teeth and reached for it, noticing that her hands were shaking.

She pressed it to her ear and merely held it there.

There was a moment of silence then the voice began again.

'You will all die,' it hissed. 'Your husband, your children and you. We will piss on your bodies as you lie dying, we will spit on you while we fuck you.'

'Shut up,' she shrieked down the phone and slammed it once more, this time running into the sitting room where she pulled the phone lead from its socket. She moved into the bedroom and did the same thing, then back into the kitchen.

As she was reaching for the lead she heard the front door open.

She pulled the lead out and dropped it, tears in her eyes.

'What are you doing?'

She spun round as she heard Chang's voice then she ran to him, throwing her arms around him.

He felt her sobbing against him.

'What's wrong?' he demanded, his own heart now thumping more heavily.

She told him about the phone call.

Chang swallowed hard, the knot of muscles at the side of his jaw pulsing angrily.

'They're just trying to frighten you,' he said, his own tone none too convincing.

'They got this phone number, Joey,' Su said, wiping her eyes with the back of one hand. 'What else do they know?'

'Do you want me to call the bodyguards up here?' he said.

She shook her head.

'I'll be okay,' she told him.

He hugged her tightly, kissed the top of her head.

'Leave the phones unplugged,' he told her. 'If I need to contact you I'll call you on the portable.'

She nodded.

'When you go to pick up the children, one of the bodyguards will go with you,' Chang added. He looked at his watch and exhaled deeply. 'I have to go. Are you sure you'll be all right?'

'You go,' she told him.

'This will be over soon, I promise you.' He kissed her again. 'If you have to go out, one of the bodyguards. . .'

She raised a hand to silence him.

'I'll be fine,' Su told him, her face set grimly.

He squeezed her hand tightly for a second then turned and left.

Su crossed to the kitchen window and peered out into the curtain of drizzle falling over the city but, after a minute or two, she stepped back.

She wondered who might be down there looking up at her.

# Sixty-One

*Northern Ireland*

A cold breeze was blowing off Lough Neagh, an icy chill which stirred the leaves of trees near the water's edge and scattered those that had already fallen. The water lapped against the shore, its surface choppy, its expanse as grey as the sky overhead.

Trees grew thickly on this part of the easterly shore, in some places right up to the lough's edge. A steep bank sloped upwards towards a road that was little more than a dirt track which ran through the woods. Little traffic passed along it.

They had parked their cars there.

Each one a few hundred yards apart, slightly off the track, hidden by bushes if possible.

Anyone passing would think they were just visiting the lough, fishermen perhaps or a family out together for a walk. There was nothing untoward about the three vehicles.

Marie Leary ran a hand through her long hair, brushing strands from the corner of her mouth as she walked, her collar pulled up against the chill.

Beside her, Paul Riordan strode along, glancing occasionally out across the lough. His vivid blue eyes looked watery, his face ruddy cheeked.

Declan O'Connor walked beside him, hands dug deeply into the pockets of his coat, his curly black hair constantly ruffled by the strong wind. He kept looking down at his feet, muttering to himself when his boots sunk into mud on the shore. He kicked at a fallen branch, stooped to pick up part of it and flung it ahead of him as if he were waiting for some invisible dog to retrieve it.

Marie had called the two men earlier that morning and said she wanted to meet. What she had to say couldn't be said over the phone.

Riordan had sounded intrigued. O'Connor had been less enthusiastic.

They walked slowly, their steps almost synchronised, across the muddied bank, through the fallen leaves. It was quiet on the shore, and a watery sun was hidden behind grey clouds which were gathering like muted warnings.

'So, how much do you know about this Jack Fagan?' said Riordan, looking out across the lough once more.

'His brother was killed by the UVF,' Marie said. 'He's angry, Paul, he wants to do something about it.'

'Talking and doing are two different things,' Riordan said, dismissively. 'How long have you known him?'

'A couple of days.'

'And he wants to join us? You told him you were with the organisation?'

Marie nodded. 'He already knew, Binchy had told him.'

'You're fucking crazy, Marie,' Riordan said, sharply. 'He could be anybody.'

'Was it him at your house last night when I called?' O'Connor asked.

'What are you talking about?' she demanded.

'There was someone with you. Was it him?'

'That's none of your business,' she snapped. 'It's got nothing to do with this.'

'It's got *everything* to do with this,' Riordan told her.

'Just because he fucked you doesn't make him all right,' O'Connor added.

'He's genuine, I know it,' Marie said, angrily.

'You *can't* know,' Riordan stressed. 'And until you can, I'm not putting the organisation at risk. We have to know more about him.'

'Then check him out. I know where he lives,' she said, giving them the address in Malone Road.

'O'Connor, you go there, get inside any way you have

201

to,' Riordan instructed. 'Search his room, find out anything you can. See what ID he's carrying, that sort of thing.'

The other man nodded.

'If he turns out to be shite, Marie, you're in fucking trouble,' Riordan said, irritably.

'I'm taking him with me to Donegal tonight,' she said.

'My arse,' snorted Riordan. 'We don't even know who the fuck he is and you're talking about taking him on a job with you. No way.' He reached for his cigarettes and lit one, cupping his hand around the lighter flame to shield it from the wind. 'We've got important business coming up. I don't want some stranger fucking it up and I don't want *you* fucking it up either. There's too much at stake, I thought you would have realised that too.'

'I do realise it, why do you think I'm so keen to prove to you that Fagan's what he says he is?' Marie snapped. 'He wants to join us, we need men, we always need men. Why turn away one who's so keen to help us?'

Riordan looked past her, fixing his icy blue eyes on O'Connor.

'After you've searched Fagan's place, you call me,' he said. 'I'll be at the usual place. No matter what time it is, you call.'

O'Connor nodded.

'I'm taking him to Donegal with me, Paul,' Marie insisted.

'I told you, no way.'

Marie shot out a hand and grabbed Riordan by the shoulder, turning him to face her. She looked deep into his eyes, seeing not the slightest flicker of emotion there.

'I'll take him,' she said. 'I'll find out as much as I can about him.'

Riordan shook his head almost imperceptibly.

'Listen to me,' she snapped. 'It's the only way.'

'And if he's not who he says he is?' Riordan wanted to know.

Marie held his gaze.

'I'll kill him myself,' she said, softly.

# Sixty-Two

Doyle's mind hadn't been on his work that day. He hoped that Binchy hadn't noticed, that he'd managed to perform the few tasks required of him adequately, but he couldn't get the incidents of the past couple of days off his mind.

More to the point, he couldn't get Marie Leary off his mind.

*Even though she is the enemy?*

He knew that part of his job was down to luck. Coincidence. Call it what you will but along with anticipation, speed of thought and a knowledge of how your opponents operated, Doyle had always felt that his work required at least a small portion of luck.

Marie Leary had been that piece of luck.

She was his way into the IRA. A way of reaching Riordan and O'Connor, and ultimately, he hoped, a way to find the stolen army weapons.

He'd left her place about seven that morning and walked back to his lodgings in Malone Road. He'd showered, eaten breakfast then come straight to the pub. Mrs Shannon had made some joke about him not coming home, but Doyle had just smiled at her and changed the subject.

It was none of her business what he did. Fortunately she had no idea she was sheltering a member of the Counter Terrorist Unit inside her house.

He wondered what she might have done if she *had* known.

Thrown him out? Spat in his face?

*Contacted the IRA?*

He smiled thinly at the thought.

She hadn't had to.

They'd come to him, albeit unwittingly, in the shape of Marie Leary.

Now he had to be careful. Play it as cannily as possible. Make her trust him.

He couldn't afford to fuck up now. He was too close.

Doyle waved goodbye to a couple of men he'd been chatting to about football during the lunchtime session as they left the pub together. He continued washing glasses, putting them on the towel which stood on the bar top before him.

At the other end of the bar, Binchy was still serving, pulling pints, pushing them across to the men before him.

Doyle could hear them talking, but he didn't take much notice of the words. His mind was elsewhere.

The jukebox was still pumping out noise and Doyle heard the words coming from that more clearly than he heard the conversation near him:

*'Loving you is like fire, but I'm tired of getting burned . . .'*

He washed more glasses.

*'Been a long time coming, baby, but the tables just got turned . . .'*

Binchy took money from the drinkers and headed for the till.

*'You swallowed up my soul, and you wasted all my youth . . .'*

Doyle was gazing blankly ahead.

*'The time has come to face it, it's the moment of truth . . .'*

Binchy pressed out the total on the till, took out the change and left Doyle alone once more.

The place was emptying out, as it usually did at this

time. They'd been busy at lunchtime, but Doyle had coped efficiently with the customers considering his mind was elsewhere.

The pub door opened.

Marie Leary smiled as she walked across towards Doyle.

He looked at her admiringly. At her long blonde hair, her slim hips and legs encased by tight denim.

He smiled back.

*His way into the IRA.*

'Hey, you,' he said, smiling.

She smiled at him broadly and sat down on the bar stool nearest to her.

'If you're looking for Binchy he's down there,' Doyle said, nodding towards the landlord who had also seen her enter.

'As a matter of fact I was looking for you,' Marie said.

'Aren't I the lucky one? What can I do for you? Apart from what I'd *like* to do for you.'

'You did *that* last night,' she grinned. Then the smile faded slightly. 'It's something to do with what you said the other night about . . .'

*About what? About the IRA?*

'About . . . joining us.' She had lowered her voice slightly.

Doyle held her gaze.

'I've got to go to Donegal tonight, I was wondering if you wanted to come with me.

She thought about mentioning her meeting with Riordan and O'Connor earlier that day, but decided against it.

'I could pick you up from here tonight,' she added.

Doyle nodded sombrely.

'About ten?' she said.

'I'll ask Binchy if I can get off an hour early,' he told her.

She got to her feet.

'You don't know what this means to me, Marie,' he said.

*And you never fucking will.*

She smiled.

'Ten o'clock out the front,' she told him and turned to walk away.

Doyle smiled to himself.

*One step closer*.

'What did she want?'

He turned to see Binchy standing beside him.

'I'm meeting her tonight,' Doyle told him.

Binchy shook his head. 'Be careful of that one, Jack.'

'Don't worry,' Doyle replied, wiping glasses. 'I just need to nip back to my lodgings later and pick up some clean clothes. Is that okay?'

Binchy nodded.

'Like I said, Jack, just watch yourself, you don't know what you might be getting yourself into.'

'I know *exactly* what I'm getting myself into,' Doyle said.

It was all he could do to suppress a smile.


# Sixty-Three


*Heathrow Airport, London*

The flight in from Belfast was early. As Paul Riordan moved slowly up the central aisle of the 737 he heard the captain announce that the aircraft had landed ten minutes ahead of schedule. He wondered if they'd have been so keen to report on a ten-minute delay.

The stewardess smiled at him as he left the plane and Riordan returned the gesture, gripping his holdall tightly, stepping back to allow an elderly woman through the exit door before him. She smiled gratefully and made her way down the metal stairs that had been pushed up beside the plane.

Riordan followed, glancing around the rain-spattered tarmac through the gloom. The sheet of drizzle draped over London made the approaching dusk look even more unwelcoming. The Irishman moved briskly down the steps and across to the waiting shuttle bus, taking up position inside for the short drive to the terminal building.

Most of his fellow passengers, it appeared, were businessmen, besuited and bearing expressions ranging from weariness to indifference. Riordan scanned the array of faces briefly as the bus came to a halt. The automatic doors hissed as they opened and the occupants streamed out into the building.

There was one uniformed security man just inside the door and another close to the bottom of the escalator which led towards Customs.

Riordan passed them both, keeping his eyes fixed straight ahead.

He continued on, up the escalator, the small holdall he carried held beside him.

He wondered when O'Connor would ring him, when the other man would get around to searching Jack Fagan's room. It would take more than a character reference from Marie Leary before Riordan would trust anyone. Once they knew this Fagan was on the level then he would speak to him. And *only* then.

They couldn't afford to take any chances.

Especially now.

At the top of the escalator dozens of people were gathered round the electronic screens that would announce which baggage reclaim area would deliver their luggage.

Riordan watched people pushing trolleys back and forth, bumping into others' legs, sometimes apologising, sometimes not, and felt relieved that he only had hand luggage.

He headed for the Gents' toilet, which was already busy.

He ducked into an empty cubicle and emptied his bladder then pushed his way through the throng to one of the sinks where he splashed his face with water and then dried it on a rapidly diminishing stock of paper towels.

Beside him a man with very little hair was trying to comb

what thinning strands he had over the top of a considerable bald patch but having little success. Aware of Riordan's eyes upon him he finally gave it up and swept the thin strands back from his shiny pate.

The Irishman smiled, ran a comb quickly through his own hair, then exited the toilet.

Riordan headed towards the green nothing-to-declare Customs sign. Two Customs officials watched him. The one closest to him, a woman, made a move towards him.

The Irishman kept walking.

The uniformed woman smiled officiously at a tall, balding man behind Riordan, asking him if he'd mind opening the briefcase he carried.

Riordan continued with an imperceptible sigh of relief. He headed for the exit, pausing at a newsagent's to buy a paper and some cigarettes. He dropped them into his holdall.

Yellow signs ahead of him directed Arrivals towards buses, taxis or the Underground, but Riordan kept walking, checking his watch to ensure that he wasn't too early.

As yet he couldn't see who he sought.

There was a small café to his right and he decided to wait there but scarcely had he ordered a coffee than he saw two figures scurrying towards him.

One of them spotted Riordan and he raised a hand in acknowledgement, approaching them.

The three men shook hands.

'My flight was early,' Riordan told them as they walked out of the exit towards the waiting car.

The two men merely smiled.

The driver started the engine as they climbed in.

Riordan slid onto the back seat.

Frankie Wong sat beside the driver.

Joey Chang took up position beside Riordan.

As the car pulled away, Chang nodded at the Irishman.

'It's good to see you again,' he said, smiling.

# Sixty-Four

*Northern Ireland*

Declan O'Connor had watched the house in Malone Road for over an hour but, fortunately for him, patience was something he possessed in abundance.

When he finally saw Mrs Shannon leave he leisurely finished his cigarette, dropped the butt on the pavement, then sauntered across the street.

O'Connor wandered past the house, glancing briefly at its black front door, then he increased his pace as if anxious to be away from the building.

He knew there was no way in through the front. In such a narrow street, with houses pressed together so tightly, it would be impossible to enter through either the front door or one of the front windows without being seen. Although the street was relatively quiet he was sure that, behind the rows of net curtains, inquisitive eyes would be watching.

O'Connor reached the end of the road and turned right, heading down the narrow thoroughfare separating the back of the houses in Malone Road and the rear of those in the next street.

Endless backyards, all identical, faced him.

He began walking slowly down the narrow alley between the two sets of backyards, counting the numbers as they decreased and he came closer to the back of the house he wanted.

Each one was protected by a high stone wall, the brickwork on most chipped and scarred, breaking away. There had been precious little in the way of repair work done on any of these houses for more than thirty years. Dustbins, some overflowing with rubbish, stood like silent sentinels at each back gate.

Somewhere a dog was barking. In another of the yards he could hear voices. To his left he could hear the steady thump of a football being kicked against the yard wall.

Ahead of him a baby was crying.

Along the top of one of the high walls, O'Connor saw that the occupant of the house had cemented pieces of broken glass.

He was grateful it wasn't the one he had to climb.

He reached the back gate of the house he wanted and looked to his left and right.

No one about.

If there was someone watching from one of the back windows then that was too bad. He had to get into this fucking place somehow and, besides, he'd be in and out as quickly as possible. People usually kept themselves to themselves around here. Everyone knew what the others were doing but any discussion of it was furtive.

O'Connor had grown up in an area very similar in Derry.

The gate facing him was painted black, like the front door, but the paint was peeling away at the bottom of the partition.

He tried the lock but found, to his irritation, that it was secure.

Glancing quickly right and left again, he pulled one of the dustbins across to the gate and using it as a step up hauled himself over the high wall.

He sat there for a second, peering down into the yard, then dropped onto the paving stones beneath.

A small shed was jammed into the small backyard, a cold frame with no glass resting against it, and a washing line stretched across from the back of the house to one corner of the yard. Apart from that, it was empty.

He crossed to the back door, pushed gently against it, and was not surprised to find that it was also secure.

There was a glass panel in the back door and, peering through, O'Connor could see that the key was still in the lock. He smiled to himself and slipped off his jacket, wrapping it around his elbow, both to protect his own flesh and to deaden the impact.

He broke the glass with one swift blow.

Several pieces of glass fell into the kitchen, one shattering on the tiled floor, but O'Connor ignored it, snaking his hand through the broken pane and twisting the back door key.

He stepped inside, closing the door behind him.

The house was silent. It smelled of furniture polish and air freshener.

He moved swiftly through to the staircase and then up towards the first floor.

O'Connor knew he would have to be quick. The woman might be gone five hours or five minutes. He had no way of knowing.

But, right now, all that concerned him was finding out as much as he could about the man he knew as Jack Fagan.

## Sixty-Five

*The Savoy Hotel, London*
Paul Riordan thanked Joey Chang and took the glass of Jamesons from him, raising it like a salute to the other men in the room before taking a sip.

The Irishman turned and looked out of the large picture windows behind him. The view from the suite was impressive and he watched a small boat chugging its way along the dark waters of the Thames. As a child he'd watched similar vessels moving along the Liffey and wondered who was on board, where they were going or where they'd come from. As he watched the boat bobbing along on the choppy water he was reminded briefly of his childhood. But then, as if annoyed with himself for allowing such flights of fancy, he turned to face the six men who occupied the sitting-room area of the suite. His eyes moved swiftly from face to face. Faces he knew well.

'Won't you sit down, Mr Riordan?' said Wo Fen, motioning to one of the armchairs close to him.

'I've been sitting for the last two hours,' Riordan said, smiling. 'First on the plane, then in the car from the airport. Thanks anyway.'

He took another sip of his drink. 'You said on the phone this meeting was important. What's going on?'

Wo nodded in Joey Chang's direction.

'As you know, Mr Riordan,' Chang began. 'Our organisation and others like it have been forced out of Hong Kong. Now the situation here in London has become . . . difficult, for want of a better word. Another group like ours has been trying to take over some of our operations. They've already killed a number of our men.'

'So what do you want from us?' Riordan asked, finishing his drink.

Chang took the empty glass from him and refilled it.

'You have something we need,' the Chinaman said, handing back the glass. 'Weapons.'

Riordan smiled.

'What *exactly* do you have, Mr Riordan?' Frankie Wong asked.

'Rifles mainly,' he told them. 'Seventy-five Enfield L70s and Sterling AR-180s, and six thousand rounds of ammunition, but they're not all for sale.'

'We would give you the best price,' Wo Fen interjected.

'We need some ourselves, probably more than *you* do.'

'We're at war, Mr Riordan,' Wong said.

'And what the hell do you think *we're* doing?' the Irishman snapped.

Wo Fen raised a hand as if to quell the rising tension.

'What can you let us have?' he asked.

'Forty of each,' said Riordan. 'But they won't be cheap.'

'We are both businessmen, Mr Riordan. I'm sure we can

'come to an arrangement, after all, there are things we have that *you* need too,' Chang told him, quietly.

'So who's the fight with?' the Irishman wanted to know.

'A rival organisation called the Hip Sing,' Wong told him.

'I don't understand why you need our help with weapons.'

'The Hip Sing are more heavily armed than we are,' Wong continued. 'And they are becoming stronger all the time. If we do not strike at them soon, it will be too late.'

'Why have they started attacking you?' asked Riordan.

'They wanted to establish themselves here in London,' Chang told him. 'They obviously felt their best way was to strike at *us*. We are the most powerful organisation here. They must have thought that if they could defeat us then the other groups would not challenge them.'

Riordan nodded.

'How soon do you need the guns?' he asked.

'As quickly as possible,' Chang said. 'We cannot waste any more time. How quickly can you get them to us?'

'Once we've agreed a price, you can have them,' said Riordan. 'But you'll have to organise transportation.'

'That's no problem,' Chang assured him, looking at Frankie Wong who nodded in acknowledgement.

'Then let us make arrangements now,' Wo Fen interjected. 'We must move quickly.'


## Sixty-Six


*Northern Ireland*

The first two rooms Declan O'Connor searched were unoccupied. The beds were neatly made, the covers smoothed out so thoroughly it looked as if they'd been ironed while on the bed. He checked the drawers and wardrobes in the rooms all the same but found them empty.

Moving back onto the landing he opened another door and peered into a small bathroom. Like the rest of the house it was immaculate, nothing out of place. The room also smelled strongly of air freshener, a cloying sickly odour which O'Connor wrinkled his nose at.

He moved to the next room.

It belonged to Mrs Shannon.

He made only a cursory search, knowing this wasn't the room he sought. A small wooden crucifix hung over the bed, a set of rosary beads hanging from it. On the polished wood dresser a photograph of Mr Shannon watched him impassively as he opened the drawers, lifting out clothes carefully, then sliding them back once he'd assured himself there was nothing there he should know about.

The room across the landing was, he found to his relief, unlocked.

O'Connor turned the handle carefully and looked in.

There were clothes scattered about, some folded in neat piles on the end of the bed, others dropped on the carpet. On the edge of the small sink in the room were shaving foam and disposable razors. He found more toiletries in the cupboard beneath.

He opened the bedside cabinets and rummaged through the underwear there, wrinkling his nose when he found some socks which would have been better placed in the washing basket.

The chest of drawers by the window held more clothes. Shirts, all neatly folded. Sweaters and more socks.

O'Connor moved to the wardrobe.

A small key was in the lock and he turned it, pulling the doors open.

There were shoes in the bottom of the wardrobe and also a cardboard box, the top of which was closed.

He reached in and lifted it out, setting it down on the floor as he pulled it open.

He smiled as he looked inside.

There must have been more than a dozen men's magazines in there. He lifted the first couple and glanced at the covers. Pouting and smiling young women in various stages of undress looked back at him. On the cover of one a girl with long red hair was posing in a French maid's uniform. MAID FOR PLEASURE the bright yellow lettering across her breasts proclaimed. Another was dressed as a nurse. OUR SEXY NURSE WILL COME QUICKLY, O'Connor read.

He flipped open the magazine, glanced at the naked flesh on show then replaced the glossy periodical in the box, slipping it back in the wardrobe.

There were three or four jackets hanging up in the wardrobe and he searched quickly through their pockets.

In the second he found a slim wallet and opened it.

There was no money, but there was a driver's licence. He pulled it out and inspected it.

The name on it was Donald Hughes, as it was on the library card he found and a business card. Mr Donald Hughes was, according to the cheaply printed card, a sales representative for cutlery.

O'Connor stuffed the things back into the wallet then dropped that back into the jacket pocket.

He hurried out of the room, aware that his time to search the last room might be running short. The landlady could return at any minute.

*And what then?*

He touched the butt of the Smith & Wesson automatic jammed in his belt.

The door to the last room was locked and O'Connor muttered irritably to himself then stepped back a pace and threw all his weight against it.

The wood groaned but held firm.

He tried again.

The door swung inwards, the lock dropping free as he burst through.

This *had* to be Fagan's room.

He began his search.

# Sixty-Seven

The bus stopped at another set of traffic lights and Doyle shifted uncomfortably in his seat. He seemed to have been sitting on the fucking thing for hours. There were another five or six stops before the bus reached the one near to Malone Road, but the counter terrorist had already decided that he'd get off at the next stop and walk the remaining distance. The constant stopping and starting was pissing him off. So too was the kid sitting opposite him.

Doyle guessed he must be in his early teens. He'd already spent most of the journey from the centre of the city picking his nose, carefully inspecting the contents of his nostrils on the end of one finger. Now he contented himself with burping or breaking wind noisily every few minutes, looking round to see the reactions of the other passengers. Little shit.

Apart from Doyle and the kid there were two other people on the bus. An elderly woman and an overweight man who had his nose buried in the evening paper.

Doyle wondered what Marie was doing now.

Her suggestion that he should come with her to Donegal that night had been both a surprise and a bonus.

*What the fuck was she going there for?*

The drive would take them a good three hours, probably longer.

*Into the Republic itself.*

Doyle felt closer to his target now than he had done at anytime so far during the job. He wondered if he should notify Major Wetherby, tell him he was close to actually infiltrating the IRA, not just to getting back the stolen army guns.

*No. Fuck him.*

No point in letting army intelligence know anything until he was sure himself what was going on. Just because he'd been right about Riordan, O'Connor and Christie working together before didn't mean that they were the ones responsible for the attack on the convoy.

No, Wetherby could wait. There was too much he had to discover for himself yet.

The lights changed to green and the bus moved off.

Doyle glanced at his watch.

The youth opposite broke wind loudly.

Compared to the last room he'd searched, O'Connor found that Doyle's room was surprisingly uncluttered both by personal possessions and clothes. O'Connor didn't have to be a genius to figure out that the occupant of the room wasn't planning a long-term stay here.

A leather jacket, some trainers, boots, a few T-shirts and some underwear just about made up the contents of the wardrobe and the drawers. Nothing unusual there though.

No ID either.

O'Connor crossed to the window which looked out into Malone Road and peered right and left watching for any sign of Mrs Shannon returning. Satisfied that he had plenty of time, the Irishman continued with his search.

He checked the bedside table.

Nothing.

He checked under the bed.

Under the mattress.

Nothing.

The floorboards creaked loudly under him as he crossed to the wardrobe once more. He took the jacket out and tossed it onto the bed then rummaged through the pockets again. He ran his hands over the lining, over the arms, the . . .

*Christ, that fucking floorboard was creaking.*

O'Connor set about searching through the pockets of the other jacket.

Still no ID.

He stepped back and noticed there was no sound.

Moved to his left.

The board creaked.

To his right.

Silence.

*It was just that one board, wasn't it?*

He kicked the rug back with his foot and pressed the floorboard with the toe of his shoe.

One end rose slightly.

The screws holding it in place had been removed then put back, but not very securely.

O'Connor dropped to his knees, fumbling in his pocket for his penknife. He inserted the end in the groove of the screw nearest to him and began to twist. It kept slipping but, gradually, the board came loose.

Doyle pushed both hands into his jacket pockets as he got off the bus, careful to avoid a puddle in the gutter.

The kid with wind peered through the grimy glass at him as the bus pulled away.

The counter terrorist set off towards Malone Road, past a group of young girls standing in the doorway of an off-licence. One of them whistled as he passed and Doyle smiled to himself and kept walking. He heard the girls laughing behind him.

Not far to go now.

'Jesus Christ Almighty,' O'Connor breathed as he lifted the floorboard away.

He could see the guns clearly in the area below.

Each one was wrapped in a plastic bag, as was the ammunition.

He reached in and picked up the .357, hefted it before him then laid it to one side.

He did the same with the burst-fire Beretta.

'Jesus,' he murmured again as he felt the weight of the .50 calibre Desert Eagle. The weapon looked enormous, even in *his* powerful hands.

For long moments, O'Connor stared down at the guns then, eyes narrowed, he got to his feet.

They'd been right to be suspicious of Mr Jack fucking Fagan or whoever the fuck he *really* was. That much they would probably never know. But it didn't matter any more.

He knew what he had to do now.

## Sixty-Eight

Doyle reached into his jacket pocket and pulled out a packet of cigarettes, flipping it open.

He muttered irritably under his breath when he saw it was empty.

There was a small shop on the corner. It sold most things and Doyle had bought cigarettes there before. He wandered across and into the shop, noticing how warm it was inside. Several other people were moving about within the cramped aisles, taking food from the shelves to drop into their baskets. One woman was balancing several cans of baked beans one on top of the other and she nearly collided with Doyle as he passed her, smiling at him as he apologised.

He got into the small queue at the till behind a woman with dozens of tins of cat food and a man who looked as if he was arranging his purchases in order of size on the counter.

There was a television screen high up on the wall and Doyle glanced up to see monochrome images of a soap opera being played out before him.

He waited his turn.

O'Connor had seen the phone as he'd passed through the hallway of the house, on his way up the stairs.

Now he hurried down the steps towards it, snatching up the receiver, almost knocking the phone from its position on the small polished wooden table.

He jabbed out the required digits.

Mr Jack fucking Fagan.

What was he? Plain-clothes cop?

*No. Coppers wouldn't carry guns like those he'd discovered.*

The phone rang once then he heard a sharp crackle of static and the line went dead.

Cursing, he pushed down the cradle and began pressing once again.

UVF man?

*Why would a Proddy be hiding out in a place like this?*

He continued pressing the digits.

What about SAS?

*Possible. But they didn't usually work like that.*

The phone started ringing at the other end once again.

Counter terrorist?

*It had to be.*

O'Connor smiled crookedly as he heard the receiver picked up at the other end.

He recognised the voice of Paul Riordan.

'It's O'Connor, I've just finished searching Fagan's place.'

Riordan wanted to know if he'd found anything.

'Fucking right I have. Guns *and* ammunition. I don't know who he is, but he's well equipped.'

Riordan speculated that it was probably the mysterious Mr Fagan who'd killed James Christie.

'More than likely. Shall I wait here for him? Take him out now?'

Riordan told him to warn Marie Leary, to ring him back when she'd been told.

'I reckon he's a fucking Brit,' O'Connor said, scathingly.

Riordan repeated the urgency to get in touch with Marie.

'Don't you want him taken care of?' O'Connor persisted.

Riordan said that as long as he wasn't aware his cover had been blown he was no threat. They could take him out at their leisure.

'I'll call Marie,' O'Connor said.

Riordan instructed him to call back after he'd done so.

O'Connor pressed the cradle down and began jabbing out a new set of numbers.

The phone started ringing at the other end.

And ringing.

'Come on, Marie,' he hissed.

It was picked up.

O'Connor spoke quickly, barely pausing for breath, struggling to expel all the words but his call was suddenly interrupted.

Behind him he heard a loud click as a key was turned in the front door.

O'Connor hurriedly put down the phone and ducked into the room to his left, leaving the door open a fraction so that he could see out into the hall.

He eased the .459 from his belt.

The front door opened.

## Sixty-Nine

*London*

'Is something wrong, Mr Riordan?' Joey Chang asked, watching as the Irishman replaced the receiver.

Riordan exhaled deeply then looked at the Chinaman.

'There *could* be,' he said, quietly.

The other men in the room looked at him as he took a sip of his drink, swirling the whiskey around in the crystal glass.

'A man, we don't know his name, is trying to infiltrate our organisation. One of my colleagues has just found positive proof.'

'How did this happen?' Wo Fen wanted to know.

'I don't know, but it might cause problems,' Riordan told him.

'Problems with our business?' Cheng asked.

'We need to get this guy off our backs, that's all.'

'Are you sure there are no other problems, Mr Riordan?' Chang insisted.

'I told you,' the Irishman snapped. 'Anyway, it's under control. He doesn't know we're on to him.'

'Will it affect the movement of the weapons?' Frankie Wong wanted to know.

'It might delay moving them for a day or two, that's all.'

'We can't afford that,' Chang said. 'We need those guns as soon as possible.'

'I said we'll take care of it,' Riordan said, defensively.

He crossed to the phone, picked up the receiver and dialled.

It began ringing.

'Nothing must be allowed to jeopardise this business, Mr Riordan,' Chang persisted.

The phone was still ringing.

'Nothing will,' Riordan snapped wondering where Marie Leary had got to.

He waited a moment or two longer then put down the phone.

Chang regarded him warily, watching as he crossed to the large windows overlooking the Thames. The Irishman was standing with his hands clasped tensely behind his back.

'You say you have no idea who this man is?' Wo Fen asked.

'He could be security,' Riordan said. 'Counter terrorist or anything.'

'And you didn't know he was onto you?' Chang said, a little too much sarcasm in his voice for Riordan's liking. The Irishman turned quickly.

'If we'd known, we'd have done something earlier,' he snapped. 'We'll handle it, all right?'

Chang raised a hand.

'May I make a suggestion, Mr Riordan?' he began. 'As this man, this intruder, could be a threat to both our concerns in this matter, why don't you let *us* take care of him?'

Riordan looked puzzled.

'As a sign of good faith between our two organisations, let us remove this . . . obstacle to our business,' he chuckled.

The other men in the room smiled and nodded enthusiastically.

Riordan frowned but then his expression relaxed slightly.

'You're going to hit this guy?' he said, quietly.

'As I said, it will be a sign of good faith between us,' Chang repeated. 'A cementing of our alliance.' He laughed.

Riordan smiled.

'I'll need to tell my people,' he said, picking up his glass.

Chang nodded.

'We understand,' said the Chinaman. 'But once that is done, we will take care of this man.'

Riordan raised his glass in salute.

'Here's to you,' he said, chuckling.

'To the removal of the last obstacle,' Chang echoed.

The room was filled with laughter.

# Seventy

*Northern Ireland*

Declan O'Connor had the pistol gripped in his hand and, as the door opened further, he raised it and squinted down the sight.

From where he stood, the door was opening towards him, masking his view of the entrant, but he could see the silhouette of the arrival framed like some kind of animated cameo in the glass of the front door.

*Come and get it, you fucker, whoever you are.*

He heard the key being removed from the lock.

*Mr Jack fucking Fagan.*

He tightened his grip on the trigger.

Mrs Shannon sighed as she struggled in with bags of shopping. She pushed the door behind her with her shoulder but it caught on the doormat and remained slightly ajar.

O'Connor pulled back, an expression of surprise and disappointment on his face.

He stepped back inside the room, leaving a large enough gap between door and frame to see that the woman had bypassed him and was heading into the kitchen.

*Where the fuck was Fagan?*

Mrs Shannon put the shopping on the kitchen table.

She noticed the broken window in the back door immediately and looked down to see pieces of shattered glass spread across the floor.

She swallowed hard, her bottom jaw quivering slightly.

She could see no other damange in the kitchen apart from the smashed window. Nothing, it seemed, had been disturbed.

She turned and hurried back into the hallway, reaching for the phone.

As she picked up the receiver, her finger already poised over the first of the three nines she intended to dial, O'Connor stepped from the cover of the room.

Mrs Shannon screamed.

'Put it down,' O'Connor shouted, motioning to the phone.

Doyle heard the words as he stepped in through the front door.

O'Connor heard him enter and turned.

For fleeting seconds the entire scene was frozen.

Mrs Shannon stood with the phone gripped in her hand, her mouth still gaping open.

O'Connor finally got a good look at the man he knew as Jack Fagan, and Doyle realised that he was less than two feet from one of the men he had sought so badly.

The counter terrorist was the first to react.

As time began to move again, he jumped forward, slamming into O'Connor with his shoulder, knocking him backwards, tearing the breath from him.

Doyle saw the gun as the Irishman went down and he threw himself onto his foe, knocking the weapon from O'Connor's hand. Doyle's hands found the Irishman's throat, thumbs pressing inwards.

Mrs Shannon screamed again and stepped back three or four paces.

O'Connor brought one hand up and clamped it across Doyle's face, trying to force his head back, all the time aware of the crushing force on his windpipe as the counter terrorist squeezed. Doyle felt a finger push into his mouth. He clamped his teeth down so hard on it he nearly severed the tip. O'Connor let out a strangled scream, his blood spurting into Doyle's mouth but the counter terrorist ignored the metallic taste, using all his strength instead to haul the Irishman upright.

Doyle slammed his opponent back against the wall with all the energy he could muster.

O'Connor grunted in pain but struck low at Doyle, aiming a punch at his groin.

He connected with the counter terrorist's thigh but struck again, a blow which smashed into Doyle's testicles with enough force to make him lose his grip.

Teeth gritted with anger as much as with pain, Doyle stepped back slightly.

He saw O'Connor's hand reach for the gun.

Doyle flew at him, both of them crashing against the door and into the dining room, colliding with the table which overturned. Plates that had already been laid there spun into the air then smashed as they struck the floor. Cutlery rained down around the fallen men.

The .459 spun away.

O'Connor shot out a hand to pick it up.

Doyle grabbed a fork and brought it down with incredible power.

The prongs pierced the back of O'Connor's outstretched hand, snapped two metacarpal bones and burst from the palm. Blood spurted from the torn appendage and as the Irishman rolled over, the fork was still firmly embedded in his hand.

Doyle kicked the gun away, rising to his feet quickly.

O'Connor was screaming, trying to pull the fork out of his hand, blood pouring from the wound and running down his arm.

Doyle drove a powerful kick into his groin, watching with satisfaction as the Irishman doubled up with renewed agony.

O'Connor went down heavily, his face contorted, landing near the gun. He shot out his left hand and grabbed the automatic, swinging it round towards Doyle.

There were two massive retorts as he fired.

The first bullet blew a hole in an antique bureau which stood in the corner of the room, the second powered into the wall blasting away a lump of plaster.

Doyle dived for the hall, rolling over as he reached it, pushing himself towards the stairs.

Two more bullets followed him, blasting into the stair rail, splintering one of the wooden steps and pulverising part of the balustrade.

Doyle snatched up the broken stair rail, grasping it like a baseball bat.

As O'Connor came hurtling from the other room Doyle swung the wooden stanchion and struck him across the chest with it.

The gun went flying once more and the impact winded the Irishman but now he turned towards the front door, desperate to escape this madman, this crazy Jack fucking Fagan.

O'Connor hauled open the door, taking another heavy blow from the wooden rail across his back in the process.

But he made it to the street.

Doyle followed, hurling the rail away.

O'Connor ran as fast as he could, cradling his damaged hand, aware that Doyle was speeding after him.

There was a main road at the bottom of Malone Road and O'Connor bolted towards it. He could see cars speeding past ahead of him.

Doyle gritted his teeth and drew nearer to his quarry.

O'Connor glanced round to see how far behind his pursuer was.

In that split second he took his eyes off the traffic in front of him.

He heard the blaring of a horn, the shriek of brakes then something which sounded like a water melon hitting stone.

The car that hit him must have been doing almost fifty.

It struck him and sent him flying into the air, puppet-like, for precious seconds, suspended on imaginary wires. Then he fell back to earth, striking the roof of the car and falling into the road.

Doyle saw him hit the ground, saw another car that had tried to stop skid over him.

O'Connor's head simply burst as the tyre ran over it.

There was a vivid explosion of blood and brain as the

skull seemed to detonate. Like a balloon into which someone has pumped too much air, it seemed to swell then burst, ejaculating its contents everywhere.

Doyle forced himself to a halt at the roadside, looking down at what was left of O'Connor's head.

'Fuck it,' he hissed under his breath.

He'd lost another one.

*Now there was just Marie left.*

She was his last link to Riordan.

He stood, hands on hips, catching his breath.

Watching the blood wash thickly across the street.


## Seventy-One


If anyone saw Doyle step away from the kerb and walk briskly back up Malone Road, no one said anything.

Drivers of vehicles on the road were more concerned about the hold-up caused by the accident, and people drawn from their houses by the sound of hooters and shouting paid Doyle little heed as he made his way back towards the boarding house.

He'd lost O'Connor, another lead.

However, Doyle realised he had more to worry about than that. He wondered how much the IRA man had seen. Not that it really mattered now because most of his head was smeared across the road, but if O'Connor had been at the house then he'd been there for a reason.

Doyle had no choice but to assume that his cover was blown.

*Or was it?*

Did Marie know about him yet?

If she did, would she be the next one to try and kill him, or would he be forced to kill her first? And he was still no closer to finding the fucking guns.

Questions tumbled around in his mind, all without answers.

He had to leave the boarding house now, that much he *did* know.

And the police? Surely someone would have heard the shots fired by O'Connor and called them. Mrs Shannon would want to know what was happening.

Doyle wondered if he could bluff it out.

He saw people gathered around the doorway of the boarding house as he drew closer. Someone was shouting something he couldn't make out. He quickened his pace and pushed through the group of women standing there.

Mrs Shannon was lying flat on her back in the hall, another woman about the same age crouching over her.

'What's wrong with her?' Doyle asked.

'I think it's her heart,' the woman said, cradling Mrs Shannon's head in her arms. 'I've called an ambulance.'

*Heart attack.*

Doyle nodded.

At least it gave him some breathing space. Mrs Shannon was going to be in no state to ask questions now. Besides, as far as she was concerned, the intruder had been a burglar.

'Someone broke in,' Doyle said. 'He took a shot at us. I chased him but he got away.'

*Do you really think this bullshit is going to work?*

The woman looked up at him and nodded.

'Did he hurt you?' she wanted to know.

'No, I'm okay.'

*For fuck's sake. It was working.*

'I'm going to check upstairs, see if he took anything,' said Doyle.

He hurried up to his room, saw the guns lying there, the torn-up floorboard alongside.

So, O'Connor had known.

*Had he informed Marie?*

Doyle gathered the weapons together, replaced them in

their hiding place then moved quickly back downstairs again.

'I don't think he got anything,' he said, looking down at the woman once more.

Outside he could hear a siren.

Someone called out that the ambulance was on its way.

'You go with her in the ambulance,' Doyle said to the woman. 'I'll get in touch with the police. I'll wait for them.'

The woman nodded.

Doyle moved slowly through to the dining room.

The .459 was lying close by the door. He pushed it beneath a chest of drawers with one foot, hiding it from view. He'd take care of it when the house was empty.

As he moved back into the hall two ambulancemen, one carrying a furled stretcher, moved towards Mrs Shannon.

They spoke words of encouragement to her as they lifted her onto the stretcher.

As they passed by, Mrs Shannon looked up at Doyle and smiled weakly.

He hoped the old girl didn't die.

She'd been useful to him.

Perhaps he should ring Binchy, tell him that his sister was being taken to hospital.

*What the fuck. It wasn't his problem now.*

He watched as they carried her out to the waiting emergency vehicle then he pushed the door shut and headed back into the dining room.

He picked up the automatic and carried it out, holding it by the trigger guard. In the backyard he dropped it into the dustbin, pulling the soggy newspapers and potato peelings over it, then he headed back inside and upstairs to his room.

Doyle packed his holdall, laying the guns and ammunition carefully in the bottom, covering them with his clothes.

He had to leave. If O'Connor had told the others then they might come looking for him.

*If* he had.

*And if he hadn't?*

Doyle was closer to Riordan than he could have hoped. Close to Riordan and close to the guns.

Marie was his only link.

*If she knew who he was she'd kill him.*

It was a chance he had to take.

He made his way downstairs to the hall, glancing at the bullet hole in the wall on the way.

He picked up the phone and dialled.

Soon he would know.


## Seventy-Two


*London*

Paul Riordan raised his glass in salute and seemed to sink further back into the chair. It was pleasantly warm in the room and the Irishman also felt relaxed due to the amount of whiskey he'd drunk, but he was far from being intoxicated. He never drank to excess and to do so while in the middle of a business transaction would be stupid. It would be unprofessional, and his professionalism was something he prided himself on.

He was a soldier. He had responsibilities. Soldier, businessman. Riordan saw a number of facets to his personality.

His proficiency in military matters had been proven during the last twelve years, his role in the IRA having grown from that of trainee to Active Service Unit commander. His business abilities were attested to by this meeting, which he now found himself the centre of. It was the latest of many such meetings which had been going on for almost eighteen months.

He looked around the room, studying each of the faces carefully.

Riordan trusted these men enough to do business with them, but that was it. One of the first lessons he'd learnt, even before joining the IRA, was to put his faith in no one. Even those in his own organisation he found difficult to trust completely. Perhaps that was why he'd survived so long.

Trust was a luxury he couldn't afford.

And he knew the feeling was mutual. Men like Chang and Wong felt the same way. The two organisations existed for different reasons, they had different goals and ideals. Riordan didn't know too much about them. He didn't care too much either. All he was interested in was how they could be mutually useful to one another.

Right now, business was the only thing that interested him.

'We haven't discussed payment,' he said, taking a sip from his drink.

Chang and the others looked at him.

'For the weapons,' Riordan clarified.

'You haven't been able to give us a definite date for delivery,' Chang reminded him.

'I said in a couple of days.'

'And *I* said that wasn't good enough,' the Chinaman reminded him. 'We must have them tomorrow.'

'Are you serious about this offer to get rid of Fagan?' Riordan wanted to know.

Chang nodded.

'Consider it part of the transaction,' he said, smiling.

Riordan regarded the man blankly for a second.

'Have you got the stuff here?' he asked, finally.

Chang nodded.

'Let's see it,' Riordan demanded.

'The terms first,' Chang said. 'We need eighty guns, as you suggested. The same men who travel with you to take care of this man, whatever his name is, will return with the guns. Tomorrow.'

Riordan didn't speak.

'Is this acceptable to you, Mr Riordan?' Wo Fen enquired.

The Irishman nodded slowly.

Chang got to his feet and walked towards the door that led into the bedroom of the suite.

He beckoned Riordan to follow him.

There was a black attaché case lying on the bed. Chang crossed to it and turned the small dials, fixing all six to the combination number then he pressed the catches and opened the case.

Riordan smiled thinly as he looked inside.

'How much is there?' he wanted to know.

'Ten kilos,' Chang told him.

'Dope for guns,' Riordan murmured, smiling.

Chang looked at him blankly.

'It's the title of a song,' the Irishman told him. He reached out and picked up one of the bags of cocaine. 'I don't want any fuck ups with this lot,' he said, his tone darkening.

'What happened before was nothing to do with us,' Chang said. 'What happened to your courier after he left here is not our concern.'

Riordan tossed the package of white powder back into the case.

'Tomorrow,' he said, flatly.

Chang nodded.

# Seventy-Three

*County Donegal, Republic of Ireland*
As the dark blue Maestro sped along the deserted roads, Doyle glanced to one side and looked at Marie Leary.

Her eyes were fixed firmly ahead, her concentration unbroken as she guided the car through the darkness. High above a watery moon tried to force itself free of some enveloping cloud but, apart from the car headlights, there was precious little light to illuminate the country thoroughfares along which she drove so skilfully.

Doyle glanced out of the side window at the lowering shapes of trees, some of whose branches were so close they scraped the roof of the car. Twigs, like bony fingers, scratched against the paintwork.

He looked at her again.

Did she know about him?

Had O'Connor contacted her as soon as he'd discovered the guns?

Doyle tried to consider both possibilities.

If she knew then chances were she'd have tried to kill him already.

*Right?*

He stroked his chin thoughtfully and laid his head back.

Why do it in the city when she could kill him here and his body wouldn't be found for days?

He exhaled deeply.

*Kill her now. Assume she knows. Get her first.*

And lose another fucking lead?

If she didn't know. What then?

He knew he would have to allow her to take him to Riordan eventually. Mind you, that was what he wanted.

*And you think Riordan will tell you where the fucking guns are?*

Riordan wouldn't. Marie *might*.

*If* she didn't know who he really was.

*If.*

Doyle shifted in his seat.

He hated uncertainty.

The first time he would know if she was aware of his true identity would be when she pressed the gun to his head.

*Not the best way to find out.*

He looked at her again.

Nothing to do but wait.

*And wonder.*

'Penny for them.'

Doyle turned his head as she spoke.

'You've hardly said a word since we left Belfast,' she told him. 'Is there something on your mind?'

*You could say that.*

'Sorry,' he said. 'As a matter of fact I was thinking about you.'

'Anything I should know about?'

'It's too filthy to repeat,' he laughed.

Marie chuckled too.

Doyle lit a cigarette.

'I was thinking about what you told me about your sister,' he lied. 'You know, being shot and all. We *do* have a lot in common, what with me losing my brother.'

'Everyone's got a sad story to tell, Jack,' she muttered. 'Nobody can expect to go through life without getting hurt in some way. Some worse than others.'

'That's very philosophical for this time of the night,' he said, smiling.

*Pain.* Doyle knew all about pain.

'You're right though,' he echoed. 'Whatever you do or say you end up getting hurt. If you get too close to anyone or let *them* get close to you . . .' He let the sentence trail off.

'Like the girl you mentioned?' she wanted to know. 'What was her name?'

'It's not important.'

An image of Georgie flashed into his mind.

'How long ago did she die?' Marie enquired.

'Does it matter? Four, five years, maybe longer.'

'How did she die?'

'What is this? A fucking interrogation?' he snapped, angrily.

*Cool it.*

'I didn't mean anything by it,' she said, glancing at him.

Doyle shifted in his seat once more, aware that the vehemence of his outburst had unsettled Marie.

'I'm just interested in you,' she continued.

'You make me feel as if I'm on trial, with all these questions.'

*Maybe you are.*

Again she looked fleetingly at him.

'Did you love her?' Marie said, flatly.

Doyle gritted his teeth.

*What was her fucking game? Was she deliberately pushing him?*

'Maybe,' he said, quietly.

*Had he ever really known?*

They rode in silence for a few miles then Doyle spoke again.

'Where are we going?'

'A place just outside Cloghan,' she told him.

'What for?'

'I've got business there.'

'What kind of business?'

'Now who's doing the interrogating?' she said, looking at him, briefly.

He smiled and nodded gently.

'I can understand you not trusting me, Marie,' he said with as much conviction as he could muster. 'If I was in your position I'd be the same.'

'Why *shouldn't* I trust you, Jack?'

'Because you don't know me. I understand that. But if there's anything I can do to *make* you trust me, then tell me.'

He reached out and squeezed her knee gently.

She reached down and gripped his hand for a moment.

Doyle looked at her, trying to make out some kind of expression on her face in the darkness.

Did she know who he was? Was she as convincing a liar as he was? His holdall was on the back seat, the guns still in the bottom of it.

He would have to ensure that, when the time came, he could reach them quickly enough.

Marie drove on.

# Seventy-Four

As Marie brought the car to a halt, Doyle sat staring out of the windscreen at the house.

Even when she climbed out of the Maestro he remained in his seat. Only when she opened the boot did he finally push open the door and step out into the coolness of the night.

There was a strong wind gusting across the open ground in front of the house and the branches of the trees that grew so thickly around it rattled agitatedly.

Doyle could see just the merest hint of light behind the thick curtains of one of the upstairs rooms. Other than that, the place appeared to be in complete darkness.

'Give me a hand with this,' said Marie, lifting a box from the boot and nodding towards another one beside it.

Doyle picked it up and joined her as she headed towards the house.

The box wasn't heavy.

*No weapons in here?*

He wondered what the fuck this place was.

A number of deep ruts marked the muddy drive, evidence that vehicles had been coming and going with reasonable regularity.

*But why?*

The house was shielded from the road by trees and a high, overgrown hedge. If you didn't know it was here you'd easily miss it, even in daylight, Doyle thought. At the moment, the only natural light was from the moon, which cast a cold glow over everything.

And inside, just that single dull lamp struggling to penetrate the material of the curtains.

Marie approached the front door and knocked loudly, the sound reverberating through the silence.

For fleeting seconds, Doyle had the uncomfortable thought that he was being led into a trap.

Marie *did* know who he was. She had tricked him.

The door would open and he'd find himself looking down the barrel of a 9mm.

*End of fucking story.*

Doyle looked across at her. She saw him and smiled.

He heard movement on the other side of the door, a bolt being pulled back then silence.

He waited.

*Now or never.*

The door opened.

'Who the fuck is he?' demanded the man standing there.

'He's okay, he's with me,' Marie said.

'I can see that, but who is he?' the man persisted.

Doyle regarded him coldly. Thick set, mid-twenties, shoulder-length hair. He was wearing a black sweatshirt and jeans.

'Does Riordan know about him?' the man wanted to know.

Marie nodded.

'Just let us in,' she snapped. 'I'm not standing out here all fucking night.'

She pushed past the man and Doyle followed, glancing at the man as he did. They locked stares briefly, the other man looking away first, pulling at the end of his moustache.

As they passed through what Doyle took to be the sitting room of the house he saw a television and video there. A number of tapes were scattered around. Ash-trays were overflowing with butts. Several dirty glasses and mugs were dotted about. The room smelt of stale smoke and sweat.

Marie set down the box she was carrying on the kitchen table and Doyle did likewise.

He scanned the room briefly, trying not to make his interest too obvious. There was washing-up in the sink, more unwashed utensils on the draining board and table.

More than one person was living here, Doyle realised.

He heard movement upstairs, footsteps descending the stairs.

'How much fucking longer are they going to be here?' Moustache wanted to know. 'I'm getting sick of baby-sitting them.'

'You just do what you're told,' Marie said, taking clothes from the box: jeans, T-shirts, sweaters. She laid them on the table before her.

Doyle suddenly understood.

The secluded house, the guard, the fresh clothes, evidence of a number of men cooped up in one place and unable to leave.

It was a safe house.

Somewhere for IRA men to lie low after they'd carried out a job.

It *had* to be the answer.

He heard movement from the sitting room, saw a figure moving about in the gloom there, searching for something.

Marie continued unpacking the box.

Moustache looked on with concern and irritation when Doyle wandered towards the other room.

'Where are you going?' Moustache snapped.

'Just having a look round,' Doyle told him. 'Any fucking objections?' He shot the man a withering glance.

Moustache looked at Marie as if for confirmation of what he should do, but she ignored him and began to unpack the second box.

Moustache followed Doyle into the sitting room where the other man was still searching for something, pulling at the sofa cushions in his quest.

He paid little heed to Doyle who stood watching him, wanting to see his face.

'If this is what you're looking for,' said Moustache,

pulling a lighter from his pocket, 'you left it in the kitchen.' He tossed it towards the man who turned and caught it, nodding gratefully.

He looked at Doyle.

The counter terrorist held his gaze, trying to control the surprise which he felt must have swept over his expression as he looked at the man's face.

The man who stared back at him was Chinese.

## Seventy-Five

Doyle watched as the Chinaman flicked the lighter, held the orange flame to the end of the cigarette dangling from his lips, then turned and headed back out of the room.

*What the fuck was all this?*

Moustache saw the expression of surprise on Doyle's face.

Marie joined them.

'We're after going now,' she said. 'There's clothes for all of them. They can sort them out.'

Moustache nodded and followed Marie and Doyle to the front door.

As they reached it, Doyle glanced up the stairs and caught sight of someone peering down at them.

It was another Chinaman, younger than the first. He was tall and wiry. He looked quizzically at Doyle who tried not to pay too much attention to him.

*What was going on?*

'See you,' said Marie.

'I'm sure you will,' Moustache murmured, watching her tight buttocks as she walked back towards the car.

'See you again,' Doyle echoed then followed her.

Moustache remained silent, waiting until they'd

climbed into the car. From inside, Doyle saw him close the front door. In the first-floor room, that sickly yellow light still burned and Doyle saw the curtain move slightly as Marie started the engine.

'Jesus,' he said, smiling thinly. 'Who are they?'

Marie swung the car round and guided it out onto the road, switching her lights to full beam in an effort to illuminate the gloomy thoroughfare.

She didn't answer at first.

'Or don't you trust me enough to tell me *that* either?' he added.

'Ah, come on, Jack,' she said, irritably. 'You've probably seen more than you should already. If Riordan knew . . .'

'Who's Riordan?' Doyle asked, looking convincingly vague.

'He's a cell commander.'

'What's so wrong if he knows I've seen those Chinamen? What's the big deal, Marie? What's so fucking important you can't tell me about them? When the hell *are* you going to trust me?' He looked at her, complimenting himself on the tone of indignation in his voice.

She sighed deeply, but kept her eyes on the road.

*Did* she know about him? Was that why she was so reluctant to answer him?

But why go this far if she knew his real identity?

*If she was going to kill him what difference would it make?*

'They're Triads,' she said, flatly, still not looking at him. 'You've heard of them, haven't you? The Chinese Mafia.'

Doyle did his best to remain impassive.

*Don't push it now, you're too close.*

'I don't get it,' he said. 'Why here?'

*Jesus, there were so many things he wanted to ask her.*

'We've been working with them for the last eighteen months,' she said.

*Take it easy.*

'What kind of work?' he asked, trying to suppress the urgency in his voice.

'Trading. We have things *they* want, they have things *we*

want. It's as simple as that.'

'So who were the guys in the house back there?'

'They're from a gang called the Tai Hung Chai, or however the hell you pronounce it. That place is a safe house for them. There are others here in Ireland, mostly around Dublin, but there are some on the west coast too. We offer them protection while they're here.'

'In exchange for what? You said it was a trading arrangement.'

'It is. We offer protection, they give us money or drugs.'

'Drugs?'

*Murphy and his stomach full of heroin. Jesus Christ.*

'It's big business, Jack,' Marie continued.

'But your funds have always come from donations or the rackets you run. Why drugs?' Doyle wanted to know.

'The money potential is enormous. The more money we have the more equipment we can buy.'

Doyle nodded.

'I understand that,' he said. 'But how did you get mixed up with the Triads in the first place?'

'I don't know the whole story. It was mostly to do with Riordan. He set it up. He travels to London two or three times a month sometimes to meet with them. To do business.'

'But you don't sell drugs on the streets. You're soldiers, not pushers.'

'*We* don't sell them, but there are plenty who are willing to do it for us, not just in Ireland either. Some of the drugs are shipped to Germany, France, even the States. The money that's collected from their sale comes back here to the organisation.'

Doyle nodded.

It was all he could do to contain his excitement.

'And that's all the Triads want in return?' he said. 'Protection over here?'

'Somewhere to hide. Usually after trouble in England. They just run. We take care of them while they're here, until they can go back. That's not all they want though.

We supply them with guns too.'

'I thought you had problems getting enough equipment for yourselves,' Doyle said, lighting up a cigarette.

'We used to. Not any more. And that last shipment . . .' She allowed the sentence to trail off.

'You hit that British convoy outside Newry a couple of weeks back.'

She nodded.

Doyle felt suddenly stupid. So stupid he was furious with himself. Jesus fucking Christ it had been staring him in the face all this time. *She'd* been staring him in the face. Major Wetherby had said that four men had been involved in the attack. Four *men*. Four fucking men. Bullshit. Four *people* had been involved and Doyle was astounded at his own ineptitude, his inability to realise until now that the fourth person had been Marie Leary. Christ, he felt stupid.

'You hit it to get arms for the Triads?' he continued.

'We hit it for ourselves, but we knew the Triads would be willing to trade for some of the weapons.'

'And that's where this Riordan is now.' It came out as a statement rather than a question.

'He's in London meeting with them, doing a deal.'

*So fucking simple*.

Doyle took a long drag on his cigarette.

The attack on the arms convoy, the drugs he'd seen inside Stephen Murphy. It all tied in.

*God, you were so fucking dumb not to see it earlier*.

'What else do you want to know, Jack?' she said, softly. 'Or have you finished asking me questions?'

Doyle glanced across at her, found she was looking at him.

*Did she know?*

Did it really matter any more?

'I'm sorry,' he said, finally. 'It's a lot to take in.'

She nodded slowly.

Doyle glanced down at the dashboard clock and noticed that it was a little after one. It might take them another three hours to get back to Belfast.

He glanced over his shoulder at the holdall.

His guns were safe inside.

Now all he could do was wait.

# Seventy-Six

*County Derry, Northern Ireland*

Doyle lay back in his seat, questions whirling through his mind. His brain felt like an out-of-control spin-dryer. He couldn't seem to focus on anything for more than a few seconds at a time. There was so much to consider.

*The IRA doing business with the Triads.*

*Drugs for guns.*

Christ, it was never-ending.

And those guns, those guns he'd been sent here to track down, most of them, it seemed, were destined for Britain.

Wait until fucking Wetherby found out about this.

Doyle suppressed a smile.

*And then there was Marie.*

He glanced across at her, saw her rubbing one eye with the back of her hand. She must be tired.

If she'd known his true identity, would she have told him so much? But then, if she *did* know and intended killing him, what difference did it make?

*If she knew.*

But there were still things Doyle needed to know, but to continue with his questions would arouse her suspicions even more.

*Take it easy.*

He knew far more than he could have hoped already and yet, there were still some crucial points which eluded him.

*Go easy.*

'So, what did Riordan say about me?' he finally said, breaking the silence.

'What do you mean?' Marie asked.

'I take it you spoke to him about me joining you. What did he say?'

'He says we don't know enough about you.'

'And what do *you* think?'

She kept her eyes on the road.

'I want to believe what you've told me, Jack,' she said, quietly. 'I want Riordan to be wrong about you.'

'But?'

'You're talking about joining the organisation, not some bloody boy scout group.'

'Let me meet Riordan. Let *me* talk to him.'

*And when I've finished talking, I'll blow his fucking head off.*

'You can't,' she protested.

'Why, because of this business with the Triads? Because *you* don't trust me? If you don't believe what I've told you then why did you let me know about the Triads, the safe houses, the drugs, the guns?'

She didn't answer.

'You believe me, don't you, Marie?' Doyle persisted. 'You know I'm telling the truth.'

'Can you blame me for being cautious, Jack?' she said, irritably. 'I've known you for less than a week, we've slept together and that's it. You told me your brother was killed by the UVF, that you hate them and the Brits, that you'd be prepared to kill. And they're your qualifications for wanting to join the organisation. Hatred, one fuck and a lot of chat, *they're* your credentials. What would *you* think if you were in my place?'

'Then why bring me here tonight?'

'Perhaps I was trying to prove to myself that I trusted you.'

*Careful.*

'Then let me go with you when you meet Riordan,' he said. 'When the Triads pick up the guns, let me be with you. I'll help. I'll convince Riordan too.'

'I can't take you with me, Jack,' she said, exasperated.

'When is the exchange being made?'

She sighed, shook her head.

'Marie?' he persisted. 'When are they making the switch? Tomorrow?'

'Jack, forget it.'

'Just tell me where. I'll be there, I'll speak to Riordan. He doesn't have to know *you* told me.'

'And how the fucking hell else would you know where the switch is taking place without me telling you? Riordan's not a fool, Jack. He'd kill us both.'

'I'm willing to take the chance he kills me,' Doyle lied. 'That's what it means to me, Marie. And if that's what it takes to prove to you and Riordan that you can trust me, then that's the way it has to be. Tell me where the switch is being made, I'll be there, I'll talk to Riordan. If he believes me, that's great. If not, then he'll kill me and if he does then it's nothing to do with you. You're safe. The organisation's safe. You've lost nothing.'

She glanced at him.

'It really means that much to you?' she said, quietly.

Doyle nodded slowly.

*Nearly there. Just take it easy.*

'Where's the switch going to happen?' he asked, slowly.

She inhaled, as if the gravity of the words she was about to speak needed clean breath.

Doyle watched her intently, saw her shake her head.

'Jack, maybe I'm not thinking straight,' she said. 'I'm tired. I need to rest. There are so many questions I need answered.'

Doyle knew how she felt.

'Pull over,' he told her. 'I'll drive.'

'There's a place about a mile from here, a guesthouse. It's small. We could check in there for the night. Rest. In the morning we could talk.'

Doyle smiled and reached out, resting his hand on her thigh.

*Shit.*

'I have to be sure about this,' she said. 'For both our sakes.'

'I understand,' he murmured.

A few minutes later they reached the guesthouse.

Doyle's patience was beginning to run out, but he knew he must hold on to his temper, must resist the temptation to beat out of her the location of the meeting.

He picked up his holdall from the back seat and followed Marie towards the front door of the guesthouse, up an ornamental path flanked by flower beds and immaculately kept lawn.

*So close now.*

Before morning he would know the truth.

## Seventy-Seven

The room was small but functional. Sparsely furnished but comfortable. Just a wardrobe, dressing table, bed and a couple of chairs, but the bed was the only thing Doyle and Marie were interested in.

She undressed and climbed beneath the sheets, asleep almost immediately.

Doyle lay beside her, the holdall on the floor by the bed.

He didn't sleep, wouldn't allow himself to. He lay with his hands clasped behind his head, occasionally looking down at his own, naked, scarred body. Sometimes glancing across at Marie who slept without stirring.

Once or twice Doyle drifted into a kind of half-sleep. An uneasy twilight between consciousness and oblivion, but with that semi-stupor came dreams.

*Of Georgie.*

He fought to wake himself up, to chase her vision from

his mind, but as he slipped back into the arms of sleep the vision came again.

He saw her laughing.

*Dying.*

The thought of her naked body pushed him towards arousal and when he snapped open his eyes he looked down at Marie, stroked her blonde hair gently, for fleeting seconds unable to separate dream from reality. Unsure who this woman was beside him.

He sat up, rubbed both eyes and looked down at her once more, her features appearing to change, to swim into sharper definition. It was as if her face was reforming itself, the visage of Georgie being replaced by that of Marie Leary.

She reached out sleepily and snaked an arm across his torso, pulling herself closer to him. Doyle contented himself with stroking her cheek.

She stirred and nuzzled against him, he felt her lips against his chest, kissing lightly.

She traced the outline of a deep scar from his shoulder then, pulling him down towards her, trailed her tongue across his throat to his face.

Doyle responded ferociously, pulling her close to him so that she could feel his erection pressing against her. She slid one hand down to envelop it, squeezing with increasing firmness, slipping her slender fingers around it, rubbing lightly but quickly until she felt him grow even stiffer.

He moved one leg between hers, allowing her to grind her pubic mound against the muscles of his thigh and he felt the wetness between her legs as she slithered against him, her breath now coming in light but rapid gasps.

Doyle used both hands to grip her buttocks, pulling her more tightly against him as her own hand continued to stroke his hard shaft.

Then he slid his hands up her back to her shoulders, pushing her onto her back and he kissed her forehead, then her lips and her chin. She tilted her head back, allowing him to flick at the flesh of her neck with his lips and tongue, then he licked down to her breasts, teasing the swollen nipples, drawing each one in turn between his lips, circling them with his tongue while she gasped softly at the pleasure of it all.

He licked down her chest, across her belly, pushing his tongue into her navel briefly before sliding down to kiss her hip bones which seemed to jut out towards him as she arched her back off the bed.

As he kissed still lower he smelled the musky scent of her sex, saw the tightly curled pubic hair. He tasted her soft liquescence with his tongue, flicking the hardened nub of her clitoris while one hand glided softly along one slender thigh and his first two fingers pushed gently past her swollen, slippery lips.

Doyle felt her body stiffen as he began to pump his fingers gently in and out, fastening his lips around her clitoris now, lapping at it with his tongue until he felt her hands clutching at his shoulders.

He heard her gasp something he couldn't make out as she climaxed.

He remained where he was as her body shuddered, finally kissing his way back up to her face, letting her taste herself on his lips and tongue.

She opened her legs, guiding his stiffness into her, coaxing his movements inside her as he sought his own release.

He looked down at her as he moved rhythmically within her, wanting the pleasure but also anxious these feelings should be prolonged.

She smiled at him, kissed him.

Doyle closed his eyes and ejaculated into her.

He finally withdrew and lay beside her, his breathing harsh. He felt her stroking his chest, again running her fingers over the scars.

*So many scars.*

'I don't want to be wrong about you, Jack,' she said, quietly, still running her hands across his flesh.

Doyle didn't answer.

'Just tell me that you understand why it has to be this way,' she continued.

'I understand why you can't trust me,' he said. 'I just want the chance to prove to you that you can.'

She propped herself up on one elbow and looked into his eyes.

'My dad used to say that you could see a man's life story in his eyes,' she said, gazing into Doyle's steely grey orbs. 'The joy, the pain. You could tell whether a man was genuine or not by the way he looked at you when he spoke or when you spoke to him.'

She ran one index finger over his eyebrows.

'Riordan's meeting the Triads tomorrow at Harland and Wolff,' she said, quietly. 'The meetings are usually there.'

'Why the shipyards?' Doyle asked.

'The guns are normally taken out by boat or by sea-plane. The drugs come in the same way most of the time.'

Doyle nodded.

'I don't want anything to happen to you, Jack,' she continued.

He smiled and took her face between his hands, kissing her lightly on the lips.

'Will *you* be there?' he wanted to know.

She touched one of his hands with her fingers.

'I'll be with Riordan,' she said.

The movement was so fast that even if she'd realised what he was doing she'd have been unable to stop him.

Doyle slipped the heel of his hand over her mouth and then, using all his strength, twisted her head savagely to one side.

There was a loud crack as two of her vertabrae snapped.

The counter terrorist held her in that position for a second longer then laid her back down on the bed, her eyes still staring open, the skin at the base of her skull already beginning to discolour due to the heavy bleeding beneath the flesh. A number of the veins had been ruptured when he broke her neck.

Doyle swung himself off the bed and dressed quickly, then he fumbled in Marie's jeans until he found the keys to the Maestro.

He left her naked on the bed, glancing down at her before picking up his holdall.

He closed the door quietly behind him and crept down the stairs, out of the house.

The car started easily enough and he guided it onto the road, looking down at the dashboard clock in the process.

The sky was beginning to lighten as the first hint of dawn coloured the clouds.

He fumbled in his pocket and pulled out his cigarettes, lighting one, sucking the smoke deep into his lungs.

Another hour or so and he should be in Belfast.

## Seventy-Eight

*London*

Joey Chang pulled his robe more tightly around him and pushed open the first of the doors slightly.

From his position in the doorway he could see his daughter sleeping. She was lying on her back, arms stretched out on either side, her mouth slightly open. He watched the gentle rise and fall of her chest for a second longer then moved across to his son's room.

Inside, Michael was also sleeping, his backside pointing out of the bed, dangling off one side it seemed, threatening to send him falling out at any moment. Chang crossed to the boy and pushed him back into bed, pulling the covers up around his neck, retrieving the large stuffed dinosaur which had been discarded. He set it beside the boy then left the room.

In the kitchen he moved without switching on the

lights, walking around assuredly in the gloom, taking ice from the fridge and dropping it into a glass. The light from the fridge illuminated the kitchen briefly but Chang closed the door as if anxious to be surrounded by night once again.

He moved through into the sitting room and poured whisky over the ice, swirling the liquid around before taking a sip.

The glowing figures on the video clock announced that it was 5.46 a.m.

Chang crossed to the window and looked out over a capital city still waiting to burst into life. He could see lights on here and there, the odd street lamp still burning. Every now and then a car or taxi would pass by below, the first in what would become a trickle of traffic, then a steady flow and finally a tidal wave.

There was a pleasing peacefulness to this early hour but as Chang sipped at his drink, he felt not peace but uneasiness, as if the stillness was nothing more than a prelude to some great and ghastly explosion.

*Like gunfire?*

There would be much of that in the coming days and weeks. He would have been a fool to think otherwise.

He crossed to the drinks cabinet, still moving about in the gloom, and poured himself another whisky. Then he made his way back to the window and looked down again on the almost deserted streets.

What would his father have said about this situation?

That he deserved to be involved in it? That he'd had it coming?

How the passing years had blurred the image of that man's face in his mind. It was as if, every year, a little more of the colour and shape of the photo drained away. He hadn't seen his father for more than twenty years. Certainly not since he left Hong Kong. In the five years leading up to his departure he had spoken to the old man just twice, both times in anger.

His father had hated his involvement with the Tai Hung

Chai. He'd kicked him out of the house when he'd discovered his closeness to them. They were scum, his father had said. All the Triads were. They didn't protect ordinary people, they sucked the life from them.

Chang's father knew little of life. He'd been working in one of the sweatshops in Kowloon making cheap silk shirts for tourists all his life. What had his honest way of life ever brought him except poverty and frequent illness. That was not to be Joey Chang's way.

His own brother had been killed by a rival Triad when Chang was sixteen, but he'd single-handedly tracked down the perpetrator and exacted his own justice. He'd caught the youth in an alley in the Sheung Wan district and cut his throat. Then he'd cut off his hands and his testicles, making sure he jammed the severed testes into the dead man's mouth. It didn't bring his brother back, but it made *him* feel better.

Chang wondered, to this day, if his father would have shopped him to the Royal Hong Kong Police if he'd known about the killing of the other youth.

And now, more than twenty years later, he was ready to kill again if he had to.

He turned round quickly when he felt the hand on his shoulder.

Some whisky slopped over the side of the glass onto his hand.

'Shit,' Chang hissed, breathing hard. 'You scared me.'

Su Chang saw the glass in his hand.

'I heard you get up.'

'I couldn't sleep.'

'Do you want to talk?' she asked, sliding her arms around him.

Chang kissed her forehead.

'No,' he said, smiling. 'You go back to bed.'

She held him tightly for a moment then padded back towards the bedroom.

Chang finished his drink then followed her, turning his back on the street below.

Had he taken one last look he may have seen the thick-set man standing across the road watching the window.

As Chang disappeared from view, the man dissolved back into the shadows.

# Seventy-Nine

*Northern Ireland*

Doyle had pulled the Maestro into a country lane about ten miles from the outskirts of Belfast, driven up a heavily wooded dirt track then climbed into the back seat to snatch three hours' sleep.

He had woken up aching, cursing a gnawing pain in his neck and the small of his back. He'd clambered out of the car and walked around for a few minutes to clear the stiffness, grateful at least that he had been able to get *some* rest. He'd always been lucky enough to get by on the minimum of sleep and many times during the course of his work he'd found that a blessing. As was his ability to doze in the most uncomfortable of surroundings and situations.

He'd sucked in a few lungfuls of the crisp morning air, taken his holdall from the back seat and begun the long walk to the main road. The Maestro was abandoned. He had no further use for it.

If the IRA knew about him by now (which they surely did), then they'd be on the lookout for one of their own vehicles. He'd be a sitting duck and he was too close now to finding what he sought to commit such an elementary mistake.

He had walked to the road and crouched down on his haunches then as each car approached, he stood up, his thumb hooked into space.

The first three had passed him and Doyle had sworn at them as they'd sped away.

As he'd stood smoking his fifth cigarette he'd managed to secure a lift.

The man who had picked him up talked cheerfully throughout the journey into Belfast, but Doyle took little notice of him. He smiled and nodded where he thought it appropriate, but otherwise the man may as well have been speaking a foreign language for all the interest Doyle showed.

Doyle had trotted out some story about his own car having broken down, not really caring whether or not the man believed him.

When he'd finally dropped him off the man had said goodbye but Doyle had merely nodded and slammed the passenger door shut, lighting another cigarette as he got out.

Now he stood across the street from The Bowman, sucking on the Rothmans and trying to catch some sign of movement from inside.

*The pretence had to be kept until the very end.*

He finished his cigarette and dropped it to the ground, stamping it out beneath his boot. Then he crossed the street and knocked on the locked doors of the pub.

There were a few people about. Shoppers mainly. Cars came and went from the Europa nearby. Looking up, Doyle could see someone looking out from one of the third-floor windows.

Cars sped by. Doyle saw a police car among them.

He knocked again when there was no answer.

Finally there was some movement from the other side and he heard the sound of bolts sliding back.

Jim Binchy pulled the door open wide enough to see out.

'We're not open yet,' he said then recognised Doyle standing there.

'Morning, Jim,' the counter terrorist said, matter of factly.

Binchy let him in then locked the doors again.

'I didn't expect to see you again,' said Binchy, retreating

back behind the bar where he was fitting some new bottles onto the optics. 'What the hell happened at my sister's place yesterday?'

Doyle shrugged.

'A burglar,' he said. 'How is she?'

'She's okay. Thank God. They said it was a mild heart attack. Shock.'

'I'm not surprised. It scared me too.'

'I heard the bastard was armed,' Binchy continued.

Doyle nodded.

'Don't you think that's a little unusual?' Binchy persisted. 'Unless he knew what he was looking for.'

'Meaning?'

*Did Binchy suspect him now?*

Doyle pushed the holdall with his boot, keeping it close to him.

'Perhaps he knew about you and Marie Leary,' Binchy said. 'Maybe he wasn't a burglar, maybe he was fucking UVF. Did you think of that?'

Doyle smiled thinly and relaxed inwardly.

'I doubt it, Jim,' he said.

'So, how is your new friend?' Binchy said, sarcastically. 'How did your little trip last night turn out?'

Doyle shrugged.

'It was okay,' he said, tapping his fingers against the handle of the broom which was propped against the bar. 'Listen, Jim, I came in here this morning to tell you something. I'm going back home. Back to Ennis. With my brother gone, there's nothing for me here.'

Binchy studied him silently for a moment.

'It's her, isn't it?' he said, finally. 'She talked you into it. You've fucking joined them.'

Doyle shook his head.

'I'm going back, that's it,' he lied.

*Keep up the pretence to the last.*

There was another knock on the pub doors.

Binchy glanced at his watch.

There were a couple of minutes until opening.

'Hold on,' he called.

'When are you going?' he wanted to know.

'First train or bus I can get,' Doyle said.

The banging on the door came again.

'All right,' Binchy shouted. Then he looked at Doyle again. 'And you've come for some money, have you?'

'Actually I just came to say goodbye,' he said.

'Ah, get away. I'll pay you for a day's work, it's the least I can do.'

More banging. This time more insistent.

'Jesus Christ,' Binchy hissed. 'They'll have the fucking door off in a minute. Jack, do one thing for me, will you? Let those noisy bastards in while I've still got a bloody door on the place.'

Doyle smiled and slid off the bar stool. He crossed to the front entrance and pulled back the bolts, stepping away from the doors.

There was a crash as both were flung open.

Doyle stepped back, his eyes narrowing as he saw the newcomers.

'What the fuck . . .' Binchy began, but the words were choked off.

Three Chinamen burst into the pub, one of them shouting something, pointing at Doyle.

Binchy froze, his eyes fixed on the newcomers, startled by their appearance and ferocity.

Doyle met the gaze of the leading man but his eyes, like Binchy's, were drawn not to the faces of these intruders but to the razor-sharp cleavers each one carried.

# Eighty

Doyle was first to react.

He hurled himself towards the bar, trying to reach his holdall.

*His guns.*

The first of the Chinamen, a tall wiry youth with long black hair shouted something and ran at the counter terrorist who, even as he hit the ground, thought he recognised this leading attacker.

*Jesus Christ. The house in Donegal.*

The skinny fucker who was trying to slice him up was the one he'd seen peering over the landing at him as he and Marie left the safe house.

Despite his tall, gangling appearance he moved with speed and assurance, sweeping the cleaver downwards in an effort to hit Doyle.

The blade parted the air with a loud whoosh.

Doyle rolled over, kicking out at one of the tables, propelling it into his first attacker.

The other two men, one short haired, almost bald, the other bearing a deep scar on one side of his face, also chased after him.

Doyle got to his feet, grabbed a bar stool and swung it like a club, driving it into the face of his first attacker.

The impact smashed the man's nose and blood burst across his face, but Doyle had no time to press his advantage before Scarface struck at him.

The counter terrorist heard the sweep of the blade but could not avoid it. The steel sliced through the sleeve of his leather jacket and nicked his forearm, drawing blood.

He swung the stool again but Scarface ducked beneath

it, slashing at Doyle's legs, catching him across the knee, slicing open his jeans and parting the skin.

'Shit,' snarled Doyle and hurled the stool at Scarface who brushed it aside.

Short Hair swung at Doyle, but the counter terrorist moved to one side and the blade buried itself in the counter.

As Short Hair struggled to pull it free, Doyle drove a powerful fist into his face, splitting his top and bottom lips and loosening a tooth. But his triumph was short lived because as Short Hair reeled back, Doyle felt a searing pain in his left cheek as Scarface's blade laid his flesh open.

The counter terrorist spun round, kicking hard at the Chinaman's legs, and he managed to knock him off his feet, grabbing the broom which still leant against the bar.

He jabbed it towards Scarface's head with all his strength, gritting his teeth, shouting in satisfaction as the stiff bristles stuck into the Chinaman's eyes.

Scarface screamed in agony, dropped the cleaver and clapped both hands to his face, clutching at his injured eyes.

Long Hair, his face a bloody ruin from the impact of the stool came at Doyle now, but the counter terrorist used the broom as a weapon, keeping his attacker at arm's length.

Binchy, shocked into action by the bloody spectacle before him, made a dash for the blade Scarface had dropped, picking it up triumphantly. But Short Hair saw him and slashed madly at him, carving through his upper arm, slicing through the bicep almost to the bone. Blood exploded from the wound and Binchy screamed in pain, dropping the cleaver again. It landed with a loud clang.

He shot out a hand to grab it but Short Hair struck again. This time the cleaver severed the first three fingers of Binchy's right hand, the digits spinning across the floor, blood spurting from the stumps.

Binchy fell backwards, his bloodied hand held before him, crimson spurting from the wounds.

Long Hair swung the cleaver at Doyle and he blocked it with the broom, but the wood didn't hold and it snapped leaving him with two jagged ends.

Turning quickly he drove one into Long Hair's back just above the right kidney.

The Chinaman screamed and clawed at the thick wooden spike, trying to pull it free, blood filling his mouth as he fell forward.

Doyle could feel his own blood pouring down his face as he turned to face Short Hair who stepped over his injured colleagues to get at Doyle.

The two men faced each other both breathing heavily.

Short Hair lunged at Doyle, the blade screaming past him by inches.

Doyle struck out with the broom end, catching him a stinging blow across the knuckles, splitting the skin but not badly enough to make him drop the cleaver.

The counter terrorist backed off, his teeth gritted, perspiration now mingling with blood on his face.

Short Hair came at him once more, catching him on the shoulder, but the blade only cut his jacket and as the Chinaman pulled away Doyle caught his wrist and twisted hard, throwing the man against the bar with terrific force.

Short Hair grunted in pain, momentarily dazed by the impact which loosened his grip on the cleaver slightly.

Doyle kicked out at him, catching him in the groin.

He went over but didn't drop the cleaver, slashing out once again with a blow which Doyle only just managed to avoid.

Still they faced each other.

Long Hair was still moaning loudly, trying to pull the piece of broom handle from his back.

Binchy, one arm hanging uselessly at his side, his other hand looking like a scarlet boxing glove, tried to force himself to his feet.

Scarface, still clutching his eyes, was already upright, staggering about helplessly.

Short Hair and Doyle faced off once more, only feet apart.

They moved side to side, from foot to foot, like two boxers waiting for the right opening.

Doyle's eyes flicked back and forth from the cleaver to his opponent's face.

Short Hair took half a step forward.

Doyle hawked and spat into his face.

The reflex was instinctive.

Short Hair put up a hand to stop the projectile lump of phlegm aimed at his face and it was all the diversion Doyle required.

He brought the broom handle down with devastating force on the Chinaman's head, following in immediately, driving two punches into the smaller man's stomach, doubling him up.

Doyle grabbed at the hand that held the cleaver, gripped the wrist and tugged hard.

There was a loud snap as the bone broke and Short Hair screamed in agony, dropping the cleaver.

Doyle grabbed him by the throat, lifted him a few inches off the ground then drove his forehead into Short Hair's face.

The first butt shattered his nose, the second opened a cut on his left eyebrow.

Doyle hissed in pain as he felt cold steel slice across his back and he dropped Short Hair, turning in time to see Long Hair standing there swaying, the length of broom handle still sticking out of his back.

The counter terrorist spun round, concentrating on his new opponent.

Long Hair was moving slowly, weak from loss of blood and Doyle found it relatively easy to avoid the next stroke, ducking under it, bringing his head up with crushing force beneath Long Hair's chin. He heard bone crack again and the Chinaman fell back.

Doyle turned, reaching for his holdall which was still lying by the bar. He managed to unzip it, diving a hand inside, his fingers closing around the butt of the .50 calibre Desert Eagle.

'Jack!'

He heard Binchy's shout, turning in time to see Scarface swinging at him.

Binchy leapt forward, pushing Doyle to one side.

The blow intended for him caught Binchy across the forehead with such terrifying force that the cleaver split his frontal bones and scythed through to his brain, jamming in the thick bone of his forehead.

As Scarface pulled it free there was a sound like breaking wood and part of the landlord's skull came away, briefly exposing greyish-pink brain beneath. Blood poured down Binchy's face and he fell in an untidy heap, the crimson fluid already spreading rapidly around him.

Doyle swung the Eagle round and shot Scarface.

The bullet hit the Chinaman in the stomach, burst the membranous sac then powered through his lower body, erupting from his back, severing his spinal column.

He dropped to his knees, his body twisted, his sphincter already opening, spilling excrement amongst the blood which was gushing from him.

Short Hair, his face looking as if it had been dipped in red paint, ran for the door.

Doyle fired at him but missed, the bullet tearing its way through the door, blasting one of the panels out.

'Fucking bastard,' Doyle roared and made to follow him.

Long Hair shot out a hand and grabbed the counter terrorist's ankle, tripping him.

Doyle went sprawling but kept a grip on the Eagle, rolling over, firing at Long Hair.

The bullet hit him in the chest, punching in the sternum and ripping through one lung, bursting the fleshy balloon and erupting from the man's back carrying blood, pulverised bone and pink tissue with it.

Doyle put another one in Long Hair's face then snatched up his holdall and dashed out into the street, colliding with a woman outside who was pushing a pram.

She screamed as Doyle knocked her to the floor, but all he was concerned with was the escaping Chinaman.

He spotted him twenty yards ahead, clambering into the back of a grey Montego.

The car sped off.

Doyle ran into the road, arms raised, ignoring the blaring hooters of onrushing cars, the screams of the woman who was crouching on the pavement being helped by another passer-by.

There was a red Astra speeding towards Doyle, but he stepped forward, the gun aimed at the windscreen.

The driver hit the brakes, the car screaming to a halt.

'Get out,' roared Doyle, the Eagle aimed at the man.

His face pale, the driver fumbled with his door, aware of the warm wetness spreading across his groin.

'Get out of the fucking car,' Doyle bellowed again, dragging the door open, hauling the driver into the street, sending him sprawling on the tarmac.

The counter terrorist tossed the holdall onto the back seat, the Eagle onto the passenger seat, then he got in, slammed the door and stamped on the accelerator.

The wheels shrieked for a second then gained purchase and the car shot forward.

Doyle, ignoring the pain that was beginning to take hold, gripped the wheel tightly, his eyes fixed on the grey Montego weaving in and out of traffic ahead of him.

He pressed down harder on the accelerator.

Ahead of him, the Montego shot through traffic lights which were flickering on amber.

By the time Doyle reached them they were glaring red.

*Fuck it.*

The Astra screamed across the junction doing nearly eighty.

Cars on either side sounded their horns in anger and alarm, but Doyle was oblivious to them.

All that concerned him was catching that fucking Montego.

And, already, he was gaining.

# *Eighty-One*

Ahead of him, the Montego was weaving in and out of traffic, now forced to slow down slightly because of the density of vehicles clogging the road in this part of the city centre.

Doyle gripped the steering wheel more tightly, his eyes fixed on the fleeing vehicle as surely as a homing device locked onto its quarry.

He had little or no idea whereabouts in the city they were, his mind was focused fully on controlling the Astra at high speed, his eyes narrowed in concentration. He had even forgotten about the pain from his wounds.

Apart from the one on his back, none of them were too deep. He'd been lucky.

*Luckier than Binchy.*

He could smell his own blood in the hot confines of the car though and there were splashes of it on the dashboard and the wheel.

Every now and then, the man in the back of the Montego would look out, peering at Doyle to see if he was still following. The counter terrorist could see him slapping the driver on the shoulder as if to urge him to greater speed.

The Montego slowed down to take a corner and Doyle took his chance, accelerating past a truck, and slamming into the back of the other car, jolting it hard.

One of the rear lights splintered and the housing came free, skittering across the road.

Doyle grinned as he saw the grey car skid slightly before speeding on. As he took the corner he heard his own wheels scream, and black rubber burned across the road for several yards as he wrestled with the wheel.

The Montego turned again, into a much narrower street. The side of the car scraped against the wall of a building as it turned, sparks flying off the chassis, paint ripped off.

Doyle followed unhesitatingly.

The street led out onto a pedestrianised area, but the Montego sped across, shoppers screaming in fear as the vehicle roared past them.

A mother snatched her small child into her arms as the grey car ploughed into her pram, sending it flying.

'Get out the way,' roared Doyle, banging on his horn as he too sped across the square.

He saw people bolting for the safety of shops, heard their shouts and screams even above the roar of the engine and his own frenzied bellowing.

The Montego shot down another street and out onto the road again, skidding as the driver turned it.

As Doyle emerged from the street he accelerated and, again, succeeded in slamming into the rear of the car.

This time the impact was even more powerful and he grunted in pain as he was thrown hard against the steering wheel but he held on, the needle on the speedo now nudging seventy as he kept up his pursuit.

For the first time he heard sirens somewhere behind him.

*Fuck them.*

Doyle didn't need their bloody help.

The speeding cars raced towards another set of traffic lights, hurtled across the junction and roared on.

There was a lorry reversing out into the street.

The Montego swerved round the rear of the juggernaut, scraping one wing on the huge vehicle, ripping off a wing mirror and cracking a side window.

Doyle saw the occupants of the car rocked by the impact.

He floored the accelerator and almost made it past the lorry intact.

Part of the tail-board stove in one side of his windscreen.

Glass came hurtling into the Astra and Doyle raised a hand instinctively to shield his face. He felt small pieces of glass cutting into his hand and arm like crystal shrapnel but he ignored it, more concerned with keeping control of the car which skidded violently, its rear end smacking hard against a parked car on the other side of the road.

Cold air rushed in through the riven windscreen, blasting into Doyle's face, causing his long hair to trail out behind him like reptilian tails. The breeze swept over him, making him aware again of the warm wetness running down his cheek from the wound on his face.

He was still within sight of the Montego and, better still, the lorry had blocked the path of any pursuing police cars.

Doyle knew he had to reach the Montego before the police did.

He could still see the bloodied face of the passenger in the back peering out at him. The little bastard was the only one of his attackers who'd escaped.

At least for now.

They were leaving the city centre, that much Doyle *was* aware of. But where they were heading he still didn't know. Where were these bastards trying to run to?

He saw Scarface steady himself on the back seat, saw him lift something.

Saw the rear window being shattered, knocked out.

Glass spilled onto the road but Doyle drove through it, pulling closer to the Montego, realising that it was slowing down slightly.

*Why?*

Then he saw the shotgun.

As Scarface fired, Doyle hit his brakes, the Astra dropping back several car lengths and swerving to avoid the massive discharge.

The blast missed.

Scarface fired again and blew out one of the Astra's front lights.

Another discharge peppered the radiator grille.

Doyle gripped the steering wheel with one hand, moving it from side to side, trying to make the Astra a more difficult target to hit.

*If one of those blasts should take out a tyre . . .*

With his free hand he reached quickly onto the back seat and grabbed the holdall, pulling it forward onto the passenger seat. He rummaged in it and pulled out the Beretta, flicking off the safety catch.

With one hand he raised the pistol, aiming through the portion of shattered windscreen.

Doyle gritted his teeth and fired, the recoil jerking his arm upwards slightly.

The burst-fire mechanism spewed out three 9mm slugs within split seconds of one another and Doyle smiled as he saw all three strike the rear of the Montego, one blasting out a light, another punching a hole in the boot and the third screaming off the roof.

Scarface ducked down as Doyle fired again, the recoil slamming the pistol back against the heel of his hand, the retort deafening him. The onrushing wind sent the stench of cordite into his nostrils.

Empty shell cases flew upwards, striking the Astra's roof, some of the hot brass cases landing around Doyle. He fired another burst and heard a loud bang as one of the Montego's tyres was burst.

The grey car skidded violently out of control and Doyle smiled as he saw Scarface flung across the back seat of the vehicle.

The driver was fighting to regain control but without the use of one tyre it seemed impossible. Pieces of shredded rubber flew from the rim and hurtled through the air, then Doyle saw sparks scorching up from the road as the wheel rim scraped along the tarmac.

He put his foot down and rammed the stricken Montego.

What was left of the rear window was sent crashing inwards by the impact and Doyle gritted his teeth, steadying the Beretta again.

He squeezed the trigger, the muzzle flash blinding him.

Scarface was hit in the throat, blood erupting from the wound like a crimson fountain.

The driver took one in the shoulder, the bullet smashing his scapula before erupting from his chest spattering the windscreen with blood.

The Montego hurtled out of control, skidding across the road.

Doyle saw it strike something, flip and fly into the air like some child's toy tossed away. The car seemed to rise ten or fifteen feet into the air where it spun uncontrollably before crashing back down to earth, skidding on its roof, glass from the remaining side windows flying in all directions.

'Jesus,' he murmured, slamming on his own brakes, leaping out of the car, the automatic still gripped in his fist.

What the fuck had made the Montego flip like that? What had it hit?

A train track.

Running not alongside the road, but in the tarmac itself.

Doyle looked up, saw the cranes towering above him like dinosaurs. Huge, rusted, abandoned skeletal steel monsters seemed to prod their booms accusingly at the sky or at the water which slopped against the dockside.

*Dockside*.

It took a few seconds for Doyle to realise where the chase had led him.

He looked round at the abandoned machinery, the piles of rusted metal.

All that remained of Harland and Wolff shipyards.

# Eighty-Two

The switch was to be made at the shipyard.

Marie Leary had told him that.

*'The guns are usually taken out by boat or by sea-plane.'*

Her words echoed in Doyle's mind as he hurried back to the Astra.

She'd said that the changeover was to be made in the afternoon.

*Had she lied?*

Even if it was to be here, the shipyards were huge. You could hide a fucking army amongst the abandoned machinery.

But *not* a sea-plane.

Doyle pulled away, scanning the dark choppy water for any sign of just such an object. As he drove, he slowed down, slammed a fresh magazine into the Beretta and worked the slide to chamber a round.

Maybe the Triads who'd tried to kill him had decided to run when the hit had failed. Run back to their one sure-fire way of escape.

He guided the car along the wide thoroughfares marked out by piles of container crates, most rusted, their paint long since flaked and gone.

Doyle glanced at his face in the rear-view mirror, saw that the worst of the bleeding had stopped.

*Another scar.*

As if he didn't have enough already.

*Sean Doyle. The human fucking jigsaw puzzle.*

He turned the car into another high-walled steel corridor, the empty containers piled up to twenty feet in height around him. They seemed to glower down at him from all sides. The chain and pulley of a crane straddling them creaked in the wind.

*Engines.*

The sound of powerful turbos cut through the ghostly silence and Doyle looked from side to side in an effort to locate the source.

The sound was growing louder and Doyle swung the car around another tower of containers.

He saw the sea-plane cutting across the dark water of the harbour, leaving a foam wake behind it.

Doyle hauled himself out of the car, watching the Dornier Seastar pass within a hundred yards of him.

He could see into the cockpit.

Could see faces looking out at him.

Chinese faces.

Marie had lied to him. The switch had already been completed.

Doyle raised the Beretta, drew a bead on the plane, thought about firing but, even as he watched, the Dornier seemed to gain the thrust it needed and he saw it rise into the air, water skimming from its fuselage. Like some enormous gull, it left the harbour, the 650 horse-power Pratt and Whitney turboprops lifting it effortlessly into the grey sky.

The counter terrorist lowered the automatic, muttering angrily.

The engines roared in his ears as he turned to watch the plane soaring ever higher, glancing quickly down the dock in the direction from which it had come.

He saw the car there.

The boot was still open.

About five hundred yards away, the blue Volvo was motionless.

Doyle saw two men there. Saw one of them aiming.

*Saw . . .*

There was a staccato rattle of automatic fire which peppered the ground around his feet.

Doyle ran for the cover of the Astra, the Dornier almost

forgotten as it pushed its way up into the low-lying cloud. He swung himself into the driving seat and stepped on the accelerator, driving straight for the Volvo.

Bullets spattered the front of the Astra, screaming off the bodywork, thudding into the bonnet. One of them ripped away the rear-view mirror and blasted out the back window. Doyle, hunkered down in his seat, kept his foot pressed against the accelerator and gripped the wheel tightly, preparing for the impact.

He looked up a few seconds before it came.

He saw one man standing in front of the Volvo, the sub-machine-gun still gripped in his hands.

He hadn't time to move.

Doyle threw open the driver's door and leapt out, hitting the concrete hard, rolling over and over, his hands and arms tucked tightly around his head for protection.

He heard the two cars collide.

The Astra practically cut the other man in half. It slammed into him, crushing him between it and the Volvo, splintering both his legs in several places, pulping his femurs and hips, his upper body snapping forward to thud against the Astra's bonnet, blood jetting in all directions.

The sub-gun went flying.

Doyle, his head spinning, looked round and saw the damage wrought. The pulverised body of the gunman, the battered cars.

And Paul Riordan.

The Irishman was climbing into the Volvo, clambering across the passenger seat to get to the driver's side, trying to start the car.

Doyle staggered to his feet the Beretta still gripped in one fist and advanced as quickly as he could towards the Volvo, noticing that blood had sprayed the front of it.

He also noticed that the gunman's right leg had been severed just below the hip. It lay a yard or so from him.

Riordan started the engine.

*No way.*

Doyle steadied himself, raised the Beretta and, as calmly as if he'd been on a firing range, began pumping the trigger.

Bullets thudded into the car and into Riordan, each spent cartridge case flying into the air.

The windscreen was blown in.

The case landed with a clink on the concrete.

Riordan took one in the chest.

Doyle kept firing.

Another bullet took away most of the left side of the Irishman's face.

*He was deafened by the retorts.*

Riordan's chest and stomach were holed again.

*Blinded by the muzzle flashes.*

The left eye socket was drilled empty.

There was blood everywhere, great arcs of it spurting from gaping wounds.

Doyle saw the slide fly backwards as the hammer finally struck down on the last shell.

It caught Riordan in the throat.

*Cordite. Smoke.*

Doyle walked over to the car and peered in at the bullet-riddled body of Riordan. He reached into his jacket and took a fresh magazine, slamming it into the butt of the automatic.

His own breath was coming in gasps and he could no longer ignore the pain from his wounds.

*So much pain.*

It felt as if someone had set him on fire, pumped burning fuel into his veins.

He looked up and saw that the Seastar had disappeared into the clouds.

Doyle coughed and spat blood into the water.

He moved around to the rear of the Volvo and pulled open the door. There were five or six small cardboard boxes inside, just a blanket draped over them. Doyle ripped one of the boxes open.

He guessed there were about three kilos of cocaine in

there. The other boxes contained the same.

So, they *had* made the switch.

And he'd been too late.

He heard sirens approaching, drifting on the cold air, carried by the breeze. The same breeze that blew in off the water. He walked to the edge of the dock, looked down into the choppy, dark depths then up towards the sky.

He'd lost the guns again.

*So near, and yet so fucking far. Ha. Ha.*

Two RUC cars were speeding up the dock towards the carnage, sirens blaring.

Doyle pushed the Beretta into his belt and walked towards them, both cars skidding to a halt, armed men spilling out, seeking cover behind their opened doors.

'Stand still and get your hands up,' shouted one of the men.

Doyle didn't need to be told twice.

He stood and waited for them.

# *Eighty-Three*

Doyle grunted more in irritation than pain as he walked across to the window and peered out.

In one of the tall oak trees close by the building a crow sat in the uppermost branches, its feathers ruffled by a wind which threatened to hurl it from the tree. It let out a few mournful cries as if to summon others of its kind, but none came.

It flew off, disappearing into the distance.

Doyle blew out a stream of smoke and winced slightly as he felt a twinge from the wound on his face. That and the others had been treated and bandaged where necessary. A small dressing was taped to his cheek.

As he moved back towards the bed he was aware of Major Wetherby's eyes upon him. The army intelligence officer was doing his best to ignore the patchwork of scars which seemed to cover most of Doyle's body and arms, but even he couldn't help wonder at the pain some of those scars must have caused.

Wetherby had arrived about an hour ago, not long after Doyle.

The counter terrorist had been brought by ambulance to the army base just outside Belfast, accompanied by two RUC men.

The chain of events following his confrontation with Riordan at the docks had been as Doyle had expected. He'd been arrested and taken to the nearest police station. There he went through a series of interrogations, growing ever more impatient when the officers questioning him refused to believe his story and, even more infuriatingly, refused to check it out. They'd left him sitting in a fucking cell for two hours, in considerable discomfort from his wounds, before investigating his story properly.

Doyle had reclaimed his weapons before being put in an ambulance and brought to the base.

The RUC had not apologised to him, the officer in charge insisting that because Doyle had no ID he could have been anyone. Doyle had sworn at them as he'd left the station.

Once at the army hospital, the nurse there had patched him up. Cleaned and dressed his wounds.

*It seemed so familiar.*

She'd offered him pain killers but he'd declined, making do with a cigarette instead.

Wetherby had arrived fifteen or twenty minutes later. He'd listened in silence as Doyle told him what had happened.

'And you're sure the Triads had the guns?' he said, finally, watching as Doyle stubbed out one cigarette and immediately lit up another. 'You said you didn't see them loaded onto the plane.'

'The drugs were in Riordan's car,' Doyle said, irritably. 'They'd already made the switch.'

Wetherby shook his head.

'I understand what you say about the IRA and the Triads working together, Doyle, but I still find it hard to believe,' the Major said.

'Why? They're both business organisations, what's so strange about it? It's a mutually beneficial situation.'

'Well, you did your best. It's up to us now.'

'What the fuck are you talking about?'

'You found the guns, but you lost them. We know where they're heading. It's army business now, Doyle.'

'In less than twenty-four hours, probably even as we speak, those fucking guns are going to be in London. This business hasn't *solved* the problem, Wetherby, it's just shifted it somewhere else.'

'Well, it's not *your* problem anymore.'

'And who's going to get them back? You?'

'I told you, Doyle, it's army business now. We'll take care of it.'

Doyle shook his head.

'So what are you going to do?' he said, challengingly. 'Invade Chinatown?'

Wetherby held his gaze.

'You put me on this job to get those guns back,' Doyle continued. 'And that's what I'm going to do. Besides, those slit-eyed bastards tried to kill me. That makes it *personal*.'

'There's more at stake here than your own private vendettas, Doyle,' Wetherby told him. 'You're supposed to be a professional. Just do your job.'

Doyle smiled.

'Don't you worry,' he said, quietly. 'I will. You can bet money on it.'

# Eighty-Four

The two men who emerged from the rear entrance of the house in Newport Street were both in their early twenties. One was a little taller than the other but apart from that they were very similar in appearance, even down to the clothes they wore. Both men were dressed in jeans and sweatshirts. The shorter one had a leather jacket draped around his shoulders and as he emerged into the early morning air he pulled the jacket more tightly around him to protect himself against the chill that hung in the air. The coolness outside was even more noticeable after the heat inside the building.

The house had been used as a Hip Sing gambling den for the past eight months. Like so many other rackets it had grown larger over the years and the basement of the house they'd just left seemed the perfect meeting place for such a set up. Men packed in there day and night, their money swelling the coffers of the Hip Sing.

The two young men who now walked from the building knew that some of the profits from that racket and the many others the Hip Sing operated in London would come their way.

There were cars parked across the street, bumper to bumper in places. The two men headed towards one of them. Leather Jacket fumbled in his pocket for the keys.

The loud crack of a rifle retort was deafening in the early morning stillness.

Both men stood immobile for a second, as if the sound had robbed them of the power to move, but then they heard another shot. And another.

A bullet hit the taller man in the face, staving in one cheek before exploding from the back of his head.

Another bullet hit him before he struck the ground, powering into his chest, shattering two ribs, tearing into his heart.

Blood sprayed over the car as it spouted from the wounds and Leather Jacket spun round, not knowing whether to see where the shots had originated or try and seek refuge in the car.

He had time to do neither. A bullet caught him in the small of the back and punched through his spine, killing him instantly.

There was no need for the three which drilled into his head and stomach.

The car from which the shots had come sped off, the sound of the gunshots still ringing in the air.


6.34 a.m.

The three men who approached the front of the restaurant in Wardour Street had no idea how many of their enemies they would find inside. They didn't really care.

Four, perhaps half a dozen at most, they'd been told to expect.

It mattered little to them.

The Ming Wah restaurant was on the corner of Wardour Street and Winnet Street. The blinds at both windows were pulled shut, as were those at the door.

The first of the three men raised the Sterling AR-180 and, gripping it tightly to his shoulder, squeezed the trigger.

The hail of fire that followed blasted in both windows, blew off the lock and obliterated one hinge of the front door. The gunman kicked it in and pushed the remains of the door aside, striding into the darkened restaurant, his companions behind him.

He counted quickly the number of Hip Sing men inside,

all seated at one large table, drinks laid out before them as if it were the middle of the day instead of early morning.

Five men saw the trio enter.

Five gazed in astonishment as the guns began to blaze.

The three men with the AR-180s raked the area before them, bullets ploughing through men easily, blasting lumps from the furniture and the walls.

A cloud of dust and smoke filled the restaurant. Even the screams of pain were drowned out by the thunderous roar of the automatic fire.

The first man noticed that there was a woman seated at the table.

Early twenties, pretty. Long black hair.

He shot her too.

6.44 a.m.

The lift rose to the third floor of the Meridian hotel in Piccadilly and the room-service waiter stepped out, rubbing his eyes with one hand as he pushed the trolley laden with breakfast into the corridor. He checked the room number he sought and set off down the corridor towards room 326.

He hated these early shifts. He'd been up since four, his uniform immaculately pressed and brushed. What the hell did it matter; anyone who ordered their breakfast this early in the morning would probably be half asleep anyway, he reasoned. Who was going to notice the odd wrinkle here and there? Besides, hardly any of the guests even looked at him when he brought their meals anyway. Pompous bastards. Like that jumped-up little shit in 216. Who the fuck did he think he was? Asking him to take back his steak last night *twice* because it wasn't cooked. And then he didn't give a tip.

The room-service waiter trundled the trolley past the emergency exit, noticing that the door was slightly open. He paused a moment and thought about closing it, but decided he'd do it on his way back.

As he drew nearer to the room he sought he lifted the

silver plate cover and peered at what lay beneath. A bowl of bran flakes and some dry toast. It scarcely seemed worth the ceremony.

He paused beside the door and prepared to knock.

As he did so he saw that the door to 326 was open an inch or two.

From inside he could hear voices. Low mutterings, conspiratorial whispering.

The waiter cleared his throat, preparing to knock.

There was a moment's silence then the door was wrenched open and two men burst out, crashing into him, knocking him to the floor as they dashed past. He shouted something, swinging his arm after one of them, noticing that they both disappeared through the partially open emergency exit. He could hear their steps as they hurried down the stone stairs away from him. He was sure they were both Chinese.

The door of the bedroom was open and he hauled himself to his feet, noticing that one or two other doors down the corridor were being eased open as inquisitive guests peered out to see what the commotion was about.

The waiter moved cautiously into the room, coughing theatrically as he did so.

The coughing turned almost immediately to a loud shriek of horror.

There was a body lying spreadeagled on the bed. Naked.

The man had been stabbed repeatedly, blood having soaked into the mattress and overflowed onto the floor to form a sticky pool around the bed.

His genitals had been hacked off – nothing but a blood-clogged mess remained between his legs. Just before he passed out, the waiter noticed that they'd been stuffed into the mouth of the dead man, causing his cheeks to bulge obscenely. Crimson fluid had congealed around his lips and chin.

The stench was appalling.

Like his attackers, the victim was Chinese too.

But that hardly seemed to matter to the waiter.

He fainted.

## *Eighty-Five*

Detective Sergeant Nick Henderson ran a hand through his hair and sat back in his seat.

'Shit,' he murmured, staring at the reports laid out on his desk.

He'd read them all two or three times and they didn't improve on repeated inspection.

Eight murders.

All within a three-mile radius.

All Chinese.

All members of the Hip Sing Triad.

Henderson exhaled wearily, got to his feet and headed out to the vending machine which stood in the corridor outside his office. He leant against it, feeding coins into the slot.

*Eight fucking murders all in one morning.*

He shook his head, ignoring the sound of footsteps approaching from behind him. The D.S. retrieved his coffee from the machine, only turning when he heard a voice;

'D.S. Henderson?'

He looked round.

The man who faced him was in his mid-thirties, he guessed. Thick set, unshaven, hair just past his shoulders and sporting a fresh dressing on his left cheek. He was dressed in jeans, a T-shirt and a leather jacket. Henderson also saw that the man was wearing cowboy boots. Ones that could do with a touch of polish, he observed as an afterthought.

'I'm Henderson,' he said. 'Can I help you?'

'My name's Doyle. Sean Doyle,' said the newcomer. 'I'm with the Counter Terrorist Unit.' He flipped open the slim leather ID wallet he'd pulled from his pocket and brandished it towards the policeman.

Henderson nodded, satisfied that Doyle was indeed who he claimed to be.

'I wondered if you could spare me a minute,' the counter terrorist said. 'I know you're busy. What with all the shit that happened this morning. But this *is* important.'

'Come through,' Henderson said, ushering Doyle towards his office. 'Do you want a drink? It's crap out of the machine, but it's better than nothing.'

Doyle smiled.

'Cheers. Coffee. White, one sugar,' he said.

Henderson fed more coins in.

'You haven't got decaffeinated, have you?' Doyle asked.

Henderson raised one eyebrow and Doyle smiled again, ducking into the office.

The policeman joined him a moment later, handing him his drink then sitting down opposite.

'So, tell me, Mr Doyle, what can I do for you?' he asked.

'I need some information. About the Triads.'

Henderson regarded him curiously for a moment, almost warily.

'What interest are the Triads to the Counter Terrorist Unit?' he wanted to know.

'It's a long story,' Doyle said. 'I just want to know what you can tell me.' He took out his cigarettes and lit one up. 'I need to know how they're organised, how they operate. What they're into. That sort of shit.'

'What makes you think I can help you?' Henderson said, looking almost longingly at the cigarette smoke drifting through the air.

'You're in charge of this investigation; you're supposed to be the expert.'

'There *are* no experts on the Triads. Not over here

anyway. We've got a pretty good idea of how they work, some of their scams, stuff like that, but it's only scratching the surface. The thing is we can't infiltrate them like we could other criminal organisations because there aren't that many Chinese coppers on the force. A white guy wouldn't last five minutes if he tried. They call us *gweilos*. It means white ghost.'

Doyle saw the policeman glancing at his cigarette and offered the packet.

'I *was* trying to give up,' Henderson told him. 'Fuck it,' he muttered, resignedly, taking one of the Rothmans. Doyle flicked his lighter and held it out.

The counter terrorist smiled.

'So, you don't think it would be possible to get close to them?' Doyle said. 'Get inside.'

'Impossible,' Henderson told him. 'Like I said, you're the wrong colour for a start. You might as well be a pork chop at a fucking bar mitzvah.' He blew out a stream of smoke contentedly.

Doyle sipped at his coffee.

'The other thing is, the Triads aren't bound by honour or family like the Mafia. With them it's a religious thing. That's why it's stronger,' the policeman continued. 'Years ago they were freedom fighters, patriots.'

*Like the IRA, Doyle mused.*

'They were all Buddhists,' Henderson went on. 'They were bound by oaths, not loyalty to some family. Also, there's no central headquarters for all Triads. They're all separate units, working autonomously, and they answer only to their own officials. Every group has a sister organisation in Hong Kong, but that's where the links end.'

'I thought you said you weren't an expert,' Doyle said.

'I know what I have to know. You could find this out from a fucking library. It's my job to know it. I know how a car engine works, but that doesn't make me a mechanic, does it?'

Doyle took another sip of his drink.

'You said they answer to their officials. What did you mean by that?' he wanted to know.

'The hierarchy of the Triad they belong to. The management if you like.' Henderson smiled. He took a piece of paper from his desk and laid it in front of Doyle, his pen poised on it. 'You've got your top man here, the *Shan Chu*, the leader. Then the deputy leader, the *Fu Shan Chu*.' Henderson wrote both names down, constructing the beginnings of what looked like a rough family tree. 'Then there's the *Heung Chu*, the incense master, him and some bloke called the *Sin Fung* or the vanguard, they're the ones responsible for things like administration, lodge rituals, stuff like initiations.'

Doyle watched and listened with fascination.

'The other two most important positions,' Henderson continued, 'are these two. The *Hung Kwan*, which means the Red Pole, is responsible for organising hits on other Triads, people who've fucked them about, or the poor sods who owe gambling debts. He arranges punishments inside *and* outside the lodge. Then there's the *Pak Tsz Sin*, they also call him the White Paper Fan. Now he's a very important bloke. The leader's right-hand man, no Triad will make a move without consulting him first. He's the equivalent of the *consigliere* in the Mafia. Usually well educated.' Henderson sat back in his seat. 'All the Triads in London are run the same way.'

'How many are there?'

'At least five that we know of. The 14K Society, the Shui Fong, the Wo Shing Wo, the Sun Yee On and the Tai Hung Chai.'

Doyle sat forward.

*That rang a bell.*

*What had Marie Leary said?*

*'They're from a gang called the Tai Hung Chai . . . We offer them protection while they're here . . .'*

Doyle dropped his cigarette butt into the bottom of his empty cup.

'How many members?' he wanted to know.

Henderson shrugged.

'Your guess is as good as mine,' he said. 'Somebody reckons there could be over fifty thousand Triads in London alone.'

'Jesus,' Doyle murmured.

'We have regular meetings and conferences with other forces around the country to share information on the Triads, and usually someone from the Royal Hong Kong Police comes over two or three times a year. But there's still so much we don't know about them, probably never will.' He took a drag on his cigarette. 'We're pissing in the wind and the worst thing is, we all know it.'

'You know who their top men are?'

'Oh yeah, some of them have even got records, but usually they're well protected. They're too clever to spend time in jail. We've managed to arrest a few of the foot soldiers over the years, but we can't get near their bosses.'

'What sort of scams do they run?'

'The usual. Illegal gambling, brothels, loan-sharking. They're big in pirate video too. Only their own stuff of course.' He chuckled. 'Fucking Chinese soap operas are the biggest movers apparently. They've got a big thing going with computer software too.'

'And drugs,' Doyle said, flatly.

Henderson nodded.

'It's their biggest interest,' the policeman said, stubbing out his cigarette. 'Believe it or not seventy per cent of all opium and heroin in the *world* passes through Chinatown here in London. You wouldn't believe some of the ways they bring it in. Hollowed out sanitary towels, melons. We've found couriers with it shoved up their arses.'

*Or swallowed in condoms, like Stephen Murphy?*

'What about guns?'

Henderson looked puzzled.

'They don't trade in weapons?' Doyle asked.

'Not that we know of. Why do you ask?'

Doyle ran a hand through his hair.

'Have you had ballistics reports on the guns that killed

those Triads this morning?' he wanted to know.

'Yes, why?'

'The bullets came from Armalites didn't they? 5.56mm AR-180s.'

'How do you know?' Henderson demanded.

'Because I know where those guns came from.'

## Eighty-Six

Henderson listened intently as Doyle told him what had happened over the past couple of weeks, the counter terrorist keeping detail to a bare minimum. After all, his offer of help to the police was limited by his desire for revenge against the Triads. He didn't give a fuck if they were overrunning London, all that concerned him was that they'd tried to kill *him* and in order to find the men he sought he needed Henderson's help.

Doyle sat back in his seat when he'd finished the story, or at least as much of it as he was prepared to relate.

'The IRA and the Triads,' murmured Henderson, quietly. 'Christ, it doesn't bear thinking about. You don't think the IRA are involved in this Triad war, do you?'

Doyle shook his head.

'Not actively involved. They've supplied the weapons to the Tai Hung Chai, that's as far as it goes,' the counter terrorist told him.

'Christ,' Henderson repeated.

'Those guns are in London and they're being used. I need to find them and the only way I can do that is by getting closer to the Triads.'

Henderson shook his head.

'Forget it,' he said, dismissively. 'Like I told you, even *we* can't do that. You wouldn't get within a mile of them.

Besides, I don't think my superiors would be too happy about you rampaging through Chinatown blowing away anyone with slit eyes.'

Doyle smiled thinly.

'You said some of them had form,' the counter terrorist noted. 'Have you got files here I could look at? If I knew who I was looking for it might help.'

Henderson nodded slowly then reached for the phone on his desk, jabbing one of the digits. Doyle lit up another cigarette as he watched.

'Bill, I want all the information we've got on the Tai Hung Chai Triad,' Henderson said into the phone. 'Yeah, files, arrest records the lot. Cheers.'

He put the phone down and took another cigarette Doyle offered him.

'Why did the Tai Hung Chai try to kill you?' the policeman asked.

'Maybe I was too close.'

'You were fortunate to get away from them, not many do. They run their whole organisation on fear and violence.'

'Perhaps I was just lucky,' Doyle said, sardonically.

'If you find the guns, what then?' Henderson wanted to know.

Doyle shrugged. 'Ask them to hand them back.'

'Call me. Don't try to do anything on your own, besides it's not your job now, they're on *my* territory. *You're* on my territory.'

'Meaning what, I play by your rules?'

There was a moment's silence, finally broken by Doyle.

'I told you, they tried to kill me but my first priority is the guns.'

*Like hell.*

There was a knock on the office door and a uniformed sergeant entered, carrying a pile of black files which he laid in front of Henderson, casting a curious glance at Doyle before leaving.

'Everything we know about the Tai Hung Chai is in here,' said Henderson, tapping the pile of files.

'Including the name of the geezer who ordered the hit on me?' Doyle asked. 'You said that punishments inside and outside the organisation were sanctioned by one man. I want to know who that was.'

Henderson flipped open one of the files, laying it before Doyle.

'I told you that no Triad makes a move without the okay from its *Pak Tsz Sin*,' he said. 'If someone ordered the hit on you, it would have been him.' Henderson prodded a small black-and-white photo stapled to an arrest sheet.

Doyle studied the face, every contour, every line.

He ran his index finger slowly around the outline of the features of Joey Chang.


## Eighty-Seven


She saw them as she stepped from the lift into the underground car park.

Both men were seated in the dark blue Cortina, one of them reading a newspaper, the other smoking, one arm dangling from the open window.

Su Chang raised a hand to acknowledge them, pulling her jacket a little more tightly around her as she walked towards the Daimler, her heels clicking loudly on the concrete of the car park.

She saw one of the men swing himself out of the car. He hastily dropped his cigarette, crushing it beneath his foot as he advanced towards her.

Su turned to face him, the key already in the door of the Daimler.

'I know what you're going to say,' she began, smiling at the first of the bodyguards. 'But there's no need for you to come with me. I'm just going to pick up my children from school. I'll be ten minutes.'

'We could fetch them, Mrs Chang,' the bodyguard said.

'No, it's okay.' She slid behind the wheel. 'Besides, I've been cooped up in here all day, I'll go crazy if I don't get out soon.'

'But your husband told us to keep you safe and . . .'

She cut him short.

'I'm sure he did and you're doing a very good job, but I'll only be gone ten minutes,' Su insisted.

'Then we must follow. Escort you.'

Su smiled.

'If you must. Thank you.' She pulled her door shut and started the engine, the Daimler roaring, the sound of its engine amplified in the subterranean garage. She guided it towards the ramp which led out into the street, glancing in her rear-view mirror to check that the Cortina was following. She would make sure she kept her speed down so they could stay close. They were, after all, only doing as her husband had instructed.

She smiled as she thought about Joey, but there was concern too in her expression. He had warned her that things might well get worse during the next two or three days. He had even suggested that she and the children leave London until he felt it to be safe again, but she had refused. She didn't want to be away from him now and she knew the children wouldn't. Whatever was going to happen, they would face it together.

There had been no incidents since the night of the phone calls. No more threats. Su had become bored sitting at home. There was only so much she could do around the flat. She'd asked the bodyguards to fetch some shopping for her earlier in the day and one of them had obliged while his companion remained behind, ever vigilant.

She looked into her rear-view mirror again and saw the Cortina a couple of car lengths behind, the driver and passenger clearly visible. The passenger was glancing to his left and right constantly, as if scrutinising not only the cars that passed but also the pedestrians.

Su wondered if either of them was married. Probably not, she concluded. One always wore a shirt with frayed cuffs, the other looked as if his clothes had not seen an iron for weeks. She couldn't imagine either man having a woman to see to such small needs for them and the men themselves obviously didn't feel the need to rectify these failings. Perhaps there was no one to impress.

Su smiled, amused at her own attempts at detective work. She slowed down as she came to a set of traffic lights, the Cortina also slowing down.

The sky above was overcast, threatening rain, and she peered up as if expecting to see the first drops spattering the windscreen.

The lights changed and she drove on.

The Cortina didn't move.

Su slowed down slightly, but she could see that the other vehicle was still stationary.

The passenger clambered out and motioned to her, perhaps to turn back.

Behind her she could hear whirring as the driver tried to get the engine going.

The passenger was running after her now, waving for her to wait but Su sighed and glanced at the dashboard clock.

The children would be waiting for her.

She didn't want to leave them standing about. The guards could follow when they'd got the car started. She might even pick them up on the way back. She smiled to herself and drove on.

As she turned a corner the passenger disappeared from view.

The school was up ahead, she could see the first few children crossing the playground towards the gate where other parents waited.

Other cars were parked, their passengers awaiting their wards.

Su found her own space and got out of the car, locking it, feeling how cold the wind was now. She pulled up the collar of her jacket as she headed towards the gate.

Even if she'd seen the Citroën moving slowly along the street she would probably have paid it no heed.

Or its three Chinese passengers.

The one in the front seat nodded to the driver.

The car slowed down as it drew nearer to her.

# Eighty-Eight

The driver of the Cortina thumped the steering wheel angrily as he turned the ignition key once more. The engine merely whined hopelessly.

'Again,' shouted his companion who was peering into the engine.

Traffic was beginning to build up behind the stricken car, some drivers sounding their horns angrily as they tried to get past.

One man shouted to the two Chinamen to get the car off the road, but they merely gestured angrily to him as he passed and continued with their futile attempts to restart the engine.

'Come on,' the driver snarled, aware that Su Chang was now well out of sight. He and his companion would be in big trouble if anyone found out about this. Their orders had been specific. She was to be escorted at all times, not to be let out of their sight when she was out of the house.

And now, *this*.

From under the bonnet the man raised an oily hand towards his companion and waved agitatedly at him, stepping back as the driver twisted the ignition key once again.

The engine whined, caught, then died. But the driver didn't stop trying.

It whined more loudly, fired and roared as he floored

the accelerator, although as soon as he withdrew his foot a little the engine died once more, but at least they were getting close.

He heard horns sounding behind him, saw his companion nodding furiously at him.

*How much longer?*

Su saw her daughter first.

Anna, her satchel over her shoulder, emerged from the main building and began ambling across the playground. Michael followed a moment later, hurrying to catch up with his sister.

Su moved forward a couple of steps, watching her children as they crossed the playground, surrounded by many others. All around her parents were waiting for their children. A small minibus was waiting to pick up others.

A young woman in jeans and a thick sweatshirt smiled at her and said something about the weather. Su nodded in return and murmured something about it being cold. The wind whipped around her as if to reinforce her musings, flicking at her long dark hair.

She glanced behind her at the Daimler. She'd left her hazard lights on to indicate that she wouldn't be parked there long. A number of the other drivers who'd parked their cars nearby had done likewise.

She saw the Citroën pull up just behind her car and wondered if she'd blocked the road.

It didn't even strike her that the man in the rear of the car was watching her.

She saw the other car drive on after a few seconds, disappearing around a corner.

'Mum.'

The joyful shout had come from Anna who was now running towards Su with Michael scuttling in her wake.

Su turned back and smiled broadly as her daughter came through the gates, then she walked back towards the car holding their hands, listening as they both babbled on simultaneously about what they'd done that day.

It was warm in the Daimler and Su waited until the children were safely strapped in before she pulled out into the road again, heading home.

The first spots of rain splashed the windscreen.

The Cortina started.

After another bout of prolonged spluttering, the engine turned over and rumbled into life.

The driver smiled broadly, relief as much as anything causing his reaction. His companion slammed the bonnet shut then hurried to join him in the car. They pulled off immediately, but they'd hardly got twenty yards when they saw the Daimler heading towards them.

The driver looked at his companion and blew out his cheeks in relief, slowing down, allowing the Daimler to draw closer.

Su smiled and waved to the two men as she passed them.

The driver checked his rear-view mirror then swung the car round in the road, pulling in close behind Su.

His companion was wiping his oily hands on some cloth he'd found in the side pocket, but the driver reminded him that they'd have to take another look at the engine when they got back.

However, for now, all that mattered was that Mrs Chang and her children were safe. They could see both the kids in the back seat as they followed.

In fact, their relief at seeing her safe was so great that neither of them noticed the Citroën that had pulled in behind them, less than two car lengths away.

Had they been able to see the faces of the men inside perhaps they would not have felt so relaxed.

The Citroën kept a respectable distance, its occupants watching as the Daimler and Cortina drew nearer to the underground garage in Cadogan Place. They saw the first of the cars swing left and disappear down the ramp, followed closely by the Cortina.

The Citroën drove past, the man in the back seat

peering after the other two vehicles.

As the Citroën slowed down he reached inside his jacket.

The driver hesitated a moment longer then sped off.

Inside the underground car park, Su guided the Daimler back towards its parking space, the children still chattering happily.

In the rear-view mirror she could see that the driver of the Cortina was also parking, his companion already out of the car, walking across towards the Daimler. Probably to apologise, Su thought.

She smiled and switched off the engine.

It was then that the Daimler exploded.

## Eighty-Nine

Within the confines of the underground car park the ferocity of the blast seemed even more devastating.

The Daimler disappeared beneath a shrieking ball of orange and white flame, the vehicle torn apart by the massive detonation. Thick black smoke filled the underground chamber as blazing petrol ejaculated into the air before spreading across the concrete in a burning pool. Portions of the car's chassis were sent spinning, hurtling about like searing, red-hot shrapnel, some of it ploughing into the other cars parked there, a huge portion of the bonnet staving in the windscreen of a nearby Jag.

One wheel, the tyre ablaze, was sent flying across the garage, bouncing over the concrete, trailing smoke behind it.

The bodyguard who had been approaching the Daimler was lifted off his feet by the concussion blast that followed. He was hurled backwards, crashing to the ground and lying still as the hot wave washed over him.

Still in the Cortina his companion ducked low in the seat, part of his windscreen and one side window splintering as they were hit by flying debris and he noticed, with horror, that the burning petrol from the riven Daimler was flooding across the garage towards the damaged Jag, fiery tentacles of petrol enveloping the other car, creeping up towards its petrol tank.

The second explosion wasn't as savage as the first but, again, in such a confined space it seemed to be intensified. It felt as if the whole of the underground car park was ablaze. The concrete floor was hot, such was the fierceness of the fires raging all over it.

Twisted pieces of metal littered the ground and smoke was now swirling so densely it was difficult to see more than a foot or so in any direction. The stench of burning was overpowering, stronger even than the reeking petrol.

The first bodyguard pulled himself to his feet, feeling something warm running down his face. He touched two fingers to his cheek and saw blood, felt it running from a cut on his head. He didn't know whether it had been caused by him hitting the concrete so hard or by flying glass or metal.

He didn't care much either.

He staggered towards the Daimler, shielding his face against the blistering heat.

The remains of the vehicle were almost invisible behind a wall of flames which drew beads of perspiration from his skin. He moved closer but was forced back.

His companion clambered out of the car and ran across to join him, the heat from the blazing Jag adding to the choking atmosphere inside the garage. Smoke filled their lungs. A poisonous black cloud billowed from the wrecks and littered the air with millions of tiny cinders. Like black snow it settled on their clothes and faces, stinging their eyes.

The first bodyguard stared into the flames for a moment longer, not quite sure what to do.

Was he looking for some signs of life?

He knew in his mind that this was impossible.

There was no way of getting near the burning hulk. As he took a step to one side he saw something else covering the ground along with the burning oil and petrol.

Blood.

Spots of it were sprayed all over the concrete, some of it already blackened by the fire, congealing in the heat.

Closer to the car there were thicker, longer splashes of it.

He murmured something under his breath, but it was lost beneath the roar of the flames.

The driver tried to pull him away, realising that it was useless, but for a moment the other man hesitated, still trying to see through the sheet of fire. Finally he gave up and turned away, standing on something in the process.

Looking down he saw that it was a watch.

The strap was broken, bloodied and part of the face was missing.

It was a woman's watch. A Cartier.

He bent down to pick up the watch, feeling the heat from the metal as he held it in his hand, then he glanced at his companion who merely shook his head slowly, his eyes watering, red rimmed from where the smoke had stung them.

The driver pulled his companion away from the flames, seeing the blood streaming down his face.

The first man dropped the remains of the watch and allowed himself to be led back to the Cortina where he slumped against it, the sound of the explosions still ringing in his ears.

His companion told him to wait then he dashed off up the ramp leading out of the car park. Smoke was billowing thickly upwards towards the light now. The bodyguard felt perspiration stinging his forehead as he stood trying to suck in deep breaths. It was as if the fire had torn the breath from his lungs, scorched it away. Every inhalation stunk of petrol and cinders and he coughed, hawked and spat. The mucous landed a few feet from him, close to an object he couldn't make out at first.

Then he saw that it was part of Anna Chang's satchel.

He closed his eyes and despite the fires raging all around, he felt an icy chill creep over him.

## *Ninety*

It seemed to take him an eternity to reach the hospital. Chang didn't wait for a driver to take him. Upon hearing of the explosion he ran to his car and drove as fast as the rush-hour traffic would allow him, his mind racing, his thoughts tumbling. He tried to concentrate on the road, on the maddeningly slow trickle of cars. Anything to keep his mind off what he might find when he got to the hospital.

He'd left the car at the main entrance of St Stephen's hospital in the Fulham Road and bolted for the main doors, his heart thudding so hard against his ribs it threatened to burst.

As he entered the building his thoughts began crowding in on him. The stark reality of his situation crushing him like a huge iron first.

There'd been an accident. A bad accident. That was all he'd managed to take in. During the brief phone call he'd heard words like car bomb, explosion and fire but somehow they seemed unreal. He'd asked repeatedly about his wife and children, but had been given no answers.

Anger had given way to desperation then those emotions had become fear. Blinding, stomach-turning fear.

In his urgency to find Intensive Care, he almost collided with a man on crutches who was leaving.

They had all been brought here, that much he knew.

*His family.*

He punched buttons on the lift panel and stepped in, pressing himself against the rear wall, his eyes watching as each number lit up during the ascent.

*Please God let them live.*

He felt tears in his eyes.

*Tears of apprehension. Were such things possible?*

He felt as if his mind had been wiped clean, like a school blackboard. He couldn't even force a mental picture of his children into his thoughts.

*Let them live.*

The lift thumped to a halt and Chang hurried out.

There was another reception area head of him, a nurse seated behind it. A number of green lights were flashing on a console behind her, but she seemed unconcerned by them. Chang crossed to her.

'My name is Chang, my wife and children were brought in an hour or so ago . . .'

'Mr Chang.'

He turned as he heard his name and saw a young doctor approaching him.

The man was younger than Chang, in his late twenties perhaps. He had large green eyes which seemed to glow as if lit from within.

'My name's Jackson,' the doctor told him. 'Will you come with me, please?'

The doctor didn't avoid eye contact with Chang and as he stared into the Chinaman's eyes he saw the tears there.

'What happened to my family?' Chang said, breathlessly.

'There was an explosion.' Again the doctor tried to usher him along the corridor.

'Are they hurt?' Chang said.

'Mr Chang . . .'

'Tell me,' Chang snapped, gripping the doctor's arm tightly.

'Your son and daughter are dead. I'm very sorry.'

Chang clenched his teeth, his eyes bulging. In that expression the doctor saw not just pain but rage. He felt

Chang's fingers digging into his flesh.

'And my wife?' he said, his voice low but demanding.

'She's in intensive care. It doesn't look good, I'm afraid.'

Chang loosened his grip slightly.

'I must see her,' he said, quietly, allowing himself to be led along the corridor to a room with a glass panel in it. Peering through Chang could see a figure lying in the bed, but due to the bandages that covered the features, it was almost impossible to make out its sex let alone its identity. There were tubes running from the arms, nose and mouth, connected to a life-support unit. Even from outside he could hear the steady blip of an oscilloscope.

'Mr Chang, we've done as much as we can,' Jackson told him, wearily. 'I wish to God we could have done more.'

'My children,' Chang said, his voice catching. 'Did they . . . were they killed instantly?'

'Your son was, your daughter lived for fifteen minutes after she arrived here. There was nothing we could have done.'

Chang nodded, the first tear trickling down his cheek.

He followed the doctor into the room and looked down at his wife.

The nurse sitting at her bedside rose and left the room.

Chang sat where she had been sitting, the blip of the oscilloscope growing louder now.

*Don't die.*

'What are her chances?' he asked, never taking his eyes from her face.

The skin he could see was red. Burned.

Jackson merely shook his head.

'I have to be honest with you, Mr Chang,' he said. 'It's just a matter of time.'

'Why can't you do something for her?' Chang said, angrily.

'The injuries are too severe. She was almost dead when she was brought in. I'm very sorry.'

'So now I sit and watch her die. That's what you're telling me? That's all I can do?'

Jackson could only nod.

'Please, leave us,' said Chang, softly, his gaze still fixed on Su's ravaged features.

Jackson hesitated a moment then stepped outside.

Chang held Su's bandaged hand, his gaze never leaving her. He felt numb, as if his body had been pumped full of iced water. Every now and then he looked at the screen of the oscilloscope and watched the glowing dot there. All other sounds around him seemed to fade. The world could have disappeared for all he knew or cared. Everything he knew was inside this room.

*Except his children.*

For fleeting seconds the image of their faces came to him and he had difficulty fighting back the tears.

*Not Su as well. Please.*

The oscilloscope bleeped, faltered then bleeped again, levelled out, rose then fell again.

Chang got to his feet, leant over Su.

The blip levelled out.

*Don't die.*

Rose once more.

He leant forward and kissed her gauze-covered forehead.

'I love you,' he whispered.

The screen was showing a flatline.

There was a single strident whine in the air. No rhythmic bleeping, just that one unbroken, discordant electronic scream.

Chang heard footsteps hurrying along the corridor.

Tears flowed down his cheeks.

'Don't die,' he murmured.

The electronic scream seemed to grow stronger.

'Su, please,' he said, more loudly, gripping her hand.

Two nurses and the doctor hurried into the room.

'You'll have to leave,' Jackson told him.

Chang wouldn't let go of her hand.

'Don't die,' he shouted.

One of the nurses tried to pull him away.

Jackson was already pumping her chest with both hands.

'No,' Chang roared, his cheeks glistening.

The oscilloscope remained flat.

Jackson pressed his stethoscope to Su's chest, shook his head. Pumped her chest once more. Listened.

He bowed his head wearily.

Chang closed his eyes and bellowed at the top of his voice, a sound of raw suffering which drummed in the ears of those around him.

He dropped to his knees beside the bed and wept.


# Ninety-One


Sean Doyle took a large swig from the mug of tea then sat back in his seat and reached for a cigarette.

The half a dozen other tables in the café were unoccupied and Doyle had just the sound of a radio for company, but his mind was not on his surroundings. He was more concerned with the photo of the man before him. It lay on the Formica-topped table, looking up at him challengingly.

Joey Chang.

Doyle lit his cigarette and blew a stream of smoke towards the photo.

*The man who had ordered his death.*

He'd asked D.S. Henderson for a copy of the picture and the policeman had complied. He'd also promised to get in touch with Doyle if there were any further developments regarding Chang or any other members of the Tai Hung Chai.

Doyle took a bite of the sausage roll now going cold beside him, wiping pieces of pastry from his mouth.

*Why had Chang ordered his death?*

What fucking quarrel did the Triads have with him?

He kept his eyes fixed on the photo, committing the features to memory, storing them away for future reference.

The stolen army guns were in London now, in the hands of the Tai Hung Chai, but Doyle really didn't give a shit about the guns. He'd find them when he found the Tai Hung Chai, but their recovery was secondary to him. He wanted to find the fuckers who'd tried to kill him. Chang in particular.

First the IRA, now the Triads.

*Popular, aren't you?*

He turned and looked out of the window of the café, watching the people pass by on the pavement beyond, illuminated by the red neon sign on the café front.

Doyle picked up the photo of Chang and pushed it into his pocket then headed out into the street, his hair ruffled by the cold breeze which blew through the city.

He walked down Shaftesbury Avenue, hands dug into his pockets. When he reached Gerrard Street he crossed the road, walking slowly beneath the huge Pagoda entrance to Chinatown. For every white face now, he saw one Chinese.

How many of the men he passed belonged to a Triad?

Judging by what Henderson had told him probably most of them. Doyle walked on like some kind of spaced-out tourist looking around him at the endless array of restaurants and shops, all brightly lit.

He saw two or three men standing in a doorway talking animatedly and slowed down as he passed, aware of them gazing at him.

A dizzying combination of smells filled his nostrils as he walked along, each restaurant belching out a different aroma. He glanced through windows to see people inside eating, laughing, talking.

Doyle wondered how many of these places were owned by the Tai Hung Chai.

He could see Henderson's problem. How the fuck did

you infiltrate something like this? Behind every legitimate business there was probably another illegal one.

And somewhere here were the Tai Hung Chai and those army rifles.

Doyle stopped on a corner and lit a cigarette, meeting the gaze of two youths who passed him, casting disdainful looks in his direction. He watched them as they rounded a corner out of sight then he walked on, past the video shops, the grocers' shops, the tailors' and yet more restaurants. All of them displaying their names in dazzling neon: MING WAH BAKERY, LOO FONG CANTONESE CUISINE. Many of the signs were in Chinese. Doyle could only guess at what they said.

He knew those guns were here somewhere, maybe not hidden in one of these shops or restaurants, but someone in this seething community knew their location. And Doyle intended finding them.

The guns *and* Joey Chang.

And if it meant ripping the whole fucking place apart, he'd find them.

## Ninety-Two

They had arrived at his flat thirty minutes earlier and at first Joey Chang had been surprised to see them, but he had overcome his initial shock and now stood with his back to them, peering out the window blankly into the road below, a drink cradled in his hand.

On chairs and the sofa behind him, Wo Fen, Frankie Wong and Jackie Ti sat in silence, Wo looking around the flat, Ti sipping at his drink, Wong watching Chang.

They had offered their sympathies when they'd arrived and Chang had been thankful, telling the elders how they graced his home with their presence. His words may as well have been those of an automaton. He spoke without realising what he said, his mind occupied only with thoughts of his dead family. Every time he turned he saw photos of them dotted about the sitting room and the renewed realisation of their loss seemed to hit him like a sledgehammer. He felt as if the life had been wrenched from him and, if he was to feel this way for the foreseeable future, then he wished that life would indeed leave him. At least in death he wouldn't have to endure such pain.

He sipped his drink, trying to push thoughts of Su and the children aside but also feeling guilty when he attempted such a difficult task. Why should he deny himself the thoughts of them? Thoughts and memories were all he had left now.

'We came to speak with you because we respect your opinions,' Wo told him. 'You have great wisdom for one so young.'

Chang didn't speak, merely took another sip of his drink.

'We realise how difficult things are for you at the moment,' Ti added.

*Do you? How could you ever know?*

'It is not a matter which can be delayed though,' Wo persisted.

Chang nodded slowly, his gaze still fixed, his back to them.

'When did the Hip Sing come to you?' he said, finally, turning to face Wo and the others.

'Representatives approached us last night,' Wo told him.

'And they asked for peace?' Chang said.

'They know they're beaten,' Wong added, triumphantly. 'They want an end to the war.'

'We have regained face,' Ti added.

Chang seemed unimpressed.

'And if you agree, how long do you think you can trust them?' he said. 'How long before they try to take over again?'

'What are you saying?' Wo wanted to know.

'There has been enough killing,' Ti said.

'I know that,' Chang snapped. 'I know it better than anyone.'

'We understand how you feel . . .' Wong began.

'No you don't, Frankie, and I hope you never have to,' Chang told him. 'None of you know how I feel. Everything I ever loved has been taken from me. Taken by the Hip Sing.'

'But now they have offered to make peace, we can be sure there will be no more killing,' Ti said.

'I don't care if there's more killing,' Chang shouted. '*I've* got nothing left to lose.' He ran a hand through his hair and sighed.

'The war is over, Joey,' Wong said. 'The Hip Sing have lost, they want peace.'

'And you?' Chang demanded, looking at each man in turn. 'What do *you* want?'

'We have what we wanted,' Wo told him. 'We are in control again, there is no one else to challenge us now.'

'I don't want peace,' Chang said, flatly. 'I want the war to go on. I want it to go on until every single member of the Hip Sing is dead.'

'At the beginning you were the one who did not want violence,' Wong reminded him.

'It would serve no purpose to continue fighting the Hip Sing,' Wo added.

'It would serve *my* purpose,' Chang shouted.

'Which is?' Wo enquired.

'Revenge,' Chang snarled.

There was a long silence, finally broken by Wo Fen.

'We came here to speak reasonably of this offer made by the Hip Sing,' he said, quietly. 'To seek your guidance, your wisdom and your advice. Is that advice that we continue fighting? For if it is then we must discard it.'

'So you will make peace with the Hip Sing?' Chang snapped.

Wo nodded.

'I will have no part of it,' Chang told him. 'I will have revenge on them.'

'You are supposed to be a reasonable man, do not forget your office,' Ti reminded him.

'Fuck my office,' Chang snapped. 'And fuck all of you if you think I will make peace with the men who murdered my family.'

'There is still much we can do,' Wo said. 'This war must end now.'

'So you are accepting the Hip Sing's offer?' Chang said.

Wo nodded.

'Then I want no more part of the Tai Hung Chai,' Chang said. 'We are brothers no longer.'

'You don't know what you're saying,' Wong said, getting to his feet.

'I know *exactly* what I'm saying, Frankie, I've never been more sure of anything in my life,' Chang told him. 'I will have revenge against the Hip Sing, even if I have to fight them alone.'

Wo did not speak, he merely pressed his fingertips together contemplatively.

'And if you try to stop me I will fight you too,' Chang said, defiantly. 'Now, get out of my home.' He glared at Wo who got to his feet.

Jackie Ti followed.

Wong hesitated a moment.

'How long have we been friends?' he said. 'Ten years?'

'Longer,' Chang told him.

'I cannot let you do this, Joey.'

'Then help me.'

'How? I cannot go against the elders, if they want to accept the Hip Sing's offer to end the war then I cannot violate that wish.'

'I don't want you to help me fight the Hip Sing.'

'Then how *can* I help?'

Chang held his companion's gaze, his eyes filled with tears.

'Understand me,' he said, quietly. 'That is all I ask.'

Wong nodded slowly then extended his right hand.

Chang shook it warmly.

Wong turned and walked out. Chang heard the door close behind him.

'He isn't thinking straight,' said Frankie Wong, looking at the two older men. They sat on the back seat of the limo, Ti looking distractedly out of the side window.

'He must not be allowed to destroy this peace, this victory. We have fought too hard for it, too many people have died for it. *You* should know that,' Wo said. 'Decisions are made for the good of the whole organisation, not just individuals.'

'Joey isn't a fighter,' Wong told them.

'Men with vengeance in their hearts are dangerous,' Wo offered. 'If Chang seeks vengeance against the Hip Sing then he betrays us all. I cannot allow that to happen.'

Wo reached for the car phone and dialled.

It was answered almost immediately.


# Ninety-Three


What did they know?

What did *any* of them know?

They didn't understand the pain he felt, the sense of loss. The most important thing in *their* lives hadn't been torn from them.

Joey Chang downed another glass of whisky and sat down on the edge of the bed, looking around.

There was a photo of Su on the dressing table. It had been taken three years earlier. A little surprise she'd arranged for his birthday. She was wearing a red dress, her face immaculately made up, one hand on her hip the other pushing up her hair at the back. She could have passed for a model in that shot. He had a smaller version of the same picture in his wallet.

What did *they* know about losing a woman like that?

On the bedside table closest to what had been his side of the bed was a framed picture of himself and Su on their wedding day.

The years had been kinder to her than to him, Chang thought. Where he had unmistakable lines and creases around his eyes and across his forehead, Su seemed to have escaped unblemished. He sat looking at the picture for long moments then got to his feet and walked across to it, sliding the drawer open in the bedside cabinet.

Beneath several shirts and handkerchiefs, all arranged with the neatness Su had been so proud of, was a 9mm Mamba automatic in a shoulder holster.

Chang took the pistol out and laid it on the bed carefully, studying the sleek lines of the gun for a second. He slipped on the holster, took a box of ammunition from the drawer and flipped it open, regarding the 9mm slugs blankly for a moment. Then he reached for the pistol, pressed the magazine release button and caught it as it fell from the butt. Sitting down on the edge of the bed once more he began pushing shells into the magazine.

From the other side of the bed Su and the two children watched him impassively from a black-and-white photo.

Chang finished his drink and, still holding the Mamba, he got to his feet and headed towards Anna's bedroom. He paused before the door, as if she were inside and his intrusion might disturb her.

*If only that could be.*

He reached out and turned the door knob, noticing that his hand was shaking slightly.

The silence inside the room seemed to close in around him, as thick and oppressive as his grief. He crossed to her wardrobe and looked in at her clothes. He reached out and touched one of her coats.

Chang felt tears brimming in his eyes. He swallowed

hard, gripped the Mamba more tightly in his fist.

He spoke her name very softly then turned and walked out of the room, closing the door reverently behind him, pausing a moment before repeating a similar ritual in his son's room.

Toys were scattered over the bedroom floor. Toy soldiers, cars, tanks. A Game-boy. Chang picked it up and switched it on, studying the brightly flashing images for a second.

Michael had loved it.

He hurled the machine away, his anger now seething inside him, competing with his pain for mastery.

And they told him that the war against the Hip Sing was over.

They who had lost nothing.

The elders. The men of the Tai Hung Chai who were to be respected.

Fuck them.

Chang jammed the Mamba back into his shoulder holster and wandered back out into the hall.

How dare they tell him it was over?

It would never be over for him. Only death could release him from his pain.

But he would not die in vain. He would kill as many of the Hip Sing as he could before he gave up life. He owed it to his murdered family.

The ringing of the doorbell startled him and he froze for a moment, looking towards the front door.

The two-tone chime sounded once again, followed by a loud banging on the woodwork.

Chang moved towards it, squinting through the spy-hole there.

He saw two men on the other side.

White men.

They knocked again, more insistently.

Chang slipped on the chain but hesitated before opening the door.

'Who is it?' he called.

'Police,' one of the men shouted back. 'Let us in, Mr Chang.'

*A trap?*

'Show me some ID,' he snapped. 'Hold it up.'

The first of the men produced a slim wallet and held it up to the spy-hole in the door.

Chang could see the initials CID on it.

*It could be fake.*

Something told him to take off the chain. He reached for it slowly then let it fall, pulling open the door.

'Mr Joseph Chang?' said the first man and now Chang could see that not only were there plain-clothes men there but two uniformed officers as well. They pushed past him into the flat.

'We're arresting you for illegal possession of a firearm,' said the first man. 'Also for conspiracy to commit murder. You have the right to remain silent.' He took the gun from Chang. 'Anything you say may be used in evidence.'

Chang did not resist. He knew it was futile.

The other plain-clothes man handed him a jacket which he slipped on, standing obediently in the hallway as the uniformed men performed a brief search of the flat.

They were still there when the first plain-clothes man took his arm and pulled him towards the door.

Chang shook loose angrily, glaring at the man.

'I can walk without your help,' he hissed.

There was a photo of Su and the children on a small table just inside the hall.

He looked down at it as he walked out.

Behind him the second plain-clothes man walked out, accidentally knocking into the table.

The photo fell to the floor with a thud.

# Ninety-Four

Doyle heard the phone ringing as he stepped from the shower. He quickly snatched up a towel and wrapped it around himself, leaving a trail of wet footprints across the carpet as he made for the phone. As he reached for it he glanced across at the clock opposite and frowned slightly.

9.46 p.m.

Who the fuck was bothering him at this time?

He wiped his hands on the towel then picked up the receiver.

'Hello.'

'Doyle. This is D.S. Henderson from Bow Street.'

'What can I do for you?'

'It's more the other way round really. Something's happened, I thought you might be interested.'

'Go on.'

'We pulled in Joey Chang earlier today, we've got him here now for questioning. Someone blew his family away.'

Doyle gripped the receiver more tightly.

'Where did you pick him up?' the counter terrorist wanted to know.

'At his own gaff about four hours ago. The weird thing is we were tipped off.'

'By who?'

'They didn't leave their bleeding names,' Henderson said, chuckling. 'But I reckon someone's stitched him up. Whoever called told us where to find him. They even told us what kind of fucking gun he'd be carrying.'

'Somebody in his own organisation?'

'It looks that way.'

'Has he said much?'

310

'That's the curious thing. He's hardly stopped talking since he was brought in. Most of these Triads, they usually keep quiet but he's answered all our questions about the Tai Hung Chai.'

'Has he mentioned the IRA or the stolen guns?'

'That's one thing he *hasn't* talked about, but he's given us names of the high-ups in his organisation, which makes me even more convinced that he was set up and I reckon he knows it too.'

'I want to talk to him.'

'Forget it, Doyle, there's nothing he'd tell you that he wouldn't tell us.'

'I can be very persuasive.'

'I bet you can. Thanks for the offer but forget it. Chang's more use to me with all his fucking teeth and I get the feeling that if you came down here he might be missing a few by the time you'd finished.'

'I need to talk to him.'

'Why? I just told you he's been cooperative.'

'Some of the shit he's involved in is my business, Henderson.'

'No way. At the moment it's strictly police business. It's got nothing to do with you or anyone else in the Counter Terrorist Unit.'

Doyle kept a firm grip on the receiver, the knot of muscles at the side of his jaw throbbing angrily.

'If you come down here,' Henderson continued, 'I'll make sure you don't get past the front door.'

'Yeah, right,' Doyle hissed, irritably. 'Has anybody asked him about the fucking guns?'

'I don't know yet.'

'Well don't you think you ought to check it out?'

'It'll be taken care of. I'll let you know what happens.'

'What happens to Chang after you're finished questioning him?'

'He spends the night here. He's due to be transferred to the Scrubs at nine o'clock tomorrow morning.'

Doyle nodded to himself.

'Look, thanks for the call, Henderson,' he said, reaching for his cigarettes and pushing one between his lips. He didn't light it.

'My pleasure. You just take it easy now. Chang's not going anywhere,' the policeman said, smugly. 'Not until the morning anyway.'

'Cheers,' said Doyle and hung up.

He finally lit the cigarette and sucked on it gently.

*The Scrubs, eh?*

He headed back into the bathroom.

# Ninety-Five

'We betrayed him.'

Frankie Wong's voice was loud, full of anger as h paced back and forth.

'We all swore oaths of blood when we became a part ( the organisation. We vowed to help one another and ye we have betrayed one of our own.'

'It was not betrayal,' Wo Fen said.

'Joey Chang is sitting in a *gweilo*'s jail even now. H needs our help, yet we turn our backs on him,' Won continued.

'He gave us no choice,' Jackie Ti offered.

'He would have done harm to the organisation,' Wo Fe added.

'So you betrayed him?' snapped Wong.

'We had no choice,' Wo told the younger man. 'There no point in going over what has happened. Chang wou not accept our way. We could not risk the enti organisation for his sake.'

'So, instead, you make peace with our enemies. You down with them,' Wong hissed.

'Where is your respect?' Ti snarled.

'You have my respect, master. All of you have my respect,' Wong said, raising his arm in a sweeping gesture designed to embrace all of the older men who faced him. 'But Joey Chang has my respect too, *and* my loyalty.'

'So, Chang has your loyalty, but we do not?' David Lun said.

'Where is *your* loyalty to Chang? If you had any you would not have betrayed him,' Wong said, challengingly.

There was a babble of conversation finally quelled as Wo Fen raised one hand.

He studied the faces of each of his companions carefully before speaking, his words slow, as if each one were being selected for maximum effect.

'We have won a victory against the Hip Sing,' he said. 'We have won the war, let us not lose the peace by squabbling amongst ourselves. Chang gave us no alternative. He would not see reason. He could not be allowed to endanger what we have fought so hard for.'

There were murmurs of approval from some of the others in the room.

Frankie Wong was unimpressed.

'You would discard a man so easily who has helped you so much?' he said.

'He knew the rules of our organisation, he was bound by the very oaths of which you spoke,' Ti said. 'He chose to disobey them.'

'He disobeyed nothing,' Wong snapped. 'He merely spoke of his feelings and for that he is punished with betrayal.'

'Would you have the war against the Hip Sing continued?' Wo demanded. 'Would you turn away their offer of peace? For the sake of one man?'

Wong swallowed hard.

'He is our brother,' he said, quietly. 'And we betrayed him. That is all I know.'

'If caring for the rest of our organisation is betrayal then so be it,' Wo told him.

313

'Well, I want no part of it,' Wong said, defiantly. 'I will not sit around and watch him rot away in one of the white skin's jails. He is a good man.'

'We do not dispute that, but his anger was harmful to us,' Wo said. 'He spoke not with reason. His thoughts were those of an unbalanced man. He did not consider his reactions, nor how they would affect the rest of us. He spoke and thought selfishly. He has no place amongst us now.'

'Why do you find it so difficult to see this?' Ti added.

'I see only your treachery,' Wong snapped.

'Then perhaps there is no place for you here, either,' Wo told him.

Wong held his gaze for long moments then turned and headed towards the door.

'*I* will not turn my back on Joey Chang,' he snapped, angrily.

And he was gone.


# Ninety-Six


Joey Chang woke from a fitful sleep, aroused by the hand shaking his arm. He rolled over, his eyes opening myopically, glancing around for the source of this disturbance.

As he pulled himself up he saw the uniformed officer looking down at him.

Chang regarded the man balefully for a moment then lay back down on the bed.

It was small, narrow even for a man of average size and Chang had to be careful not to fall off when he turned over.

The cell which housed the bed was less than twelve feet

square and, beside the bed, it was home to just a bucket (which Chang had been forced to use during the night) and a small table. On this table stood the remains of his breakfast, brought an hour earlier. Pieces of bacon and egg were sticking up from thick, rapidly congealing grease. Chang looked at the food and felt sick.

'Come on, time to go,' said the uniformed man, reaching for him, touching his arm.

Chang pulled away and sat up, rubbing his face with both hands. He felt as if he hadn't slept for a month. He could taste something sour in his mouth and, as he got to his feet, he spat into the bucket nearby.

'Can't I even wash?' he said, irritably.

'You can do that when you get to the Scrubs,' the policeman told him, snapping on a pair of handcuffs.

There was another uniformed man standing in the doorway watching impassively.

Chang ran his handcuffed hands through his hair and yawned, allowing himself to be prodded from the cell by the first guard. The two uniformed policemen walked behind him as he moved into the corridor, passing other cells, their doors tightly closed.

There was another door up ahead, guarded by yet another policeman. As Chang and his two warders approached, the man opened the door, stepped back to allow them through, then joined the melancholy little procession.

Beyond, Chang could see that they were heading towards the rear of the police station, the back door opening out onto a concrete yard still dark from recently fallen rain.

High above, the sky was filled with cloud, great thick grey expanses which threatened to drench the capital once again. The buildings surrounding the yard seemed to have been fashioned from stones the same colour. Despite the overcast weather, Chang shielded his eyes as he stepped out into the daylight, the handcuffs rattling as he did so.

A black transit van and a single police car were parked there and the rear doors of the van were open. Inside Chang could see another police officer.

There was a narrow thoroughfare leading into and out of the yard, hardly wide enough to get the van through, Chang thought. Two more uniformed men were standing beside the car, watching as he was escorted to the van. They both climbed in and Chang heard the car's engine start up.

One of the policemen close to him nodded towards the van, an indication that Chang should get in.

It was then that he heard the roar.

The black Astra sped along the narrow passageway into the yard, the driver twisting the steering wheel savagely, bringing the car around almost full circle, its tyres screaming on the concrete.

Chang stood, dumbstruck, as the Astra shot forward, slamming into the side of the police car, the impact hurling the driver across his companion in the passenger seat. The Astra reversed, narrowly missing one of the uniformed men who leapt to one side, trying to pull Chang with him but the Chinaman stepped away.

The Astra thudded into the van, the man inside toppling forward, sprawling on the concrete.

Chang saw the driver's side of the Astra open, saw the figure jump out.

Whoever it was wore a balaclava, just the eyes and mouth cut away.

The Chinaman saw the gun that the driver held.

He felt a hand grab his arm, felt himself being hurled against the Astra and then across the back seat.

One of the uniformed men ran at the driver and Chang saw the man swing the pistol round, using it like a club striking the policeman hard across the bridge of the nose. Blood burst from the shattered appendage.

Then the driver was inside the car again, stomping on the accelerator, causing the Astra to hurtle forward. The back wheels spun madly for a second time then gained

316

purchase, and the car roared up the narrow alley and out into the road.

Chang kept ducked low across the back seat as the Astra sped out into traffic, slamming into a taxi, sending it skidding across the path of some oncoming cars. A chorus of horns filled the air, punctuated by the sound of broken glass as headlights were shattered in collisions.

The Astra weaved in and out of cars, bumping those it couldn't overtake, shunting them aside in an effort to get away.

The driver looked into the rear-view mirror to see if he was being followed and even when he was satisfied that no police cars were in pursuit he still didn't slow down, dragging down hard on the steering wheel as the car headed into Drury Lane.

Chang also looked out of the rear window to see if they were being tailed, his mind reeling.

Someone had taken a great risk to get him out.

*But who?*

Chang was aware of the car slowing down. He saw the driver pulling at the balaclava, tugging it free.

'We've got to change cars,' the man told him.

He turned and looked at Chang.

'Keep your head down and your fucking mouth shut. Got it?' hissed Sean Doyle.


## Ninety-Seven


'Who are you?'

Joey Chang's words echoed around the empty buildings, bouncing off the walls, amplified by the stillness within.

He had no idea where he was or what this place was. All he knew was it stunk.

The red-brick walls were dark with mould and damp and the whole place smelt fusty, as if he and his captor were the only people to enter it for many years. The windows, those that weren't boarded up, were so filthy they were opaque. Outside they were spattered with bird shit. Inside, the grime looked as if it had been applied with a trowel.

There were oil stains all over the floor and Chang fancied that he could smell petrol in the air. Piles of rubbish – empty cans and crisp packets, pieces of yellowing newspaper – covered most of the dust-shrouded floor. The stench of rotting matter adding to the overall odour of neglect that permeated the place.

Every now and then he heard a rumble from overhead, a sound he finally managed to place as that of trains. Each time one passed by tiny flakes of discoloured plaster would drift from the roof like filthy snow, some of it settling on him.

He was seated on a battered wooden chair, one of the back legs held on by just a length of string wound tightly around it. There were a number of orange boxes scattered about the place, two of which had been pulled across in front of him and upturned.

Sean Doyle sat on one of them, a cigarette jammed between his lips. He watched Chang impassively, his steely grey eyes betraying no emotion. Doyle took another drag on the cigarette then ground it out beneath his boot.

He saw the uncertainty in Chang's expression, but found that the Chinaman held his gaze.

*So, you're the fucker that ordered me to be killed, eh?*

'If you're going to kill me, you've gone to a lot of trouble about it,' Chang said.

'Maybe,' said Doyle, quietly. 'But that's my business isn't it, *Mr* Chang?'

'You know me?'

'I know every fucking thing about you. Your name

318

what you do, what you are. I know about your organisation. I know about your links with the IRA.'

Chang swallowed and Doyle was not slow to catch the brief expression of concern which flitted across the Chinaman's features.

He smiled thinly.

'Yeah, I know about that shit,' Doyle continued. 'I even know about those fucking guns that Paul Riordan traded you for the drugs.'

'You know so much about me, you have me at a disadvantage.'

'You're fucking right I have,' Doyle snapped, reaching for another cigarette.

Chang shifted uncomfortably on his seat, the handcuffs jangling as he moved his arms. He looked down at his wrists and saw that there were red marks where the cuffs had chafed his skin.

'What do you want me for?' Chang asked.

'I need some information. About those guns you bought off Riordan.'

'Who *are* you?'

'You're not really in a position to ask questions, Chang, but since you asked I'll tell you. My name's Doyle. You ordered my death. I want to know why?'

'It was part of our arrangement with the IRA.'

'You are the *Pak Tsz Sin* for the Tai Hung Chai Triad, right?'

The Chinaman nodded.

'And all hits are made with your say so,' Doyle continued. 'I know because I've done my homework. Three of your slit-eyed cronies tried to kill me in Belfast about a week ago. Ring any bells?'

Chang didn't answer, he merely held Doyle's gaze.

'Your boys fucked up, as you can see,' the counter terrorist said, blowing out a stream of smoke.

'So you went to the trouble of springing me from the police just so you could kill me?'

'Like I said, I need information.'

'You seem to know everything. How can *I* help you?' There was scorn in Chang's voice.

'Those guns, where are they?' Doyle demanded.

'I don't know.'

'Bollocks.'

Doyle slid a hand inside his jacket and pulled out the Beretta. He worked the slide on the 92F, chambering a round.

'Kill me,' Chang said, defiantly. 'Death holds no fear for me now.'

'What is that? Some kind of Eastern Confucius bullshit? You have no fear of death. Join the fucking club.'

'My wife and children are dead, there is nothing left for me now anyway. Do you expect me to be afraid of dying?'

'I don't give a shit what you're afraid of.'

A train rumbled by overhead, the sound filling the entire place momentarily. More fragments of plaster fell from the roof.

'When you've lost everything, Doyle, death is to be welcomed, not feared,' Chang said.

'Don't try to tell me about loss,' Doyle rasped.

*I lost Georgie.*

The counter terrorist leapt to his feet and kicked out at the chair on which Chang sat. It went flying, the Chinaman crashing to the floor. He rolled over in the dust and filth.

As he looked up he saw that Doyle had the Beretta pointing at him.

Chang raised himself up slightly, handcuffed arms supporting him.

'The guns?' Doyle snapped.

'I can take you to them,' Chang said.

'Why should I trust you?'

'You have no choice.'

'Bullshit,' snapped Doyle and pulled back the hammer.

He took aim and fired.

320

# Ninety-Eight

The retort of the pistol inside the building was deafening. The barrel flamed, the Beretta bucking in Doyle's hand as he fired.

The 9mm bullet struck the handcuffs close to the right-hand steel band and split the chain. Pieces of metal flew into the air and, as the bullet powered into the floor, dust erupted upwards like a tiny geyser.

Chang rolled to one side, his ears ringing, blinded momentarily by dirt and dust.

Doyle looked down at him, the automatic still aimed at the Chinaman.

'Just to let you know,' the counter terrorist said. 'I could kill you any time I wanted to.'

'And once I've shown you where the guns are hidden, how can I be sure you won't kill me then?' Chang wanted to know.

'You can't. But what's the big deal? I thought men who had nothing didn't fear death,' he said mockingly.

Chang raised himself up onto his knees then stood up, brushing the dust from his clothes.

'You know who set you up?' the counter terrorist asked.

'What are you talking about?'

'You were arrested at home, right? The police said whoever tipped them off gave them details. They even knew what kind of gun you'd be carrying. It'd have to be someone pretty close to you to know *that* kind of information, wouldn't it?'

Chang exhaled deeply and reached for the broken chair. He perched on the edge of it.

'You knew you'd been set up, didn't you?' Doyle

continued. 'That's why you named names in your organisation when you were questioned. Why did they blow the gaff on you, Chang? What makes you so fucking dangerous to them?'

'Another organisation, the Hip Sing, killed my family,' Chang said, quietly. 'I wanted revenge against them. My own people said no. They couldn't afford the bloodshed between our two lodges to continue.'

'So they shopped you to get you out of the way?'

Chang nodded.

'They wanted peace, they've got it,' the Chinaman said. 'There will be talks, a meeting between the elders of each lodge and the peace will be secured.'

'When will this happen?'

'In the next day or two.'

'Where?'

'I couldn't be sure.'

'Have a guess.'

'There are a number of places where it could happen. A hotel in the Strand, a restaurant in Gerrard Street. It's difficult to say.'

'And the guns?'

'I can take you to them.'

Doyle nodded slowly and gestured towards the door of the building.

'Do it now,' he said.

'Can I ask *you* a question, Doyle?'

'What?'

'You're not a policeman, that much is obvious. Why are you so interested in my organisation?'

'I'm doing a job, Chang. Someone told me to find those guns and that's what I'm going to do, but when you tried to have me killed in Belfast you made this business personal. I'm attending to business, that's all.'

'Then why go to the trouble of snatching me from the police?'

'I needed you to get close to your organisation. You're my ticket in, Chang.'

The two men locked stares for a moment.

'And after I lead you to the guns, what then?' Chang wanted to know.

'What do you mean?' Doyle asked.

'Will you turn me in to the police again?'

'I might just blow your fucking head off. Right?'

'Let me find the men who killed my family, Doyle. At least do that for me.'

'I don't make deals, Chang. But I have got a good memory and the thing that sticks in it at the moment is that you ordered my death. So be grateful you've stayed alive this fucking long.'

## Ninety-Nine

'Didn't anybody get a look at his bloody face?' shouted D.S. Nick Henderson, angrily.

The other policemen around him could only shake their heads.

'We traced the first car,' one said. 'He'd dumped it.'

'Of course he fucking dumped it,' snapped Henderson.

'Do you reckon it was Triads, guv?' D.C. John Layton asked.

'Who the hell else would want to snatch Chang?' Henderson said, irritably.

'It doesn't make much sense though, does it?' Layton persisted. 'They grass him up then, twenty-four hours later, they spring him.'

'Don't ask me to make any sense out of how these bastards think,' the D.S. said, raising his arms despairingly. He sat down on the edge of his desk and looked at the men around him, both plain clothed and uniformed. 'Whoever it was must have been watching this place. They knew when he was being moved, don't ask me how. They took us by surprise. End of story. We fucked up. Now we have to get him back.'

'How?' Layton wanted to know.

'I'll tell you one thing,' Henderson said. 'We're not crawling around every rat hole and fucking sewer in Chinatown to do it. Chances are Chang's miles away by now anyway, he might even be on a plane back to Hong Kong. If his own Triad sprung him then they'll want to keep him hidden until the heat dies down. If another Triad snatched him then he's probably dead by now.'

'Another Triad wouldn't risk the kind of attack that was made just to get Chang,' said one of the uniformed men. 'He was out of action, they knew he wasn't going anywhere.'

Henderson nodded.

'So, odds on, it was his own people,' the D.S. said. 'Well if it was, let's see how they react to some time in the cells. Pull them in. All of them. I want all the big nobs in the Tai Hung Chai arrested. Got it?'

'On what charges?' asked Layton.

'Picking their noses in public, dropping noodles on the fucking pavement. I don't *care*,' Henderson snapped. 'Check out their form, you'll find something, but I want them *all* brought in this morning. Let's move it.'

The shutters at the two large front windows and also on the glass door of the restaurant were closed. Anyone passing by in the street outside could not see into the building.

Most of the tables in the place had been pushed to one side to make way for one large table which occupied the centre of the floor. It was spread with a freshly laundered tablecloth. There were ten seats set up around it. Five on either side.

Behind the large table was a door which led into the kitchen. To the right was another door which shielded the lounge area from the restaurant and the bar.

To the right of the table was an enormous fish tank, lit from behind by a pink light. Many different kinds of tropical fish swam back and forth in the warm water.

Frankie Wong watched one of the angel fish, smiling at its grace as it slipped through the water.

Behind him, Wo Fen, Jackie Ti and David Lun were taking up position behind the table.

Peter Sum was standing beside the bar sipping a glass of water.

'Is this what you really want?' Wong asked, his eyes still on the fish tank. 'You settle for peace when we could have driven the Hip Sing out of London forever?'

'The war is over, Frankie,' Wo Fen told him. 'That is all that matters. We have won. There is no need to spill more blood.'

'Tell that to Joey Chang,' said Wong, pressing his index finger to the glass of the tank, watching as half a dozen brilliantly coloured tetras darted away.

'The peace will be made this morning,' Lun added. 'It is over.'

'And you think you can trust them to keep that peace?' Wong asked.

'Yes,' Wo told him. 'They will be here within the hour. I want an end to this talk, do you understand?'

Wong didn't answer.

They climbed into two cars for the short journey from Beak Street. Five men from the Hip Sing. They spoke only briefly, tersely, to one another.

In the leading car, Billy Chi settled himself into the back seat and closed his eyes meditatively. He remained like that for a moment or two before reaching forward and tapping the driver on the shoulder.

The Jag pulled away, the Mercedes behind it following.

The large white transit van which followed remained two or three car lengths back.

Waiting.

# One Hundred

Doyle banged hard on the Saab's horn, glaring angrily at the car in front.

'Come on, for fuck's sake,' he hissed, peering forward to see a queue of traffic building up ahead.

A large lorry was reversing into the street, blocking most of Gower Street. Other cars were also showing their impatience and, as Doyle sat drumming on the steering wheel with his fingers, a chorus of blaring horns filled the air.

Next to him, Joey Chang sat back in his seat, peering to his right and left, only vaguely interested in the blockage that was holding them up. He looked down at the dashboard clock.

9.57 a.m.

He wondered how much longer they would be stuck in this traffic.

'And you're sure about these guns?' Doyle said suddenly, looking at Chang.

'As sure as I can be,' the Chinaman told him.

'What the fuck is that supposed to mean? You said you knew where they were.'

'As far as I know they are still there, but you cannot blame me if they've been moved.'

'Who else am I supposed to blame? I'm telling you, Chang, those fucking guns had better be where you say they are.'

'And what do you propose to do when we find them? Walk in and take them? Do you think they will allow you to do that?'

'They'd be *very* stupid to try and stop me.'

'They'll kill you.'

'Let them try. Anyway, if they kill *me*, you're going with me.' The counter terrorist noticed that the traffic was beginning to move.

He guided the Saab out into the line of cars, winding down his side window far enough to toss out the butt of his cigarette.

As the counter terrorist did this, Chang looked across at him and saw the butt of the 92F nestling in its shoulder holster.

He knew that Doyle wore at least one more gun in another shoulder holster, he'd seen it before the counter terrorist pulled on his jacket as they'd left the lock-up twenty minutes earlier.

Chang knew he would have to time his move to perfection when the moment came.

For now he sat back in the passenger seat and waited.

D.S. Nick Henderson shifted in his seat as the police car sped through the streets from Bow Street.

None of the three unmarked cars or the two black transit vans full of uniformed men was using its sirens to help aid their passage through the traffic. After all, as far as Henderson was concerned, there was no need for undue haste. The Tai Hung Chai weren't expecting them.

*Were they?*

If they had been the ones responsible for springing Chang . . .

The thought tailed off.

It didn't make any sense, Layton was right.

And yet, if the Tai Hung Chai weren't responsible then who the hell was?

*Unless . . .*

Henderson shook his head imperceptibly, as if dismissing some half-formed notion.

Once the elders of the Triad were arrested and shaken up, *then* he'd find out where Joey Chang was.

'Do you reckon we should have requested armed

back-up, guv?' Layton asked.

Henderson shook his head.

'They won't fight, they know better than that,' he said.

'That's probably because they know they'll be out again in a couple of hours,' Layton said, wearily. 'What the hell are we going to hold them on?'

'I told you, any fucking thing we can think of.' He wiped his palms on his trousers thinking how much he needed a cigarette. 'They're going to need more than some smart-arse lawyer to bail them out *this* time. None of them walk until I find out where Joey Chang is.'

Most of the short journey was spent in silence, the men of the Hip Sing preoccupied with their own thoughts. The Jag and the Mercedes moved smoothly through traffic, drawing towards Shaftesbury Avenue.

Behind them, the white transit van allowed another car in front of it, but the driver never took his eyes from the Mercedes.

The two cars stopped at the junction with Great Windmill Street, held there by the traffic lights.

In the Jag, Billy Chi glanced out of the side window, watching two young women, both dressed in short skirts, as they passed along the pavement. He nudged his companion and nodded towards the two women, smiling approvingly as they disappeared into the hordes of other pedestrians.

The lights turned green and the Jag pulled away, leading the Mercedes.

The white transit followed.

They were approaching Cambridge Circus when Chi reached for the two-way radio in the door panel of the car. He flicked it on, adjusting the volume as the sound of static filled the car momentarily.

Satisfied that he had contact, Chi pressed the 'Transmit' button.

There was another hiss of static.

'Are you receiving?' he said, holding the two-way

tightly in his pudgy hand.

'Loud and clear,' the voice rattled back.

'Tell them to get ready,' said Chi. 'We're nearly there.'

The Jag and the Mercedes turned into Charing Cross Road.

So did the white transit.

## One-Hundred-and-One

With his jacket on, Joey Chang found that the steel circlets still gripping his wrists were all but invisible. One was still cutting into his skin, but he managed to dismiss the pain from his mind.

He had more important things to occupy him.

He nudged Doyle as they walked side by side, motioning towards the rear entrance of the restaurant which was hidden by a brick wall about five feet tall. The alley leading to the yard was wide enough for the two men to walk comfortably abreast.

As they drew closer, Doyle saw two men standing outside the rear door of the restaurant, one of them smoking while his companion chatted animatedly.

'In there,' Chang said, nodding towards the building.

Doyle looked around him at the other buildings backing onto this yard. Any number of eyes might see them.

They would have to move fast.

'If you're fucking me around, Chang . . .' Doyle hissed, allowing the sentence to tail off.

'We have to get inside,' the Chinaman said.

'Those blokes will know you, won't they?' Doyle asked, motioning towards the two men guarding the rear of the restaurant.

'Well, unless you want to walk through the front door,

it's our only way in,' Chang told him.

The two men locked stares for a moment then Doyle nodded.

'You take the one on the left,' the counter terrorist said. 'And I'm warning you, Chang, you try to set me up and I'll kill you here and now.'

The Chinaman smiled thinly and began walking towards the two guards, Doyle a couple of paces behind.

As they approached, the two guards moved closer together, as if to block the way. The taller man, the one smoking, dropped his butt and ground it out beneath his foot.

His companion puffed out his chest and took a step towards Chang, one hand outstretched in a gesture designed to stop his advance.

He spoke quickly in Chinese.

Doyle saw the man point at him.

Chang replied in Chinese.

*What the fuck was going on?*

The taller man looked at Doyle then smiled thinly.

The other one shook his head, his hand sliding towards the inside of his jacket.

Chang moved like lightning.

He took a step towards the man, swivelled and drove a powerful kick into his solar plexus, hard enough to knock him off his feet.

Doyle pulled the Desert Eagle from its holster and, using the heavy barrel as a cudgel, slammed it into the face of the taller man. He pitched sideways into a dustbin, its contents spilling onto the floor of the yard.

The Chinaman tried to rise but Doyle kicked him hard in the face, splitting his bottom lip and driving two teeth backwards into his mouth.

As the other man rose, Chang struck him twice in quick succession, the first blow shattering his jaw, the second catching him on the temple. He dropped like a stone.

Doyle slid the Eagle back into its holster then moved close to the back door, easing the handle down. He beckoned Chang forward.

'You first,' the counter terrorist snapped, pushing the Chinaman ahead but making sure he stayed close.

They slipped inside and found themselves in the kitchen.

It was large. There were work tops arranged in L shapes, and countless pots and cooking utensils hung from racks on the walls and above the counters. There was a door to the right, open slightly to reveal a staircase.

Ducking low, Doyle moved towards the door but Chang shook his head, motioning instead towards the double swing doors that led to the front of the building.

Doyle could hear voices.

Keeping close to ground, hidden by the work tops in case anyone should enter the kitchen from the front, he and Chang moved towards the sound of the voices.

They were babbling in Chinese and Doyle wondered what the hell they were saying.

Chang knew.

He picked up sentences here and there as he advanced, glancing behind him briefly to see how close Doyle was.

The counter terrorist was only two or three feet behind him.

They passed a rack of knives and Chang glanced hurriedly at the gleaming blades hanging from hooks. Their razor-sharp edges glinted dully.

Doyle motioned to him to stop and the two men crouched down close to the double doors, within clear earshot of the conversation beyond.

There were round windows in the double doors that were almost opaque and difficult to see through, but Doyle crept towards them and peered quickly through the glass. All he could make out were four or five silhouettes in the room beyond. He ducked down once again and scrambled back to where Chang waited.

Chang had recognised at least two of the voices as Wo Fen and Jackie Ti.

Doyle eased the Beretta from it shoulder holster and

slipped off the safety catch.

Chang watched as he replaced the weapon.

When the time came, he knew he would have only one chance.


In the back of the Jag, Billy Chi sat gazing at the front of the restaurant.

The Mercedes was parked a few yards back.

The white transit was a little further away on the corner of the road.

Chi reached for the two-way and flicked it to transmit.

He scowled at the device as it crackled with static.

'Can you hear me, over?' he said, his eyes still on the restaurant front.

'Go ahead,' the voice on the other end replied.

'We're going in now,' Chi said. 'Give us ten minutes.' He looked at his watch. 'Do you understand?'

'Ten minutes,' the other voice echoed.

'What time do you make it?'

'Ten fifteen.'

'At ten twenty-five you come in and you kill every single member of the Tai Hung Chai inside that building. Is that clear?'

'Clear. Over and out.'

Chi switched off the two-way and dropped it onto the back seat of the Jag then he swung himself out and, accompanied by the two other men inside the car, headed for the front of the restaurant. Two more of his men joined him from the Mercedes.

They stood together for a second on the pavement then set off towards the front entrance.

Chi glanced once more at his watch.

*Ten minutes.*

# One-Hundred-and-Two

The traffic was at a standstill from Cambridge Circus to Trafalgar Square, the whole of Charing Cross Road stifled with vehicles, some of their drivers blasting on their horns in anger and frustration. Like an impenetrable wall of steel, cars, vans and trucks stretched across the side roads, blocking any oncoming traffic as effectively as if a barricade had been installed.

'What the fuck is this?' shouted D.S. Nick Henderson angrily as his car and the other police vehicles were brought to a halt at the end of Cranbourn Street. Across the road, past the array of waiting motor vehicles, he could see Leicester Square tube station and the front of the Hippodrome looking lifeless in the daylight, its neon waiting for the darkness.

Behind his own car the black transit vans had also stopped.

'Find out what's going on,' snapped Henderson, watching as D.C. John Layton snatched up the two-way inside the car.

Henderson heard little of the conversation that followed. He even pushed open his door and stepped out, trying to see what had caused the hold-up.

The blockage couldn't be more effective if it had been arranged. There wasn't room to get a motorbike between the bumpers of the cars let alone a fucking transit.

He banged angrily on the roof of the car and slid back inside.

'There's been a smash up in Trafalgar Square,' Layton told him. 'A bus and a lorry. It's blocked traffic all round.'

'Jesus Christ,' hissed Henderson.

'We'll have to get in another way,' Layton said, shrugging at this statement of the obvious.

Henderson glared at him, as if the traffic jam were the D.C.'s personal responsibility.

'Get us out of here,' he barked at the driver.

The door of the restaurant creaked slightly as it was opened and, inside, all eyes turned towards the newcomers.

There were five of them, all Hip Sing men, all of similar office to those men of the Tai Hung Chai who waited to greet them.

Billy Chi was the first in. He nodded respectfully towards Wo Fen and then the others assembled around the *Shan Chu*.

Frankie Wong watched them indifferently as they entered. He saw his opposite number, but did not know his name. The man was a couple of years older than Wong, his face thin and pinched.

It was Wong who advanced towards the five men and briskly searched them, patting their arms and legs for any concealed weapons. Satisfied that there were none he stepped back and took up his position in the line of Tai Hung Chai men.

As if at a given signal, all ten men in the restaurant bowed to one another then sat down.

'Welcome,' said Wo Fen. 'Let us conclude this meeting quickly and with good faith.'

Billy Chi smiled thinly.

'Let our meeting show our intent,' he said.

Both sets of men regarded each other uneasily across the table, some of them watching as Wo Fen filled ten small glasses with saké from a glass decanter.

Chi glanced down at his watch.

10.19 a.m.

He smiled at Wong.

Inside the white transit van there were four men. All in

their twenties. All casually dressed.

All armed with Ingram Mach 10 submachine-guns.

The inside of the van smelled of perspiration and the man nearest the door swallowed hard, his heart pounding against his ribs. He checked the safety catch on his sub-gun, glancing round to see that his companions were also gripping their weapons tightly.

Time was ticking away.

One of them looked at his watch.

Six minutes.


Doyle edged the kitchen door open a fraction of an inch, squinting through the crack in an attempt to pick out the faces of the men beyond.

He had seen the newcomers enter, seen the greetings and now he watched as Wo Fen filled the last of the small glasses, getting to his feet once he'd done so.

Billy Chi did likewise, facing the older man.

'What the hell are they doing?' Doyle whispered.

'They are making peace,' Joey Chang told him, watching the silhouettes through the opaque glass of the kitchen door. There was venom in his tone and Doyle heard him hiss something in Chinese.

'Who are they?' Doyle wanted to know.

'They are Hip Sing council members.'

'The top men?'

Chang nodded.

Doyle glanced around at him, saw the darkness in his expression.

'They are the men responsible for murdering my family,' Chang said, quietly.

Doyle returned to gazing through the crack in the door.

Chang looked down.

He knew his time had come.

Doyle saw Billy Chi and Wo Fen facing each other.

'They are the men I must kill,' whispered Chang.

He struck quickly, before Doyle realised what was happening.

The counter terrorist felt a stunning impact to the left side of his neck, as if he'd been struck by a lump of very smooth, very hard wood.

He pitched to one side, still clinging to consciousness but feeling as if his muscles had ceased to obey him.

In this dazed state he was aware only of his own inability to move and of Chang crouching over him, sliding a hand inside his jacket, pulling the Desert Eagle from his holster.

Doyle opened his mouth to say something but it seemed that the blow Chang had struck had robbed him not only of his power to move but also his ability to speak. He could merely mouth the words silently as he saw the Chinaman brandishing the large weapon in his hands.

The counter terrorist saw Chang looking down at him and thought that he was going to kill him but then he realised that the Chinaman's attention was directed beyond, into the restaurant.

*You fucking idiot, you let him take you by surprise.*

Doyle clenched his fists slowly, like a cripple learning how to use limbs that have been dormant for many years.

That numbness still enveloped his body, but it was beginning to fade slowly.

He tried to raise himself up onto his knees.

He saw Chang push his way through the kitchen doors which swung back on their hinges.

Doyle saw the men inside the restaurant turn to see what the intrusion was.

He saw the smile fade from Billy Chi's lips.

Saw Chang raise the Desert Eagle.

Saw his finger tighten on the trigger.

The retort of the pistol was thunderous as he fired, the muzzle flash blinding white.

Chang grunted as the massive recoil slammed the Eagle back against the heel of his hand.

Travelling at a speed in excess of 2,500 feet a second, the nitro-express bullet struck Billy Chi just below the left eye.

It penetrated the bone easily, staving in the zygoma,

bursting the eye and ploughing effortlessly through the brain before erupting from the back of the skull sending a thick spray of blood, pulverised bone and thick grey matter across most of the floor behind him.

Chi's body seemed to sway for interminable seconds, those around him rooted to the spot by the suddenness of the incident, riveted by the awesome power of the Desert Eagle. Then, as if in slow motion, the body fell forward, crashing across the table, spilling the saké and spouting blood high into the air.

Chang took a step closer and fired again.

## One-Hundred-and-Three

Doyle was on his feet by the time Chang got off the third shot.

Like the other two it thundered into the table, blasting off a sizeable portion of the wood. The Hip Sing men dived to the ground as the bullets hit the floor around them, the noise deafening.

Chang shot one of them in the back, the bullet shattering the man's spine, exploding from his stomach carrying a thick porridge of pulped intestine and blood with it.

Wo Fen shouted something which Chang couldn't hear. The massive retorts from the Eagle had deafened him, his eyes were seared by the muzzle flashes.

He saw Frankie Wong running towards him.

The remaining Hip Sing men seemed to favour running for it and the first of them scrambled to his feet and lunged for the door.

Chang fired, missed and could only watch as the bullet shattered the glass of the door sending huge shards spraying out into the street. The sound of smashing crystal now mingled with the shouts of the men inside and the boom of the pistol.

Doyle kicked open the kitchen door, pulling the Beretta from its holster, his head still spinning.

*What the fuck was going on?*

Through the broken door he saw men running towards the restaurant.

Four of them.

The first of the quartet burst in and Doyle saw that he was holding a Mach 10.

The counter terrorist dropped down instinctively as the first staccato rattle of machine-gun fire erupted. Bullets sprayed the inside of the restaurant, several drilling into the table over which Billy Chi was slumped. Indeed, three of the 9mm slubs ripped into Chi's thigh. More hit the fish tank to the left and the glass exploded, water and fish spilling onto the floor which was already stained with blood.

Another man entered and opened fire, empty shell cases raining down as he emptied the weapon with one swift jerk on the trigger.

As he reached for a fresh magazine Doyle saw his chance.

He got off two shots from the Beretta, the first of which hit the man in the chest, the second screaming past his head to shatter what glass was left in the door. He pitched backwards, colliding with another onrushing Hip Sing man who was trying to fire the sub-gun with one hand.

The spray of bullets was erratic and cut across the restaurant floor, drilling into the polished wood, punching holes.

Peter Sum was hit in the knee, screaming as one of the bullets pulverised his patella and sent him crashing to the ground.

Doyle saw another man entering the restaurant and the air was suddenly filled with a deafening fusillade of automatic fire.

Bullets sliced through the air, most of them hitting their targets.

Wo Fen went down, clutching a wound in his stomach, blood pouring through his fingers.

Jackie Ti, attempting to run for the kitchen, was hit in the small of the back and the base of the skull. He pitched forwards, blood spraying from the wounds.

Doyle leapt behind the bar, resting the Beretta on the polished surface to fire more accurately at the incoming Hip Sing men.

He saw one of their men on the floor snatch up the dropped Mach 10, but before he could get a shot off Doyle put two slugs into his back, one of them puncturing his lung, the other macerating a kidney before ripping through his stomach as it exited.

A burst of fire peppered the bar top and Doyle ducked down, keeping low as more bullets shattered the glasses behind him, covering him with fragments of crystal.

Chang shot another of the gunmen, the impact blasting his victim sideways, sending blood spurting from the wound in his chest.

In a desperate effort to find some cover, David Lun overturned a table and sought escape behind it but the bullets merely ploughed through. He was hit in the face and stomach.

The air was thick with the stench of cordite, a grey mist of smoke now settling inside the building as guns continued to flame, men barely aware of who their bullets were striking the place was so tight packed. They were deafened by the sound, blinded by the muzzle flashes.

Chang saw one of the Hip Sing changing magazines and took his chance, throwing himself at the man, crashing into him, bringing him down. The Ingram went spinning away across the floor.

Chang gripped the man by the throat and slammed his head down repeatedly against the wooden floor but, so intent was he on pummelling the life from his opponent, he didn't notice the man slide a hand inside his belt. He pulled the cleaver free and struck out at Chang, laying his right arm open to the bone and forcing him to relax his grip.

Doyle could hear screaming from close by and saw one of the Hip Sing gunmen crawling towards the door, his lower body shredded by bullets.

Frankie Wong stood over him and shot him twice in the back of the head, turning from his triumph in time to see another of his enemies turn an Ingram on him.

The burst sent bullets cutting into Wong. He was hit in the chest, stomach and shoulder, thrown backwards by the multiple impacts, finished off by a shot which ploughed into his groin, blasting away most of one testicle. He hit the floor and lay still in a spreading puddle of blood.

Doyle swung the Beretta round to bear on the Hip Sing man but was too slow. They fired simultaneously.

One of Doyle's shots caught the man in the shoulder, but the counter terrorist felt a white hot pain in his arm as a bullet punctured his wrist, shattering bone there and causing him to drop the automatic.

'Shit,' he bellowed as pain seared up his arm, the limb numbed by the wound. He gripped at it, shouting with renewed agony as he felt a portion of bone grate against his fingers. Blood was running down his hand and dripping to the floor.

He saw the Hip Sing man staggering towards him, pulling a cleaver from his belt.

In another part of the restaurant, Chang was backing away from a similarly armed opponent, using a chair leg as a weapon to counter the attack.

It was hard to tell who was dead and who was alive, thought Doyle. There were bodies everywhere. The air was dense with the smell of blood and excrement. The sound of gunfire had ceased.

All that seemed to matter now was the bastard with the cleaver who faced him.

He screamed angrily and ran at Doyle.

# One-Hundred-and-Four

The counter terrorist ducked down behind the bar, his hand searching through the piles of broken glass, the shards slicing open his fingertips. But, finally, his hand closed around a broken bottle, the neck still intact, the bottom splintered to form a dozen sharp spikes of glass. Leaping up, Doyle brandished it before him as the Hip Sing man advanced.

'Come on you slit-eyed bastard,' Doyle hissed, watching the cleaver as it hovered in the air.

The Chinaman brought it down, missing Doyle by inches.

The counter terrorist stepped back, aware of how useless his damaged right arm was. It flopped beside him, dripping blood onto the carpet of glass both men walked on.

The Hip Sing man lashed out again.

Doyle jabbed the broken bottle forward and raked the jabbed ends across the Chinaman's forearm, splitting the skin and watching with satisfaction as four wide gashes yawned, blood pouring from them.

The Hip Sing man kicked out at him, catching him in the stomach, but Doyle managed to stay on his feet, winded by the blow.

He gritted his teeth, anger now driving his resistance as much as a need to stay alive.

Close by, Chang ducked beneath a swipe of his own opponent's blade and struck out hard with his left hand, cracking two of his attacker's ribs.

He pressed his advantage, slamming into the man with his shoulder, knocking him off his feet.

They hurtled into a table and fell over it.

Chang hissed in pain as he felt the cleaver cut into his back, but he was on his feet first, kicking hard into the groin of the Hip Sing man.

Doyle and his attacker faced each other once more.

Doyle saw the next blow coming, and knew he could only block it with his injured arm.

The pain was excrutiating.

He parried the downward swipe with his forearm, teeth gritted against the agony, then with his other hand he drove the broken bottle forward, slamming the jagged points into the throat of his attacker.

Blood ejaculated from the gashes, spraying Doyle and the bar.

The Chinaman dropped the cleaver and clutched at his throat as if trying to hold the ragged edges of the wound together, but the cut seemed to yawn open like the gills of a fish. A rent in the soft flesh widened until it exposed the man's larynx. He dropped to his knees, blood pouring down his chest, bubbling on his lips.

Doyle stepped past him and snatched up the Beretta from the mass of broken glass on the floor.

He pressed it to the Chinaman's head and fired once, blowing most of the top of his head off.

His right arm still dangling uselessly at his side, Doyle staggered forward, his clothes drenched in blood and perspiration.

He saw Chang backing away from his opponent, watching the cleaver.

Doyle raised the pistol and shot the Hip Sing man twice.

He went down like a stone at Chang's feet and the other man turned to face Doyle.

They were both panting for breath.

The floor was awash with blood. Dead and dying men lay all around them.

'Is this what you wanted?' Doyle said, sucking in a deep breath.

Chang didn't answer. He looked down at the body of

Billy Chi. Close by Wo Fen was lying on his back, both hands frozen on his stomach wound, dead fingers slipped into the hole.

There was sweat dripping from the ends of Doyle's long hair.

Chang, his arm bleeding badly, was also spattered with crimson fluid. He dropped the chair leg he'd been clutching and stood facing Doyle.

Close by, drawing nearer, the counter terrorist could hear sirens.

'The guns,' he said. 'Where are they?'

'They're here,' Chang told him. 'Upstairs.'

Doyle nodded.

'Those guys you sent to kill me in Belfast,' he said, quietly.

Chang looked puzzled.

'What about them?' he wanted to know, his brow furrowing.

'You should have picked better ones,' Doyle told him.

He shot Chang twice in the face.

Doyle turned, saw the first policeman running towards the restaurant. He felt his head spinning, his legs giving way.

There were more policemen out there now.

Doyle hoped one of them had a cigarette.

He blacked out.


# One-Hundred-and-Five

The strong breeze that had been blowing when he'd first parked the car had eased slightly, but Doyle seemed unconcerned either way. He stood beside the black marble headstone, hands dug deep in the pockets of his jacket, the ash on the end of the cigarette between his lips threatening to drop off.

Doyle was surprised that, even at such an early hour, there were other mourners at the cemetery. It wasn't even ten in the morning and yet he had passed half a dozen other people attending to graves.

He himself had finished his tasks.

The usual things. Clean the plinth, change the water, add fresh flowers. Wipe down the stone so that the words could be read clearly:

GEORGINA WILLIS
AT PEACE

It was a simple enough inscription.

Doyle took the cigarette and knocked off the ash, catching sight of someone watching him from the path nearby.

It was a woman in her thirties and she smiled at him.

He'd seen her here before and he nodded to return the greeting. She passed by, heading back towards the main walkway that ran through the centre of the necropolis. He heard her footsteps crunching on the gravel, dying away as she moved further from him.

He was alone again.

*What else is new?*

As he took the cigarette from his lips he felt a slight twinge from his right wrist. It was still heavily strapped.

*More pain.*

Doyle dropped the dog-end and ground it out beneath his boot, looking down at the headstone once more.

*Georgie.*

He would come again, he told himself. Visit more regularly.

Why not spend more time here? At least *here* there was something he had cared about. There was fuck all for him amongst the living.

He stuck his hands in his pockets again, noticing that

344

the wind was growing stronger again. There was moisture in the air.

Doyle looked down at the gravestone.

At her name.

Georgina Willis.

He smiled thinly.

'See you soon,' he whispered, then he turned and walked away.

It was beginning to rain.

'Under conditions of peace the warlike man attacks himself.'

Nietzsche